Serge Joncour is a French novelist and screenwriter. He was born in Paris in 1961 and studied philosophy at university before deciding to become a writer. His first novel, *Vu*, was published by Le Dilettante in 1998. He wrote the screenplay for *Sarah's Key* starring Kristin Scott Thomas, released in 2011. His 2016 novel *Repose-toi sur moi* won the Prix Interallié. *Wild Dog* (*Chien loup*), also published by Gallic Books, won the Prix Landerneau des Lecteurs.

Louise Rogers Lalaurie is a writer and translator. She is based in France and the UK.

D0993422

# Human Nature

Serge Joncour

Translated from the French by Louise Rogers Lalaurie

# Human Nature

Serge Joncour

Translated from the French by Louise Rogers Lalaurie

Gallic Books
London

A Gallic Book

This work has benefited from the support of the Institut français'
Publication Assistance Programme.

First published in France as *Nature humaine*
Copyright © Flammarion, 2020
English translation copyright © Louise Rogers Lalaurie, 2022

First published in Great Britain in 2022 by Gallic Books Ltd
12 Eccleston Street, London, SW1W 9LT

A CIP record for this book is available from the British Library

ISBN 9781913547196

Typeset in Fournier MT by Gallic Books
Printed in the UK by CPI (CR0 4YY)

2 4 6 8 10 9 7 5 3 1

*For Lewis John Rogers (d. 1993),*
*Hubert Lalaurie (d. 2006)*
*and their farms:*
*Red Hill, near Monmouth, south-east Wales*
*Pech' d'Ancou, near Monpeẓat, south-west France*

Friday, 24 December 1999

For the first time, he found himself alone at the farm. There was no sound whatsoever from the livestock, nor from anyone else, not the slightest sign of life. And yet, within these walls, life had always won through. The Fabriers had lived here for four generations. It was here on the farm that he had grown up with his three sisters. Three straight-talking bright sparks, utterly unlike each other, who illuminated everything.

Their childhood had burnt out long ago. Years of laughter and games, of family gatherings, and the high points of summer when everyone came for the tobacco and saffron harvests. Then the sisters had all left for new horizons in the city, and there had been no sadness or bad feeling at their departure. Once they were gone, just four souls remained on the whole hillside: Alexandre and his parents, and the other one, the crazy old guy in his shack by the woods that he owned. Crayssac, whom the family had always kept at a distance. But now Alexandre was the only person living up here, beside the high meadows. Crayssac was dead, and their parents had quit the farm.

That evening, Alexandre dragged the sacks of fertiliser from the old barn to the new equipment store. Then, sticking carefully to Anton's plan, he checked the mortars, and the fuel. Now everything was ready. Before returning to the farmhouse, he glanced down the valley, alert to the slightest sign, the tiniest sound. The wind

7

was strong, so he walked out further. Blasting from the west, the din echoed snatches of sound from the blasts in the bedrock, the racket of the trenchers and diggers. In the loud gusts tonight, it seemed he could hear them again for real, rising from hell, barely five kilometres away. The noise was hideous. Each time it resumed, it sounded like a great drill spinning furiously from the depths of space, an ear-splitting asteroid ready to crash to earth and shatter before his eyes.

He set off once again towards the farmhouse and wondered if the police were hiding somewhere on the other side of the valley, beyond the expanse of razed ground. Perhaps they had been watching him since yesterday, waiting to intervene. He peered into the darkness but could see not the faintest speck of light, nor the tiniest movement – nothing. Yet he was sure he had been spotted– not by the camera at the top of the tall white pole, but by the little one over the barrier across the site entrance. He'd been so careful, though, when he took the detonator: he'd stuck sackcloth to the soles of his shoes, just as Xabi had told him. The concrete plant was far out on the limestone plateau, but he would have to go back. With these high winds – which were set to last, according to the forecast from Météo France – the site would be closed for another whole week, giving him ample time to take the tape out of the camera, or check the angle and calm his nerves. Time enough to see to that, coolly and calmly. Alexandre sat down at the big kitchen table, resting on his elbows as if someone had just poured him a drink. But the only thing in front of him was the fruit basket with its sad-looking winter stock. He took two walnuts and squeezed them one against the other in the palm of his hand, crushing their shells effortlessly, with a loud crack.

Every life stands looking, from a distance, at what might have been. How close things had come to working out another way. Alexandre thought about Constanze often, of what his life might

8

have been if they'd never met, or if he had followed her around the world, always on the move. He wouldn't be here now, for sure. But he had no regrets. And anyway, he'd always hated travelling.

1976–1981

Saturday, 3 July 1976

It was the first time that nature had thumped an angry fist on the table. There had been no rain since Christmas; the drought had hardened the soil and brought the country to its knees, not to mention that, in June, the scorching heat had cracked the enamel of the tin-plate thermometer on the wall. All along the hillside, the meadows were gasping. The cows grazed their own shadows, casting frightened, sidelong glances.

The heatwave was wringing their bodies of moisture, and at Les Bertranges the eight o'clock television news became more important than ever. For Alexandre, the endless reports of record temperatures were a chance to see the massed bodies of young women in short skirts and bikinis. The clips were filmed mostly in Paris: bare-legged girls walked the city streets, others lounged in squares or on café terraces, and some were even topless at the side of a lake. A dream-like prospect for a young man of almost fifteen. His sisters gazed at a world they longed for, too: the busy streets, pavements lined with cafés, every terrace like Saint-Tropez – the very opposite of boredom, so they thought. If nothing else, the heat had united the nation in a great throwing-off of clothes: no one, in town or at Les Bertranges, was afraid to unbutton their blouse or bare their torso.

Many thought the furnace-like temperatures were the result of nuclear tests, and the atomic power stations springing up across

13

England, France and Russia, boiling the rivers and steaming up the sky like great, demented kettles. But their father reckoned the fiery heat had been caused by the space stations the Russians and the Americans were firing up through the atmosphere, factories floating around up there, disturbing the sun. The world had gone mad. Their mother trusted no one but white-haired Captain Jacques Cousteau, the doom-laden Father Christmas who blamed progress and industrial pollution, when frankly, it was hard to see what smoking factory chimneys had to do with the sweltering nights they endured at Les Bertranges. On television, as everywhere else, superstition was rife, and the only practical solution to the heatwave were the mountains of Calor fans piled up in the entrance to the Mammouth hypermarket, with the added attraction of Tang orange-juice sachets (*just add water!*), and Kim Pouss ice pops which rose magically from their cardboard tubes – there was hope for this world after all.

Their grandparents, reluctant ancestral sages, remembered that during the great drought of 1921 the farmers in the valley had arranged for a special mass to be said. Back then, they had all roasted through a two-hour service celebrated in full sun, out in the fields. Say what you like, but three days later the rain returned. God had brought the cracked earth back to life. Except that now, in 1976, there was no direct line to God: the church at Saint-Clair had lost its curate, and in the absence of an intercessor, the candles lit for St Médard on 8 June had no effect whatsoever: not a drop of rain fell. The nightly weather forecast showed a huge sun symbol over the entire map of France, and yellow zig-zag cartoon lightning – storms that no one ever seemed to see for real, proof of the extraordinary disconnect between the television, in Paris, and the rest of the world, out here.

## Sunday, 4 July 1976

Their father had taken the animals down to the lower pastures, on Lucienne and Louis's land. It was never a good idea to let the cattle drink from the river: the cows' hooves would slip on the banks, or they would get fluke, or spread TB by mixing with other herds. But from their small, newly built house, the grandparents could keep a careful eye on the beasts. Lucienne and Louis had just left the old farm on the high ground above the valley to the children. They had reached retirement age, but they had not given up farming altogether. At sixty-five, they declared themselves perfectly capable of working the silt-rich valley soil and keeping a market garden, especially now, with the new Mammouth and its vast self-service vegetable section.

That Sunday, 4 July, marked a turning point at Les Bertranges. They were planting saffron for the last time. In this heat, the bulbs were guaranteed not to rot, and once they were in the ground, the crocuses would be unaffected by damp; on the contrary, they would slumber, tucked up warm, and wake with the first rains on the other side of summer. To the Fabriers, this last crop felt like the end of an era. The red gold was imported now, ten times cheaper, from Iran, India and Morocco. Growing it here was no longer profitable. In France, the labour costs for a half-hectare of the flowers were too high, even as a family. There was no point spending days at a time picking the flowers, then stripping them, seated around the table. Up at the farm, Alexandre's father and mother knew what

15

they were about: the bulbs lived for five years. They could plant them now in the certain knowledge that their children would be around for another five years, that things could stay as they were for another half-decade. This last planting of the crocuses would ease the transition for Lucienne and Louis. They were keeping on with the walnut oil, and the blackcurrants – activities that had filled the long evenings before television – for the same reason.

For the last time at Les Bertranges, three generations worked side by side. Caroline, the oldest sister, had turned sixteen. Already, they could see from the way she constantly dusted herself down that she was distancing herself from their world. At just eleven years old, Vanessa was never without her Instamatic camera, worn cross-wise on a strap. She looked through it every couple of minutes to check the picture she would take if she pressed the shutter. Which meant that she was not much help. From time to time, she would stare at a bulb clasped between the tips of her fingers, then hold it further away and frame the image. Hers was an expensive hobby – it cost a lot to develop the films, so she would always think twice before pressing her finger down to take a picture. Six-year-old Agathe was the baby girl. Her parents reprimanded her every time she put a bulb in upside down or peeled it inquisitively before planting it in the ground. But Alexandre was busy everywhere at once. He had hoed and raked the soil the day before, and now, as well as helping with the planting, he fetched new boxes of bulbs while everyone emptied out and planted the ones he had already brought. Lucienne and Louis had come up from below for the occasion, leaving their brand-new three-bedroom house with steps up to the front door, a fitted bathroom, and a lingering smell of paint. As country people, custodians of practices handed down over a thousand years, they knew that, tomorrow, those same practices would cease.

The land at Les Bertranges had been in Lucienne's family for four generations, but now the future looked uncertain. Caroline was talking about teacher training in Toulouse, Vanessa dreamed of one thing only: becoming a photographer in Paris. And Agathe would follow her sisters, no doubt about that. As luck would have it, Alexandre had no such plans. He studied farming and land management at the agricultural college, and he loved the soil. Save for him, the family's days at the farm would be numbered. The absence of anyone to take over would have spelled a death sentence for the land, the cattle, the woods. And the entire estate – fifty hectares, plus ten hectares of woods – would have been abandoned. Alexandre never spoke about it, but he felt a great weight of responsibility on his shoulders. If the girls felt free to dream of a life elsewhere, they owed it to their brother, the sacrificial son, preparing to take up the burden and carry on.

Alexandre was fetching a fresh load of bulb crates when he heard the blare of sirens in the distance. Strange, because the police never showed their faces around here, least of all in an emergency. From the end of the field there was a view right across the valley, but the big trees were in leaf now and obscured it. Through a gap, he saw his grandparents' small new house down below, and the narrow road that followed the river. He ran his hand over his face, which was streaked with sweat. Just at that moment, he spotted two police vans emerging from a tunnel of overhanging trees, sirens howling as they sped around a bend in the road, a sure sign that they were heading for Labastide, unless they had taken the turning to come up here.

His father called to him: 'Hey! Alexandre! What the hell are you doing?'

'Strange, down there, there are two—'

'Two what?'

'No, nothing …'

'Bring us some more boxes! Can't you see we're running out?'

Alexandre said nothing about the police vans. Two of them. That meant something serious. He wondered if they were headed for Crayssac's place. Last week, the old Red had gone up to the Larzac plateau – he was an activist in the struggle against plans to extend the military camp up there. Thousands had attended the protest, it seemed, and caused a fair bit of trouble. The militant rebels had broken into the army buildings to try and tear up the deeds expropriating the farmland, and that same evening the police had thrown them all in jail. But the very next day, Prime Minister Jacques Chirac had infuriated the cops by ordering the farmers' release: their flocks were dying of thirst in the drought. The Fabriers never discussed such things, but Alexandre knew Crayssac had taken part in the protest. Without admitting it, even to himself, he was fascinated by the struggle – a kind of Woodstock closer to home, with girls and hippies travelling there from all over, and tons of weed, so he'd heard. It must be a wild scene up there, for sure.

'Get a move on, for goodness' sake!'

Alexandre hurried back and forth, fetching crates full of bulbs and placing them beside each of the team of planters out in the field. They were down on all fours, planting the bulbs one by one. Alexandre passed close to the viewpoint a second time, and saw a third van racing along the road. Impossible, surely, that a whole company of gendarmes would turn up just for Crayssac.

'Don't stand there dreaming, bring us some bulbs!'

This time, he knew he had to go. He had to find out.

'I'll be back in a minute!'

'What the …?'

'I'm thirsty, I'm going to fetch some water.'

'There's some Antésite cordial here.'

'No, I want fresh water, not that stuff. And I need the toilet. I'll be right back …'

'The toilet?' Jean stared at Angèle in bemusement. 'The heat's affected that son of yours.'

Alexandre's mother shrugged.

## Sunday, 4 July 1976

Alexandre walked back up to the farmhouse, but rather than fetch a drink of water, he jumped onto his Motobécane scooter and raced over to Crayssac's place. When he got there, the police were nowhere to be seen. Perhaps the track was blocked, or the vans' narrow tyres had got stuck in the deep ruts that had hardened to concrete in the drought. Alexandre found the old man sitting indoors, pouring with sweat, his gun across his knees.

'Jesus Christ, Joseph, what's going on?'

The old man sat immured in ice-cold rage. 'This is all your fault!' he spat furiously.

'What are you talking about?'

'You and your blasted telephone.'

'Did the PTT technicians call the police? You haven't shot at them, have you?'

'Not yet.'

Alexandre was bewildered. Lately, in their conversations, the old goatherd had talked of nothing but non-violent protest.

'Joseph, the gun ... What happened to the spirit of Gandhi?'

'Well, you know what? You can stick your non-violent resistance. Because it doesn't work, does it? Non-violence ... The Corsicans, the Irish, they know ... Only way to make your voice heard is to blow it all sky-high.'

'But you didn't shoot at the guys rigging up the telephone cables, surely?'

'We've lived for two thousand years without the telephone. I won't have it here, I tell you.'

Old Crayssac sank deeper into his rage, accusing Alexandre. He was a landowners' brat, and it was their fault the rubber cables were being strung along their lanes. His parents were materialist good-for-nothings who wanted it all for themselves, two cars, new fences, aluminium feeders, a television set, two tractors, shopping trolleys crammed full of stuff from Mammouth ... And now the telephone. Where would it all end?

'So did you shoot at them, or didn't you?'

'Don't you go spreading shit about me all over the neighbourhood, boy. I just sawed through their blasted poles, fucking great tree trunks laced with arsenic. No one's sticking arsenic round the edge of my land! Same fucking wood as the Americans used in the forties that brought us the canker. Their munitions crates were infested with it. Those tree trunks are death ...'

'But the gun?'

'My father's old rifle. It's what we do here. Resist! Your grandfather was a prisoner in the war. But me, my father was a *maquisard*. Not the same thing at all.'

'That's ancient history.'

'Ha! Well, no point counting on you to stand up for anything, that's for sure. I've seen you with your green tractor and your Motobécane. That modern world will eat you up, you'll see, eat you alive like all the rest.'

'What's that got to do with the telephone cables?'

'The telephone, Larzac, nuclear power, it's all the same. The nuclear plants at Golfech, Creys-Malville. All that. And the mines and the steelworks? They're closing them down! But people are taking a stand, can't you see? Everywhere, people are rising up against that world. You can't just take it lying down, like your lot do. You'll see, one day, if no one protests, they'll put a fucking

21

motorway through your fields, or build a nuclear power plant right here.'

Alexandre was sitting in front of the old man now. Was seventy really as old as all that? He looked at Crayssac. Was he what his father would call an old fool, or some prophet of doom, a communist Christian, the sort dismissed locally as *fadorle*, wrong in the head, a goatherd to whom a world of change had not been kind?

It was plain to Alexandre that they needed the telephone, just as they needed their sleek Citroën GS, the John Deere tractor, the television set. If nothing else, they needed a direct line to Mammouth on the main road to Toulouse, so they could sell their vegetables, and perhaps meat one day – why not? But old Crayssac didn't want black rubber cables hung along the sides of the roads. The electricity pylons were enough of an eyesore already.

'The state wants us on its leash. In ten years there'll be so many wires along all the roads, they'll have to cut down the trees.'

'But you've got electricity and running water here.'

'Running water! Ha! The wells are dry, the tap dribbles dark-brown piss, that's all. Take a look if you don't believe me.'

Alexandre picked up a glass and turned on the tap. Sure enough, Crayssac's water was a dirty brown colour.

'The wine's under the sink, mix it with that. Help yourself.'

It was so hot everywhere else that the bottle felt cool. Alexandre poured the *vin de soif* – cheap, thirst-quenching stuff, but a fine ruby red, nonetheless.

'Time was, you could drink from the springs, but now they've cut off the aquifers to make cretins like your lot buy their water in bottles at Mammouth. They sell water at the price of wine and you all buy it. Fools.'

Crayssac's hunting spaniel had lain motionless under the table since Alexandre's arrival, sprawling with its nose pressed against the cool tiles. But now it sprang to its feet and began to bark, standing right in front of its master, staring him straight in the eye. Then the dog tore outside, baying as it did so when it caught the scent and gave chase. The greeting was well in advance of the police vans that the dog alone had heard. Until now.

'I know they're going to give me trouble. They've got me in their sights over at Saint-Géry, even at headquarters. Heh, what d'you think? We scare them, people like me, d'you see? Even up there in Paris. They're frightened we'll blast this world off its tracks.'

'Joseph, get rid of the gun, quick! Or this really will go all the way to Paris ...'

Soon, the three vehicles came into view at the far end of the lane. Alexandre and Crayssac peered through the window, watching their slow advance. Three Renault vans, bizarrely tall and narrow, lurched wildly – pathetically – along the deeply rutted track. Dizzied by the sight of them, and his gulps of cool wine, Alexandre waxed philosophical:

'Best you can do is apologise. The gendarmes are military men, they command respect.'

'You sound like Michel fucking Debré.'

'What's that supposed to mean? They're here to protect us.'

'Against what? The Soviets, is that it? Are you like all the rest, scared of the Russians?'

Outside, the van doors slid open. Almost before he had time to think, Alexandre grabbed the gun from the table and slipped it out of sight, on top of the kitchen cupboard. The gendarmes appeared in the doorway, and though Alexandre could tell they were surprised to see him, he felt incapable of extricating himself from the situation, assuring them he had nothing to do with it. He remembered the words Crayssac had breathed on his return from the very first protests with the guys at Larzac: 'If ever the gendarmes get you in their sights one day, you're screwed. They never forget, never give up ...'

Sunday, 4 July 1976

At mealtimes, Alexandre was the audience for his three sisters. Outside, on the farm, he was the one who felt most at ease, but indoors it was the girls who took the lead, filling the farmhouse with their laughter and fun, united by a bond of glee while he watched from the sidelines. The girls were closer to their parents, too. They were chatty and opinionated, and they could talk about absolutely anything. They discussed every possible subject, from the deeply serious to the frivolous, while Alexandre and their father and mother talked about nothing but the farm, the livestock and his studies. They wanted him to stay on at agricultural college, but he told them he already knew farming inside out, so there was no point in carrying on with his studies. His relationship with his parents was strictly professional.

They sat down to eat every evening at eight o'clock, when the television news started. It wasn't planned that way, that's just how it was. The presenter presided at the head of their table – Hélène Vila, Roger Gicquel or Jean Lanzi with his widow's peak, aviator glasses and friendly grin. Mostly, the reports were drowned out by their conversation. No one ever really listened to the 'high mass' of the eight o'clock news, except when their father or mother hissed a loud *Ssshhh!* – the unmistakable signal that something bad was happening in the world, or beyond, in space, because people were more and more interested in that too, now that the Russians had developed a rocket that could take them to Mars.

Most often, Vanessa would talk about someone she had seen while out and about, one of her best girlfriends, or a distant neighbour whom they scarcely knew, while Caroline, in her teacher's voice, loud and voluble already, would tell them all what she'd done that day, or was going to do tomorrow, when she wasn't holding forth about some book she'd read, or a lesson she'd just finished revising. When she warmed excitedly to the subject of a film, they knew they'd be driving her to Villefranche or Cahors, or dropping her off at a friend's so the parents of Justine or Alice, Sandrine or Valérie could take their turn and drive them all to the cinema. When Caroline spoke, she expanded their world far beyond the periphery of the farm, and yet here they had everything they needed to make a life for themselves. Agathe enjoyed watching her two older sisters, eager to catch up with them. Meanwhile, she borrowed their shoes, their sweaters and their dresses. She was impatient to grow up, and ringed with the unmistakable light of the favourite, the baby of the family.

The television news was still showing footage of the protest against the Superphénix nuclear reactor in Creys-Malville, far north and east of Les Bertranges, in the opposite corner of the Massif Central. Activists from France, Germany and Switzerland had come together to camp at the site. The hippies had quickly established a second Larzac, of sorts, but the riot police had chased them out in a series of violent clashes. Alexandre seized the moment. Now it was his turn to shine. He would be the one to grab their attention, as the bearer of sensational news. He launched into an account of the incident with the three police vans at old Crayssac's place. For once, the others listened in disbelief, amazed to hear him speak at such length. He might almost have been on the news! For once, events on their stretch of hillside rivalled the reports on TV.

Alexandre relived the scene, holding their attention all around the table. Caroline listened, doubtless comparing the story to a chapter in one of her books, or an episode in a film. Vanessa imagined, regretfully, the shots she could have taken, of the sabotaged poles, the old man with his gun, and the platoon of gendarmes, ready to pounce. Agathe took it all in, sceptical and wary like her parents, and fundamentally alarmed, if the truth be told.

Alexandre was forced to admit that the old man had lashed out and called him the spoiled son of a pair of arsehole landowners, reiterating over and over that this was all his parents' fault. After all, they were the ones who had followed the will of President Giscard d'Estaing, like sheep, and ordered a telephone!

'So, did he shoot at them, or not?'

For once they were hanging breathlessly on his every word. Alexandre would have loved to embellish the story, add a spectacular shoot-out, with the gun dog tearing at the gendarmes' throats. But he stuck to the facts.

Since joining the struggle for the Larzac plateau, Crayssac had achieved a modicum of fame. Whenever the TV news reported the protests, the family would peer at the screen, hoping to pick him out. Crayssac was among his own kind up there, siding more with the communists than the hippies, fighting the fight alongside the union firebrands, the Lutte Occitane, the Catholic Young Farmers, and the arty types down from Paris. He had fasted with the bishops of Rodez and Montpellier. Even François Mitterrand had joined them on hunger strike, for about three-quarters of an hour, but the gesture had made its mark. The socialist leader had sworn that if ever he got into power, his first act would be to secure justice for the Larzac farmers. The protest was no small affair, and in a world mesmerised by modernity and progress, it gave solid proof that nature lay at the heart of everything.

'So go on, did they take him away?'

Alexandre didn't want to brag, but he was careful to point out that he was the one who, at the very last minute, had instinctively hidden the gun on top of the kitchen cupboard. He said nothing, on the other hand, about the look the gendarmes had given him when they appeared at the old man's door. A look you don't forget in a hurry. He chose his words carefully, but he made sure that everyone around the table got the message: Crayssac disapproved of their management of the farm, the expansion of the herd and their purchase of more land. It was their fault if the lanes were lined with poles of contaminated pine that would poison them all.

He read the disapproval in his parents' eyes, and his sisters' too. The family kept out of trouble with the gendarmes, or anyone at all. They had pumped water from the river lately, and that had aroused quite enough hostility, even without doing business with the hypermarket. In remote, sparsely populated country like theirs, there were still a thousand ways to provoke the dislike, even the hatred, of your nearest neighbour. The Fabriers had nothing against the gendarmes, still less against the military proper – on the contrary, since the start of this damned drought they knew full well that without the infantrymen from Angoulême and Brive, and their Berliet trucks, farmers like them would have been short of feed. For the past two months, the military had been bringing feed south from the Creuse, the Indre and the Loire, while the tanker trucks of the Seventh Marine Infantry Regiment brought water up to the drought-stricken countryside, to fill the animals' drinking troughs, and the wells. Without them, the cattle would be parched and cracked like the mud in the dried-up ponds. Larzac or no Larzac, everyone acknowledged that, since June, the army had done everything it could. Now was not the time to pick a fight with the gendarmes, or go shouting about the army camp. People needed the military – they were doing a fine job.

## Monday, 5 July 1976

July was a month of fire, endured by all. The drought was never-ending, and the heat beat down across the high *causse*. Even the wild animals were behaving strangely. At night, the deer came close to the houses to drink. They lapped at the dregs of water left out for them in tubs, but often the boars would tip the containers over to roll in the thin layer of mud that resulted. In the fields, the cattle clustered around the drinking troughs. Cows detest the heat, so they would wait until evening to drag themselves over to the mangers, knocking the galvanised metal bars with their horns to vent their bad temper. On the hillside, the springs had all run dry, and the rainwater dams were reduced to expanses of cracked earth.

At night, every window in the farmhouse stood wide open. At two o'clock in the morning, with the others doubtless all asleep, Alexandre felt the need to take a walk outside. A breeze stirred the hot air. In places, along the paths, there was a smell of death – the heady stench of a carcass, some poor beast that had strayed. He thought of old Crayssac, spending his first night in police custody. His goats would need feeding tomorrow, and milking. He didn't like taking care of the goats. When you're used to working with cattle, goats seem tiny, like keeping chickens. Sometimes he was afraid he would end up like the red-faced old man, that he would come to look like him, little by little. Perhaps that's where he'd be in fifty years, distrusting everyone and everything, living in his own small world, as they had always done here.

That night, in the light of the half-moon, he could see the suffering of nature: the trees slumped as if struggling to breathe, haunted by the dread prospect of the sun rising one more time, and the close embrace of the suffocating air after the relative cool of the night. Old Crayssac loved to predict the very worst, and perhaps he was right; perhaps progress had brought nothing good, as that politician in his roll-neck sweater had said, brandishing a glass of water to show that we would all be faced with water shortages by the end of the century and that the solution was for everyone to go back to riding bikes, like they did in China. Perhaps the crackpot prophets were right. Perhaps one day the sun would never set.

A trip to Mammouth was even better than a trip into town. In the belly of the great, ever-changing megastore, you no longer walked from shop to shop, but penetrated to the very heart of things, the *stuff* of life itself. On Saturdays, breakfast was a hurried affair and the farm buzzed with activity all morning. Ahead of the grand outing, Alexandre took charge while the others got ready: he would take the Citroën GS out of the barn and warm the sixty-eight-horsepower engine, revving it for that distinctive deep, velvety hum. Each time he drove it secretly along the lane, he would put his foot down a few times, just to frighten the cows. He never ceased to marvel at the hydraulic suspension.

At the other end of the little valley, Crayssac's goats were bleating fit to burst. Alexandre had milked them, but their udders were full once more, so gorged that their teats were inflamed. The signal that the gendarmes still had not let Crayssac go.

When it was time to set off, everyone complained that Alexandre had left the car out in the hot sun. The seats were scorching, but it took more than that to spoil the excursion to the hypermarket, and their teatime treats at the Miami Café. Saturday shopping was a ritual, a cruise on dry land, the only time when the whole family crammed into the Citroën to drive the twenty-five kilometres to Cahors. Today, the expedition had a special urgency because Angèle was worried about the tap water. It was running brown, just as it had when they were first connected to the mains. As a responsible matriarch, she declared they would pick up half a dozen packs of Vittel, the water that coursed through your body as if it was turning a millwheel (so it said in the television advertisements), eliminating toxins as it flowed. Vittel's other great advantage was its plastic bottles which, once empty, were endlessly useful around the farm: they would cut off the bottom sections for use as protective covers for the fenceposts, or paint pots, or for storing nails. Plastic bottles were better in every way than old tin cans, which rusted after six months.

Alexandre always drove from the farm to the nearest main road – a good five kilometres. After that, he would hand over to his father. His sisters had no interest in learning to drive, but Alexandre kept one date firmly fixed in his mind: 18 July 1979, his appointment with destiny, the day he would turn eighteen, the day he could take his driving test at long last. Meanwhile, it was he who drove the car along the track at Les Bertranges, and the narrow lane beyond. He said nothing, but he dreaded coming face to face with the gendarmes. They had never come around here before the incident with Crayssac's gun, but now it paid to be cautious.

No one ever objected to Alexandre's taking the wheel. On the contrary, Angèle and Jean had pinned their hopes on their son passing his test, so that he could share the burden of shopping and deliveries alike. He could take the animals to slaughter or fetch equipment and machinery, make any of the frequent, essential trips to Villefranche, Brive or Cahors. Not forgetting the girls, who were constantly in need of a lift to one friend's house or another, and had to be fetched home when the party was over. The sisters declared that, thanks to Alexandre, they could skip the school bus in the mornings. There would be no more hanging about in the rain at the end of the track. They could go to the fairs and fêtes in the other villages, even the Sherlock pub, without asking their parents, without even telling them.

31

Where the road came out at the top of the hill, they turned right and skirted around old Crayssac's fields. They saw that twenty telegraph poles had been put up along the edge, but that was all. Two large, empty trailers were still parked on the grass verge, though no one was sure why. What they noticed above all was the state of the drystone walls. Whole sections had collapsed. The vibrations from the diggers must have shaken them to the ground. The breaches were big enough in places for Crayssac's animals to get out easily.

The farm track was deeply rutted, but driving on the main road was a different matter altogether: they floated through the countryside, borne aloft on the hydraulic suspension. Alexandre drove the next five kilometres clasping the wheel in a kind of ecstasy. Their father turned on the radio, the soundtrack to this free-flowing modernity. A song by Michel Sardou came on, and he turned up the volume. With his tumbling dark locks and wounded pout, Sardou was the darling songster of the right, always on the radio, especially his new hit, 'Ne m'appelez plus jamais France', an unlikely anthem to the transatlantic liner *La France* that Valéry Giscard d'Estaing had sworn to keep afloat, during his presidential campaign, but which had since been declared unprofitable, and speedily decommissioned just a couple of years before. Whenever their father heard the song, he would turn up the volume and holler the defiant refrain, especially since, in this case, singing along to Sardou no longer marked you out as a right-winger: even the leftie trade unionists at the CGT had recognised the single as an anthem of the labour movement. In the back seat, Caroline and Vanessa would clap their hands over their ears and plead with their father to turn it down, then lunge through the gap in the front seats, trying desperately to reach the knob on the dashboard radio. This was 1976; in the era of Pink

Floyd, Clapton and Supertramp, even a couple of bars of Sardou were too much to bear. Alexandre concentrated on his driving but refereed the squabble by placing one hand over the volume button, at which point his father saw that he had not fastened his seat belt and reprimanded him. The two older sisters took advantage of the distraction to dive forward, but their father pushed them back and burst into song again immediately. And through it all, the hydraulic suspension smoothed the occasional bump in the road and muffled the commotion, while his sisters jumped about in the back.

While their mother gazed placidly out of the window, the peaceful journey became a bare-knuckle fight. Feeling a rush of premature nostalgia, she pictured what would become of her riotous family just a few years from now, when all the girls had gone. She knew already that it would end as it had for their neighbours the Jouansacs and the Berthelots, farmers whose children had left for the city and visited their parents only at Christmas and Easter, Bastille Day and All Saints'. Inevitably, sooner or later, family life was reduced to the high days and holidays of the Catholic Church, and the Republic.

The great advantage of Mammouth was that it took away any anxiety about parking. On the other hand, the large expanse of bare tarmac was hot as hell. No one had thought to plant trees. People walked across it as if it were a great, scalding pan, its surface melting in places, but the moment you passed through the glass doors, the cool, fresh air enveloped you like the waters of a lake, and the feeling was ecstatic. Perfect happiness. Inside the concrete and steel cathedral, it was as cool as the village chapel or the caves at Pech Merle. Calor electric fans were stacked either side of the entrance, each in its box, on special offer – a highly suspicious gesture of benevolent concern. The pile had been smaller the week before.

The hypermarket had restocked. Vanessa and Agathe stopped to look, as they had every Saturday for the past three weeks, and this time their mother relented.

From there, they set off along the aisles, like explorers on an expedition. Alexandre walked behind, pushing the trolley. Up ahead, they seemed the embodiment of the ideal family. He followed them through the different departments, never losing patience in the clothes sections, or household goods, just going with the flow, released from desire or impulse, floating free and light, especially as there was air conditioning throughout the vast space. He felt a sense of unparalleled well-being. With gentle music playing in the background, the aisles were lined with objects of interest, like some endless enchanted cavern. In town, reality intruded every time you crossed the road. And while the air shimmered and burned over the arid hills outside, here people and merchandise alike were cool and serene. The whole thing seemed unreal.

Living as they did, on a hill farm far from anywhere, it heartened their parents to show the children that they were part of the modern world, the life of the TV adverts, the life of steam irons, electric coffee machines and carving knives, carousels of T-shirts, and yoghurt makers.

At four o'clock sharp, their father left them and made his way to the administrative offices – he had arranged a meeting with one of the head buyers to negotiate Lucienne and Louis's contract to supply fresh vegetables, but above all to talk about meat. Here, the meat counter had its own cutting room, and they were sure to be able to make a deal. The head food buyer wanted fresh, local produce, and though breeders were never in a position to name their price, their father knew that working with a giant like Mammouth would ensure regular orders.

Inside the hypermarket, everyone walked on the flat. After a week at Les Bertranges, going up and down the stony hillside tracks, it was restful to feel the smooth floor underfoot. At the meat counter, their mother inspected everything but bought nothing. Two men dressed up as butchers were shrink-wrapping pre-cut portions in plastic. At the next-door counter, two women were slicing cold meats and cured sausage. Twenty metres away, a Breton fisherman in a striped top and yellow rubber boots spoke in the gravelly, landlocked tones of Gers. Alexandre observed the scene. He envied his sisters' excitement. Their chorus of pleading carried more weight than he could ever muster to secure packs of Mamie Nova desserts or Chocolate Fingers. Backstage, in the offices, their father would be talking time frames and bulk orders, making commitments, saddling himself with constraints. It was a risky business: he had to stand his ground and not settle for anything under fifty francs a kilo. Their mother guided her flock onwards around the store, casting a wary eye over the food offers, certain that the flaccid, drab-looking steaks (not a trace of marbled fat) had come from dairy cows at the end of their working lives. She recoiled at the sea bream held out to her by the fake Breton fisherman. She had been tempted at first, but the poor fish had clearly suffered on its long journey to the point of sale. And besides, her instinct told her that the real bargains were elsewhere, on the stands at the ends of the aisles. Five packets of Grand-Mère coffee for the price of two, all bound together with thick red tape.

At five o'clock, everyone met at the cafeteria as planned, for the unmissable treat of a peach melba or a banana split. Agathe flew round and round in a helicopter amid the flashing bulbs of the miniature fairground ride – ten turns for five francs. A perfect afternoon. In this land of promise, the heatwave and the drought ceased to exist, and anyone who dared to complain about the air-conditioned atmosphere was a killjoy, like old Crayssac.

Back at the farm, they hurried to unload their new purchases.

Alexandre gave it some muscle, carrying the five packs of water all at once and basking in a heady mirage of adolescent omnipotence. The splendid new fan was lifted from its box and plugged in immediately. The three sisters tried it out, sitting down to face the miraculous blast of air, as they were watching a film. Their mother was unconvinced. The fan created a draught, for sure, but it was very noisy. The sisters thought it was perfect. Already, they each wanted to keep it on all night in their room. Except they had a bedroom each, and there was only one fan.

When everything had been put away, Alexandre and his father went out into the yard. The unbearable heat knocked them back straight away. Late afternoon was the very worst time: when the sun had beaten down relentlessly since morning, the earth could take no more, and nature sank into a complete, exhausted silence. The cows clustered at the bottom of the field, the two dogs had taken shelter in the barn, no birds flew. Alexandre sensed defeat. His father seemed tense and nervous, which was unlike him. He kept rubbing his forehead with the flat of his hand.

'So how did it go with the buyers?'

'Not sure. We're going to have to choose.'

'Oh? Choose what?'

'I'll be frank with you, Alexandre, from now on. Like a business partner. If you're sure you want to take over the farm, it's probably going to be worth your while extending the cattle shed or building a new one.'

'Why?'

'Mammouth aren't interested in taking one beast every few months. We need store cattle if we want to make this work, even dry cows, cull cows. Buy them in, fatten them up. We've got the space, we just need to double the arable, grow corn instead of the tobacco. We've got the river, so water's never going to be a problem. If we put three beasts a month their way, it'll be worth it.'

Alexandre had sensed his father's renewed ambition for some time now. He was thinking big, ready to move Les Bertranges out of the old-style polyculture practised by Lucienne and Louis. Alexandre would benefit from his father's ideas, but he could be a hostage to them, too. He would have to commit to working with his parents, and his grandparents down in the valley; he would take over in twenty or thirty years, and that meant spending his whole life in the same place, right here. No small decision. All so they could supply Mammouth with beef. And not only Mammouth — everyone swore that more hypermarkets were coming; there was already talk of a Radar, and Euromarché, because in the future, people would do all their shopping in vast cathedrals like these, with parking facilities and trolleys right next to the car. The silence around them felt heavier still, like lead. And then Alexandre remembered.

'Notice anything?'

'No. What?'

'The goats, they've stopped bleating.'

'Roasted alive, like the hedgerows.'

His father glanced up at the sun, its intense glare still high in the sky, radiating heat like a flow of lava.

'Another eight days of this and we'll all be roasted alive, for sure.'

## Monday, 19 July 1976

The rains returned, borne on the west wind. From now on, summer could proceed as usual. The fan was put back in its box and consigned to the barn, forgotten about that very evening, as cool, fresh water filled the troughs and welled up from the springs. The cattle emerged from the shade and felt the grass beneath their hooves. Life went on.

For weeks, the nation had been united in dread. Town and country had suffered alike in the catastrophe. City dwellers endured temperatures of 59°C aboard crowded buses, while country folk watched their harvests and forests wilt. For weeks, city dwellers and farmers were united in thirst, and now it seemed the experience had sealed their fellowship for evermore. The townies had taken Larzac to their hearts. At last, they understood the militants' cause. More than a protest over an extension to a military camp, the struggle opposed the forces of modernity that were disfiguring the planet as a whole. The government sought to appease all sides, and the court nearest the site, in the town of Millau, released the last few activists who had been awaiting sentence. This new compassion for Larzac was a sign: city dwellers no longer denied their rural roots. The natural world was close to their hearts, and the French nation felt a profound respect for rural life. Or a deep-seated nostalgia for the land.

And yet, just a few weeks later, in the middle of August, the government voted in a 'drought tax' (a clumsy phrase coined by the Ministry of Finance). It was decided that 2.2 billion francs would be raised from the taxpayer and distributed to the farmers, and to them alone, as if they were the only ones who had suffered in the heat. In the middle of the nation's summer holiday, Giscard decided to open the veins of the workforce, blue-collar and white-collar alike. The CGT was furious at the right-wing government's decision to clear the farmers' debts by siphoning off employees' pay, and to do it in mid-August, when the workers were on holiday. The exceptional one-off tax provoked outrage, and the resignation of Prime Minister Jacques Chirac. The angry backlash extended to the farmers themselves: the sums proposed were pathetically inadequate set against the damage they had suffered. The summer of fire had thrown everything and everyone out of joint. Nobody knew which way to turn, including Crayssac. Communism coursed through his veins, and it sickened him to feel more kinship with Giscard d'Estaing (the 'Baron' himself) than with his fellow countryman Georges Séguy, the Toulouse-born union leader and hero of the Resistance. Truly, the summer of fire had turned everything on its head.

It was four years since the arrival of the telephone. The girls had wanted an orange one, but their parents chose grey, alarmed, so they said, at the prospect of a bright-orange device that might ring at any moment. And anyway, coloured telephones were for Paris. In the provinces, you'd wait weeks for anything other than the standard-issue concrete-grey Bakelite model. The girls had got used to the grey in the end. But it was a big, ugly thing, with its hollow casing and rotary dial, like a moulded plastic breeze block.

Most irritating of all, everyone had the same grey colour: Monsieur Troquier the bank manager at Crédit Agricole, and the vet, and the shop at the Antar service station – all with the same ring. Enthroned on its small stand in the hallway, the telephone looked more like a piece of office equipment than a link to the rest of the family. Still, the phone meant that Caroline's absence was less of a wrench. It was good to know they could get in touch. The sisters called her at least twice a week, on Tuesday and Thursday, and each time they fought over the handset, though the sound was like pressing your ear to a door or listening in from the boot of a car.

Caroline came home every other weekend from Toulouse. As a rule, she would arrive late on Friday afternoon at the station in Cahors, or be dropped off by the Chastaing girl's parents (she was studying there, too). The rest of the time, it was strange to see the empty place at the end of the table, their big sister's chair, silent now. Caroline had occupied that spot because she was the eldest, but also because she would get to her feet throughout the meal to help. Caroline took an interest in everything, led the conversation on every possible subject. Of the four siblings, she was the family's very own talk-show host, the sister-in-chief. She took her place every second Friday now, and she had more to tell than ever. About her studies, of course, and life in Toulouse, all the new friends she had made, not kids from around here, but foreigners. She told them a thousand things about the big city, and the big apartment they all shared in an old townhouse in Saint-Cyprien, the working-class neighbourhood that faced the historic city centre, on the opposite bank of the Garonne. People were always coming round. Usually, the apartment was crowded with far more than the five housemates. Caroline told them everything: she had nothing to hide, and no subject was taboo. She'd got a room in the commune (which was basically what it was) by sheer luck, and she talked constantly about the crowd of students who hung out there – Diego, Trevis, Richard, Kathleen and two or three others. Most of all, she talked about the girl from Germany, Constanze. Provocatively, on purpose. Each time Caroline pronounced the tall, blonde girl's name, she would glance at her brother. She had seen all too clearly, on the Sunday evenings when he drove her back to Toulouse and stayed for a drink before heading home, how sometimes he hung around late into the evening too, but only when Constanze was there. If not, or they knew she wouldn't be there later, Alexandre would leave much sooner.

'It's true, admit it!'

'Shut up! You're talking rubbish. I leave earlier sometimes because I'm tired, that's all.'

'No! Absolutely not. Don't listen to him, he's so secretive! I swear, whenever Constanze's around, he's never in a hurry to come back here.'

'Is she really that tall?' Agathe reached a hand high above her head.

'Thing is, little brother, she's a high-flyer, she works hard – biology and law, she's out of your league.'

'Those German girls are very sporty ...' their mother added. 'They won everything in Moscow, they were faster than the men in the swimming.'

'Yes, but those were the East Germans,' their father corrected her. 'Built like fridge freezers, and necks as thick as a bull's.'

'Not all of them,' said Caroline, slyly. 'Proof: Constanze's from Leipzig.'

'So?'

'So Leipzig is in East Germany!'

'Watch out, Alexandre,' their mother laughed. 'You'd better get into training!'

Whenever the subject arose, the sisters kept up their banter, but in truth they were just a little jealous. Not only had Alexandre passed his driving test, but he went to Toulouse twice each month, a magical thing in the eyes of the two younger girls. They knew perfectly well that Constanze had caught his eye. Teasing him about the German goddess had become a game. Their parents went along with it, but they knew that little by little they were being excluded from their children's talk. Unconsciously, the girls were distancing themselves from the things that really mattered: the farm, the weather forecast, the water level in the river, calving, how well the grass was growing, and the maintenance of the buildings. Things that had set the pace of life here since forever. Angèle and Jean observed the change and accepted it as inevitable. Alexandre and the two little ones were still living with them, but everything – their interests and plans, the music they listened to – seemed to take them in another direction, away from the path their parents had trodden.

What caught Jean and Angèle off guard more than anything else was the talk about people they had never met, and probably never would. Perfect strangers like this Constanze girl, unknown to them, but clearly someone of great importance to Caroline and Alexandre. Before, country parents would know everyone their children knew, and not only that, but everything about their families. Everyone knew everything about everybody, for several generations back. But now Caroline talked endlessly about her housemates, and students from Spain, England or Germany, distant people they would never see, though they heard about them constantly.

Still, the evening came when their mother wanted to know more about this Constanze. And what she heard was far from reassuring. Their son's probable crush came from the other side of the Wall. Her family lived in Leipzig, or East Berlin, which made her more foreign than they could possibly have imagined. Under questioning, Caroline told them that Constanze's mother worked for the East German railways. She travelled on both sides of the Wall, but she lived in the East, where she took care of her ailing parents. The father was a highly qualified aeronautical engineer, based at Toulouse–Blagnac Airport. Perhaps he was a spy, working for the Russians, said Caroline, purely to wind Alexandre up. Her sisters laughed, but Alexandre did not, and neither did their parents.

Angèle and their father pondered the matter constantly, though they never spoke about it. Would Alexandre find a girl one day, a girl who would agree to live here on the farm, or somewhere nearby, at least? Would he find a girl to marry, when all the young people around here were getting out fast, one after the other? Alexandre was almost nineteen. They knew he had had a couple of girlfriends at the college, and probably one or two flings he'd kept secret, but nothing serious so far.

As for the German girl, their mother knew already that home-

43

sickness, and the need to care for her family, would catch up with her one day, especially if they were behind the Wall. Besides, a girl who had never lived anywhere but Berlin, Toulouse and Paris would never settle out here in the country.

The non-existent love story between their brother and Constanze preoccupied them all, not least Alexandre himself. Twice they had found themselves alone together in a room at Caroline's apartment, but his strategy for getting her to like him was to appear aloof, say nothing, play hard to get. A subtle approach instilled by Monsieur Roger, the rugby coach, who had taught his players that to seduce a girl, you should never try to talk to her, and better still, you should pretend not to notice her at all. Inevitably, he said, her curiosity would be aroused, and she would ask herself, 'Who is this guy who won't even look at me, when the others have been hanging around me all evening?' The trouble was, Monsieur Roger was full of advice before a match, or at half-time, but over the three seasons that Alexandre had played in the college team, they had won precious few games, so perhaps the coach's advice wasn't so great after all.

More than ever, all through the weekend, Caroline was the Big Sister in the eyes of the other three. Not only was she the oldest, but she enjoyed the status of one who has crossed to the other side, to the promised land. She had taken the first step towards independence, and the city, and her talk was full of the new places that filled and expanded her life: Place Wilson, built in a circle, with its vast Gaumont cinema, the sun-drenched quaysides of the Garonne at La Daurade, the university buildings at Mirail; and the main square, Place du Capitole, where the cafés and their terraces were open late. At night, the brightly lit streets thronged with people. Viewed from Les Bertranges, Toulouse was truly a land of promise – the birthplace of Concorde, humanity's greatest accomplishment, and if one day people could fly to New York in an hour, it would be thanks to Sud Aviation. Toulouse would carry civilisation forward into the year 2000. Perhaps, one day, Europe's aviation industry would swallow Boeing and McDonnell Douglas, and Toulouse would lead the world.

It bothered their parents that on the weekends when Caroline was home, she never went to look at the cattle. Not even the newborn calves. The saffron was finished now: the rains had caused the last bulbs to rot in the ground, and the tobacco harvest was no more either – the Chinese had undercut the selling price and Europe was no longer subsidising the crop. They had abandoned all the labour-intensive work, all the tasks that brought families together in the past. It was the same with the potatoes: no need to spend two entire days down on all fours now, when the machine harvested them a hundred times quicker, and their grandparents had tripled the area devoted to Bintjes and Rosas down in the valley. The loose vegetable racks at Mammouth took some filling – you had to produce more and more to keep up with the orders. Same with the animals, and because grass was still the best feed for beef cattle, the Fabriers had focused on grazing pasture. They could plan ahead now, growing the grass when they needed it, rather than waiting for it to show. They sowed the right quantities of seed grasses, clover and ryegrass, so that the pasture had the correct ratio of stalk to leaf, making it more digestible, more easily assimilated by the animals. Soya meal and maize silage made up the protein; everything was precise and planned, no room for uncertainty. The seed drills were calibrated down to the last millimetre. Progress wasn't only for Hong Kong, Taiwan and Singapore. It had its place here, too, on the farm.

Saturday, 12 July 1980

On that point, Giscard had won. He would forever be the president who strung black rubber telephone cables between dead pine trees along the roads of France. Thanks to him, everyone had the telephone – in town, down in the valleys, even high up in the mountains. Giscard's black cables covered the countryside. A pole-less, wire-less track leading to someone's place was almost shameful, a sign that they were hopelessly far behind the times. Another struggle old Crayssac had lost. A bit like Larzac, where the fight went on as before, but the war was far from won. Still, the old countryman organised his committees up there in Aveyron, and each time he was away, Alexandre would help him out, saying nothing to anybody. He took the goats out in the morning, brought them in at night, even milked them when their udders were full. The old man never stayed up on the plateau longer than was necessary, anyway. He would come home late at night, getting a lift from their former postman in his battered Citroën Ami 6 Estate.

Crayssac's brushes with the gendarmes had done nothing to calm his zeal. He returned to the fight every couple of weeks, with the retired postman or a bunch of hippies who lived out towards Lalbenque. He had never asked Alexandre to drive him, so far. The struggle had lasted a decade, and the activists were always searching for new ideas to keep it going. There had been marches and masses, picnics and concerts, sit-ins and 'lightning strikes', like the release of flocks of sheep into the regional administrative headquarters.

46

Since the previous summer, legions of city dwellers had been coming to lend a hand on the farms threatened with expropriation, working in the fields or renovating buildings, clearing tracks and replanting telegraph poles.

For ten years, the militants had kept the sacred flame alight, but the enemy was strong: none other than the army of the world's fifth most powerful nation – soldiers equipped with machine guns and tanks. At times, they would launch into exercises, firing 105mm shells, though happily so far only blank rounds had been used.

Alexandre had listened to Crayssac's talk of violent uprising since he was a child. The old man's obstinacy commanded respect. He lived as people must have done for centuries on the hillside. Apart from electricity and his short-wave radio, his cottage was set firmly in the Middle Ages. When Alexandre visited, he would sit opposite Crayssac and accept a freshly rolled cigarette, as if it were some kind of splendiferous offering.

'You know why I like ewes better than farming folk?'

'No!'

'They have nice kind faces.'

'What do you mean?'

'A sheep has a pleasant, kindly look about it. It's like a big, soft clump of wool.'

'So what?'

'So, ever seen anyone afraid of a sheep? No, eh? Well, up at Larzac, the farmers have got all that support – the hippies, and the townies, the Catholics and the Commies, all of them – because of the sheep. Mark my words, if they'd been rearing turkeys, or pigs, or bulls, Larzac would never have got off the ground.'

'Sheep are cute-looking, but they're really stupid.'

'For sure, but Debré's cops don't know that!'

Crayssac had fought in the Second World War, in the Resistance with his father, it was said, but the only battle he liked to recall, his personal Austerlitz, a jubilant, treasured memory, was the episode of the great flock of sheep they had released into the prefecture buildings, in the departmental capital. A hilarious sight, according to him, with the cops and the riot police completely overrun by columns of leaping ewes, the animals so terrified that they scattered all over the place, and the cops' peaked *képis* falling off as they ran after the animals, which got them even more excited, and some of the sheep were so nervous that they knocked the riot police to the floor and trampled them as they bolted.

But with the presidential election less than a year away, the fun was well and truly over. The government was flexing its muscles and making ready to implement the threatened evictions. The only way to turn the spotlight back onto the struggle was to organise a rerun of the sheep, not in Rodez or Millau this time, but in the heart of Paris.

'Yep, thousands of sheep released on the Champs-Élysées, or the Champ de Mars, under the Eiffel Tower, perhaps even the president's own garden, the Élysée Palace itself, why ever not?'

Alexandre was fascinated by the old man's revolutionary fervour; it both captivated and frightened him. He had no desire to get into trouble with the gendarmes. The very thought of them turning up at the farm one day, or calling him in, even for some minor act of revolt, like setting a STOP sign on fire, scared him half to death.

Crayssac pictured the scene, the chaos of sheep streaming through the ministries, while Giscard struggled to restrain his Weimaraner and his Labrador, the classy pair of dogs he had introduced to the nation on TV, on the animal-lovers' programme *30 millions d'amis*, as proof that he really did have a heart.

'That would be a fine fucking mess, wouldn't it? The Paris cops are trained to tackle gang bosses armed to the teeth, and left-wing militants, and the PLO, but not sheep.'

'But sheep can't carry banners and placards.'

'No, but they're there. They've been there from the very beginning. And that's what matters. Never giving up the struggle, being sure you can hold out for ten years, twenty years if you have to. It's what the sheep do.'

Crayssac liked to put on a show, and Alexandre enjoyed watching. He finished his cigarette. He wasn't sure exactly what it was he admired about Crayssac – perhaps the survival of a bygone world, a time when farmers made their own cheese and sold only what they didn't need, when self-sufficiency was the goal of every farm, nothing more. Alexandre was afraid he might see himself in the old man, one day, that he might come to resemble him in thirty or fifty years. Perhaps he, too, would be a hardened bachelor, as people said, having lived all his life alone.

'You know, Alexandre, I'm not telling you all this for nothing. Perhaps you'll find it applies to you, too, one day.'

'Protests, marches, they're not really my thing.'

'Fine, but if ever you get into a scrape one day, you can bet no one will come and pet your cows. You think you're the kings of the hill over at Les Bertranges because you've got cattle and a few hectares. Granted, you've done all right, you've got plenty, but you're on your own. And if the state decides to stick an army camp on your land one day, or a dam in your river, well, it's like I said, you'll be on your own.'

'They'd never put an army camp here.'

'What do you know? They've been talking for ten years about building a motorway from Paris to Spain, and they're getting on with building the northern end right now – Châteauroux, Limoges, Orléans. Soon enough, you'll see, they'll be making a start on the southern section.'

'And why would it come this way?'

'Because we're surrounded by empty land, and empty land can

easily be expropriated. We're right in its path. They've got plans to bridge the river valleys – the Dordogne, the Lot – so I reckon stepping over us here, in the Rauze valley, won't pose too much of a problem.'

Alexandre had heard talk of the motorway since he was a boy. Every summer, at the end of July, when the first wave of holidaymakers headed back home, up north, and the August contingent drove south, there were two-hour tailbacks at Cahors, Brive, Caussade and Gourdon. Tens of thousands of cars inching through the city centres. Alexandre knew the old man was telling him this to lure him into the struggle, too, for some unknown purpose. His face lit up every time he brought up the proposed motorway route. But not for one second could Alexandre picture a viaduct straddling their valley, nor a four-lane highway ploughing through their fields. It was impossible.

'See, I swore I'd never let the telephone come past my fields, and the result is there for us all to see. Progress is like a great machine. It will crush us all.'

## Sunday, 21 September 1980

That Sunday, Caroline wanted to set off early for Toulouse. A party was planned at the big shared apartment. Her housemates had invited their crowd, students from Montpellier, Barcelona, even Germany, together with some who hung around with the trendier lecturers, the self-appointed guru types on the teaching staff at Mirail – left-wing activists. Caroline wasn't too happy about that. She wanted to get back before everyone arrived, make sure everything went OK. She was vague about the reason for the party, including with Alexandre, but she needed him to drive her, especially since she was heading back to town with four crates of vegetables and conserves. Alexandre intended to make the most of the evening. For him, it was a chance to see other people and savour what was, for him, an exotic, even alien atmosphere. If possible, he would get closer to Constanze. Later, he would drive back along the Nationale 20, windows wide open, in the dead of night, no worries. Driving at night was no problem for him, any more than going to bed at three o'clock in the morning, even when he had to be up two hours later to take a cow to slaughter.

Caroline only came back to the farm once a month these days, with no great desire to be there at all. She was a child of the city now, in her second year of modern languages and literature at the University of Toulouse, and she left town only rarely. They had barely seen her that summer. In July, she had taken a job as a supervisor at a children's summer school, and then as a waitress in a Hippopotamus steak house, where she spent her days serving greasy slices of meat that the restaurant received vacuum-packed, stewed in its own blood.

For the drive to Toulouse, Alexandre was allowed to borrow the Citroën, a far more comfortable ride than the Renault. Driving the Citroën was pure pleasure, especially on the long, straight stretches of the Nationale after Caussade. There were no straight roads around Les Bertranges: the whole area was threaded with sinuous, winding lanes and no one ever exceeded fifty kilometres an hour.

Once they were on the Nationale, Caroline lit a cigarette. She never dared smoke her filterless Camels in front of her parents, nor on the farm track or the smaller roads, for fear of being seen and judged by one or other of their neighbours. Above all, she was afraid that if she smoked at the farm, her parents would see it as another irrefutable sign of her newfound freedom. Yet their father had his daily ration of six Gitanes Maïs, wrapped in yellow corn paper, two of which he lit at the table after lunch and supper. The thick smoke had an appealing aroma of fresh straw and leaf mould. Smoking was not forbidden at Les Bertranges, but Caroline's departure from the nest was hard enough to bear, and she had no desire to ram the message home by dragging on a cigarette in front of the family.

At seven o'clock they reached the big old tenement building in Saint-Cyprien and parked in a side street. The sounds of the party reached them straight away. The music escaping through the open windows was much livelier than usual: Madness and The Police, not the gentle, more mellow stuff they generally played in the daytime. They never usually had the volume up so high, either. Alexandre's arms were loaded with the crates of food. He closed the boot with his elbow and caught up with his sister who had hurried on ahead, looking anxious. Already, he felt he had entered another world. Suddenly, the farm seemed far away — more distant than ever, that life of patient husbandry and slumbering hillsides. Caroline was worried her brother would stay for the party, leave late and drive home through the night after drinking or smoking dope. Their parents would worry, and so she did too. Alexandre followed her, saying nothing, As the one carrying the big crates, the vegetables and jars of preserves prepared by their mother, he had every reason to come up to the apartment. They entered the courtyard planted with tall trees, like the grounds of a splendid town mansion. But the space was neglected, like the dilapidated facades and high windows staring down all around. Alexandre was impressed by the decor each time he visited. The old brick-and-stone tenement must have been a fine building once; it had the timeless look of a small country house set down in the middle of the city. Birdsong competed with the sounds from the avenue on the other side of the carriage entrance, but louder than both this evening was the noise of the party, reverberating through the open windows.

The moment they entered the apartment, Alexandre felt assailed by conflicting emotions. He wanted desperately to soak up the heady atmosphere, mingle with the diverse crowd. But cruel preconceptions, and his own shyness, held him back. Not being a student disqualified him from any number of conversations. Among these university types, all a little older than him, he felt horribly young and, most of all, horribly uncool, an outsider.

He deposited the provisions in the kitchen, drank a glass of water from the tap and followed the loud hubbub of voices to the big living room. It was quite a gathering, at least forty people, students he'd seen before, and others, older than the rest. One group in particular stood apart, all of them apparently in their late twenties, perhaps even thirty. On the drive from the farm, Caroline had explained that she was not happy about the party. It was then she told Alexandre about a particular crowd who would be there, militant types who spent more time on politics than they did studying. Alexandre walked over to Antoine and Sophie, whom he knew already. Two others joined them. In spite of the din, he quickly gathered that people had arrived in town the day before for the launch of a place called La Rotonde. And for a big protest that had been held the day before, against the planned nuclear power plant at Golfech, an hour's drive north-west of Toulouse. Alexandre felt a strange sense of déjà vu. It was like listening to the spectre of Crayssac. These people were young, but like Crayssac they seemed thoroughly agitated, and they spoke the same language. They talked about the nuclear plant the way Crayssac talked about the telephone: as a kind of evil curse that would threaten all mankind. As far as Alexandre could tell, La Rotonde was a plot of land that the anti-nuclear protestors had managed to buy in the middle of the proposed site. The group had passed themselves off as agriculturalists, with help from the Larzac farmers, well versed in the occupation of contested land. The plan was to build a House of Resistance as the centre of operations for the protest. The atmosphere there had been cheerful and good-natured, they said. However, a few Molotov cocktails had been thrown at the diggers, and some of the EDF electrical installations had been set alight, though no one knew by whom.

'The cops do it themselves. Anything to discredit the struggle. They start the fires, then tell everyone it was us. Everyone knows that.'

Antoine was waiting for him to agree, but the only thing that interested Alexandre was whether Constanze would show up that evening, or not. He glanced casually all around the room, but there was no sign of her. He longed to explore further, down the corridor that led to the bedrooms. Caroline had disappeared that way as soon as she set foot inside the apartment. He was intrigued. But instead, he opened a can of Schweppes and wandered from group to group, never settling, daunted by the multitude of new faces. More than ever, people seemed to stare straight through him, and he found almost nothing to say, even to those he already knew. He decided to save face and return to the kitchen to keep an eye on the food he had brought. There, he found more new arrivals, four guys busy stocking the fridge with beer. They seemed to be German, but Constanze wasn't with them. The guys glared at him, even stopped talking when he entered the room, so Alexandre retreated. In the corridor, there was no hint of the cloud of patchouli that followed Constanze everywhere she went, a heady fragrance that suggested she had wafted in, freshly sprayed, from paradise. He liked her more than the other girls, but she was unattainable, as he well knew, for any number of reasons. First, she was a student, and German, plus she was a year older than him. Not least, Caroline would hate it if he slept with one of her pals. For all these reasons, he liked Constanze more than anything.

Caroline still hadn't reappeared. Alexandre knew already that if he went to find her, she would ask him not to hang about. Or tell him to leave. He sank deep into the battered sofa, not wishing to join in with the people who'd started dancing. He felt the absolute discomfort of a person alone in a crowd where everyone else is talking and having fun. Worse still, he actually dreaded the possibility that someone might talk to him, ask him where he was from, what he was studying. If he said he was a farmer, a cattle breeder, they would sneer, or think he was joking. He'd been right to stay for a while, soak up the atmosphere – if nothing else, he understood now that there was nothing for him here. But a guy sat down next to him on the sofa. Short, dark, full of beer and evidently keen to talk. He was surprised that he hadn't seen Alexandre at the protest yesterday, nor at La Rotonde that afternoon. He seemed on edge, given to flights of warlike rhetoric, and had a strong Spanish accent. Alexandre had to concentrate hard, over the music, to make out his words. The guy handed him a cigarette, and Alexandre took it, though he didn't feel like smoking. He listened while the guy told him about his family. Spanish Republicans. He seemed proud of that. So you could be proud of your Republican ancestry, like aristocrats or the grand bourgeoisie here in France? Alexandre had no wish to say that he was from a family of farmers, and if no one asked, he wasn't telling. The guy told him about the protest the day before. He made it sound like a war zone: there had been grenades and lines of armed soldiers. Giscard was Franco in his eyes. Alexandre thought about last night's television news. In the closing round-up there had been a brief report about diggers sabotaged at a site near Agen. But things got blown up every day in France. The Spanish Republican continued, seemingly trying to convince Alexandre that the nuclear plant would never happen. They had started to build a camp from recycled materials. La Rotonde would be a proper encampment, dug in, right in the middle of all the work – an international symbol. They could hold out under siege for months if required. The more the guy talked, the more Spanish he sounded and the more excited he became. He rolled his r's, eyes flashing as he described how the EDF installations had caught fire the night before, how the Molotov cocktails had set the builders' vehicles alight, sending balls of flame into the sky, because their tanks were full. Alexandre listened, and felt he could see Crayssac all over again. Faced with these rebels, old and young, these firebrands from across the generations, he wondered why he was not like them, why he didn't mobilise to resist the march of progress, why he felt none of their cultivated, defiant scorn. In that, at least, he felt closer to his parents than to the protesters. Like them, his focus, above all, was the future of their farm.

'In the referendum, eighty per cent said they were against the plant. Eighty per cent, can you imagine! Only one word for it when the word of people is ignored ... Dictatorship!'

'Yeah. Absolutely.'

Alexandre felt not the slightest urge to battle the nuclear industry. He wasn't the least bit interested. This guy and his high-strung tales of rebellion were getting on his nerves. The Spaniard had noticed, it seemed, and recoiled a little on the sofa. He was surprised when Alexandre told him he'd never set foot in Golfech, and astonished when his lack of concern became obvious.

'Are you part of the struggle, or not?'

'Not. No time for it, anyway. I work from six in the morning to eight o'clock at night, out in the middle of nowhere. I have to be there, every day.'

'What do you do?'

'Farming. I breed cattle.'

'Oh, I get it. Veal stuffed with hormones, all that.'

Alexandre failed to see the joke.

'This isn't Spain, or Italy. My cows eat grass and the calves drink their mothers' milk.'

'So you're on a real farm, then, you're a proper *campesino*, a cowboy?'

'Sort of.'

'How big's your farm?'

'Quite big, fifty hectares, plus the woodland, a river, eighty head of cattle. Plenty to keep me busy.'

The Spaniard stared at him in amazement. He straightened up and shook him by the hand. He said his name was Xabi. He wasn't Spanish, as such, but Basque. Then he stared thoughtfully at Alexandre, saying nothing, as if suddenly struck by something he was keeping to himself. Alexandre could see he was wondering what to do. Then the guy got to his feet and crossed the living room, slaloming between the knots of people standing or sitting on the floor. He went up to the four who had been standing to one side, the guys from the kitchen. They were sitting at the big dining table now, talking amongst themselves. Alexandre looked around the

57

room. Still no sign of Constanze. She must have gone somewhere else. Caroline had told him she sometimes went into town to call her family in Berlin. Often, at the central post office, you had to wait to get a phone booth, and the call would cut out all the time, but if she rang them direct, from a telephone box, it cost a fortune in coins. So she would go to the university buildings and make a discreet call from a desk in the administrative offices. From what Alexandre had understood, the other housemates didn't want her to call from the apartment. Perhaps they were right to be paranoid. Perhaps frequent calls to East Germany from the shared telephone would get them all a file with the Renseignements Généraux, the security police, maybe even a tapped line. Or perhaps that was just the kind of crazy nonsense they believed.

From the other side of the room, the Basque was signalling for him to join the group at the table. Alexandre was suspicious of the four of them, but it gave him an excuse to stay at the party, at least. He threaded his way through the dancers. When he reached the table, three of the guys stood up to greet him. They were about to sit down again when they all agreed there was too much noise, too many people. They told Alexandre to follow them back to the kitchen, where they ordered everyone to take their bowls of crisps and get out, then opened the fridge and took out a round of beers. Alexandre felt obliged to take one, and they all raised their cans and drank.

It was quieter in the kitchen. The guys all had German accents, but they spoke perfect French. They began talking to Alexandre about the Golfech power plant, asking him what he thought about it. They were interested in the views of a regular citizen, not an activist. Alexandre said he had nothing against nuclear power. They seemed surprised. On what grounds? Alexandre admitted that he didn't really follow it all – atomic energy, nuclear power plants – he didn't know much about it, except that they'd been talking about it on the evening news, on both channels, since the end of the summer. One of the regular journalists, usually Elkabbach or Léon Zitrone, would explain that the Iran–Iraq War and the closing of the Strait of Hormuz posed a serious threat to oil supplies, and so France needed nuclear power. He spoke, and the guys learned that French TV was full of reports that explained how the nuclear 'generators', as Zitrone called them, worked. With a ton of diagrams for the benefit of the viewers, too: 'Understanding, not fear,' as they always said.

'So you're not afraid?'

'Of nuclear power? No.'

'You understood it all?'

'Well, no. But it's cheap and clean.'

'And you believe that?'

'Seems obvious to me that atoms aren't as polluting as oil. I know about oil; when I put my foot down in the John Deere I send fifty litres of diesel up in smoke for every hectare worked, and you should see the black stuff it belches out. Two hundred litres of fuel when I'm ploughing, and believe me, it smokes ...'

The four guys looked perplexed. Alexandre sensed this was the wrong answer.

At that moment, the kitchen door opened and Constanze appeared. She was surprised to find them there, apologised for bursting in and said she just wanted to get some bottles of Coke from the fridge. Clearly, she respected the group and was surprised to see Alexandre chatting with them in private. More astonished than surprised. Plainly astonished, in fact, to find him sitting with them, in conclave, in the kitchen. She went around the table, air-kissing each of them in turn, but with no show of warmth or real affection. They exchanged a few words in German. They sounded serious, but Alexandre couldn't understand what was being said. She shot him a discreet, incredulous glance on her way out. Clearly, he had scored a point.

On the few occasions he had seen her in recent weeks, Alexandre had realised it would be hard to get her to notice him, precisely because, each time, what seemed to interest her most was the talk among Caroline's most militant group of friends. She was obviously a political type, exceedingly unlikely to be interested in talking about alfalfa silage or soya meal. Just then, the apparent leader of the group pulled his chair closer.

'Tell me, Alexandre – Alexandre is your real name, is it?'

'Why, do you all use false names?'

'Listen, Alexandre, you've been watching too much TV. The problem with nuclear power is not how polluting it is or isn't, the problem is, it centralises energy – the means of production – in the hands of the state, and energy is the engine of industrial capitalism, with which *you* don't think you have a problem, or at least not yet ...'

From there, they launched into yet another rehearsal of the points Alexandre had picked up here and there already, whenever he sat in on the students' conversations. He scarcely listened.

'But wait, I'm just out there on my farm. I don't expect anything from anyone, and no one comes looking for me. I'm a free man: I can do what I please.'

'Exactly – that's what you think, but with nuclear power, the state controls everything, because it controls the energy that controls everything else, and whoever controls electricity in the future will be even more powerful than the controllers of the world's oil today. Besides which, you'd better believe that by the year 2000, there won't be a drop of oil left!'

Alexandre had never thought of that. One day, there would be no oil, no diesel, a world without petrol, the end of everything.

'They'll keep drilling, and one day they'll be drilling into nothing, and on that day, electricity will be the only thing left, and even your tractor will be electric. That's why, if you attack the nuclear industry today, you're striking at the very heart of the system.'

Xabi took up the thread. Alexandre felt he was being ensnared.

'We can't let them get away with it, d'you understand? We must not be oppressed, and as soon as the work gets underway at Golfech, we'll be taking action, every single day. Boom, boom! D'you see?'

The Basque mimicked the explosion by flipping the top off a bottle of Kronenbourg with a five-franc coin.

Alexandre was adrift on a tide of confusion, but he knew one thing: if he kept in with the group, he would rise in Constanze's estimation. Even sitting with them here, plotting in the kitchen, had elevated him in her eyes. He was among the movers and shakers, the leaders. The conversation continued, and finally he began to understand why they had taken an interest in him.

'We need to take action. Sit-ins, squats, clashes with the forces of law and order, they're all very well, but the struggle demands decisive action. The rest is just folksy nonsense, tree-huggers lying down in the road to stop the trucks going in, when the best thing is to blow them up before they even get started. Always go for the most radical solution – do you see what I'm getting at?'

'Not really. I get the ecological argument, nature, that makes sense, but not blowing up trucks.'

'Alexandre, the tree-huggers are against nuclear power because they're tree-huggers. They're so naïve, they think the real threat from nuclear power is nuclear power, but that's not it at all. The real danger lies in handing the keys to all that over to the state.'

At this, the guy who had been leaning against the wall in silence since the beginning looked across at Alexandre and summarised the situation in a thick German accent.

'Let's be clear, Alexandre, the only answer to everyone's cause, the tree-huggers and all the rest, the very best thing we can do, is to blow the nuclear plants sky-high before they're even built – do you get that?'

'OK, but why are you telling me all this?'

'Fertiliser, Alex. Fertiliser.'

Sunday, 21 September 1980

'In the year 2980 the people of earth live in luxury ... Space robots exploit the resources of distant planets, and the harvest is given freely to all. But still their overlords fear that humanity will rise, stand proud and hold its head high again one day. Their answer? The mondio-visual brutaliser device, that blocks the minds of mankind. The people are slaves – they do not think, therefore they are content ... But I, Albator, and my loyal crew have broken these bonds of steel. None but we can alert our fellow men to the danger they face ... Now, I am known to all as the Space Pirate Captain, wanted dead or alive, wherever I go ...'

Sunday evenings were sacrosanct. No one turned on the television after supper, and Agathe would read aloud from her comic book, reliving the adventures of the lean, long-legged Japanese cartoon hero, with his boyish charm and tousled hair forever falling into his eyes. That evening, at supper, the parents found themselves alone with Vanessa and Agathe. Sitting opposite their two youngest daughters they felt young at heart, too. Now, they had a chance to hone the parenting skills they had first used on the other two. They made both girls read aloud.

Without Alexandre and Caroline the games were different, and the conversation, too, even the background noise around the house. Everything reverted to childhood. After supper, the air was warm and languid, with a lingering fragrance of summer, though there was school tomorrow. In the glow of that Sunday evening, with the remaining swallows swooping high above, anyone would have thought they were deep in the month of August. Before sunset, their father went to check on the muddy hollow at Les Bras. The cattle drank from the river, and their hooves dug out the banks. Before long, someone would be forcing him to fence off the river and install drinking troughs down there. Under the new regulations, cattle were no longer free to drink where they pleased. Vanessa and Agathe decided to follow him down, but they ran while he walked and were ahead of him now on the track, scampering back and forth with their back-to-school gift, a little butterfly net, oblivious to everything but their own eternal present. Watching them, it comforted Jean to think that Vanessa would be there on the farm for another two or three years. And it would be another six or seven before Agathe flew the nest. Their father felt no bitterness. He thought of Alexandre. The son, the boy they were counting on. Perhaps he needed no further enticement, but still, they could buy a new tractor. The steering on the old John Deere was as stiff as a lock gate on the Canal du Midi. A new tractor would be a grand gesture to his son, Jean could see that, but it was tantamount to bribery, forcing him to live on the farm. Perhaps one day, he, too, would feel an overwhelming desire to leave. All those trips to Toulouse, meeting all those new people, discovering lives that were brighter, more up-to-the-minute than his own. Perhaps he, too, would develop a taste for a different life altogether. It was obvious: the purchase of a tractor that didn't break its driver's back or threaten to slide or tip over on the steep hillsides would bring a more modern aspect to the work they did there.

The track ran down the hillside, and the horizon broadened to a vista of the setting sun. The gaps in the trees afforded glimpses of the valley, with its rich pasturelands. The cows were just below, dotted about the hillside, grazing peacefully. The pasture had grown steadily through the summer that year. The warm days and cool nights were good for the grass. Nature is a fragile balance that will not be dictated to. She is bountiful, or not, from one year to the next. Gazing at the landscape, their father felt a kind of foreboding. Whenever his son was in Toulouse, Jean dreaded the possibility that he would meet someone, that he would take up with that German girl once and for all, and change his mind, and not take over the farm. There would be no continuity then, no future. All country people knew this. Once the children got a taste for the city, they never came back.

With no one left here on the farm, all he could see from where he stood, all the bright meadows and hedgerows, would very soon spread out of control, smother their own growth, and die. No one would move to a farm around here. Quite the opposite. They would all shut down one after the other. One day there would be no cows to keep the pasture in check, no goats or ewes to trim the higher ground, no countrymen to maintain the tracks. This whole world would run wild, wild enough to suffocate.

Vanessa and Agathe ran towards him, proud of having caught something in their little butterfly net.

'Look, Papa, it's a yellow one, that means it's going to rain!'

Their father stared at the setting sun, then glanced at the butterfly. There would be no rain, not that night at any rate, nor tomorrow. At least that's what the television forecast had said.

'Let it go now. They're fragile things, butterflies. Very fragile.'

'No, I want to take it home. We can put it to bed in a jam jar.'

'Well now, Agathe, would you like to sleep in a jam jar, hmm? Would you like it if someone put you in a big glass pot?'

Agathe's face froze in an expression of sweet perplexity. The sight of the butterfly caught in the net brought another image to mind – those poor, crated veal calves, and the scandal of hormone-fed veal that had erupted lately, as a result of which the authorities had ordered the slaughter of 2 million beasts over the next six months; 2 million calves brought into the world for nothing, slaughtered as a precaution. Jean told himself this would all end badly one day.

'Agathe, please do as I say. Let it go.'

Agathe turned the net inside out like the sleeve of a coat, but the butterfly was still caught. It refused to fly away.

'You see, Papa, it doesn't want to go!'

'Let it recover, it's in shock. You've given it a terrible fright.'

'Oh, really?'

The insect was stock-still. Petrified, or dead. The three of them stood motionless for a moment. The cows were still some distance away, three fields along, and all around, far in every direction, there was not another soul, just their grandparents' new little house, down in the valley out of sight. And everything in that vast space hung on the butterfly's fate. Would it, could it fly away? At last, after a few minutes, it began to beat its wings and pick itself free from the net. Then it rose high into the sky. Usually, at that time of day, butterflies kept close to the ground, but the tiny yellow speck went on rising, rising through the darkening air, bright and alive, like an answered prayer. Vanessa and Agathe set off again, out in front, returning straight away to their games and their laughter. He was lucky to have them, Jean thought to himself, these two little girls with their endless chatter, bubbling with life.

Sunday, 21 September 1980

Alexandre came out of the kitchen shocked and stunned, as if he'd been slapped. At least it was clear to him now. While the other guys talked, he pictured his mother the week before, peeling potatoes over the outspread pages of *La Dépêche du Midi*, dropping the peel onto a photograph of a railway station that had blown up in Italy, possibly due to a faulty boiler or, more likely, a bomb. An explosion so powerful it had overturned trains and killed eighty people in the heart of Bologna.

But more than those hideous scenes, what Alexandre had taken from their talk was the fascination the guys exerted over Constanze. She had come back to join them, and sat listening, grave and beautiful, while Anton spoke.

In the big room, the music was playing louder and louder – Pink Floyd and Yes covered puddles of words, bursts of laughter, a sea of conversations conducted by spirits wandering free. The chillum was being passed around eagerly from smoker to smoker, and most were lying on the floor rather than on the sofas. The few still dancing performed vague, almost abstract moves, as if entranced.

An hour went by, and then Constanze emerged from the kitchen. She joined Alexandre where he sat, alone, on the battered sofa. In a show of concern that he had not seen in her before, she asked if everything was all right. It was difficult to hear above the noise, but Alexandre didn't dare move closer. She was talking about music, wanted to know what he liked, whether there was something he wanted to listen to. She was beautiful, and Alexandre noticed that when she raised her voice to compete with the music, her German accent seemed stronger. In the shared apartment, you never knew who would put a record on, but sooner or later, someone would want to play some of the old stuff. Just now, someone had set the stylus down on Crosby, Stills, Nash & Young, a plaintive, nervy vocal that rattled the eardrums. For the whole of the A-side, Alexandre felt his knee brush against Constanze's. She had sidled closer to talk, so close that he could smell the fragrance of her hair, breathe its aroma while struggling not to bury his face in its warmth.

At one o'clock in the morning he was still there. Caroline had appeared only once, to ask them to turn it down, shooting a disapproving glance all around the room. That autumn, after the summer activity club and the Hippopotamus restaurant, she was working from eight in the morning to midday at a café on Place Wilson, which left little time for her studies. She was a conscientious student and never stayed late at parties. Studying was far more important to her than smoking dope and listening to music for hours on end. Alexandre loathed hashish, hated the sensation of losing control, but he dared not refuse the joints that were held out to him – he didn't want to look weird – so he took a drag each time one came around, determined to blend in with the crowd, but sucking more air than smoke. He was in with the activists now, almost on a par with Anton, Xabi, Gerhard and Esteban. Refusing a joint or a puff on the chillum would single him out as someone not to be trusted, when what he wanted more than anything was the exact opposite, to be accepted into their small circle.

Monday, 22 September 1980

Alexandre left the party at three o'clock in the morning. Settling into the driver's seat in the Citroën, he shook off the noise and the smoke all at once, and realised that he was very stoned. Stoned. He liked the word, and now he was experiencing for real that feeling of floating outside yourself, just above, or just below. There was no one out on the streets at this hour, no cars on the exit roads, or on the Nationale. He just had to cover the 120 kilometres with the windows wide open, filling his lungs with oxygen to shake off the effects of the psychoactive smoke he had been breathing for hours.

He drove, and he thought of Constanze, wishing he had taken her hand during the long time they had sat so close. But his regrets were soon forgotten when he thought again of the topics he'd discussed with the guys in the kitchen. He realised he'd been stupid, really monumentally stupid this time, and he revisited the scene with mounting apprehension. Taking it right back to the beginning, he remembered they had talked about the nuclear power plant – just that – and that the state would hold the key to everything in future. The old familiar chit-chat to get him on their side, but after three or four beers he'd sensed they were testing him out, questioning him with some specific purpose at the back of their minds. At one point, sitting around the table, Xabi and Anton had begun asking him about the farm, how he worked, how much fertiliser he used, or kept in store. Alexandre hadn't seen straight away what they were getting at. But now, he was surprised that Caroline hadn't spelled it out to him, that she hadn't warned him to keep his mouth shut. Perhaps she didn't know. Perhaps it had never occurred to her that not everyone at the party was a student or a tree-hugging anti-nuclear protestor, that some of them were militant activists who knew all about explosives. She had never made the connection between ammonium nitrate and revolution. But she knew all the precautions they took around the huge sacks of fertiliser on the farm. Whether they came from Bayer in Germany, or the AZF factory in Toulouse, the giant sacks were marked all over with red warning signs and skulls, symbols that had terrified them all as kids, not to mention the safety leaflets their parents kept in the drawer in the old dresser, which explained the precautions to be taken each time the products were handled, and especially in relation to their storage. Alexandre and his sisters had always heard their father say that ammonium nitrate had to be kept bone-dry, and away from any electric wires, any Walkman device. Above all, they must never play with firecrackers or rockets of any kind nearby. On stormy days, the doors to the big barn were checked and shut tight. If thunder or lightning struck one of the bags there would be a gigantic explosion, and a firestorm that would blow the barn and all the other buildings to smithereens, and all the trees in the area … Handling ammonium nitrate was even worse than DDT, which had long since been banned, though like everyone else, they continued to use their stock rather than let it go to waste. The farm was a veritable arsenal.

Alexandre turned onto the narrow country roads and relaxed. He felt his confidence return. Sometimes he wondered if he could ever live anywhere other than the countryside. The further he drove, deep into the pitch-dark landscape, the greater his relief at leaving the noisy, frantic city behind. But Toulouse, with its thousand hot-headed struggles and fights, its parties full of new faces, was fun and tempting as hell for all that.

On the road that climbed towards Les Bertranges, he felt his strength return. The same strength that deserted him whenever he left the natural world behind. He was breathing clean air once again, and it was his alone. He and Constanze had talked about many things. She told him that her way of loving nature was to protect it. She held the word 'nature' long and lovingly in her mouth. It was an inspiration, a dream. She spoke of it as a distant realm that she seldom visited, but a realm to be saved nonetheless. Alexandre told himself that a girl like her could never live anywhere but the city. He had even, almost, asked her the question out loud.

He hadn't the faintest idea what she thought of him. She was intrigued, that much was clear, or she would never have spent so long sitting beside him. At the same time, while they talked, he had found himself wondering whether she was a part of the gang in the kitchen, trying like them to reel him in. He knew what they wanted now. Fertiliser to blow up EDF substations, or the trucks at the building site, no doubt. Thinking about it, he would have no difficulty passing them ten kilos of the dry granules, but he'd leave it to them to mix it with the fuel, so that the fertiliser swelled up and made ANFO explosives. He was ready. All they had to do was supply the containers and guarantee that nothing whatsoever could be traced back to Les Bertranges.

Alexandre continued driving due north, fast along the deserted tarmac road, one elbow resting on the open driver's window. He felt like a character in one of the American shows he watched on TV – Mannix or Napoleon Solo, a solitary type, high on the adventure of some wild, improbable mission. Roger Moore as Lord Brett Sinclair, a noble player on the stage of history. Doing something this crazy opened up new, unexplored terrain, it took a man out of himself, made him great. Others looked at you completely differently. Supplying the fertiliser would take things to a new level – already, that evening, he felt that Constanze had noticed him, whereas on the other Sundays, she hadn't noticed him at all.

Mireille Mathieu's sleek, black bob shone as the singer moved from room to room, followed closely by a figure in a diving mask, shirt and tie. The unlikely pair were threading their way through a maze of large terracotta statues, giant dolls with frozen expressions, like terrified children. Alexandre followed their progress, rubbing his forehead. For once, this lunchtime, he had sat down before the table was laid. He could not summon the energy to lay it himself, though he had slept until eleven o'clock that morning. But the joints he'd smoked the night before had left his head in a spin.

'What the hell is this? It's horrendous.'

'That's Mireille Mathieu.'

'No, over there.'

'It's a terracotta statue.'

'Not that ... The person in the diving mask, wearing the tie?'

'Can't you see? That's Plastic Bertrand, obviously!'

The Belgian singer was a fixture on TF1's live lunchtime show, a regular star of its legendary, accident-prone outside broadcasts. But today's offering plumbed new depths of weirdness. Angèle shrugged and set the roast chicken down on the table. Its aroma had wafted over the hillside.

'Alexandre, I asked you to lay the table. Hurry up, for goodness' sake. Where have the others got to, anyway?'

'Who?'

'Danièle Gilbert and all the rest of them … On the programme! Do wake up.'

'I think it's coming from somewhere in Alsace. A museum with statues. I'm not really sure.'

The worst of it was that Alexandre knew his parents could see he was half asleep. It was plain as day. They were looking at him strangely. Never in his whole life had he got up at eleven o'clock in the morning, even when he had the flu. Doubtless they were wondering if he'd had too much to drink. Or perhaps he'd met a girl in Toulouse. They were itching to find out what he'd been up to the night before, but were reluctant to ask.

*Ça plane pour moi, ça plane pour moi …!*

Poor Plastic Bertrand had come on the show to present his latest single, but each time he appeared he was forced to sing the punk hit that had made his name and haunted him ever since. Their parents suffered his appearances, the very picture of scepticism, but if his sisters had been there, no doubt about it, they would have been jumping up and down and singing along. The song meant something to them. Alexandre kept his head down, hiding his bloodshot eyes, avoiding his parents' gaze and their horrified protests at the song's chorus. Never had the song sounded quite so sinister.

On a normal day, *Midi Première* was a minor miracle of variety and entertainment in the hour leading up to the one o'clock news on TF1. Infinitely less controversial than the latter, it offered little to spark disagreement among its lunchtime family audience, besides the outfit chosen by one or other of the guests: men plastered in orange Pan-Cake make-up, and skimpily dressed young women. Typically, Alexandre would dismiss them all as hideous has-beens, while his parents found them far too with-it for their taste. *Midi Première* occupied the lunchtime slot, a splendid, glittering paradox, simultaneously too old-fashioned and too trendy, at the crossroads of its time.

After coffee, Alexandre said he was going to lie down. He could barely stand. His father lit his Gitane Maïs and got straight to the point: why had he got back so late last night; what was so extraordinary in Toulouse that he had to go to bed in the early hours of the morning?

'A party.'

'You were with your sister, at least?'

'Yes.'

'Oh really? I thought she didn't like to stay up late.'

Alexandre said nothing. He went to his room. The family hierarchy weighed heavily upon him. Living with your parents until you were twenty-five, thirty, forty years old meant putting up with reprimands and comments that took him back to the worst scenes of his childhood. And the most terrifying thing of all was the knowledge that this could last a lifetime. Perhaps it would never end: his parents would never see him as anything but their little boy. While he lacked the money to rent a house somewhere, he was forced to stay on the farm, trapped and labouring under the same old yoke. He would need to bring in far more money if he was to break free one day. Or pray his grandparents would move to a retirement home so that Angèle and Jean could take their place in the smaller new-build down in the valley, with its fitted bathroom and broad front steps. Then they could be the older generation in their turn.

Alexandre lay down fully clothed on his bed. Wherever he looked, the future seemed mapped out for him, with no possibility of breaking free. True, the farmhouse was big, there were five bedrooms, but just one television set, one kitchen, a single hall along and across which everyone moved throughout the day. And above all, there in the hall, was just one telephone, squatting like some fucking great toad for all to see and hear. Whenever anyone made a call, the others listened in.

At moments like these, overcome with anger, Alexandre swore he would find a way out. Sometimes, he promised himself he would leave one day, find a place of his own, some old shack he could renovate, even an old caravan. He felt angrier than usual right now, out of guilt for this morning, or shame that he had failed to get up at dawn as promised, so that his father had taken the cow to slaughter instead.

He stayed in his room for half an hour with the shutters closed, unable to sleep, listening to his parents moving about, talking outside. Then his father started up the air compressor, and it was hard not to think that he was doing it on purpose. Alexandre needed some space. He got up, took his ghetto blaster, with its giant built-in speakers, one at each end, and went out to fix the fences around the fields on the western slope, the land above old Crayssac's place. At least there he could work uninterrupted. This wide-open landscape, these vast spaces bathed in sunlight were his, he knew that. And they were a godsend when he needed time alone. All he had to do was fire up the tractor and go to work in one of the fields, off at the far end. No one would come looking for him. There, with the old tractor making more noise than ever these days, he could turn the volume up loud, play Supertramp full blast, and no one was bothered at all.

Tuesday, 30 September 1980

Alexandre and his father were cross with one another that evening. There had been a shouting match after lunch, about the fences. Entire stretches needed mending and his father had refused to help, saying he was too old to be messing about with jobs like that. They sat staring at their plates, listening absently to the eight o'clock news while Angèle continued negotiations with the girls, bickering endlessly about their homework. At the opening frames of a new report, their father got to his feet and turned up the volume. He had caught the name of the Malause dam, where an explosion that July had blown up the hydro-electric plant. The investigation had uncovered new links to protests over the future nuclear power plant at Golfech, work on which had just begun. The attack had forced EDF to release tens of millions of cubic metres of water, draining the reservoir throughout the summer months. Crops had been left unwatered in the heatwave, and the harvest had collapsed. The camera lingered obscenely over the vast expanse of mud, four hundred hectares of dead fish, their spawning grounds destroyed, yet those who were responsible called themselves environmental campaigners. Their father raged at the spectacle of the disaster. Alexandre had stopped eating and listened. He felt bizarrely involved. His mother and sisters paid no attention.

In the evenings, after dinner, Jean often went down to see his parents. A good ten minutes' walk along the track, but twice as long to get back, and so more often than not he took the car. At the wheel of the old Renault 4L he took a moment to smoke his after-dinner Gitane and check the hedges, the trees and above all the fences, just as he would if he were on foot.

It was strange to think of Louis and Lucienne in their new house. They had always prided themselves on their old-school ways. Jean would never have believed them capable of living within neat, smooth concrete walls, but they were happy and comfortable, as it turned out. Far more comfortable than at the old farm: they had even said as much. There was a bathtub, for one thing, and about time, at nearly seventy years of age, though they never took baths themselves. The greatest luxury of all was the small flight of steps that descended directly from a door inside the house to the lockable garage, a convenience they felt was richly deserved.

With Jean, they reviewed the produce to be picked that week: the lettuces, spinach and the few remaining tomatoes. But the real concern was their old farm up on the hill. Before thinking about buying a new tractor, the drainage under the buildings needed replacing, and extra income would be needed to pay for that. With all the talk about hormone-treated veal, Jean told them, now was the perfect time to show everyone that they did things differently. They possessed a treasured resource that other breeders seemed to have forgotten, a thing of wonder, worth more than all the cake feed and steroids in the world. Grass. Vast expanses of lush, rich pasture. He spoke to them again about his project to buy some store cattle for fattening. Old dairy cows could easily put on a hundred kilos if they were fed good grass and maize sileage.

'You know, Jean, the way things are now, I'm not convinced it's a good idea to bring dairy cattle into the herd. You've got to be careful mixing the animals like that, it's a sure-fire way to bring disease in with them. Remember what they always say, "Buy the beasts, buy their bugs." Introducing new livestock is never easy, you'll have a discontented herd.'

'Well, we could keep them apart. We can take at least twenty more. Minced beef is all the rage; twenty old milkers will be perfect.'

Jean had always reared his cattle on grass. More than was recommended, if anything. And thanks to the river, their maize grew well. The yields were good, Les Bertranges was a gold mine for vegetables and crops – a valley of green gold. They'd have no trouble at all fattening twenty dairy cows, he insisted, even taking the herd up to a hundred head of cattle altogether. And with the milder, snow-free winters, there would be no need even to refurbish the barns. The animals could spend their lives out of doors.

'Listen, Jean, it's your place up there now, but you can see the grass isn't growing like it used to. Fifty years ago, I had grass up to my waist, and still growing on All Saints' Day.'

'Whatever do you mean? The grass will always grow ...'

'I see less water in the soil, believe me. I don't see any white clover any more, and look at the wells – we're pumping gravel by July. The weather's changing, mark my words.'

'So what? If there's not enough grass, we double the maize crop and feed the herd with that. We'll show them what naturally reared cattle look like.'

'There you go again. If you grow maize for the herd, you need more water.'

'We can pump the river. The river's ours.'

'The riverbed, not the water.'

Lucienne had made a nightcap: chicory coffee with a shot of eau de vie. Since handing the farm over to his son, Louis had been restless, distracted. Not that he was worried about Jean, but there were new regulations everywhere they turned, and hours of paperwork. Forms to be filled in, applications to submit if you wanted to move so much as a pile of twigs on the farm. Jean breathed in the aroma of the eau de vie and said nothing more. But the thoughts jostled in his head. Was he right to keep searching for new ideas? Where would a deal with the hypermarket take them? Was fattening cattle from Normandy or who-knows-where really as risky as all that?

'Reckon the buyer at Mammouth put that idea in your head.'

'Which idea?'

'About fattening store cattle.'

'You never thought about it yourself?'

'Certainly not. You'd get poor, soft meat anyhow.'

'Precisely. The biggest demand nowadays is for mince – everyone wants minced beef for *tartares*, burgers, Big Macs, frozen ready meals. You've seen all the ads on television.'

'I don't watch the ads.'

'Old people with no teeth. Kids. Mince is all the rage, even in the top restaurants.'

Lucienne stirred her fake coffee. She often disagreed with her son, but she did not want to upset him.

'What about you, Ma? What do you think?'

'I think minced beef breeds germs. You saw what happened with the butcher in Uzerche: they closed his shop, the mincing machine wasn't clean. He poisoned the whole town. They say it might even have killed some children. It's the worst thing out. Meat wasn't meant to be minced.'

'But, Ma, no one has time these days to cook a *bœuf en daube*, a collar or a blade roast, stuff that takes two hours to cook. It all goes to mince now, or it won't sell at all. The world's changing. Women go out to work.'

'And I don't work, I suppose?'

'That's not what I meant. But women in the city, they haven't got the time to make a *pot-au-feu*; that's not how it is today.'

'Well, the world's turned on its head if you ask me. Freezing meat so it can be eaten by people a hundred, two hundred, two thousand kilometres away, I'll have none of it.'

'Listen, you can't change the world. There's nothing we can do. The fact is – and I'm telling you straight – we have to go for two hundred kilos of mince per cow, anything less and there's no point. There's no point breeding fine, muscly beasts with great hind quarters on them if you can't sell the meat at the right price.'

Jean felt bad lecturing his parents. He was standing at the crossroads of two eras, two worlds. He knew that all right. He was running the farm, with its old buildings, its old ways, but at the same time he had to adapt to the new regulations, prepare for tomorrow's world, for his son, and build higher stalls and a quarantine shed for the incoming store cattle. Jean knew his generation would be forced to choose – to go down the new road, or not. His was the generation that must accept progress or watch the world move on without them.

He reproached his parents for their refusal to face the facts. Even in their brand-new house, they had installed the old wood-fired range from the farm, in which dishes would be left to simmer all day long. When the weather turned cold, his mother always had a pot on the stove. In the same way, his father refused to understand how a steak could be frozen before leaving the abattoir, how the cold chain nowadays allowed a beefburger to be kept for months at a time, and even go halfway around the world without defrosting.

Conversations like these always finished the same way. Old Louis would get to his feet, pressing a hand into the small of his back and declaring that something in there wasn't quite right. He would say he was off to bed, even if it was still light, and then he would go outside to stroke the dog, knowing full well that his son – his only son, since Pierrot killed himself – would join him after pecking his mother on the cheek. And the two of them would make amends by talking about something else.

The light was fading and the air was mild, with not a hint of damp. But down in the valley it was two or three degrees colder than up at the farm. The land was set deep between the hills, and faced south-east, which meant sun in the morning and afternoon, but not the baking sunlight of the summer months. Louis fondled the spaniel's ears and took a short walk around his plot. All the well-schooled, obedient plants, ready to produce a crop. He sensed Jean walking behind him.

'You know, Jean, there are rumours going around about the dairy cows.'

'Hormone-treated veal. It's what I told you!'

'No, about the Holsteins, and the *Normandes*. Listen, I don't know anything for certain, but it seems to me they're doing some strange things with dairy cows these days.'

'But that's a load of nonsense. And anyway, it's in England. Seems they feed them meat and bone meal over there, but we don't do that.'

'Still, you shouldn't go mixing the herd. You know your own cattle, but you don't know the rest. It does the animals no good travelling like that. They're not like us, they're not made for travelling, and they bring in all kinds of filth when they do. Mark my words, if they really are feeding veal calves with eggs, if it's true they're raising heifers on fish meal, then we're all done for ...'

'And straight away, your imagination's running wild.'

'You shouldn't go taking in cows when you don't even know what they've been eating.'

'If you say so.'

'You know, before, we used to keep goldfish in the bottom of the drinking troughs to clean the water. Your son told me he wants to go back to that.'

'So?'

'So you never saw a cow eat one of the goldfish. Never. Nor the horses, either. You mark my words, folk who think they can play at that game will ruin everything, and the day will come when no one wants to eat cow meat any more. So think big if you like, Jean, but not that big.'

Wednesday, 1 October 1980

There was adequate sun, but not enough rain. If nature was not more generous, she would damage the seedlings, and if the fodder grasses were thin, they would be ruined in the first frosts. The cows were still down below in the valley. Autumn was just beginning, but if it granted them some rain they could get a third cutting of the alfalfa. Next year Jean would sow an additional two hectares of forage and hire the new round baler. Everyone was doing it now, but the slope here was steep and they would have to drive the tractor hard to pull the machine along. It would cost them in diesel. There was no end to it.

Gazing out over the fields, Alexandre tried to picture them with an artist's eye, like his Uncle Pierrot, his father's brother who had found himself with no farm, no land, all because Lucienne and Louis thought he drank too much and was muddle-headed. Pierre (his proper name) had worked here from time to time, and talked as a painter would have about the crops to be sown. 'Next year, we'll plant rape along the wood, a stripe of yellow against the green, with poppies in the middle …' To him, the hillside was painted with the fleeting purple of the saffron crocuses; the flowering tobacco was a field of white clusters tinged with mauve. Pierrot used to pick the tobacco flowers and keep them in vases; he'd make a huge bouquet in the big basin outside. It smelled good, like amber honey. Pierrot had been a true poet, a good countryman, but a countryman who never set his alarm and often rose later than the sun.

Alexandre decided that next season, they would sow alfalfa as well as clover. There would be a mass of flowers. Flowers were important, they were easy on the eye from a distance, and a treat for the bees. Lately, in country areas, plenty of people had installed hives – but the craze meant that with all the new colonies of bees, a mite had infiltrated their ranks in a devastating attack. It had travelled from Asia via Siberia in the 1960s, and now it was invading Europe. People were terrified the parasite would kill all the hives – as if some Asian mite meant that one day there would be a shortage of bees on earth. Les Bertranges was teeming with bees, and so Alexandre would grow flowers, boosting them with fertiliser so they could take three cuttings from the crop. Perhaps his father was right, with his plan to fatten extra cattle. Especially since it had dawned on Alexandre that with twenty more animals, he might even be able to rent a new house, instead of doing up some old shack. Nothing huge, but not a ruin like old Crayssac's place. With twenty more cows, he could have a proper two-bedroom bungalow, with a brand-new fridge and an eighty-watt Technics hi-fi system in grey metal, tall as a skyscraper, with a pair of Cabasse speakers ...

Alexandre pondered the idea, and his forehead beaded with sweat. Time and again, he wiped it away. Since the party, the slightest effort had worn him out. Perhaps that shit the Basque had slipped into his pocket to take home was too strong for him. More than anything, he was worried about the business with the fertiliser. He should never have got mixed up in it; perhaps he should never even have spoken to those guys. The sweat trickled into his eyes and, instead of driving the staple into the wooden stake, he bungled it almost every time, shattering the metal and narrowly missing his fingers. He had already hit them three times in half an hour. There was blood. But the fences absolutely had to be mended. The worst was when he bent down to hammer the nails at the bottom. Each time he straightened up, his head spun so hard that he had to support himself on one of the fence posts. He felt dizzier still at the thought of what he had got himself into. He would be seeing them again at the apartment a week on Sunday. Anton had said he'd be there at any rate. Apparently, he was crashing in the big bedroom for a few months. With hindsight, Alexandre had no desire to pass them the ten kilos of fertiliser, because he knew it would not end there. It would never end. Sunday after Sunday, they would ask for more. He was caught in their fucking web now. Unless he stopped going to Toulouse, never contacted them ever again, never saw Constanze … Alexandre set the hammer down on the ground, tossed the roll of barbed wire and the rest of the stuff into the digger, but instead of driving home in the tractor, he left it where it stood and walked across the fields and through the wood to see Crayssac. The old Red was the only person in the world he could talk to about this. He at least had some experience of struggle, protest and activists. He'd spent time with militants of every stripe, not to mention the rebels up at Larzac.

Alexandre found the old man in his dairy, making his miserable little rounds of cheese. Crayssac didn't care for visitors, but they gave him an excuse to have a drink and slake the thirst that never left him, the thirst that came from the dusty salt he handled every day to stabilise the cheeses, the salt he rubbed over the milky spheres. This man spent his life steeped in goat's milk and salt.

'*Oh là là*, you poor sod, don't you get caught up in that. Believe me, the anti-nuclear lot are a hornet's nest, what with the anarchists and the Maoists and the German agents, not to mention the Basque hotheads from ETA, and all the bourgeois papa's boys playing at guerrillas and dreaming about knocking the shit out of the cops. Just you watch out … Nuclear power is the last thing they're worried about, you mark my words.'

'I don't know, I mean, they're like all of you up on the plateau, they're protecting nature.'

'Oh, are they? The whole nuclear thing's more complicated than that.'

Crayssac's reaction was unexpected. Alexandre had hoped for a measure of approval, the complicity of brothers-in-arms, but the mere mention of the anti-nuclear crowd seemed to infuriate him. He carried on turning his cheeses over a big pail as he spoke, sending clouds of powdered salt up into the air. He explained his thinking to Alexandre: while he was against telephones and military camps, and hypermarkets, he had nothing against nuclear power stations.

'So ... you're in favour of nuclear power?'

'No. I'm against the people protesting against it.'

'But the struggle at Creys-Malville was a bit like Larzac — there were farmers fighting to stop the power station ...'

'Tell me about it.'

'We saw them on TV!'

'The ones who showed up were only there to leer at the German girls showering under a hosepipe in front of their VW combis. They wanted an eyeful, and they met their Waterloo — one dead, hundreds injured, complete chaos. The pacifists and the far-left firebrands will never see eye to eye, anyway. End result, we've had a bomb attack a week for the past three years.'

Alexandre took his words to heart. For the first time, he felt directly affected by the bomb attacks, the endless explosions reported on TV. Pylons, EDF substations, hydro-electric dams, construction vehicles blown apart, the *nuits bleues* in Corsica — bombs detonated simultaneously or one after the other, right across the island, all on the same night. There were attacks in Germany and Italy, too. So much violence, so many bombs and kidnappings. It had been going on for so many years that people scarcely bothered about it now.

They left the shed for a drink in the cottage. In the distance, Alexandre heard the familiar sound of the school bus, stopping at the crossroads at the top of the hill. The bus drove away and he knew that Agathe and Vanessa had just got out. He pictured the scene, the bus disappearing into the distance behind them on the Pastura road, and the girls climbing the rest of the way on foot, almost two kilometres. Two kilometres that set them apart from the rest of the world, the track that everyone in the family had walked. Two kilometres from the road to the farm, which the local council had never tarmacked because of some ancient business about water rights on the dam, dating back to the days when there had been other farmers on the hillside, and jealousy towards the Fabriers, who could pump the river and take their cattle to the water. As payback, the old earth track to Les Bertranges was left unmade. Now there were no other farmers nearby, besides Crayssac, and still no tarmac on their lane.

'Something the matter?'

'No, just the girls coming back from school. I wanted to wave, but your hedges are too high.'

Old Crayssac shrugged. He had no interest in children.

'Don't you go talking to them about all this ...'

'To who?'

'Your sisters. Don't go telling them about the guys you see in Toulouse. You shouldn't talk about it even to me, I'm telling you. You start hanging around with that lot, you keep it to yourself.'

'But I've got nothing to do with them really. I've only just met them.'

Whenever he stepped inside the ancient, ramshackle cottage, Alexandre was struck by the earthy smell of straw and old tobacco, intensified by the cold floor. It was a smell he liked, in a way – the aroma of a timeless lair, unchanged for centuries, but one that people nowadays had eliminated by tiling every possible surface, even the goat sheds and the dairies, so that they looked like laboratories for the manufacturing of cheese.

'I'm in no position to advise, but hear this anyway ...'

Old Crayssac took his bottle of wine out from under the sink and poured two glasses.

'Stop, stop! Not too much, thanks.'

'See, when you join a struggle, the first thing to know is who you're fighting alongside. Most often, guys get involved because they're empty-headed and shallow. So they make a lot of noise. Not out of the goodness of their hearts.'

Alexandre ran water from the tap until it was fresh and cold. He drowned his wine in it when the old man wasn't looking.

'Even me, at Larzac, I only went along at first for my sister and brother-in-law. Basically, I didn't care about Larzac one bit, but I go back there now to fight the bastards who want me to put my milk in aluminium cans, and filter it through sterilised nylon stockings, the fucking technocrats who tell me my cheese is full of bacteria – well, of course it fucking is, bacteria are the source of life. Soon they'll be telling me to make my *cabécous* wearing a bloody hairnet and a surgical mask ... See, when I go up to Larzac, I'm taking a stand against that world, not their military camp. Even I'm not honest about my motives. I'm sincere, but I'm not honest. Don't fool yourself, militants are selfish bastards. Fighting for the common good? Don't make me laugh.'

It was dark inside the cottage. Alexandre peered around the spartan room, but he couldn't see the gun that was usually left in plain sight, hanging by its strap on the wall. The old comrade had been more careful since his spell behind bars. Finally, four years ago, the Post Office labourers had installed their poles while Crayssac brooded in police custody. Then he had paid the fine.

'So tell me, kid, how come you're so concerned about nuclear power all of a sudden?'

89

'It just interests me, that's all. It's our future at stake! You're the one acting strange, anyway. Before, you'd point a gun at the guys putting up telegraph poles, and now you don't have a problem with nuclear power. A nuclear plant is more than a few pine poles treated with arsenic, surely?'

Crayssac said nothing about his own contradictions. The idea of the nuclear power plant infuriated him, for sure, like any form of progress. It was just that there had been so many bomb blasts for which the fake commies had claimed responsibility, the 'anti-nuclear communists' as they called them on the news. Dozens of attacks all over France, and he could not bear the violence. Above all, the real communists, the apparatchiks at party HQ on Place du Colonel Fabien in Paris, had decided what their stance was vis-à-vis nuclear power. Now, the official line was that the reactors would be a gold mine for the workers. Sixty reactors by the year 2000, two hundred thousand jobs guaranteed ... The first miracle worked by nuclear power was the hundreds of thousands of new workers who would never have been hired without it. More than enough to compensate for the collapse of the steel industry, right across France. And EDF had promised to give one per cent of its turnover to the unions, through the workplace committees, so there was no question of blowing them all sky-high. And if that social traitor Mitterrand persisted in distancing himself from the nuclear industry, it was only so he could grab a handful of votes – environmentalists, hippies who only go to the polls if they can spare the time. Someone should stop Mitterrand in his tracks, send him packing, sabotage his presidential campaign instead of helping to get him elected.

They sat for a good while longer, saying not a word, each immured in his private contradictions. Then old Crayssac filled their two glasses again.

Without looking up at Alexandre, he observed dully: 'You know, boy, in life, when you look too far all around, you see too many things that are beyond our control. And getting into politics means learning not to think for yourself. Do you see?'

Alexandre gave no reply. The goats were calling from the shed; they wanted to get out into the open air. Framed in the doorway, the world outside was like a painting. The five o'clock sun burnished the early autumn leaves, and the last green ones were still bright, pulsing against a backdrop of serene blue sky.

Tuesday, 31 December 1980

'All aboard for the year 2000!'

With an array of special editions and excited headlines, the magazines were full of the year 2000, as if the date would somehow mark a pivotal moment, a tipping point into a new and different world, the third millennium. In exactly twenty years' time, change would be inevitable, unstoppable. A host of feature articles showed what the world might look like in 'the year 2000'. Illustrations and photomontages evoked cityscapes, with futuristic sketches and editorials obsessed with 'vertical cities'. There was nothing, anywhere, about the countryside, nothing about trees or forests, as if by the year 2000 nature would no longer exist and the world would be one vast conurbation. None of these stylish futuristic drawings showed what open fields and hillsides might look like in the third millennium. Perhaps, for the futurologists, country life remained frozen in time, outdated for all eternity. Besides, no one would need nature in the year 2000: people would get their nourishment from gel capsules, everything would be grown in laboratories, the countryside would serve no purpose at all.

Caroline read from her copy of *Paris Match*, and scared them all half to death. 'The year 2000 is tomorrow!' The phrase rang out over and over again, a cry of hope for some, and sheer dread for others. In the scramble to predict the future, Caroline was the only member of the family who felt confident, optimistic. Up to now, in the farming world, the only visible sign of the forced march towards modernity and all things new had been the ever-increasing burden of standards and regulations, buildings to be updated, the endless checks and controls. True, there had been genuine progress in seeds, with an unending supply of new hybrid varieties that produced new grains with impossible-sounding names, apparently worth more than their weight in gold, to judge by the prices. For the rest, the march of progress continued, further and further from Les Bertranges. Cities were swollen on credit, and elected politicians found the money to build motorways and roundabouts that would shorten their own journey into town. Here, the dirt tracks were still untarmacked, and grass invaded the lanes.

Caroline was more forward-thinking than the futurologists. Why wait till the year 2000 for things to change? They could make change happen far sooner than that, in May 1981, and even if Giscard was ahead in the polls, she had a plan to overthrow the right. Her choice of words suggested a royal dynasty, or an autocratic leader. In France, the right had always been in power. A win for the left would be a revolution indeed. In Toulouse, Caroline was a committed Socialist Party activist. Unlike most of the student unionists and the members of the Socialist Youth Movement, who were from well-off professional families, she had already taken the step from one class, one way of life, to another. Leaving an isolated farm for a city like Toulouse, while not becoming an urban exile, showed extraordinary adaptability. She was living proof that anyone could accomplish change, and she knew it. No need to wait for the year 2000.

As always, on her visits to Les Bertranges, Caroline monopolised the family's attention. All eyes were on her. More than ever, while his sister talked, Alexandre listened but held back, saying nothing, though he was itching to tell them all that he was a militant, too. He, too, was making a difference, changing the world, and in a more concrete way than his big sister. He had already passed more than thirty kilos of ammonium nitrate to Anton and Xabi, in two batches. Mixed with diesel, there was enough to rock the foundations of society, and though he did not feel much like a proper, hands-on activist himself, he knew he was indispensable to them now, as they carried their plans forward.

But Caroline shone, as always. Her bombshell to change the world was called François Mitterrand. A bombshell that would blow Rocard out of the water and shatter Giscard into tiny pieces, even Chirac if he decided to run. The man was a true revolutionary, she said, a man of letters, and a man of action. Since seeing him on television, on Bernard Pivot's literary talk show *Apostrophes*, she had read both collections of his writings, and found in them a countryman and an intellectual, a strategist and a lover of flowers, a politician who thought wallflowers more beautiful than roses, because actually he didn't much care for roses. She identified with this great man, because in his books he would recall a forest walk, or an evening with friends. Seemingly a city dweller, he was a rustic at heart, a man who had never disavowed his lifelong pact with the countryside, the lost world of his childhood.

'If a politician wants to rewrite history, first he needs to know how to write, and Mitterrand writes very well, whereas Rocard, Chirac and Giscard will never be writers.'

Her parents listened, though they were less than enchanted by Caroline's attempts at political persuasion. They admired her wholeheartedly, but they were unimpressed by her involvement in politics. No sense getting mixed up in all that. But she seemed to be doing well and studying hard, and they were determined to be proud of their daughter, no matter what.

Caroline was the family optimist. In three years she would get her first teaching post – she would try for Toulouse or Montpellier, and teach at a school in one of the outlying suburbs. Because while some people saw nothing there but gangs and stolen cars, she saw young people with no access to culture, kids desperate for distractions other than dope or scooters. A land of promise. Even Giscard had realised this and was investing at last in neighbourhoods that had never been built to last, but were here to stay.

'In Toulouse, the city council has just voted to build a metro system – no one out on the periphery will be far from the centre of town.'

Caroline said that Toulouse and Montpellier would attract more people and investment than Paris. The capital was filthy and choked with traffic, like Bordeaux and Lyon, all those bourgeois fast asleep behind their blackened facades. But Toulouse and Montpellier were investing in young people – in five years they would be the New California, the Silicon Valley of south-west France, so roll on the year 2000. Everything was in place, Caroline said: soon she'd have a flat and a salary, and she would work hard and spend every precious moment of her free time at the cinema or the theatre. She came back to Les Bertranges less and less often, but she knew that she would move on, move away, without bitterness or regret. She was untroubled by the prospect of a life far from her family, especially because she had a new family now, her fellow students at the Faculty of Education, some of whom were planning to move ahead into research, unconvinced of their power to confront a class full of pupils. For her part, she knew she could exercise authority, she would let no one stand in her way and if, tomorrow, she could be a bridge for her sisters to cross, she wouldn't hesitate. But she would do anything to dissuade Alexandre from the same path. Alexandre must stay on the farm. That was why she did not like to see him too often in Toulouse. She feared he would get a taste for city life.

## Friday, 17 April 1981

Alexandre had agreed to work with Anton's group, but he would only take part in non-violent action. Anton had no faith in non-violent action, but here, now, two days before the first round of the presidential election, there was something he had judged worthwhile. Alexandre had hesitated at first, but when the guys told him he'd be operating in a two-person cell and that the other person was Constanze, he had agreed. For twenty-four hours they would work as a team, travelling through the countryside of Gers, picking up some boxes and dropping them somewhere else. He had no further details. Twenty-four hours alone with Constanze was something for which he had never dared hope.

That morning he got the Renault 4L ready, taking out the back seats. The boxes were big, it seemed, and they would need the space. After that, he threw himself into the day's work, keeping busy so as not to think too hard about a twenty-four-hour road trip with Constanze. Luckily, there was always something to do on the farm, with the livestock, the crops and everything else. You had to be a breeder and a herdsman, an accountant, an administrative agent, a vet, builder, mechanic, geologist, dietitian, zoologist, chemist, landscape designer and a whole heap of other things ... Above all, you had to be prepared to drive for hours on end, in one vehicle or another, and not mind getting your hands dirty, because they were always breaking down or in need of maintenance. There were times Alexandre thought he could bear the endless chores no longer – the oil change in the tractor after every 150 working hours, checking the gearbox and the hydraulics, and 150 hours in a tractor soon went by, what with sowing, cutting and fertilising, tedding, baling and weeding, harvesting, taking the hedge cutter along the lanes. A hundred and fifty hours was nothing. And there were two tractors on the farm now. All these thankless tasks robbed him of even more of his time. He had to change the oil in the engine blocks, change the filters, check the axles, the hydraulic cylinders, and all the rest, and always Alexandre would discover a trickle of oil that indicated a leak somewhere, however tiny. Each time, it would take him an age to loosen the nuts and find the right spanners. His father's old toolbox weighed over twenty kilos, crammed so full it would barely close. That was another reason why Anton's crowd took an interest in him: he was good with his hands and had a plentiful supply of tools.

That morning, after draining the engine block of every last drop of oil, he noticed the tractor was not standing level, which would throw everything out of kilter. He would have to restart the engine and park it further along, on flat ground, unless he just estimated the oil levels … He was at a loss. He felt all over the place this morning. The gearbox was leaking slightly and he couldn't get at the nut to unscrew it so he wriggled underneath, wondering if he'd still be supple enough to do this at fifty or older, or whether he'd be like his father, suffering constantly with his back. He changed the seal correctly, but the oil change was a careless, rushed job, which it never should be.

Next, he took the used oil and poured it into the green container. No more tipping it into the river, soaking it into the ground in front of the barn, or pouring it into the rocky crevice at Aujolle, like before. Last year, a law had been passed: the used oil must be collected by a garage. Everything they did was governed by legislation, day in, day out. Even in the most far-flung, isolated place, the spectre of a government agent kept watch.

Alexandre shut the lid on the big barrel and his eye fell on the huge white sacks at the back of the barn. Three sacks of fertiliser, each weighing 150 kilos. Every time he saw them he felt an acute stab of guilt. He'd slipped the gang almost fifty kilos now. When he used the spreader, he no longer filled the tank up to the top, so his father would not notice there was any fertiliser missing. The crops had not received their full dose of nitrogen, and it had shown in places, towards the end of winter, so to make up for the nitrates that had gone to blow up electricity pylons and construction machinery, Alexandre had spread good old-fashioned muck.

History was being made, and his was a small role, he knew that. A secondary, secret role. And all the more secret now, because in addition to supplying the fertiliser and diesel, he had shown them how to get into the equipment hangar at the Sauvanet quarry on the road to Villefranche. The trick was to go along the top footpath, the little track that led down the side of the wood. Then you just had to slip down to the hangar and cut through the padlock. There was no night watch at the quarry, nor at the weekend, just an old surveillance camera over the gate, which had never been connected, though hardly anyone knew that. Anton's gang had no trouble busting the padlock and helping themselves. They'd taken ten electric detonators, and ten detonator fuses, maybe more, Alexandre didn't want to know. He had left it to them to get the emulsion: there were chemistry students in the group, plus their connections to ETA. All that mattered to Alexandre was the operation they had discussed, to be carried out just before the first round of the presidential election, so that it would attract maximum attention. The operation he would be carrying out with a partner, Constanze.

For the past five months, he'd opened the daily paper at the national rather than the regional news, dreading the discovery of his fertiliser pellets as an ingredient in one bomb blast or another. He wondered constantly what they had done with the stuff. And the violence was everywhere, not to mention kidnappings, hostage-takings, murders … The day before, in Corsica, a bomb had torn through the airport at Ajaccio just as President Giscard d'Estaing's plane was touching down for an election visit. People said it was a coincidence, but there had been many wounded, even one person dead. The incumbent presidential candidate had not been wounded, and attended his meeting as if nothing had happened, but the attack was Corsica's first fatal bomb blast. The thought was dizzying. Seconds later and there would have been no president, one less candidate in the election on Sunday. Things seemed crazy, terrifying and fascinating all at once. History depended on just a few seconds either way. Anyone could change its course with a single violent act.

Violence was all Alexandre saw now, in the paper, on television. The Red Brigades, the Baader–Meinhof gang, and in France the Armed Proletariat, the Breton Revolutionary Army, not to mention ETA and the activists on the far right. There were bombings and arson attacks daily. In the litany of terror, he saw a great EDF pylon ripped to pieces in Gers, and the umpteenth explosion at the Malause dam. He shuddered each time he saw pictures of pulverised cars, wrecked substations, banks and offices. It was as if since supplying them with the nitrate, things had been blowing up all over the country, on the Champs-Élysées, at the stock exchange, the doors to a synagogue, the headquarters of Chanel, a series of bombings outside the homes of Turkish diplomats and the Syrian ambassador, the headquarters of Aeroflot, the Hôtel de Ville in Paris … He felt involved now, each time he came upon a photograph of a man sprawled on the ground – like that nuclear physicist who worked for the Iraqis and had been murdered in Paris – or a bombing, like the far-right attack on a workers' hostel, or the headquarters of an association for Muslim students from North Africa. But despite his mounting fear, he had said yes to Anton and his crew. Next Friday he would go into action and there was no turning back this time. Desertion would be seen by them as treason, and that would mean cutting himself off from Constanze, forever.

Friday, 24 April 1981

Alexandre woke at four o'clock in the morning, with no hope of going back to sleep. He could no longer tell which was the stronger – his dizzy excitement at being with Constanze, or the dread of greater involvement, more danger, of allowing himself to be manipulated by the gang. But there was no going back. He would meet Constanze at two o'clock in the afternoon, in front of the little train station at Dieupentale. The boxes were stashed in disused hangars there, and after collecting them they would set off on a circuit that Constanze knew in advance. Some sort of supply mission.

Caroline had walked in on him during a talk with the activists a couple of weeks ago, but she couldn't have known what they'd been discussing. It would never cross her mind that he might be mixed up with them for real.

At six o'clock in the morning he was still in the barn, changing the blades on the hedge cutter so that everything would be in perfect working order. His father would be using it to cut the hedges along the lanes. It would take him two whole days. Alexandre wanted to get to the rendezvous ahead of time. Constanze had classes that morning, after which she would take the train to the little station, and from there they would cover a handful of electoral districts in Lot-et-Garonne and the southern end of Gers. There would be about twenty pairs operating across the whole of the south-west, each with their own route. Alexandre had lied when he said he knew Gers and Lot-et-Garonne like the back of his hand. In reality, he had only a vague knowledge of the area. He just knew the mission would take him far from Toulouse and its surrounding sprawl.

He arrived twenty minutes early. The station serving Dieupentale was on the main line from Toulouse to Paris, a long way from the village. The boxes would be in one of the old freight hangars, and they were to take them to five drop-off points, except for the last box, whose contents they would distribute themselves on an extended round trip between Lauzerte and Mauzevin, about two hours north-west of Toulouse. Constanze knew the precise route. Alexandre reviewed his cassette tapes. Rummaging in the glovebox, he had his doubts about the music he'd chosen: *Simon and Garfunkel's Greatest Hits* and *Breakfast in America* by Supertramp. He worried Constanze would think it was dated. *Music for oldies!* That was what she'd said the other night about Pink Floyd and Dire Straits. But his system was terrific, anyhow. That summer, he had installed a K7 Pioneer radio, a great block of metal with forty-watt speakers, and the sound was fantastic.

Alexandre got out of the car and stretched his legs. There was no one about. The stationmaster seemed to be shut away in his office with the door closed. He might even be taking a nap after lunch. The disused hangars stood over to his left. This must have been a big, important station once. Below him, on the other side of the tracks, flowed the Toulouse-to-Bordeaux canal, with the remains of a freight jetty, abandoned like everything else. In the past, wine casks would have been loaded onto canal barges there, while the hay fodder travelled by train. Alexandre walked over to the old buildings. It was dark inside, and there were no boxes at first glance. He suddenly felt intimidated: Constanze was really something. She could speak three languages and she wanted to do a doctorate, or train as a university lecturer – he didn't really understand the difference, but she was a true intellectual anyway. He had no idea what they might talk about.

The train was late. There were no houses anywhere near the station, and the gantries over the tracks were all rusted. The sky was overcast, but the sun broke through the clouds from time to time, warming the air, then disappearing. The grey clouds thickened, and it was dark again – almost night – inside the old hangars. Alexandre felt a sudden dread. Perhaps there was a bomb in there, or perhaps the gendarmes were hiding, ready to pounce. He was no longer playing by the rules, he had broken the Fabriers' long line of fine, upstanding citizens.

The dark hangars and deserted station terrified him now. He told himself he'd better give the whole thing up. He had been lucky so far, no one had come to the farm to check the accounts for the fertiliser. But the gendarmes might well have launched an investigation – how could he know? One day the trail would lead back to him, and if Anton and his crew got arrested, they would tell the police who it was that had supplied their nitrates, sooner or later.

A door creaked. The stationmaster emerged from his office with his cap tucked under his arm. Alexandre watched him from the shadows. He didn't know if the man could see him. Then he walked over to the platform, too.

'No one about!'

The man stared at him and said nothing. Perhaps he had taken the remark as a wounding reminder of the lack of travellers through the station these days.

'I'm meeting someone.'

'Really …'

The stationmaster donned his cap and straight away he looked taller, more impressive, more official. He glanced at Alexandre, as if somehow he knew about the boxes. Then he checked his watch and stood waiting with his green-and-white stationmaster's baton wedged under his arm. Alexandre thought he should never have parked right in front of the station building. The stationmaster would certainly have had time to note down the car's registration number. He knew now that he was totally unprepared for this type of operation. From now on, he would plan every last detail in advance. A faint sound rose from the tracks, signalling an approaching train. The red Micheline railcar appeared in the distance, to the south. Its progress seemed slow, utterly unlike the images of the future TGV that were being shown on television. Then the noise swelled to a din, mingled with the screech of brakes. Alexandre watched as three carriages passed before him, with hardly anyone on board, and no sign of Constanze. Well, that made everything easier anyhow.

Finally, she stepped down from the last carriage, taking her time, flashing the broad smile that seemed to be her natural expression. She was wearing a flowery, slightly hippy dress, with a big raffia bag over one shoulder. She looked as if she was on holiday. Alexandre made ready to brush cheeks, the conventional air kiss, but she clasped him in her arms, and the scent of patchouli enveloped him, especially as she was holding him very close, as if they were lovers and had kissed a thousand times before. Alexandre knew the stationmaster was watching them. This was for his benefit: the guy would think they were a couple who hadn't seen one another for days. Then she took his hand and led him towards the car.

'What about the boxes?' Alexandre whispered.

'They're not here,' she said meaningfully. The boxes were somewhere else. They were throwing them off the scent. This girl was a whirlwind: scarcely two minutes at her side and already everything was out of his control, everything was unplanned.

## Friday, 24 April 1981

Caroline was in class. After a morning sitting uncomfortably in the big lecture hall, she savoured the peace of the small room where her tutorial group met afterwards for study and questions. Here, she lost all sense of time, forgot about the weather outside. She was absorbed in the myth of Orpheus, who loses Eurydice on the very day they are married, a story made all the more vivid by Caroline's absolute horror of snakes, one more phobia to add to all the rest: her spider phobia, and small bugs in general … Country life had never been a pleasure for her, more of a struggle, something akin to physical combat with an army of foes determined to sting her and make her itch. She dissected the myth down to the last detail. The hero who descends into the Underworld to find the woman he loves and bring her back … She considered the possible contemporary relevance of the story's many symbols, then allowed her mind to wander at the sight of the sparse trees outside the windows, the sprouting leaves a vivid green that touched her heart. Such glimpses of nature in the city were quite enough for her. If she felt any guilt at all, it was for her own lack of regret at the life she led now, far from the hillsides and fields, far from her family. She did not miss the farm, the meadows, the woods one bit.

At Les Bertranges, their father woke from his sleep after lunch. He never rested for more than half an hour, except at the height of summer when he would sleep out of the sun until four in the afternoon. He downed a small cup of Nescafé and headed for the fields to check on the animals, rather than continue with the hedge-cutting. The calves were stronger and steadier on their feet now. They could easily slip under a loose bit of barbed wire. There were great lengths of it to repair around the fields, and the task could not wait. Twenty-five millimetres of rain had fallen in the night, twenty-five litres of water per square metre. Each time, he pictured what it would be like to pour twenty-five litres of water right there, into the ground beneath his feet. He was eternally grateful for the rain. It was a blessing from heaven. Not that he believed in God, of course, not at all.

Jean grumbled that Alexandre wasn't there to give him a hand. He was off training to drive the combine harvester, or so he'd said. He didn't believe his son's story about the Massey Ferguson, though he would never say so. Alexandre said he had been awarded a place on a two-day course, but Jean knew he was making it up. At the same time, he wanted Alexandre to feel free, and not spied upon, or not too much. Jean had worked alongside his parents throughout his youth; he knew the shame of having them always on your back. And all the more so because when he was a young man, Louis and Lucienne had never stopped reminding him that the farm was theirs, that they knew better than him how to do things. He would not inflict that on his own son. The poor kid had a right to live his own life. He was out and about on the farm every day as it was, and he kept up with the work. Of course, at twenty years of age, he needed a change of scene from time to time, to 'do his own thing', as his mother put it.

Jean took advantage of his son's absence to inspect his land. Something had been bothering him for a while now, especially after a bout of rain. It seemed that the newly sown fields were lifeless. In spite of all the fertiliser Alexandre had spread, the seedlings weren't showing. Rather than go digging by hand out in the middle of the field, he walked up to the barn where they kept the backhoe his parents had bought thirty years ago to plant the walnut saplings.

It was rusty, like a piece of old agricultural bric-a-brac. It took Jean some considerable time, and a great deal of effort, to shift the thing and hitch it to the back of the tractor. Angèle was down in the village, and the girls were indoors. There was no one to ask what he was up to, what on earth it was that had possessed him to fit the big digger to the tractor, the one used to dig very deep holes. But that was it, he wanted to see what was in the belly of the earth and so he went out onto the hillside, telling no one. Only their old bitch Fanou ran after him, tired no doubt of listening to the girls play indoors since the beginning of the afternoon. Jean didn't even notice the dog running behind him. His mind was elsewhere. At winter's end, the fields looked too smooth, like football pitches. The squiggles of soil thrown up by the worms were gone. But most worrying of all were the days after a bout of rain, when it seemed the water was eager to get away, scurrying down the slope in long streams coloured by the earth they carried along.

To put his mind at rest, he began digging at the spot he had thought seemed too compacted, too smooth. With a few strokes of the digger he dug a trench thirty centimetres deep. He climbed down from the tractor to see what he could see. In the first, clean cut, the earth was smooth and glossy as a painted wall. Since autumn, the soil had lain bare to the sky, with nothing to rot on its surface. He dug again. Anyone watching from afar would think he was digging a man's grave, or burying a horse. They would take him for a madman, or a murderer, or maybe even someone attempting suicide. He wanted a hole about two metres deep, and he kept digging until the teeth on the digger screeched loudly as they touched the bottom. As if he had pierced a sheet of metal down there, a buried vault. Jean killed the engine and jumped down into the ditch to see how things were. Fanou watched,

107

uncomprehending. She sniffed half-heartedly at the earth he had turned up, detecting no smells, no remains, no living thing to snuffle out. Jean scrabbled with his fingers and uncovered a piece of stone. It looked like part of a conduit. By scrabbling some more he made out a hard floor sealed with mortar. It gave him the creeps to uncover a built structure like that, so far underground. Perhaps it was some kind of secret burial, or an ancient sacred site. He totally forgot why he had made the hole and began digging with his bare hands. Incapable of shifting the huge sandstone slab, he saw that it rested on two supports, but that there was nothing underneath, only more earth, like a tomb for the earth, buried within itself, deep in his own soil. This was beyond his understanding, particularly since another slab was visible, leading away from the first, the beginning of an endless line of slabs, perhaps. He dug some more to see where it led, more angry than intrigued, and he thought of what his damned brother Pierrot had told him. Pierrot, who reckoned their land bore a curse; Pierrot raving in his drink, who declared that Les Bertranges was damned, that the fields covered the tombs of horses dead from the plague, or Roman witches, entire herds of cattle killed by tuberculosis; Pierrot, who uttered such abominations to get his revenge on the family, and who had refused to acknowledge the real reason he had not inherited this land – not because he was the youngest son, but because his brain was addled by alcohol.

Jean straightened up at the bottom of the hole. For the first time in his life, he stood in the very heart of the earth, its entrails. He glanced around at its lifeless flanks and saw that it was dead inside. The rain no longer reached down this far, nor the air, nor the roots. The soil was densely packed, an immobile, inert mass. Perhaps the slab under his feet marked a spring that had dried up. That would mean that here on this spot, generations ago, water had welled up, and that now it had run out, that one day there would be no water left. It meant this land could die, that they had been killing it forever, he and generations of ancestors before him; they had killed it by letting the nutrients leach out, and taking away the residue of straw, and clearing it of the debris between harvests. For the soil to absorb air and water once more, they would need to feed the earthworms, scatter organic matter to encourage them to return. And failing that, they must keep on adding fertiliser, to coax the harvests up into the light. They would befoul this earth, make it dirty again, to bring it back to life, but it would take years; it would gain a centimetre of humus every three years, five in a decade and a half, an appallingly long time. Above all it would compromise their way of working, their yields. For the farm to stay in profit, they would have to rear more cattle, double the herd in ten years, and now was not the time to turn everything on its head.

The cold earth, this buried slab ... they frightened him. Most likely it was not a spring, because other slabs seemed to be buried in alignment with the first. He should never have gone poking about, best to fill the hole back in and forget about it. Looking up, he saw Fanou above him. The dog was nervous, standing firm and tense, waiting for a sign. If the father had dug down so deep, she seemed to tell herself, it was to turn up a piece of game buried too far down, or a lost soul, a spirit, and her entire being trembled and shivered. She stood shocked and shaking on the spot, but she did not bark. She marked the spot, like the hunting dog she was.

'It's all right, everything's all right, quiet now, Fanou, good girl, there there ...'

But the dog was still trembling. Jean stood on tiptoe to run his hand along her flank, and at his touch she lay on her belly, half crouching, reassured and calm once more.

He climbed back onto the tractor and filled the hole, using the hydraulic digger. When he'd finished, the mound of loosened earth resembled a tumulus, so he ran over it a few times, back and forth, to remove any trace of the dig.

From the bottom of his meadow, hidden behind the juniper bushes, old Crayssac watched and laughed at what he saw. He knew perfectly well that idiot Fabrier had no idea what it was he had discovered – the buried slabs, the stones sealed with mortar. Plainly, he had no understanding of it at all, and the thought of it made old Crayssac laugh.

Friday, 24 April 1981

History is made in contact with the living. It shapes lives like hands model clay. Constanze came from a country cut in two, to which she thought she would never return. She dreamed of one thing only, to travel, and she talked about living in Africa or India one day. Most of all, she wanted to repair the harm caused by the green revolution, the developed world's policy to boost harvests and yields artificially in developing countries, but which had killed their soil. Coming from a closed country, her appetite for the great wide world was insatiable. She wanted to learn every language there was. Alexandre, on the contrary, knew he would never leave Les Bertranges. He was the heir to the farm and the soil needed him. They came from two irreconcilable worlds, which was why he could scarcely believe he was sitting beside her, driving through Tarn-et-Garonne and the hills and vales of Gers, even if it meant becoming an activist, a man of the shadows.

They followed the itinerary Constanze had drawn up, and she explained the purpose of the mission: a large-scale distribution of fake documents on EDF headed paper. The idea had come from a militant group she was close to, she said. They would use the first anniversary of the accident at the nuclear plant in Saint-Laurent-des-Eaux to reawaken people's fears. Just over a year ago, a piece of sheet steel had blocked the plant's cooling circuit, and the temperature had risen so high that twenty kilos of uranium had melted down inside the reactor, which threatened to explode. The event had been all the more spectacular because a television crew had filmed the alarms, the howling sirens, in footage that resembled the outbreak of war. A year later, five hundred people were still cleaning the contaminated reactor. Groups of workers took it in turns to go down inside for two minutes at a time, on the end of a rope, before being yanked back out, double-quick. They had to wait until the next day before going in again, so the teams relayed one another, never stopping. It would take years, and millions of litres of water pumped from the Loire, to flush the plant out completely. For now, the plutonium seepage was still killing fish in the river. Around the anniversary of the accident, it was vital to remind people of what had happened and stoke their fear by distributing letters on EDF headed paper – alarming letters that everyone would mistake for an official message. If the operation succeeded, a wave of panic would sweep the region around Golfech, and a great terror would stir people to action once again.

Constanze showed him the documents. Bearing the official EDF logo, the letter invited EDF subscribers to adjust the voltage on all their household appliances as a matter of urgency: television sets, heating, washing machines, toasters, all had to be adjusted in case some of the electricity supplying them came from a nuclear source. In a few lines, the document explained that with electricity from a nuclear plant, the voltage in the electric wires was boosted to over 220 volts to absorb the excess current due to the atom. Household appliances that were not adjusted for this risked catching fire or even exploding.

Clearly, the day after the letters were distributed, the EDF switchboards, and local fire stations too, would be inundated with panic-stricken calls. The mayhem and terror would spread, and atomic energy would be revealed for what it was – uncontrollable and excessive. People in the south-west were already suspicious of nuclear power, and in the referendum eighty-three per cent of voters had said no to it. And so the letter would stoke people's fears and sow doubt in everyone's mind.

Constanze had drawn green lines and blue dots on her Michelin map. A big red square marked the cache where the boxes were hidden – an old storage hut in the depths of the countryside. They identified the small drystone building from a distance, atop a hill, beside a wood. They turned onto a track and approached it in a fever of excitement. The six boxes were blank and unmarked: there was no way of knowing where the letters had been printed. Alexandre loaded them into the back of the Renault 4L with some difficulty while Constanze kept watch, making sure no one saw them. She scanned every detail of the countryside, gradually opening her heart to the landscape: the velvety, new-grown meadows, nature freshly painted in myriad shades of green, the pastures surrounded by bright hedgerows. A simple, unspectacular scene, but her eyes drank it in. She knew nothing of the countryside. She had always lived in cities – Leipzig, Berlin, Paris and now Toulouse.

Hastily, Alexandre shut the boot. Heading back down the rough track, he expected his partner to tell him what they were doing next, where they were going in order to drop off the five boxes, and to deliver the contents of the last box to people's letterboxes in a carefully defined cluster of villages. But Constanze was still in a dream.

'I've never seen anywhere so lovely, believe me. *Un endroit aussi belle …!*'

'*Aussi beau …*' Alexandre corrected her French.

'*Aussi beau …* Don't you think it's beautiful?'

'Yes, of course, there are some nice places in Gers, but it's not very … wild.'

'Is it beautiful like this where you live?'

'At Les Bertranges? It's much more beautiful there, I reckon.

113

Rolling countryside, not like here. Woods and hillsides, and, best of all, it's wild.'

'What do you mean, wild?'

'Wild means there's one house every five kilometres, isolated farms, far from everything.'

'When I was little, we took the motorway to visit my uncle, but the countryside there isn't like this. The land is filthy, and the farms are *kolkhozes*, collectives with three thousand cows.'

Alexandre shot her a disbelieving glance. There was no such thing as a farm with three thousand cows. It was true, she assured him. Crayssac, the devout Old Red, had never told him about that. This girl might have been talking about a different planet, the mysterious, unknown East, about which he'd heard anything and everything. She had decided to leave it all behind anyway, to choose freedom and never go back. Sitting with her in the car, Alexandre felt utterly out of his depth. She was here, right beside him, but he didn't dare make the slightest move. He refocused on their mission to save humanity from the insane threat of the atom, to halt the construction of a nuclear plant, with its trail of eternally lethal waste, in the midst of these lovely, open fields. She had convinced him of that at least, and especially the horror of toxic waste that lasted for thousands of years. It was difficult to put the nuclear industry into perspective, but one thing was certain – the radioactive waste would accumulate so fast that soon no one would know how to deal with it. Constanze told him, too, that others in the group were planning acts of violence. But she wanted to stop things spiralling out of control that way. Alexandre was horrified. He was himself an accomplice to the violence she was trying to stop. Constanze confided in him that the violent, militant wing found justification in what had happened in Bilbao. There, building work had stopped after the assassination of the nuclear plant's chief engineer. Proof, they said, that violence worked. In the current climate, Mitterrand swore he would halt the work at Golfech if he was elected. Constanze abhorred violence. The best way forward was to influence public opinion, hence the letters. They should fuel the fear of atomic power that everyone felt deep down inside, the little people and the powers-that-be alike.

'We just need to awaken that fear, because you can make an impact on people through fear. Do you understand?'

'I understand.'

What Alexandre understood above all was that she knew nothing about the fertiliser, and that she must never, ever find out. He stopped at a crossroads, waiting for her to tell him which way to turn, watching her as she pored over her map. He gazed at her for a long moment, fascinated and lost all at once. She was the reason he had got mixed up in this world, with its jargon of 'demos', 'bombs', 'nuclear waste', 'the Soviets', words he had only ever heard on the eight o'clock news until now.

'Best to go left, follow the signs for Gimont.'

Alexandre was still looking at her. He had never thought that a woman would be capable of leading him so far off course.

'What are you waiting for?'

'Better not to take the main road,' he said. 'Find us a route via the country lanes, the white roads on the map.'

Constanze shot him an admiring glance, convinced he was right. They continued straight ahead, along the D-road. Alexandre drove slowly while Constanze plotted a new route, trusting his judgement. She began to talk about herself, her rejection of violence. She came from a country where people who tried to get across the border were shot. No question of anti-nuclear protests in East Germany, though the situation was worse there than in France: work had begun on the Stendal plant, the craziest of them all, with four Soviet mega-reactors, in full knowledge that, for the Russians, safety regulations for the protection of the population were never the priority, but only and always to finish ahead of time.

'In the East, they'll put up a nuclear plant anywhere, any old how, it's sheer madness, but no one can do anything to stop it.'

The girl beside him was driven by a powerful social conscience. Listening to her, Alexandre felt an overwhelming desire to take her hand and kiss her neck. He had never felt especially comfortable with girls: his childhood had been spent in the shadow of his three sisters, to whom he took a back seat, and at the agricultural college there were only three girls in his entire class. He had caught the eye of one of them, and the other guys had been jealous. But the girl liked him precisely because he didn't make any clumsy attempts to come on to her as they did.

Despite their change of route, they made it to the different meeting points on time. At six thirty sharp they pulled up as planned outside a small, modern but dilapidated house near Mauzevin – their last rendezvous for the day. Two men emerged. This time, instead of shaking hands, as she had done with the others, Constanze air-kissed them both. Alexandre gave no greeting as such, but left two boxes outside the gate. They set off again in the Renault. Now, their mission was to put the remaining bundles in letterboxes, but out here in the country the shops shut early and their first priority was to find something to eat. The village boasted only one charcuterie, but there they found bread and salads, cured sausage and sliced ham, all of it tempting. There was even wine, but no Coke. Back on the road, they met the grocery van heading home from its rounds. Alexandre pulled across the road to stop it in its tracks. From a distance, the manoeuvre must have looked like a hold-up – even the van driver seemed to think so, but they paid cash for a pack of small glass Coca-Cola bottles. Constanze loved Coke.

'Do you know, Alexandre, this is my first time out camping!'

'Camping? I haven't brought a tent.'

'I know, but when you say *camper* in French, doesn't it mean sleeping in a car, too?'

'I don't know, Constanze. I don't know … But if you sleep out in the open, you can say *dormir à la belle étoile*.'

'*Ah oui!* But which is it? Which one is *la belle étoile*?'

## Friday, 24 April 1981

At Les Bertranges, it seldom occurred to anyone to go for a walk. Walking took you to the barn or the car, and always in order to do something else. Walking for no purpose, staring all around for the sheer pleasure of it, was pointless. But still, when the evenings were light, their mother would sometimes take a turn after supper. She would wander aimlessly along the hillside, or through the fields further down. In autumn she would keep an eye out for mushrooms, in spring she would spot the first daffodils or primroses, and in summer she would bask in the fragrance of wild mint – each time, a pretext to justify her need for a walk.

Typically, one of the dogs would follow her – Rex, or Belle, or Fanou, and sometimes all three. Sometimes even the cats would tag along. On fine evenings, after the heat of the day, even the animals savoured the pleasure of drifting along through the cool, sweet air.

This evening, however, the dogs showed no sign of leaving the yard. Angèle called them, but try as she might, they refused to move. Strangely, unusually for them, it appeared the animals were keeping watch over Jean, who stayed indoors. He seemed nervous, even smoking a second cigarette, as if he was waiting for something. And so Angèle set out alone for the hillside. Approaching the pasture, she gazed fondly at the cows grouped at the far end. A beautiful sight. The fields were covered with thousands of soft, feathery dandelion globes, like a dusting of snow. The animals sensed her presence. The cows were already on their feet, but the calves were still lying down serenely in the grass. At the sight of her, resting her elbows on the fence, they all rose, or tried to, adorably awkward as they struggled to their feet. The more agile, co-ordinated youngsters forced themselves up by pushing on their hind legs and trying to gain momentum. Swaying under the weight of their bodies, they would stagger forward, but their hind legs were still weak, and they were unaccustomed to the movement. They would throw all their weight back and prepare to swing forward, further this time. They were like rocking horses or big, malfunctioning wind-up toys. Angèle thought of the 2 million calves that had just been slaughtered, and all that had been said for weeks on end about the scandal of hormone-fed veal. Careless of animal welfare, forever turning its back on the countryside, France had discovered that three-quarters of the national veal herd were raised in dark, filthy crates and force-fed anabolic steroids so that they would grow to fifty kilos in three months. This wrong-headed, unregulated practice was the result of the Common Agricultural Policy, itself a product of worlds unconnected to the land, where all the talk was of increased yields and production. But for the farmers the outcome was plain to see. The media had talked of nothing else for months: veal bred from dairy cows stuck in tiny cells, animals injected with substances like cyclists on the Tour, or Olympic weightlifters, so that they would grow muscle and more muscle, but not a gram of fat, because that was another thing people expected these days. Modern man had identified two new enemies – bread and fat. Both were denounced in the magazines: bread made you fat, and fat in our food was a slow, subtle killer. The white-coated TV doctors prescribed low-fat diets and jogging or aerobics at the gym, to disco music.

Angèle felt she was swimming against the tide. At Les Bertranges, at least, the calves were never crated, they had all the pasture they needed, and hay fodder, cornmeal and water. They were free to roam as they pleased.

The calves were all standing now. They waited for their mothers to take the lead, then walked across to the fence where Angèle stood. She gazed at the land all around and thought of the generations who had lived here before. A calf pushed its head towards her and suckled her finger. The mothers were calm and quiet, partly because the dogs had not come. Angèle had always thought that the cows were scornful of dogs – servile creatures, whereas cattle had been released from all that long ago. They no longer pulled carts or wagons. Angèle looked to the west and saw misty white clouds, like cotton tulle, very high up in the sky, a sign that colder air was coming. She thought of Alexandre. She had seen him take a blanket from his bedroom and put it in the boot of the Renault 4L this morning. She hadn't asked what he was doing. Sometimes she wondered if her son was quite as strong as he seemed, if he really did have a sound head on his shoulders.

They hadn't delivered a single leaflet after all. The last box was still in the back of the Renault, not even opened. They would make an early start tomorrow. Alexandre and Constanze had found a quiet spot on a hillside, sheltered from the road and the mission they had been sent to carry out. From up here, they gazed out over the hills of Gers, a rolling landscape parcelled into small, checkerboard plots – pasture and arable, fallow areas and woodland. A tame, well-tempered canvas. Again, Constanze seemed fascinated by the immense scale of this plain, unremarkable panorama.

Alexandre assured her that when the sun sank towards the west, she'd see the whole chain of the Pyrenees against the horizon. Perhaps they already could. If you opened your eyes wide you could just make out a faint line of white summits and ridges ... Constanze was ready to believe him, but Alexandre couldn't be sure they were looking at the eternal snows. The white ridge was probably a bank of cloud, a vast front rolling in from the ocean, bringing rain. But he didn't tell Constanze that.

Damp, cool fingers of air stole between their clothes and skin. Constanze shivered. The picnic was their consolation. They had brought the packages of food out onto the grass. There was wine but no glasses. Alexandre opened the bottle with the corkscrew on his Opinel knife. Constanze didn't even flip the cap on a bottle of Coke. She stared at the landscape, and her expression was serious now.

'It makes me sad, actually.'

'Really? Why?'

'To think that all these farms and fields – all it would take is one nuclear accident for them all to be destroyed, just one explosion and it would all disappear, it's insane ...'

It had never occurred to Alexandre that this landscape might be threatened or vulnerable. Nature was there for all eternity, he was certain of that. They sat and watched the setting sun, ruminating. Cold War babies, they had lived all their lives on the knife edge of mutually assured destruction, the endless stockpiling of nuclear weapons by the Russians and Americans. But this was a war that everyone said would never come, and no one can live with a threat hanging constantly over their head. People set it to one side, forgot all about the terror of nuclear explosions in the upper air. Besides, Constanze was right about one thing – it was the reactors dotted over the landscape that made the nuclear threat concrete, visible and omnipresent.

Alexandre unfolded the blanket and spread it over the ground to serve as a picnic rug, then he unpacked the food, folding the waxed paper to use as plates. He only had one knife, and there were no paper serviettes or spoons. But he took care to lay out the meal as attractively as possible. Constanze said her father was an engineer. It saddened him, she said, to see so much groundbreaking research focused on the atom. It was immoral to devote the biggest budgets to an energy source inherited from the atomic bomb when there was still a whole pile of diseases for which they had no cure. She was warming to her subject, in full flow. She spoke not as a militant, but as a human being, a person of conviction. Alexandre listened, and spread the pâté over thick slices of bread, plunged his knife hungrily into pots of pickled red cabbage and celery, swallowed a morsel of Cantal cheese. From time to time, he offered Constanze a mini sandwich which she nibbled, still talking all the time.

At least now he knew why she was here in France. Toulouse was the El Dorado of the aviation world, and her father had switched from engineer to businessman once he settled in the West. He travelled constantly, so that Europe and Airbus could conquer the world. Business was more powerful than politics; you consolidated power through trade, simple as that. Her father talked about nothing but the future, she said, while her mother and sister had stayed where the world stood still, on the other side of the Wall. She hadn't seen them for two years. Her mother was caring for her sick parents. They were allowed to leave the East, given their age, but they did not want to move. Constanze felt guilty about not going back, not being with them, but it meant going through Checkpoint Alpha, with all the waiting around, the humiliating questions, and once you were in the East, there was the dread of not being allowed out again. It terrified her even to think of it.

Alexandre had eaten more than half the food. He lay back. The blanket felt cool against the grass.

'And what about you, have you travelled abroad already?'

'No.'

Constanze stared at him as if he'd said something extraordinary.

'Have you ever been in a plane?'

'Certainly not. And I never will.'

Constanze pondered this strange news. So you could be young and never be tempted to go travelling across Asia or America. Even now, you could be content with your own little world.

'I don't like planes,' he said. 'When I was a kid I used to ride my bike by myself, over the *causse*. I'd be gone for hours, and even when I was completely lost, all alone, away from it all, there was always a plane going by overhead, full of people looking out of their windows, and it bothered me, all those people sitting up there, all those rich bastards ...'

'You're afraid of flying?'

'Perhaps. I don't want to find out.'

Constanze wanted Alexandre to talk about himself. She asked questions, but his answers were evasive. He didn't have much to say, just that he loved the open air, being out in nature, like here. It was a genuine need, and he still didn't know all there was to know about his own valley, so why would he go off exploring somewhere else? His life was all mapped out, anyway; he would take over the farm and follow the seasons, and he didn't have a Wall to complain about, but he sensed a widening gulf between the old world, where he lived, and the new – the coming world of cities and seed companies and regulatory standards and banks. To his great surprise, Constanze did not think this was outdated or archaic. On the contrary, she thought it was a fine thing to live with nature, deep in the countryside. Free, in a way. She told him he was the freest creature she'd ever known.

The shadows were increasing all around them. Constanze was so beautiful, he thought. He liked the things she said, her voice, the accent that brought her smile to life. Even when she wasn't talking, her broad, generous mouth wore an expression of universal contentment, a permanent smile. They weren't looking at one another, weren't even trying to look into each other's eyes, but they reached out and held hands. The same reflex, at the same moment, not because they wanted to touch for the sake of touching, but a gesture of mutual reassurance. From this moment forward, they could be sure of nothing. Everything was uncertain, even whether or not it was really getting cold. As if childhood or adolescence had set them down just there, washed up on the last beach of innocence, the one from which you set sail for the life ahead, your life, though which life, you cannot know. They held hands because they had come to a sudden realisation, like falling to earth from a great height. They said nothing, but each of them was pondering their ties, their commitments, the things that kept them from being completely free. She, who felt the call of other countries in her unending flight from her own; he with his visceral connection to the land he owned. They squeezed each other's hand tighter and tighter, a wordless pact, as if resolving not to give in to the way of the world. They would fight to change everything, fight nuclear power, and fight for themselves too, fight selfishly against a life that was all mapped out. Every couple is an uprising, a rebellion.

'You know, I've never seen a night like this.'

'What do you mean?'

'Total darkness. I've only ever seen scraps of the dark, and always against the light of a city, but never like here, never a whole black night.'

Friday, 24 April 1981

Tonight Toulouse was hosting the last big campaign meeting for the presidential candidate François Mitterrand, before the first round of voting. The apartment was the designated meeting point for them all before they headed off to the stadium together. While they waited for the others, they mimicked the lyrical eloquence of the Man with the Rose. Soon, they would hear him for real, but for now, everyone had fun taking turns and proclaiming their socialist ardour, Mitterrand-style.

Antoine and Marc were the party poopers, gleefully reporting what their families had to say on the matter.

'My grandfather reckons the foul weather and wintry cold this spring signals the advent of communism at the heart of government, and the coming of the great East wind ...'

'Yeah, mine are saying that if Mitterrand is elected, France will join the USSR, and Russian tanks will roll down the Champs-Élysées on the Fourteenth of July ...'

Caroline was annoyed. 'Well, of course, that's what all the bourgeoisie think. They're afraid of socialism because socialism means real brotherhood, not the old *liberté–égalité–fraternité*. Socialism is the coming-together of people and progress.'

To which Sophie added: 'Socialism is the seedbed of the people. Death to the bourgeoisie!'

'Hey ... That's enough!'

'Well, for me socialism will come when everyone buys their share of toilet paper, kitchen sponges and washing powder,' declared Paula, solemnly.

'Yeah, socialism is when everyone stops keeping their stuff in their own little compartment in the fridge ... And especially when everyone stops passing the buck and pretending not to notice the sink's blocked!'

Sophie and Paula were not about to waste this opportunity to settle their scores with those of the household who only ever helped themselves, and never thought to buy food – apart from beer and crisps. The boys, basically.

Caroline applauded loudly, then addressed them in the solemn tones of the leader she undoubtedly was in all their eyes: 'Socialism means remembering to cast your vote in the first round, on Sunday ... So anyone who hasn't registered at this address needs to get on a train and get down to their home polling station with Pa and Ma. There's only one way to win an election – vote! Any way you can, but vote!'

A good ten or so of the assembled company broke into applause – glasses in hand – at her rousing exhortation, while the rest remembered they hadn't registered for or received their voting card, and now it was too late.

More than ever, that evening, Caroline was the beating heart of the group. They'd arranged to meet up with the other students and walk together to the stadium, not for the local rugby derby, or a concert, but for Mitterrand. The candidate had disappeared from sight over the winter, but now he was holding meeting after meeting in the main provincial cities. He recognised the rural roots of families that had moved to the towns, their deep-seated nostalgia for their home region, their sense of themselves as children of the soil. On his latest poster, he posed against the backdrop of a village in the depths of the Morvan hills, a photograph that proclaimed France was still a rural nation with cherished, long-held traditions. Countering the country postcard, Giscard was a figure of cold protocol, backed by the gilded panelling of the Élysée palace. A disdainful, elitist monarch at the heart of Paris, the overweening capital, the centre of power.

Rustic roots apart, Mitterrand was there tonight because, of all the great regional metropolitan centres, Toulouse was the only one to have said no to de Gaulle in 1969. All the city's deputies, the president of the regional assembly, and most of the surrounding municipal mayors were on the left. Symbolically, the city known to all as the Ville Rose was the last staging post in Mitterrand's conquest of France. But for that, the stadium must be full. On this cold wet night, nothing was less certain, and if the stands were empty, the three TV channels that had risen from the ashes of the old public service broadcaster, ORTF, would be only too happy to film the dismal scene.

Sure enough, the ghastly weather put off some of the party when they set foot outside. Rather than freeze in a stadium, they preferred to play cards back at the apartment. Finally, eleven of them set out for the rally – a proper football team. But there were only three mopeds.

Marc and Paula climbed onto Antoine's Piaggio. Sophie and Brigitte rode pillion behind Pablo on his MBK. They would get there! Except that Caroline refused to sit astride the big panniers on Xabi's Honda 125. She didn't have a crash helmet, for one thing, but she also had no confidence in Xabi whatsoever. He liked to look mean and moody, in a huge cape, like the Elephant Man, but worst of all, from her point of view, he was one of Anton's crowd. She couldn't understand why Xabi was coming with them at all. He was the one who claimed to have links to Iparretarrak, the Basque paramilitary group, the one who bragged about handling explosives.

He had no business attending a democratic electoral rally.

'For God's sake, Caroline, don't be so stuck up. It's just for five minutes.'

'No, we have to round up the others first, from Tortoni's.'

'That bunch of pissheads? They'd rather stay put and get smashed!'

Caroline insisted. She raised her voice very slightly, signalling that she was the one in charge of this operation.

'No, we're going to fetch them, otherwise they'll bail out, too. OK?'

Caroline planned to take a detour via the big café on the corner of Toulouse's main square, then head off to the stadium. She wanted to round up the rugby guys. At least they weren't afraid of the cold. She dreaded turning up to an empty stadium. She could already picture the footage of deserted stands on TV tomorrow, and so she unlocked the communal bike from its place at the bottom of the stairs and led the charge towards Place du Capitole. The wind buffeted them as they rode up and over the Pont Neuf from Saint-Cyprien. Like Napoleon crossing the fucking Berezina, said the boys.

At Tortoni's, the room was even more packed than usual, punks rubbing shoulders with rugby players, and everyone else. Caroline even recognised a few guys from the far-right Parti des Forces Nouvelles. An ecumenical crowd, assembled to celebrate the owner's new grand plan: he was just back from Frankfurt, he told them, where he'd signed with the European subsidiary of McDonald's. Thanks to him, Toulouse would enter the modern age, with the first ever McDo in southern France.

'The first ever what?'

'That's it, pretend you don't know.'

'You're selling out to the Yanks?'

'And so? Have you seen the state of this square? The state of

Toulouse? Somebody's got to do something or the entire city centre will fall into ruins.'

'And what if the communists get in?'

'I couldn't care less. I've secured all my loans. Mitterrand can take the Élysée— hell, Brezhnev can take the Élysée for all I care; the contracts are all signed, work starts Monday! But before we connect the pumps to the vats of Coke, we've got to drink the booze dry! Four Roses, Guinness, all the cigarettes, the Marlboros … It's all on me!'

The owner's open invitation drew a chorus of cheers … Deliberate provocation in Caroline, Sophie and Paula's eyes. The weather was bad enough, but now they had to contend with a horde of students who were more pissed than political. The owner was forging a coalition all his own, rallying his clientele to a concrete vision of globalisation: rum from the Caribbean, cachaça from Brazil, bison grass vodka from Siberia, he was giving away the whole world. He didn't care two hoots about the future of socialism. He'd lived for five years in the States: he knew that entrepreneurship was the only way to change the world.

'You've sold out!'

'Perhaps. But before that, tonight, everything's on the house!'

Caroline stepped back. She was in shock, especially when she spotted Anton's gang in the crowd. The sworn enemies of imperialism were ready to drink the bar dry to make way for a McDonald's. She was crosser still that there had been no sign of Constanze for two days now. Some of them teased her that Constanze had taken her kid brother off on a clandestine expedition. She knew Alexandre was easily led, and eager to please. Each time he set foot in Toulouse it worried her that he would be lured into something. She didn't like him hanging out with Constanze, still less Anton's gang. They were all under surveillance. If there was ever any trouble, it would get straight back to the police, and their parents would be furious – they'd never hear the end of it. A catastrophe for the farm. Alexandre was a naïve country boy, but they were all from solid bourgeois families. If they ever got into trouble there was a parent or a lawyer to step in and sort things out.

'Guinness for world peace! Bacardi for world peace! Four Roses for world peace! Malibu for world peace! Get 27 for peace! Business for peace!'

The girls left Tortoni's, sickened by such a display of idiocy. But now they had a moped each. Caroline kept the bike. Antoine, Éric and two others felt guilty now, and soon left the bar to join them, swearing they'd be back after the meeting to drain Tortoni's tanks. They wanted to ride up front but the girls made them sit on the back, given the state they were in.

At the stadium, not only were the stands full, but a mood of feverish excitement contrasted with the freezing sky. These terraces were invariably packed for a match in the depths of winter: this cold snap was nothing. A giant screen showed wide-angle views of the seating area at the foot of the podium. They vaguely recognised the top rank, their faces if not their names – Lang, Quilès, Mauroy, almost all of them men. A brotherly band of comrades clearly united by one thing: they were all frozen half to death, wrapped in thick coats, hats, scarves, projecting an image that was far from dynamic and all-conquering.

Caroline had never set foot inside a stadium before. It was packed to the very top of the stands, thirty-five thousand people in fine voice, hollering '*Mit-ter-rand! Mit-ter-rand!*' On the grass, the words MITTERRAND PRÉSIDENT were spelled out in huge white letters. But the most extraordinary thing for her was the sight, in close-up on the giant screen, and as a tiny figure far below, of Mitterrand himself stepping up to the podium. Mitterrand in the flesh, albeit no bigger than a toy soldier. On the screen, he walked slowly, holding a rose. A man with a flower in his hand didn't look very up-to-the-minute, especially with that stiff, rather affected walk, as if he was pacing behind a coffin, preparing to lay his rose on someone's tomb – but whose? Still, a shiver of excitement ran around the stadium the instant he began to speak. A simple greeting addressed to the crowd in general, and every single person in it: '*Bonsoir*, People of the Left!'

*Peuple de Gauche* – three words that united his troops and melted their hearts. Perhaps this was true leadership. Perhaps it showed in details like that. And unlike those seated down below, in front of the podium, Mitterrand was on fire. He wore only a jacket – a leader doesn't feel the cold. He lay the rose on the lectern and spoke not to the crowd, but to each and every pair of eyes trained on him from around the stadium. He modulated his voice, projecting forcefully when required, but sometimes speaking softly, resting his elbows on the lectern as if he was about to confide a secret. Caroline had never seen anything like it. This man shone with a kind of secular faith. Or he was a great actor, a method performer, speaking from the heart, taking risks, even improvising – yes, in his left hand he held sheets of paper rolled into a tight tube, his speech, no doubt, while his right hand gesticulated constantly, flickering like a flaming torch held level with his face. The flimsy lectern trembled with every move, even the podium looked shaky, but the candidate looked strong, powerful, unstoppable.

Caroline saw the man she had come to see; she heard the words she had come to hear. Politics took on a new meaning, made sense at last, in the person of this man. To engage in politics was to be swept along by a project, a mission, and above all by a leader. Only a true leader can embody a project, a plan, and she found herself listening more and more intently, closing her eyes, to the point where Sophie asked her: 'Caro, are you all right?'

'… I say to you all, and I will say it loud and clear to my dying breath, that I, I am a free man, and there is no one in this world, no force, no power that can influence my own free will, not in the East, nor in the West, not in Moscow, not in Washington, nor in Bonn, and not any individual or force here at home, not the power of money, for which I care nothing, nor capital, nor multinationals or lobbies of any kind. There is no power on this earth that will ever force me to speak anything other than my own mind ...'

Caroline was trembling, she wanted this moment to last forever. She glanced at her gang. The fervour of the speech had gripped them, too, and all the more so when they sensed the candidate was bringing things to a close, that this man standing before them was projecting himself as nothing less than the figurehead of an entire people, at the prow of history. His voice swelled now to fill the vast space. The grandstands reverberated to the tremolo rising from the podium. Their pact was sealed, their communion was complete ...

'And so I say to you all: we'll meet again. We shall meet again soon, in France, and for France. Soon! For the Republic, and for victory!'

The crowd, and Caroline and Sophie, rose as one, applauding wildly, hugging each other for joy. But the girls sprang apart in surprise when the candidate left the lectern and the loudspeakers blared the 'Internationale'. The recording sounded uncomfortably old and scratchy, redolent of the Red Army Choir, though that in no way deterred the crowd from joining in: 'Arise, ye wretched of the earth, / Arise, ye hungry and enslaved ...!' The words reminded Sophie of her righteous anger earlier that evening – the fridge back at the apartment would be empty, the boys could never be bothered to do the shopping, and some of them were propping up the bar at Tortoni's right this minute, getting blind drunk. Socialism was a daily struggle, and fraternity would only be achieved through hard work There was still so much to be done. But things would be different now, she was sure of that.

## Friday, 24 April 1981

They left the meeting, and no one could remember where they had parked their mopeds and the bike. Some said they had to go right, but Antoine, Sophie and Patrice swore it was left ... Confusion and hilarity. Being a militant was all about coming together; it was selfishness as a crowd, fraternity itself. And here, in the poorly lit vicinity of the stadium, they could literally feel the brotherhood of man. Caroline stood apart from the group, watching them, as if looking back on an episode in her life, years after it had taken place. Already, she felt a kind of nostalgia. She could picture herself in ten years' time, or twenty. She would think about the meeting, and this evening, and all the images would come flooding back: the packed stadium, the speech, the fervour, it would all come back to her perfectly intact. The great moments of history are repositories for our private memories. The little gang in front of her was walking past another group, fifty or so militants gathered outside their chartered bus, waiting for the door to open. The driver was fast asleep in his seat, and in an effort to wake him, the whole crowd was singing 'Changeons la vie', Herbert Pagani's anthem for the French Socialist Party, written at the end of seventies. They looked like a proper band of brothers and sisters, grown-ups rehearsing a chorus they'd all learned by heart, like a battle hymn, or the Ave Maria at Sunday mass, except that this melody was neither grave nor transcendental, but bright and cheery – 'Bella Ciao' crossed with a Russian folk tune: 'Why believe the promise of tomorrow? / When we can change our lives right here, today ...!'

Sophie, Brigitte and Patrice went and stood with the choir, but they couldn't remember the words. Caroline was sure of one thing: tonight, more than a political rally, she had witnessed the prelude to real change. The toppling of the old order. But this was more than a one-off revolution, it was the coming of a new age. Whether the man with the rose was elected or not, nothing would ever be the same again. With or without Mitterrand to lead the country, one thing was certain, her own life would change over the seven years of the coming presidential term – she would complete her studies, get her first teaching post in the state system, launch herself into active, adult life. Find her own apartment, a man, perhaps start a family, here in Toulouse or some other city. The next seven years would redraw her world.

Everyone met up back at the apartment. Caroline was the last to arrive. She had found the bike at last, not far from the tennis courts, leaning up against the wire mesh fence, unpadlocked. Someone must have taken it for a spin but not stolen it. All part of the magic of that evening, the euphoria of universal brotherhood.

The traitors who'd spent the evening at Tortoni's bar were just back, all of them very drunk, and even though none of them had been at the rally, they all voiced their opinions. The idea of posing with a rose was so passé, for one thing, a naked appeal to base populism, and then there was the way Mitterrand held it up, like some blushing bride, when the power of the image was precisely the contrast between the rose and the clenched fist, like the Socialist Party logo, the rose you had to grip hard, to show that nothing would hold back the forces of progress, not the thorns in the stem, nor the jibes of your enemies.

'But a man walking into power with a rose in his hand, there's something beautiful in that, don't you think?'

'Are you kidding? Smell the roses! Makes me think of bloody Wizard aerosol spray. Not Che Guevara.'

Xabi and the others took the opportunity to trot out the same old arguments, the alienating, unholy trinity of the Media, Government and the Multinationals, from which they must all free themselves. And it would take more than a rose in a clenched fist to do that. Anton said nothing. Listening to them, Caroline felt more doubtful still about the company Alexandre was keeping. She ignored Wizard and the multinationals, but asked them if they knew where Constanze had gone, and why she wasn't back.

It was Anton who replied: 'How should I know? Just because we're German, we don't spy on each other.'

His comment fired up the debate once more, with the ultra-radicals denouncing the trend for big political rallies, like some kind of high mass, an opium of the people. Patrice and Marc singled out Rocard, Mitterrand's rival in the early stages of the presidential race, but who had dropped out and served as the candidate's warm-up this evening at the stadium. He was far better equipped to fight the right. Their drunken impersonation united all the others, making them laugh so much they no longer knew quite what they'd been discussing. Anton and Xabi finished them off completely with a couple of stiff gin and tonics. At which point the telephone rang. It was well past midnight. Sophie picked up the receiver. The person on the other end sounded gruff, and spoke German, so she called Anton. The others fell silent, all listening intently to find out what was going on, given Anton's grave expression. He hung up almost immediately, then came back into the room and went straight over to Xabi and Gerhard. The three of them stuffed their things into their bags and left without a word. A short while later, around one o'clock in the morning, footsteps rang out on the staircase, heavy and loud. A group of men was hurrying up to the second floor. Looking out of the window, Caroline saw two police vehicles parked on the street. They heard loud knocks at the door, fists pounding the wood, and a raised voice ordering them to open up.

Saturday, 25 April 1981

Early next morning, the cardboard box lay on the grass behind the car, soaked with rain. That night, unable to stay out under the stars, Constanze and Alexandre had made love in the cramped Renault. At first, they kissed tenderly to the strains of the old Simon & Garfunkel compilation. Then Constanze took out the latest Talking Heads. The cassette was halfway through, so she wound it back with the tip of her index finger, causing a strange hiatus during which nothing was heard but the sinister patter of falling rain. Once the cassette was in the deck, and the volume turned up loud, things had really taken off. Not content with just kissing now, they wanted to take each other, bite one another, excite their bodies with teasing strokes of the tongue, thrusts of the hip, but in such a tight space it was very hard to get their clothes off. There was scarcely any room to move, but that only excited them more. And then Alexandre, in a moment of blind passion, opened the boot and tossed out the big box stuffed with leaflets that was taking up so much space. Now they could lie down and make love to Talking Heads, electrified by the primitive beat, driven wild by the whining, repetitive vocals – music that spread over you like a trance.

Alexandre woke at dawn, not daring to move for fear of waking Constanze. At eight o'clock she was still asleep, her head snuggled into the heap of sweaters and bags that had served as their pillow. He looked at her long, lean body. She was clinging to him. If he made the slightest move, she would wake up, and anyway it was cold. It was still raining, softly and steadily now. Alexandre greeted it like an old friend, one of those spring downpours that drenches the growing plants, the kind of rain that gorges vegetables, wheat, alfalfa and meadows alike. Though Alexandre doubted his parents were grateful for the rain right at that moment: they still had to clear out the eaves that fed the water butts and the tank. Above all, they would be wondering where their son had gone, and why he wasn't home yet. He knew they would be tactful enough not to ask questions when he got back, but they would sulk for the rest of the weekend all the same.

At length, stealthily, smoothly, Alexandre sat up and peered outside. He saw the box he had pushed out of the car, so completely soaked that it had lost its shape. Inside, the thousands of leaflets formed a compact wet block, a mass of paper sheets stuck together, with all the ink running. At that moment, Constanze opened one eye. She followed Alexandre's gaze, and seemed suddenly to realise where they were, as if she'd forgotten all the open space around them. She sat up in turn, and saw the box lying out on the hillside.

'What have we done!'

'We made love.'

She paused for a few seconds after his reply, unable to deny the fact. The natural world she cared about so much … in truth, this was the first time she had truly communed with nature, and she owed this new experience to the boy who smelled so wonderfully of trees. She sank back down, dozed for a few seconds more, then sat bolt upright again.

'Oh God, Alexandre, I've got to make a phone call!'

'What, here, now?'

'In the night, I thought that—'

'Thought what?'

'Nothing, but I need to make a call, straight away.'

'But there's no way, or we'll have to drive to a house, find a farm, I don't know …'

'No, no, it has to be from a phone box. I can't call from someone else's line.'

'But who do you need to call?'

Constanze said nothing. She stared at the landscape all around, at the small wood, the hills that seemed to run one after the other all the way to the Atlantic, or the Pyrenees. Then she lay down again slowly. Her eyes closed.

'You know what? Let's just stay here … Never leave this place.'

Alexandre knew he'd be lying if he said yes, but it would be cruel not to agree. Constanze's body tensed. Her eyes were wide open now, and staring.

'They scare me, Alexandre.'

'Who?'

'The others. Anton, Xabi, all of them …'

'Why?'

'I think they're going to do something for the election.'

'Oh? What?'

'That's just it, I don't know.'

Alexandre feared he understood. He saw again the kilos of white pellets that had brought him closer to Constanze, until now he was as close to her as he could possibly be.

This time, Constanze propelled herself up and out through the door of the car. She was clearly on a mission. She really had to make that telephone call, but first they must deal with the cardboard box; there was no way they could leave it there in the middle of nowhere.

'What shall we do with the leaflets, Alexandre?'

'Well, we can't burn them, or throw them in a river, and we certainly can't post them in people's letterboxes now.'

'This is no joke. If we get stopped with that in the car …'

Before they broke camp, they heaved the box back into the boot, a delicate operation because it was so sodden that there was no way to get a grip, and the whole thing weighed ten times what it had before the rain. Then they set out straight away on the road, with the leaflets like a dead weight in the back. Alexandre knew they would have to drive a long way before they found a call box, perhaps as far as Lauzerte. If the weather lifted, at least from up there they'd have a magnificent panoramic view from the old ramparts. But there were other things on Constanze's mind now; the outing had taken on a different tone. Still, he wanted to show her the sights. He glanced across at her as he drove. She was paying no attention to the scenery, and seemed immersed in dark thoughts. He would have liked to take her hand, smile at her, but he didn't want to look like a love-struck kid. He took great care not to touch her at all, not to stroke her cheek, or worse, try to kiss her. He had understood this girl was wild at heart: she would bolt if she felt the slightest bit cornered. Like her long, untamed mane of blond curls, Constanze's sense of freedom was the first thing you saw.

Under their combined weight, plus the box, the Renault struggled to make it up to the village square, with its church, two cafés and a call box, the latter occupied by an elderly woman. Constanze stood in front of the door, to let her know she was waiting. The grandma was speaking loudly into the handset, asking the person at the other end to repeat everything they said. Alexandre sat down at a table outside the Café du Commerce and ordered two coffees with hot milk. Croissants would have to be fetched from the village bakery, a newspaper from the Tabac-Presse across the square. He covered the two cups with their saucers to keep the coffees warm and headed for the bakery. Constanze watched him as he walked, and he watched her as she waited. They gazed at one another like two distant lovers. The bakery smelled good. Alexandre bought croissants and two brioche buns. He had no idea what she liked.

He pushed open the door of the Tabac-Presse, and the 'ting' of the bell made the trio of customers chatting beside the cash register turn around. He walked across to the wall of magazines and newspapers. Again, he felt a wave of anxiety, dreading some mention of his nitrate fertiliser. He read the newspaper headlines one by one. All agreed the world was a powder keg waiting to explode: Colonel Gaddafi was trying to unite the Arab countries to protect Lebanon against Israel; President Reagan was slowly recovering from an assassination attempt by a crazed *Taxi Driver* fan; in Northern Ireland a boy of fifteen had been killed by a plastic bullet fired by the police; and in Italy, eight months after dozens had been killed in the bomb attack in Bologna, the investigators had followed a trail from the Red Brigades to a rogue ex-Masonic lodge, the Propaganda Due or P2. In France, eighty gravestones in a Jewish cemetery in Bagneux, on Paris's south-eastern rim, had been plastered with anti-Semitic graffiti, the cold snap was set to worsen with a blast of wind from the north, and tomorrow night at eight o'clock sharp, the new CII Honeywell-Bull computer would deliver the results of the first round of voting in the presidential election – a reported 37 million votes cast, but the outcome would be known in seconds – and in all that there was no word of an explosion anywhere nearby, nothing about Golfech, or Agen, or Toulouse, nothing …

'What are you looking for, the racing results?'

'No, just looking.'

'Read my entire news-stand while you're there. Go ahead …'

Anxious not to attract any further attention, Alexandre paid for the half-dozen newspapers he had just leafed through and headed back to the café. The bar owner had taken the initiative and was giving the two cups an extra, deafening shot of steam to warm them up. Out on the square, nothing had changed. Constanze was still waiting outside the call box.

'There – drink it while it's hot!'

'Thank you.'

'Tell your girlfriend she can call from here if she likes, the phone's behind the bar.'

'No, I think she needs to call overseas.'

'Ah, that's different. She'd better have a good stack of coins. Depends where she's calling though.'

'I'm not sure. Switzerland, I think.'

'Well, best take her the coffee. Old Ma Cadelle is stone deaf, she could be there for hours.'

'It's OK, thanks though.'

Alexandre opened a newspaper, but the silence in the café disturbed him. He sensed the owner spying on them both from behind the bar.

'Not from round here, are you?'

'No, from Corrèze.'

'But your car registration is 46, that's not Corrèze, is it?'

'Yeah, that's not my car.'

Alexandre was satisfied he'd put the café owner off the scent. That would do. In the countryside, you only had to drive twenty kilometres and someone would always ask where you were from. Twenty kilometres from home, you were a foreigner.

The little old lady hung up at last. Before leaving the call box she carefully, slowly collected up a pile of papers from the shelf and put them back in her bag. Constanze dived into the cubicle as soon as she had left. Alexandre watched from the café. He saw her check her address book before dialling. So she was calling an unfamiliar number, not the apartment in Toulouse. He studied her manner, looking for clues about the nature of the call. She seemed nervous, edgy. Then she hung up, checked her address book again, redialled the number, or a different number.

Alexandre returned to his newspapers, scanning the regional

pages of *La Dépêche*. A Renault 12 had hit a wild boar on the D-road near Montcuq and two people had been slightly injured. A freight train had hit a small truck at a level crossing on the Brive–Toulouse line. A dumper truck full of gravel had overturned in the quarry near Caylus, and a grocery van had been robbed on its rounds in Villefranche. Nothing spectacular. He opened *France-Soir* and immediately came across a photograph of a huge explosion, accompanied by a lengthy article – a powerful bomb had gone off the day before, at Berlin University, causing considerable damage. He froze as he read the piece, wondering if Anton was involved in any way, directly or indirectly. His mind raced; he was unable to concentrate, but he gathered that an extremist with close ties to the Red Army Faction, or Baader–Meinhof Group, had been on hunger strike in his jail cell, that he had been force-fed, and that he had died as a result, sparking a week of rioting in West Berlin. Hundreds of young people and anti-nuclear campaigners living in squats around the city had been protesting relentlessly, all dressed in black. Dubbed the Schwarzer Block by the press, they had thrown Molotov cocktails into shops and set fire to banks, culminating in this gigantic bomb.

'Doesn't look good, does it?'

Alexandre started in fright. The bar owner was standing just behind him. Alexandre closed the newspaper but the owner carried on talking – it was just like the Brixton riots last week, a whole area of London like the front line in Belfast for four whole days, hundreds of wounded, pictures of Madame Thatcher's capital reduced to a war zone, and worst of all, the fear that the whole city would go up in flames.

'Bombs going off all over the place. It'll end in revolution, you mark my words. Best call in the army and eradicate the whole lot of them. Filth.'

Alexandre dared not reply. The bar owner was expecting an

approving nod, but he did not oblige. The guy returned to his post behind the bar. Alexandre folded away all the papers he'd spread out in front of him. All this rage was beyond his comprehension. That world was so different from his own, the world before him right here and now, this village, and the hills beyond. Everything clashed in his mind. He stared at the open space of the square, the house fronts above the vaulted arcades, the peaceful village. He was sheltered from it all here, because the connecting thread in this violence, this drama, was city life. London, Berlin, Bologna, Belfast, Washington, Beirut, Kabul.

Constanze was still on the phone. She seemed suddenly far away, and utterly different. Best to put some distance between them, get away and leave her right there. Best to act like he'd never met her before. In his mind, she was connected to the double-page spread in *France-Soir*, the collapsed buildings, the riots in Berlin, a city split down the middle. Nothing good would come of this. He felt weak, vulnerable; he thought of Les Bertranges, his cattle, his fields, his grandparents. They would need help with the market garden. He thought of the eight calves that had just been born. His place was there, with them. He should never have got mixed up in this business; it was nothing whatever to do with him.

Constanze pushed the door of the phone box shut with a quick, nervous gesture. She headed towards the café then suddenly turned on her heel. With difficulty, she heaved the door open again. She had forgotten something. Then she came towards him. You could see straight away that she wasn't from around here – her bright blonde hair for one thing, and everything about her, even her way of walking.

'Your girlfriend's beautiful ...'

Alexandre turned around. The owner was wiping glasses behind the bar, and staring out into the square, just as he had been doing.

'Could you put the radio on? Some music, or something?'

'As you wish ...'

The owner switched on his big radio set and turned the dial until he found a music station. Abba's 'Dancing Queen', an old club favourite. In this setting, its urgent harmonies sounded like a blast from another place, late at night.

From Constanze's blank, distracted expression, he knew something had happened. Fearing the bar owner would overhear their conversation, he walked out to meet her in the square, and she fell into his arms.

'Alexandre ...'

'What's up?'

'I can't go back to Toulouse.'

'What's happened?'

'The cops have been round to the apartment. I'm sure they're looking for Anton and Xabi.'

'What about Caroline? Is she OK?'

'I don't know.'

'But that's nothing to do with the leaflets?'

'No, Alexandre. Nothing at all.'

They sat down together at a table on the edge of the terrace. Constanze looked suddenly defeated, overcome with exhaustion. She needed to confide in someone. Alexandre glanced inside the café. The owner was still surveying the scene from behind his bar, probably annoyed he couldn't hear what they were saying.

'You know what, I don't want any trouble. All I want is for there to be no nuclear power station, that's it, that's all. But their violence, their bombs, I don't want any part of that. It hurts us all, do you see?'

'Of course I see, Constanze.'

'No, you don't. You don't understand. They love to stir things up. They stir up hate, the cops hate them, the state hates them, they dream of sending everything up in flames, but why, why? The violence, Alexandre. I can't stand it a minute longer.'

He put his arms around her and tried to reassure her, though she was scaring him half to death. She seemed so defenceless that the thought of abandoning her there and turning his back on this whole mess was impossible.

'I get it, Constanze. I really do.'

'I need a break, Alexandre. I can't go back to the apartment. Can I come to your place?'

'Well ...'

He hadn't thought of that. Never pictured Constanze at Les Bertranges, not for one second. His parents' looks, and his little sisters' questions, and Caroline, who would certainly get to hear about it ... It was unthinkable.

'So?'

'Yes, absolutely, if you like.'

'Are you sure?'

'No problem.'

When they entered the café once again, the owner saw a couple reunited, two young kids who had weathered a passing crisis, nothing more.

'Want me to heat those coffees again?'

## Sunday, 26 April 1981

The Sunday of a presidential election, any election, in France is a day of limbo. The hours seem to expand. Time itself is a formless vapour. Like midnight on New Year's Eve, the entire nation comes together at the appointed time, 8 p.m. precisely, to hear the result. At Les Bertranges, the atmosphere was even more unreal than usual, with all eyes on the tall girl with curly blonde hair. Her presence was enough to mark the weekend out as something extraordinary. She was quite the attraction, and Alexandre, too. He who was usually so discreet, who never told them anything about what he was up to, and had always kept his girlfriends out of sight – here he was, showing them all his new love interest. Not only that, but he had shown up with her unannounced, without even really saying how long she'd be staying. It was crazy.

The meal was nothing special for a Sunday, except in Constanze's eyes. A big bowl of potato and vinaigrette salad stood on the draining board, beside another of mixed, diced vegetables, while a big chicken roasted in the oven, filling the house with the aromatic promise of crispy skin.

'*Les enfants*, time to lay the table!'

It was never clear to whom the instruction was addressed – the advantage of a big family. You could choose to follow the order, or tell yourself it was directed at everyone else.

Alexandre heard his two little sisters vying to set out the plates and cutlery. He and Constanze were walking around the garden.

They had spent the night in the same room, something Constanze had accepted as perfectly normal, while Alexandre had felt acutely awkward at the thought of his little sisters close by, and, above all, his parents. More awkward still was the evident hint of a kind of relief, a sense of private satisfaction that their son had found a girlfriend at last, a young woman who might just, perhaps, be prepared to live here. From now on, their son would embrace the idea of staying on the farm, making his life here, as the family always had until now.

Constanze wanted to walk further, out into the fields. Alexandre didn't like to say no, in fact he didn't care to say much at all. He felt acutely uneasy, beset as he was with doubts as he reminded himself that this girl was only here with him now, at this moment, to get away from the trouble in Toulouse. She was keeping her distance in case the police came back. All she wanted from Les Bertranges, no doubt, was a safe hiding place on a farm deep in the countryside, at the end of a track that no one would find. Alexandre hesitated to ask her outright, 'Constanze, why are you here?' He was too afraid of what she might say. Her reply could shatter the magic of walking through the fields with her. To walk along the hedgerows, bursting with new spring life, was a joy. She asked him the names of all the bushes and herbs, the shrubs gorged with rain and sap. The birds, too. And he knew them all. She took his hand as they walked, and he could tell she wasn't pretending, because she held it tight, as if clinging to him for help. She marvelled at everything. She knew nothing about the trees, or the plants, or the birdsong. She walked through their natural surroundings as if this was a new world, discovering it all like a child in an enchanted kingdom. Unlike the day before, she was not miserable or confused, but revelling quite simply in the moment, transported by the lightness of a Sunday suspended in time.

'Alexandre, are you mad at me?'

'What for?'

'Because I ... how do you say it in French? Because I forced your hands just a little.'

'No, my hand, you forced my *hand*.'

'Well?'

Again, Alexandre said nothing. Deep down, he was unsure of the risk he was taking in sheltering her here. If the cops from Toulouse decided to try and find her, they would very quickly follow the trail back to the farm, and make the connection with the fertiliser. Looking back at the farm from where they stood, that matrix of mortar and stone from which all his family had come, Alexandre felt furious with himself above all. The first person to put a foot wrong in all this was him.

An odd atmosphere reigned at lunch, even odder than the evening before. Agathe and Vanessa still seemed intimidated by this young woman, this grown-up so far ahead of them in every way, and especially because their parents were plainly fascinated by the radiant stranger. Her accent which seemed to make her smile even broader, her easy, liberated manner – everything indicated that she had come here from another planet. Their parents stared at her as they might at an extraterrestrial. For one thing, she came from that improbable Other Germany beyond the Wall, and it was hard to believe that her parents and grandparents lived in that immense red stain on every map of the world, the Soviet bloc which everyone dreaded would one day leach into the free world, especially since the Red Army had poured into Afghanistan three weeks ago. The pictures were appalling. More than ever, red was the colour of fire and aggression. This girl was an entire geopolitical reality made flesh before their eyes. That whole other world was real, then ... And though Constanze spoke naturally and easily about her family, she felt a kind of guilty shame at the reality she described. She even felt obliged to tell them that she could see her mother whenever she liked. Her mother worked for the state railways in East Germany – like the SNCF – and transport workers from the East were all granted access to West Berlin. She, too, if she wanted, could go back to the East tomorrow, and come out again, no trouble at all. She played down the situation because she felt ashamed to come from such a poisonous country. Constanze filled the space at her end of the table. Unknowingly, she had taken Caroline's place. She sat before them all like some unlikely apparition, the substitute eldest daughter, and only Alexandre saw her, fleetingly, as a bird of ill omen.

The one o'clock news showed pictures of the candidates casting their votes in their home regions. President Giscard d'Estaing was in Chanonat, a tiny village tucked away in Puy-de-Dôme in central France. Chirac was in the depths of Corrèze, Debré in Amboise on the Loire, Crépeau at La Rochelle on the Atlantic coast, and the others in Poitiers, or some such. Mitterrand, for his part, was still eagerly awaited in his remote corner of Nièvre, the north-eastern quadrant of the Massif Central. Each of them drew strength from their native soil, a sign that the seat of every president's power and legitimacy was the land itself. For any of them to be elected, they must first seal their humanity by showing themselves to be made of the same stuff, the self-same clay as the people of France. The more city-centric the political class of France became, the more it proclaimed its rural roots.

At that very moment, the future of the country was being played out under cloud-filled skies. France was choosing its leader, and in the cities and countryside alike, citizens of the Republic were turning up at their local polling station. They could not know it yet, but with every ballot cast, perhaps they were changing the course of history, throwing themselves into the adventure of socialism, perhaps even communism if they voted for Marchais. Or perhaps they were playing safe, falling back on the incumbent candidate. In the first round, the field was wide open. For now, no one knew what lay ahead. Even there, sitting around the table, everyone sensed the curious, pervasive chemistry of an election Sunday – a foretaste of melancholy, or cautious, anxious confidence.

Sunday, 26 April 1981

When Caroline called after lunch, it was all Alexandre could do to get them to stick to his instructions. No one must say that Constanze was there. He feared his sister would be jealous, that she would resent him not asking her permission to go out with her housemate. And Constanze wanted none of the Toulouse crowd to know where she was. Still, Agathe and Vanessa carried on with their stupid veiled hints, being mysterious, asking their older sister if she could guess what was happening there on the farm, something incredible, yes, right here on the farm ... But down the line, Caroline wasn't really listening. She suspected nothing. She was overcome with feverish anxiety, overwhelmed with partisan emotion, and there was something else too, about which she said nothing, other than to tell them she hadn't slept very well for the past two days, because of things that were going on at the apartment. At any rate, for the moment, all she could do, to the exclusion of anything else, was wait for it to be eight o'clock so that they would know at last.

Over coffee, on the stroke of two, the sky cleared to reveal bright sunshine in a glorious expanse of blue. Everyone got up from the table and prepared to go outside. Their mother headed for the garden, and the two girls went with her, while their father said he would take advantage of the fine spell to shift the tree that had fallen across the bottom of the track to the mill. Alexandre detected a hint and walked across to the storage shed to fetch the chainsaw. Constanze stood in the doorway, unsure who to follow, more lost than ever. Alexandre looked into her face – the face of a sad little orphan girl, a child standing alone on a station platform when a train has just left. Perhaps she was seeking an adoptive family, a calmer existence among people she loved. Perhaps that was what she was missing. He signalled to her to join them, and she ran to sit with him and his father on the tractor.

They drove down the narrow earth track towards the fields. The tractor lurched unpredictably, but Constanze just laughed. His father set about the tree with the chainsaw, while Alexandre moved the animals to a new field. For the first time, Constanze heard the soft, scything sound that cows make when they crunch really long grass, cutting through the juicy stems. A wild, powerful sound. She found a piece of dead wood to use as a stick, and together they led the herd to the next field, up the hill. The new-born calves looked as soft as plush toys. Constanze didn't dare approach them, warned off by the looks their mothers cast in her direction. Alexandre helped her to stroke one of them, then another. She wanted to take them in her arms. She loved their long, poignant lashes over huge, astonished eyes. Never had she held such a big animal in her arms like this; it was a whole new experience. She straightened up and closed her eyes, filling her lungs with the pure air. Alexandre watched her, entranced by the way her top smoothed over her breasts.

'You know, in two months' time, if you come back, this field will be full of the scent of wild mint. It'll be covered in millions of little wild mint flowers.'

'Really?'

'Yes. In summer, the whole hillside is covered with millions of blue flowers. When you walk through them it's like floating in an ocean of fresh mint.'

'I don't believe you.'

'Come back in July. You'll see.'

Alexandre gazed at the field of rich, thick grass. At least here his conscience was clear. Here he'd put the ammonium nitrate to good use. Anton and the others might use it to make bombs, but he was spreading it over fields of clover and ryegrass, giving the plants the nitrogen they needed to encourage new growth at the end of the winter. And on top of that March had been warm, and April cooler but without too much wind and with plenty of rain. Now the grass was juicier than ever, and the clover was wonderfully sweet.

Constanze was surprised to see him snap off a few blades and nibble the ends. He showed her how the species of grass were all different – this kind was especially good; there would be enough to feed the cattle without supplementing their diet with cornmeal. They didn't believe in stuffing their cows with protein, like weightlifters at the Moscow Olympics, or Arnold Schwarzenegger.

Constanze had spent the most wonderful, most extraordinary day, but now she was talking about getting back. She needed to be in Toulouse that evening. She had to find out what exactly had happened. She was afraid for them all, Anton, Xabi, Gerhard and the others, and above all she was afraid for herself.

At five o'clock, everyone gathered at the farmhouse. The girls ate their teatime snack – Paille d'Or biscuits dunked in cold chocolate Nesquik, because in late spring the afternoons were getting warmer. Constanze glanced, as she had earlier, at the telephone on its stand in the hall. She really ought to get back. Alexandre's parents insisted he drive her to Toulouse in the Citroën. Already, in their eyes, she was a cherished future daughter-in-law. But Constanze wanted to take the train. It would be safer for Alexandre that way, though she did not say so of course. Before setting out for the station in Gourdon, they checked the train times on the SNCF timetable. It was from last winter, but they didn't notice. Only once they arrived did they see that the 18:56 train didn't run any more.

The schedule had changed at Easter. Now, the evening train left at 19:27. There was no bistro or kiosk. They sat and waited in the car, in front of the deserted station.

Constanze took advantage of the extra time to tell him that these three days had made her feel so much better. She'd felt light and free, as if she was being carried along on the breeze, surrounded by simple, straightforward, uncomplicated people. Alexandre searched her face, trying to understand what she was really saying. Naïvely, he'd hoped she might make some sort of declaration, unless it was up to him to take the initiative. But that was out of the question. Constanze didn't broach the subject, and so he forced himself to do the same. He sensed she would take fright at any suggestion they might see one another again, perhaps even next weekend. She was too much of a free spirit to get attached to anyone at all. But she drew close to him, nonetheless, resting her head on his shoulder, as she had done before. Alexandre tried to look tough and strong, not to show his sadness and disappointment that she was leaving.

They walked across to Platform 2, and his show of strength hardened to frost. She'd got what she wanted, hadn't she? She'd run away from Toulouse to the farm, taken shelter while she waited for the storm to pass.

'Alexandre, you look so far away …'

The old Micheline railcar pulled into the station, making a tremendous racket. When it came to a halt, the diesel engine kept up the din, puffing out hot, filthy smoke. Constanze climbed onto the first step of one of the carriages. Then she turned to Alexandre as if, suddenly, there were a hundred things she wanted to say.

'I'll have to tell Caroline I was here when I see her …'

'No. If I don't tell her myself, she'll give me hell about it. She'd hate it if she didn't hear about it first from me. Caroline's like that.'

'But it's an impossible secret. And anyway, it isn't really a secret. There's nothing wrong with us seeing one another, is there?'

The stationmaster was taking delivery of boxes brought by the engineer. The two of them were talking, apparently in disagreement. Constanze stepped back down onto the platform, drew close to Alexandre, tried to talk to him in a low voice. She was careful not to be overheard, despite the noise, and the absence of anyone else nearby or aboard the train.

'Alexandre, Caroline has to know I came to the farm. She absolutely must. Everyone has to know.'

'But why?'

'For your sake, Alexandre. If there's an investigation, the police will come to the farm, and because everyone will know we're going out, the cops will think I stole the fertiliser, do you see? This way, if they follow their leads to the farm, it will lead them to me. Do you understand?'

Alexandre was thunderstruck. So she knew about the fertiliser. She took him in her arms, and the gesture was protective and loving all at once. He was stunned by what he'd just heard. Perhaps she'd known all about it from the start. The whole gang was so secretive and conspiratorial. He buried his face in her blonde curls, suppressing the questions he wanted to ask. He knew perfectly well that this girl had no interest in him whatsoever, but he couldn't help himself.

'Caroline will be here next weekend. But it's the second round of the election in two weeks, and she'll be in Toulouse, so you could come, don't you think?'

Constanze was still holding him tight. She whispered.

'Yes.'

'You'll call me?'

'Promise.'

A loud blast of the whistle made them draw apart. Alexandre glanced at the stationmaster. There was no need to blow the thing that loudly. He probably did it on purpose to scare them.

The Micheline revved its engine, belching out still more smoke. Constanze waved and said something. Perhaps 'See you soon' or perhaps not. He realised, with horror, that the only number he could call her on was his sister's. He didn't even know her family name, or her father's address, or her mother's. He had no idea where to get hold of her, except at the apartment. He'd be the one waiting for her to call.

## Saturday, 9 May 1981

Everyone in the family was always busy out of doors, and for anyone expecting a phone call, it was a nightmare. With no one in at the farmhouse, there was no way of knowing if the telephone had rung or not, nor any way that anyone could be relied on to take a message. When the phone rang in the empty silence, the only creatures within earshot were the dogs, the cats and the chickens. The only solution was to keep within a reasonable distance of the yard, not too far from the squat grey toad. There was no other way of knowing who might be trying to get in touch with you.

That morning, the girls had gone over to the Martel place to make preparations for the school show. Their father and mother had gone to the farmers' cooperative, and then to do the shopping at Mammouth, after which they would drop in on the grandparents down in the valley, to take them everything that Jean's mother had noted on her list. Which left Alexandre alone on the farm. He drove the tractor back to the house every fifteen minutes, listening out for the telephone. He was spraying the corn in the large field on the lower ground and rode back up each time with the sprayer still hitched to the tractor. Several times, from a distance, he thought he could hear it ring. With the engine turning, about two kilometres from the house, he was convinced he could hear the rasp of the bell, but once he reached home, there was nothing. Once, he even went indoors and lifted the handset to check the phone was still working. He unwound the spiral cord that had become coiled in upon itself, and once everything was untangled, he placed his hand against the inert Bakelite, convinced that the telephone had indeed rung a few minutes before, and would ring again any time now.

Constanze had implied she would come this weekend, that she would call. Alexandre was all the more on edge because he had decided to spray the corn today, Saturday, and leave his Sunday free. The corn shoots were covered with bindweed in places – the wild flower that Constanze had thought so beautiful. Even the French word for weeds had delighted her: 'mauvaises herbes'. She thought they sounded charming. Alexandre had treated the field just after sowing, but the rains had washed the weedkiller down the hillside. If he didn't do something soon, the bindweed would take over, not forgetting the thistles and fescue, all of which would quickly choke the young shoots. Before, the weedkiller was strong stuff that stayed in the soil for weeks and could survive up to ten downpours. It would eliminate weeds by scorching them to the very tips of their roots. But the stuff they used nowadays only attacked the leaves; it was gone again after the first rain. He had told Constanze this, but the information had done little to reassure her.

Alexandre poured himself a big glass of orange squash, diluted with water from the tap. He emerged into the yard, and glanced at the three dogs lying stretched out nearby. They looked listless, as if the air was close.

'Call me if it rings, eh?'

The dogs lifted their heads, certain that Alexandre was giving them an instruction, though they had no idea what, and so each laid its head back down on its paws and returned to its reverie. Alexandre climbed back onto the tractor, cursing. Old Crayssac was right, of course. The telephone was an evil invention, a disaster. Either you did nothing but wait for it to ring, or you dreaded not being there when it did.

He forced himself to concentrate on his task. He hesitated for a second, thinking he should go back to the house and dial the number of the Toulouse apartment, but he was too afraid that Caroline would answer. Anyone else, he wouldn't have minded, but to have to ask Caroline if he could speak to Constanze was unthinkable.

Waiting for Constanze's call was like conjuring something of her presence. When you told yourself she would come, it was almost as if she was already here. The thing he dreaded most was never seeing her again. That would be like hearing a song on the radio, a wonderful, enchanting song, and then never being able to find out the title, and realising you might never, ever hear it again. Since she had been here, he felt her presence almost everywhere. Everything reminded him of her – the surrounding landscape, the golden fields and the blue sky – they actually looked like her. Here, in the countryside that had so charmed her, he felt as if he was with Constanze again, because nature itself was in her image, wild and remote. Everything around him spoke of her. At times, he even thought he could smell her perfume, that delicate scent of patchouli that filled his senses. He hurried to finish the spraying, driving the tractor at almost twenty kilometres an hour, convinced he would hear the phone ring up at the house at last. Once he even thought he saw her on the other side of the hedge, though he knew she couldn't possibly spring such a surprise. Gradually, without him noticing, the others had come back home. First his sisters, then his parents. Only the dogs knew whether the damned telephone had rung in their absence or not.

When he reached the farmhouse, Alexandre couldn't help noticing how transfixed they all were by the election. The girls weren't old enough to vote, but they asked what time everyone would be going to the town hall tomorrow? They wanted to be the ones to hold the envelopes containing the ballot papers, and drop them into the ballot box. Alexandre said nothing. He wasn't planning to leave the house tomorrow, not until the Bakelite toad had croaked. Other than that, he wanted Mitterrand to win, so that they could forget all about the nuclear power station, and Larzac and all the rest of it. Things would be simpler for him then at least. Mitterrand had promised to review France's nuclear programme. As a loyal representative of the working class, he would get the miners back to work in Décazeville and elsewhere. His parents disagreed. Coal mines weren't the issue. For them, it was up to Giscard to block the Reds, especially since Marchais had begun dropping hints about the 'solid assurances' he'd received from the socialists. With twenty per cent of the vote in the first round, the communists had become the king-makers. Already, rumours were circulating that the franc was on the brink of collapse, the borders would be closed, and Russian tanks were on the move in the East. As for the business of Bokassa's diamonds, that was a KGB plot to discredit Giscard. There was no doubt about it, the communists were operating in the shadows, France would rally to their cause and the Reds would stand poised to take over the world.

'A vote for Mitterrand lets nutcases like Crayssac into government, don't you see? With guys like him in charge, the Yanks will have plenty to laugh about, for sure!'

Alexandre didn't bother to argue. He had no choice now anyway. Mitterrand had to get into power so that Anton, Gerhard, Xabi and the rest would stop their nonsense. Mitterrand had to get into power so that Golfech would be cancelled, and all the other planned reactors. It didn't matter how; it didn't matter if he owed his victory to Bokassa's diamonds, or even whether the story, with its uncomfortable colonial overtones, was true or not. Some football matches are won on a handball.

## Sunday, 10 May 1981

Constanze hadn't called. It wasn't yet 8 p.m. but the faces of the TV presenters – Elkabbach's solemn gaze and Étienne Mougeotte's enigmatic grin – told Jean and Angèle that something big was afoot. The two journalists knew. It was plain as day that up there in Paris they already had the result. This was their smug, insufferable way of letting you know that they, in the capital, already had insider information. In fact, they had probably known for several hours already, perhaps even since noon, but they were pretending not to know, and out here in the countryside you had to wait for the big grandfather clock to chime eight before you could know too, before you could get the results. That superior attitude of theirs was repulsive. Alexandre waited more expectantly than any of the others. As soon as the result was out he would have an excuse to call the apartment in Toulouse and ask what was going on over there.

Just before eight o'clock, the TV studio fell silent. Followed by the countdown, like the NASA rocket launches at Cape Canaveral. And then, from the top down, the computer-generated image appeared, like a drawing on a Minitel screen – a bald forehead that could belong just as well to the left or the right. For just a couple of seconds, France was not so much parted down the middle as hanging by a hair, until finally the face of François Mitterrand appeared, in thousands of tiny electronic dots – blue, red and white. Silence. Then very quickly the image switched to a live camera at the Socialist Party headquarters on Rue Solférino in Paris, and their father could not bear the sight of so many overjoyed faces, so many laughing people, their arms full of roses, hugging, kissing and probably getting scratched by thorns in the process. He got up to turn off the television, but Agathe and Vanessa wanted to carry on watching, and so did their mother, who said it was just one more catastrophe to add to all the rest. Their father snapped shut the little door that covered the TV controls, as if he wanted to lock it and hide the key. In a fit of pique, he turned down the volume and went out into the yard. Alexandre eyed the scenes of joyful party activists, but more than ever, his focus was the telephone. Mitterrand's victory was the perfect pretext for a call to Toulouse, to ask how they were celebrating their triumph. He would call Caroline, and hope that Constanze would be the one to pick up.

'Shall we call Caroline?'

'What for?' said his mother.

'She's been waiting for this for so long, they must be having quite a party ...'

'Well, exactly, leave them in peace.'

'Cheer up, Ma, don't look like that! This is a victory for the youth of France! And young people are the future, aren't they?'

His mother said nothing. She thought it odd that the oldest candidate had been the one to appeal to the youth of France, that their idea of progress was to elect a president who was already past retirement age. It was incomprehensible, and above all, she wondered what the result would bring at the European level – their subsidies, the beef market, the cost of machinery, because their seed drills were old now, and badly rusted in places, and they would have to renovate all the buildings in accordance with the new standards. The left would take them towards centrally planned agriculture, perhaps even collectivisation of the land, and Crayssac, that lifelong communist, would get more than them.

Alexandre had already dialled the number but no one was picking up. He let it ring. Then he hung up again and redialled, just to be sure. Now there was an engaged tone. At least there was someone in. Everyone was there, probably. He pictured the party, the wild celebrations. He replaced the handset, dialled again. Still engaged.

'They'll be out on the streets. Look at that. My word, they all look happy in Paris.'

'It's engaged, so someone's definitely there.'

'Fifty-two per cent, dear God, it's not possible, that old skinflint ... he's never won anything until now. Impossible. He can't possibly have won now he's retired.'

'Well, he has.'

'It'll be madness tomorrow at the bank.'

Vanessa and Agathe were bored with the alternating images of overjoyed or tearful faces – Lionel Jospin, Pasqua, Olivier Duhamel ... They wanted to watch something else now, but there was nothing else on, and anyway their mother wouldn't turn over until Giscard had accepted his defeat in person. It was still in the balance. So the girls went to their room. Their mother went to the kitchen, not for coffee but an orange-blossom tisane. They needed to calm their emotions this evening. And then the telephone rang. Alexandre hurled himself into the hallway as if Antenne 2 itself was calling for his personal reaction. It was Caroline. She was hysterical with joy. She wanted to talk to their father, to wind him up just a little bit. Alexandre told her he'd gone outside, so she asked to speak to their mother, but Alexandre cut her short.

'She's busy.'

'Really? Doing what?'

'She's making orange-blossom tisane.'

'For Papa?'

'No, for everyone ...'

'Well, enjoy the party ...'

'What are you all up to?'

'We're going to get on the bikes and go out. Can you imagine, this is history! We're living through a moment of history, the left is in power, just imagine that …!'

'Yeah. So where will you go?'

'I don't know, Alexandre, anywhere the crowd takes us, probably Place du Capitole. Everyone's out on the street here, it's like a revolution – can you hear it? The car horns all sounding everywhere, listen!'

Caroline held the handset towards the open window, but Alexandre couldn't hear anything. He glanced out of the farmhouse window. It was still light here, and there was not a sound coming from outside. Even the dogs were silent. In fact the only thing they could hear was coming from the television, the mounting excitement in Paris. But just at that moment, the camera switched to Rue de Marignan, Giscard's campaign headquarters, and the contrast was striking. The place looked as quiet as Les Bertranges.

'Is everyone there, Caroline?'

'What do you mean?'

'I mean, who are you with?'

'Listen, I'm going to go now. Tell Papa he's lost the bet, eh? Promise?'

'Wait, Caroline, I'll come down and find you all!'

'I don't know where we're going, Alexandre, it's like a huge party all over town! *Salut!*'

Alexandre rushed to his bedroom, leaving the television on in the empty living room. Quickly he changed, pulling off his sweater and slipping on a cap-sleeved T-shirt, the one on the Springsteen poster. He took his close-fitting leather jacket, the one that made him look macho and well-built, then he went to the kitchen to test the water, to see whether his mother would let him borrow the Citroën.

'Wait, you're not going off to Toulouse now?'

'There's a huge party and Caroline was begging me to go down and find them. There won't be anything like this again for years!'

'Thank the Lord.'

'So can I take the Citroën?'

'No, the tank's only a quarter full – you'll never get there and back on that.'

'OK, so the Renault ...'

'You'll be back later, eh? Don't stay out like the other time.'

Alexandre had no idea whether he'd be back later or not. He was a free man after all. In charge of his own life. Like here in the fields, on their land, their territory. He was The Boss tonight, even more than Springsteen ... He walked out to the hangar to take the Renault, but was surprised to find his father sitting on the baler against the back wall, smoking his umpteenth Gitane.

'Where are you going?'

'Toulouse.'

'A Person of the Left, now, are you?'

'Why not? What do you expect? You don't think I'm going to stay here and watch you all crying into your tea, tucking the girls up in bed because there's school tomorrow?'

'If you want a drink, you can go to Le Paradou, it's not far. You can be sure there'll be a bunch of nutters buying rounds at the bar.'

'I don't care about getting drunk. I want to see people, make some noise, see the crowds in the streets. There's a party going on everywhere across France right now, millions of people out celebrating in the streets, and I'm not going to miss it!'

'And what if the last two calve in the night?'

'They're Salers, they'll manage on their own.'

'Once you're in charge around here, you'd better not be running around like this, at the drop of a hat.'

## Sunday, 10 May 1981

Alexandre drove fast. The Renault was much better than the Citroën in fact. He felt truly himself. Since sleeping in it with Constanze, the car had become priceless to him. Since they had made love, holding one another tight; since they had clung together the whole night long, a night when they'd huddled against the cold and talked like he'd never talked to anyone ever before, the Renault had become a world all its own, the only real, tangible vestige of their love.

He drove through Saint-Clair then down to the Nationale in the valley. There was very little traffic out that evening, and the cars coming the other way were flashing their headlights and sounding their horns all the more as a result. Even the French XV winning the Grand Slam a month earlier hadn't sparked joy like this. In the woods, the boar and deer would be wondering what all the noise was about. It was a strange evening. Every car seemed to feel the need to commune with the rest of the traffic. But Alexandre wasn't really heading into Toulouse to join the wild crowds and share in the universal harmony, he was driving there to find just one other person.

There were more cars on the outskirts of the city, a great stream of traffic heading for the centre. He took a turning along the canal and got lost. He always had a hard time finding his way around. Then he got stuck in a jam and headed for Place de la Daurade, the open space on the banks of the Garonne where Caroline and her crowd went drinking in the evenings, sitting by the water for hours when the weather was warm. It was chilly tonight, but perhaps in the heat of the moment, people would be diving in. The traffic was more or less at a standstill now. He decided to leave the car on the embankment that followed the river, where he could be sure to find it again later. He felt uncomfortable, constantly startled by the cars bursting out of the side streets. He began reversing into a space on a pedestrian crossing, when a crowd of revellers began to shake the Renault, bouncing it like rugby fans on a big match night. Now he felt even more lost, and afraid. He gave them all the thumbs up, pretending to enjoy the fun. There was nothing for it but to join in the somewhat alarming hysteria and share the moment, when for him the sole purpose of all this was to bring everyone out onto the streets, and for Constanze to be out there too. He was peering at them all attentively now, scrutinising the faces. She was sure to be out, and around here somewhere. He planned to start at La Daurade and follow the river, but after two searches up and down, with no sign of her, nor his sister, nor anyone else from their group, he turned off into the narrow side streets, following the movement of the crowd. The victorious left seemed to have one idea in mind – to congregate right in the centre, on Place du Capitole. All these smiles, the shouts, the explosive joy overwhelmed him completely. Cries of '*Mitt-er-rand, pré-si-dent!*' and '*On a gagné!*' rose all around him. The bars were pumping out music now, and musicians were playing in the streets. Alexandre didn't miss a thing, not a single person: he was more focused than any of them, utterly present in this moment of history. Unlike the rest, he wasn't euphoric or drunk, but not because he wasn't celebrating. No, in the midst of it all he was calm, focused on one thing only, to see all there was to see, in each and every one of these faces, and to find Constanze. He tried to imagine the emotion he would feel if he found her there, if he spotted her in the distance, and if she saw him, too, at the same moment. They would walk towards one another and throw their arms around each other, and then the party would begin for real.

He thought he saw her a hundred times, at the slightest hint of a head of blonde curls, at the slightest glimpse of a tall figure in a silky sweater, at the faintest whiff of patchouli. How incredible it would be to find each other in all this chaos. He prepared for it as for a truly great moment in his life, a thousand times more potent than a mere presidential victory.

He walked past a café and spotted Patrice, a guy who often hung around the apartment, clearly drunk, leaning on the bar in the middle of a crowd of people he didn't recognise, all of them about as drunk as he was.

'Patrice! How's it going?'

'Eh?'

'Alexandre, Caroline's brother.'

'Yeah, I know ...'

'Aren't you celebrating?'

'Look at all these suckers ... A great big dose of democracy, what a fucking con ...'

'Yeah, right. Are you on your own?'

'Look at 'em all. Suckers ...'

'Guess you didn't vote Mitterrand?'

'Vote? Me? Do my civic duty an' piss into a pot every seven years? What kinda fool d'you think I am?'

'All right, all right.'

'That's not democracy, you need to give power back to the people! Even if they never had it before, gotta give it back ...'

'Know what? I don't care about any of this either.'

'You're a good guy!'

'Hey, where are the others?'

'Ah, I get it, looking for Faye Dunaway, are you?'

Patrice had clearly been drinking for hours. Alexandre was

careful not to rise to his mocking description of Constanze.

'So where's everyone else?'

Patrice stood up straight in front of him and fingered Alexandre's leather jacket as if he was feeling the quality.

'Hey, that's real leather! You really don't wanna look like a country bumpkin, do you? Well, don't get yer hopes up, fella, she'll never fuck you ...'

Alexandre took a deep breath. The close-fitting jacket sculpted his torso, like a second skin over his muscular form. Almost unintentionally, he grabbed Patrice by his nylon K-Way and held his face close up to his own.

'Know what, you pathetic motherfucker, I never liked the look of you, and now I know why.'

'OK! Calm down.'

Alexandre gripped him tighter still.

'Where are they? Fuck's sake!'

'Hey! Relax, man ...'

Their confrontation had gone unnoticed amid the general euphoria, especially because Patrice was far too drunk to get properly scared. In truth, he would probably have laughed at the idea of getting caught up in a fight in the midst of all this. A great way to wreck the atmosphere, spoil this whole stupid pretence of a party. But Alexandre was clutching his K-Way so tight against his carotid artery that it hurt.

'Where are they?'

'I dunno, on the Capitole, or down at that Spanish joint, the one with all the *ha-mones* hangin' up. That's where they all go.'

Alexandre hurried away from the bar and pushed his way through the middle of the jubilant crowds. He resented their happiness. Around him now, all he could see were pathetic, overexcited types, a coalition of gullible partygoers, though they all seemed united by genuine fellow feeling, and in that splendid communion he

171

knew he was out of place; he could read it in their faces. They all resented his selfish quest, his pursuit of one single individual in this overjoyed multitude. On this day when history had been made, the day they would all remember, all he could think of was falling into a girl's arms. And why hadn't she called, these past two weeks? Why had she done nothing to see or talk to him again?

And just then, he felt a hand grasp his shoulder from behind.

'Hey, sorry to grab you by your jacket. Just windin' you up ... If you're looking for Constanze, don't waste your time.'

'What do you mean?'

'Listen, I'm not in the frame, but your sis has cleared out the apartment. After the cops came round, she chucked everyone out.'

Alexandre thought of how his sister had seemed the weekend before. As soon as anyone had asked her about the apartment, her housemates, she had changed the subject.

'What?'

'I don't usually tell other people what to do, but I reckon you've got yourself into some deep shit. If I were you, I'd do whatever it takes not to see any of them again.'

Alexandre was astonished by Patrice's calm, humane tone as he pronounced the words.

'Believe me. Don't try to see them ever again. They're going for it, in the next few days – Anton, Xabi, all the crowd from Mirail, they want to send the whole site up in smoke. Seems they've made six bombs.'

'And Constanze?'

'Don't worry about her. She won't get into any trouble, at least, that's for sure.'

'Why not?'

'She's gone back to East Berlin.'

## Friday, 24 December 1999

Alexandre stared at the pellets of fertiliser in the sacks he had positioned against the tank of diesel. He thought back to that evening in April 1986. Back then, they still had the hideous grey telephone with its long, twisty cord. He'd spent two hours out in the hallway, bent over the small stand, then sitting down against wall, before actually lying stretched out on the tiled floor, listening so intently to Constanze's voice that at times he felt he could smell her perfume.

She'd called him eventually, from Berlin. After five years. He heard from her at long last thanks to an explosion in a nuclear power plant. It was thanks to Chernobyl that he'd picked up the thread of a vanished love.

Without that calamity in the Soviet empire, she might never have called, never have contacted him. Without the radioactive cloud wafting across Europe, and the crazy uncertainty about the radiation it was spreading in its path, he might never have seen her again. But two days after the catastrophe, Constanze had telephoned. She wanted to know that everything was all right with him, and the countryside all around. She wanted to be sure that the meadows, and the trees, and more than anything the wild mint, were all still there. She was surprised to learn that, in France, everyone thought they were safe from the radioactive cloud, whereas in Germany and the other Nordic countries, people were panicking. There had been a rush on iodine tablets. But no one in France was worried –

the government had reassured the population that the Alps formed a natural barrier to the cloud. Yet in the USSR the talk was of thousands dead. The cloud was a threat of the utmost seriousness; people were forbidden from going out in the rain; children were not to play outside; no one was to touch or eat salad leaves. Fruit and vegetables picked in the three days following the explosion were not to be eaten. These were the words that Alexandre heard Constanze speak, after five years of silence. She had been right all along to distrust nuclear power, and for all they knew, the problems it would cause were only beginning. She told him of the desire that had never left her, to live in the countryside one day. She dreamed of it constantly, now more than ever. Alexandre dared not believe what he was hearing, but more than anything, he was astounded just to hear her voice. He could never hear enough of it, and asked her a thousand questions. First of all, he wanted to know how her studies were going. She had carried on with biology, and law, and she was happier than ever with the choices she'd made, for reasons she could not tell him over the phone. That was why she wanted them to meet. In July, she was probably going to spend a week at Anton's place – he was out of prison, and living on the high *causse* in Aveyron. After three years behind bars, he was lying low with friends in some far-flung place. He'd joined one of those groups of hippy smallholders that were flourishing all around the edge of the Larzac plateau. He had gone to ground there with two others, including Xabi, the one who knew how to handle explosives.

Alexandre had listened to Constanze as she told him everything. He'd listened to her voice at the other end of the line, and wondered if he was dreaming. Her voice was exotic, disorientating.

But without that call from Constanze, he would never have taken up again with Anton, and his personal pyrotechnician. And if he'd never seen those two again, he wouldn't be here now, tonight, heaving sacks of fertiliser and stacking them against the fuel tank

– a pyrotechnician in his own right, so that everything would blow sky-high, just as Anton had shown him.

1986

Thursday, 24 April 1986

For two years, Alexandre had gone out with the Bardane girl, Isabelle. She was the same age as him, and she was a pharmacist. They saw one another twice a week, and the plan was to keep it that way, because she wanted to live in her two-room apartment, right in the middle of Cahors, while he did not want to move away from the farm. Isabelle didn't have a driving licence. She was afraid of driving: she could never have lived out in the countryside. The arrangement suited her well – no commitment, no expectations. But then there had been the Dutch girl at the campsite at Cénevières, one rather wild August, and friends of the Bardane girl had told her everything, and she'd found the humiliation hard to bear. Their relationship ended there. Their plan to have a child, all the things they'd talked about, but no more than that, had dissolved. Alexandre's parents never understood why he'd split up with the pharmacist. Pharmacy was a good, respectable line of business.

Alexandre had had no news of Constanze for five years, but for him, 24 April was an anniversary, celebrated by him alone: their first and only night together. He wondered if Constanze remembered the date, wherever she was. Most likely she would have forgotten all about it, probably didn't even remember their time together. He'd never heard any news of her, nor was there any way of finding anything out, beyond tapping her name into the cold keys of the farm's Minitel terminal from time to time. The machine was indispensable now for registering the animals' births and managing the herd – a technological marvel. Alexandre typed at the keyboard every day: 3614 or 3615, '*trente-six quatorze*, *trente-six quinze*', followed by the relevant code in words, and he could call up anything, even the latest cereal prices in just about every market. He could also get extraordinarily reliable and precise weather forecasts, a change from the vast zones covered by the TV weather reports. Each evening he would work out the animals' food rations, or the amount of fertiliser required for the fields, but above all he watched out for the alerts from the plant protection service – destructive pests or health concerns. You could even contact a consultant via a messaging service, to the utter exasperation of his father, who loathed the very idea of 'consultants', along with the idea of being told how to rear cattle by a Minitel machine, when he'd been doing it all his life. But the most miraculous thing of all, the thing that kept Alexandre tapping away at the keyboard for hours at a time, even to the extent of setting it up in a corner of his bedroom, was the directory. The directory, and the search function, by family name or first name. Over a period of six months he had typed CONSTANZE LINDENBERG into the little box hundreds of times, exploring every available department of France. Soon, all the directories in the world would be on there. And all the while, the others thought he was busy with farm work. Up to now, the results had delivered row after row of Constances, but no Constanze. Unsure how to spell the family name, he had tried Lindenberg, and Lidenberg. Each time he got the same message: MORE THAN 200 ENTRIES CORRESPOND TO YOUR REQUEST. And he would follow up each and every lead. The quest was enough to drive him crazy. What fascinated him, too, were the hundreds of dating services that were popping up. He would waste hours on end, trying to identify her behind one or other of the German-sounding pseudonyms. He remembered she had told him her name meant 'mountain lime tree', or 'lime-tree mountain', or 'a mountain of limes' and so he

180

checked out the pseudonyms that resembled that, but had never found even one, not a single Mountain Lime or Lime Mountain. He was going mad ... Sometimes, scanning the pseudonyms, he would allow himself a moment's distraction – a tempting code name, girls looking to meet someone, or find the love of their life, if only for one night. It was a glimpse into a world far from his own, a world that more often than not arranged its meetings in Paris. The thought of so many potential one-night stands was intensely exciting but then, instantly, he would be overcome with guilt at the thought of straying from his true quest; at the thought of betraying Constanze, his one true love, the love that he couldn't forget. Worst of all, Vincent, the postman down in the valley, a regular at Le Paradou, had told him that the pseudonyms all over the Minitel system were fakes. They were employees of the state postal service, the PTT, posing as women or men, depending on their subscribers' preferences, and their sole purpose was to boost your telephone bill. But Vincent saw evil in everything, and no one ever believed him.

Alexandre feared his search was in vain. Constanze wasn't the type to waste her time on messaging services, and it was highly unlikely that she had come back to France. If she was living in Germany or anywhere else he would have to wait for Minitel to conquer the world before finding her. And the searches cost money. Each new telephone bill was a source of strife in the household. It was so high, Alexandre maintained, because of the hours he spent at 3615 La Redoute, ordering pairs of tights, blouses and bras for his mother, and things for his grandparents down below, not to mention the endless requests for the TV schedule, or the storm and hail warnings. Alexandre was the only one who knew how to use Minitel, the only one who knew how to turn the thing on, so he was constantly called upon to search or place orders for all the others, giving the date and time of the next expected rain shower, or a summary of the latest episode of *Dallas*. All that came at a price.

Most of all, he was afraid that Constanze might be married, in which case she would have changed her name as convention dictated, that appalling custom designed precisely to prevent a woman's past loves from finding her again by typing in her maiden name.

There was another reason why he found it hard to get news of Constanze: Caroline was still furious with him. She hadn't got over the fact that he'd slept with her housemate, and worse, got mixed up with the gang of militants, all behind her back, without ever telling her a thing. Now, on her visits to the farm, they talked about practicalities, nothing more, and greeted one another with a cold air kiss on each cheek. It worried their parents to see them fall out, though it was the same in any family, they knew that. Angèle didn't get on with her sisters. Once you reached adulthood, family ties strained and loosened. Brothers and sisters could be resentful, angry, sometimes even come to blows. But it hadn't come to that yet in the Fabrier household.

What enraged Caroline more than anything was that Alexandre had quite deliberately got friendly with Constanze's gang of buddies. After the police raid, tongues had loosened at the apartment. The others had told her about the fertiliser, implying that her brother had supplied the extremists with the ingredients for their explosives. That had made her insanely angry: she'd even sworn she would punch her brother in the face. She and Alexandre had only ever discussed it once, but it ended badly. He had never set foot in the apartment since. She'd even forbidden him from spending time with any of her circle, whether close friends or passing acquaintances.

Sure enough, in June 1981, three weeks after the police raid in Toulouse, the gendarmes had shown up at the farm. They had visited dozens of farms in the district. Each time, they'd found bags of fertiliser, but everyone used it here in the countryside. They had never succeeded in tracing Anton and Xabi's source of supply. Some of their questioning centred around a female German student with connections to the radical activists. They were looking to press heavy charges: a dozen bulldozers and trucks, and some of the huge earth-moving equipment, had been blown up at the Golfech site on the night of 10 May 1981. But the work had continued nonetheless. The National Assembly had debated the nuclear issue, but the deputies of the newly elected 'Pink Wave' were eager to get on with the programme, and voted largely in favour. On top of which, the regional assembly had done everything in its power to ensure the reactor was up and running as soon as possible. And so the next round of bombings had targeted not the heavily protected site itself, but the local Socialist Party headquarters. For six months, tensions mounted around the tiny, rural municipality of Golfech, population six hundred. By day, gigantic machines assaulted the land, flattening its natural relief, and by night, hundreds of riot police and security staff patrolled the site with dogs, behind miles of barbed wire and anti-tank barriers, just like in Berlin. The Golfech site was a tumour in the lush, green countryside. Protests and commando operations followed one after another, until the wild night of 29 November 1981, when a full-scale battle had broken out. A vast crowd of over eight thousand protestors from all over had bombarded the forces of law and order with Molotov cocktails, and set fire to the police station. The armed confrontations were backed by other, carefully planned acts of sabotage against pylons and electrical installations, which had plunged the region into darkness while the site itself was a nightmare of gunpowder, chlorine bombs and blazing fires. The fighting was intense, to the desperate sound of dogs howling in burning vehicles. But the craziest thing of all was that in the long, dark journey of that night, a shadow army had risen up. An army of local people who could stand it no longer, and of supporters of the project, a platoon armed with axes and picks, who had come to the aid of the police and set about attacking the militants themselves, in apocalyptic scenes. Everything and everyone had gone too far.

Now, five years on, most of the main building was complete and the first reactor would be operational in just a few years' time. Alexandre was pensive, thinking back over the episode that had sabotaged his own love story. The anti-nuclear protests had blown that sky-high, at least. And so he marked each 24 April in his own way. Today, all he did was sit and gaze at the landscape a little longer than usual, picking out the tree-lined course of the river as it snaked through the fields, tracing the narrow path that followed the contours of the hillside, the whole tableau of green, and sky, and water that had fascinated Constanze. He saw again the wonder in her face when she had come here, her utter astonishment and delight, and it had stayed with him. The scene reflected in the blonde girl's beautiful blue eyes was still here, in front of him, as if her gaze had imprinted itself on the trees, the river, the meadows. It would live here forever. Looking out over his natural surroundings, Alexandre recovered some part of Constanze herself. Even now, he saw the simple, unadorned landscape of the valley through her eyes – the elms lining the river, the hills. Back then, Constanze had stood on this spot and taken it all in, as if standing in front of a painting in a museum. This view was her, it resembled her, it inspired the same sense of freedom, the same simplicity, the same freshness. It was beautiful here. Without Constanze, he would never have realised just how beautiful it was. And so she had never left him, because he spent his life here among these hills, deep in her gaze, at the very heart of the treasure she had revealed to him.

Alexandre stood daydreaming while the water bowser filled. This morning, he was pumping water from the river, and after that he would take it up to the cattle troughs at the top of the farm, keeping the rest for the sprayer. In late April, the water was still ice-cold. Later this morning, he would spray his grandfather's potatoes down in the valley before they sprouted. That way he could avoid having to hoe weeds and damage the whole crop, like last year. But whenever he helped his grandparents, something was bound to go wrong. Now, the wind was getting stronger. The leaves had been trembling but now the branches were swaying too. If he sprayed in a strong breeze, there would be more trouble. Pesticides were always a source of strife – either his father would tell him he wasn't applying enough, or his grandfather would say he was using too much, and the next time it would be the opposite. Fortunately, Roundup had made weeding so much easier – you sprayed it on, it did the job, and that was that. It worked, and then it disappeared into thin air, like magic. No risk of it washing into the river the first time it rained. So that now, the trout had returned, and the crayfish. But it was progress at a price. The stuff had to be carefully applied. Now more than ever, a good grower had to be sure to apply the right dose, down to the last centilitre, using sprayers calibrated in millimetres. Surgical precision.

Only Crayssac swore that chemicals should be avoided at all costs. According to him, nothing beat the hoe and a good application of muck. One turn of the topsoil with the plough, at most. Everyone had their own ideas on the matter, and each outing with the sprayer was an opportunity to rehearse the old arguments one more time. That was how things were in the country: there would always be those who opposed progress and stuck to the time-honoured ways, the so-called golden age when the wheat was lost to smut or devoured by weevils. Alexandre had no particular personal creed, but he trusted the dozens of opinions he'd found on the Minitel forums. At least there, you could be sure there were no old-timers from before the war, who were suspicious of anything new. On the contrary, the forums were full of good advice and new ideas. He'd even read that soon people would be producing larvae that would eat the wireworm or grubs in the corn. The Soviets were working on it, getting the pests to destroy each other. Soon, they'd be sowing seeds with the weedkiller already inside. The year 2000 was coming. People would plant the seed and its pesticide all at once; at least then that would put an end to all the chemicals, and the squabbles they provoked between the generations.

As for what would happen when the cattle ate all these intelligent grains – perhaps their hide would repel flies, perhaps there wouldn't even be any flies – anything was possible with a little imagination. Perhaps Crayssac was right after all. Sometimes, Alexandre thought, this new world scared him, too.

## Tuesday, 29 April 1986

'The winter of the century'; in recent months, the papers had talked of little else. April had seen worse snow and hail than February, the thermometers were below freezing everywhere, and at Les Bertranges they'd had snow three weeks after Easter, with sleet and icy winds. The weather was incomprehensible. The TV bulletins tried to make sense of it all, showing great draughts of cold air marked in blue, as if a door in the sky had been left wide open and God or the Devil was refusing to pull it shut. On the farm, in the evenings, everyone looked west for the colours of the sunset. Their horizon was limited, but they had always checked the setting sun. They liked to think they could read the sky. Shades of pink meant cold air was on the way; shades of orange announced warmer weather. But in reality they were under little illusion. It was never that simple. The old barometer up on the wall had never been prodded quite so often. Everyone tapped it with their index finger to see whether or not the weather would turn fine. The old folks' rheumatism was a far better indicator, in fact, but now that Lucienne and Louis lived down by the river, they suffered from it all the time.

That evening, Alexandre had put some more logs into the big stove. He watched them, careful to contain the fire. Agathe was sulking again, up in her bedroom, even moodier than usual. Their father was outside fixing the barn door, and their mother had just finished blending soup in the kitchen, using the enormous Robotchef

187

that made a noise like a hedge trimmer. As he often did, Alexandre had laid the table before being asked, turning on the TV as he did so, in time to hear the jingle for the Antenne 2 news. Synthesised music from the studio, far away in another world. A daily breath of air from another place, something he savoured as a rule, but tonight the presenter's voice delivered the opening headlines with words that made Alexandre's blood run cold, words that cut into his consciousness like knives: 'nuclear accident', 'two thousand dead' and, above all, 'the USSR is requesting assistance from Germany and Sweden …' A TV announcement that the mighty USSR was asking for help from its enemies was unexpected indeed. Not daring to call the others, Alexandre stood staring at the set. The evening anchor, Claude Sérillon, had lost his usual twinkle – a sure sign that something unbelievably bad had occurred. For the first time ever, staring into the camera, there was no hint of merriment in his face, no hope. So a nuclear reactor had blown up in the USSR. The news had only just broken, but the core had been burning out of control for three days already. For three days, thousands of tonnes of radioactive water had been boiling and belching out a cloud of steam that could engulf the whole of Europe. The Swedes had sounded the alert, because the radioactive cloud was right over their heads, and spreading to Finland, Denmark, even down into Germany and Czechoslovakia. Alexandre froze at the thought of the cloud poised to envelop Germany, perhaps even Constanze's town, her neighbourhood, her immediate, everyday surroundings. If she was still living there, she would be right inside the cloud, right now, this minute.

Sérillon had said thousands were dead, but more mesmerising even than that was the orange cloud he was indicating now on a map of the world, a cloud that was very likely fatal – no one knew for sure, or no one dared to say. They had been living in fear of acid rain for the past ten years and more, but at least you could see when it was raining, and stay indoors. What did a radioactive cloud look like? Alexandre was speechless with shock. Living so far from everything, he had watched the ills of this world from a distance – bomb attacks, economic crises, protests, wars, even the strikes that broke out constantly in town. At Les Bertranges, they knew they were shielded from such disturbances. But this cloud signalled an end to all that. If it decided to float this way, there was nothing to protect them, not even their splendid isolation.

His father and mother came into the room, ready to sit down for supper. Alexandre summarised the situation so far: the explosion at the nuclear power plant, the radioactive cloud, the two thousand dead, as reported in the nearby town of Chernobyl. Chernobyl, a hitherto unheard-of town whose name was now on everyone's lips. Already, Antenne 2's Moscow correspondent was on the line, playing down the news with a reminder that, for now, the Soviet authorities were confirming just two casualties. But he said nothing about the cloud that was spreading across Europe. According to Moscow, there was no cloud. In the USSR, reality was whatever its leaders wanted to make it.

It was a lot of information for Alexandre's parents to take on board. Neither of them heard the rest of the bulletin. They both had the same instinctive reaction, to go back outside to stare at the sky they had checked earlier on. But now they were looking east, not west, searching the sky obscured by the great oak trees that were powerless to flee if the radioactive cloud came, no more able to move than the hedges, the cattle, or the great patchwork of fields. In the west, the sun had sunk below the horizon and the sky was a deep red. It would be clear tomorrow. Only the wind could say if the cloud was coming or not. But there was not a breath of wind now.

A radioactive cloud spreading out of control was worse than a war, an enemy so subtle that no one would hear it come. Watching his parents through the window, Alexandre felt a sudden urge to laugh at their concern. It was hard to picture the threat posed by a cloud full of radioactivity. TF1 was giving no more details than Antenne 2, or perhaps they knew the reality of the danger, and were keeping quiet. The Soviets were doing all they could to cover up the threat, no doubt about that. An invisible threat, by definition. The prospect was terrifying. Five years on, Alexandre saw how right Constanze had been. He knew now that she had foreseen the future, that he had been right to risk getting mixed up with her gang of activists, right to give them the ammonium nitrate. At least now there was proof that a nuclear reactor could blow up, and now there were nuclear power stations all over the place; there would be dozens of them soon in France. More than the Cold War, or the distant images of Hiroshima, this was the threat they should be afraid of. The reactors could blow up at any moment, Golfech or any of the others. Not since the war had the world seemed such a frightening place.

None the wiser for their scrutiny of the sky, his parents came back indoors to see what the weather report would say. They would have to talk about the cloud on there. But Laurent Boussie, the weatherman, was even chirpier than usual.

'Well, look who's here!' he exclaimed, twisting his hands like a glove puppeteer.

He was referring to the anticyclone out to the west. Fortunately, this would be strong enough to hold back any cloud formations coming from the east. And to ram the message home, he matched actions to words and pushed both hands out in front of him, as if to shoo away the clouds in the east, clearly visible on the map. As if the TV weatherman truly had the power to save them from such peril. The bulletin made no mention of the rains referred to in the news, the rains that would come down from Sweden, towards Germany and Czechoslovakia. That was how lucky they were, here in France. Alexandre went outside to assess the situation for himself. The clouds did seem to be moving away towards Aveyron, as if in response to the weatherman's sweeping gesture. The grey, overcast mass was plainly shifting slowly away to the east. Indoors, he heard his parents addressing Caroline on the telephone, then Vanessa. An anxious message on the answering machine each time. Then they called out crossly to Agathe who was still in her room, as if they had only just realised.

'Agathe, for goodness' sake, come down and have something to eat!'

Agathe was above all this, anyway. She couldn't care less about a cloud passing their way, or not, any more than she was interested in the French cup final that Alexandre and their father planned to watch the next day, monopolising the television for an entire evening, as they did for every match, with the commentators yelling and all the noise from the stadium, and the sound turned up far too loud. There were six TV channels now, and Agathe wanted a second television because every night there was a battle over what to watch, a battle that was never resolved by democratic means. Now that Caroline was in Toulouse and Vanessa in Paris, she dreamed of following in their footsteps, especially Vanessa's. It had become an obsession with her: Paris was even wilder than Toulouse. But she had two more years of school to complete. She felt trapped, incarcerated with her parents who never talked about anything but the farm, and Alexandre who talked of nothing but buying old Crayssac's place, who was interested in nothing at all, and didn't seem to care if he ended up old and alone. Let the cloud come, why not, it wouldn't bother her. Let it put an end to all the chaos and confusion of this world that threatened to overwhelm them all.

The next morning, their father found two dead birds on the doorstep. Anyone else would have taken it as an ill omen, proof that the Devil's cloud had passed in the night. But after recoiling for a moment in disgust, he quickly identified the culprit: Madonna, Agathe's murderous cat.

Agathe had wanted a cat, not the semi-strays that already lived on the farm, but one like the kittens in the calendar they got each year from the Post Office, with delicate features and fine, long hair. She had wanted a kitten that would stay indoors with her, up in her room, but this creature was a wild little thing, always off outside. She'd called it Madonna, but it turned out to be male. The natural world was his to roam, but strangely he always came back to use his litter tray. It didn't matter that he went outside, except that he was constantly catching birds and field mice, and depositing them at the front door. Madonna had all the Whiskas pellets he could eat, and soft food twice a week, but he couldn't resist killing and leaving his victims' mortal remains at the front door. The dogs would sniff the tiny cadavers in bafflement. Only Agathe was allowed to yell at the killer, and shut him in her bedroom, but half an hour later, Madonna was off on the road again. The vet said he needed a purpose, that he felt useless on the farm, and was having a hard time finding his proper place, what with the humans, and the cows, the chickens, the dogs and the other cats. Madonna felt the need to demonstrate that he, too, could serve a purpose.

*

Alexandre buried the two birds that evening at the bottom of the garden. He dug the holes deep as a mark of respect. He was glad Agathe's cat was a killer – it was a blessing. It put things in their place. Agathe was growing up fast and she never held back from telling them all that cattle-rearing and caring for the cows, only for them to end up being sent for slaughter, was a vile way to make a living. Lately, she had come close to implying that she lived with a whole family of murderers. At least now, with a serial killer all her own, she, too, was implicated in the vicious cycle of death.

Alexandre stopped short of putting up a cross, but he packed the earth down tight and lifted his eyes to the sky. The clouds were thinning. Today was one of those days that turns bright and radiant on the stroke of six o'clock in the evening. At the sight of the tiny graves and the mottled stratus clouds dispersing overhead, he thought about the people who had predicted that Golfech would blow up one day, and how on that day they would watch the trees die for tens of kilometres all around, and the population would be forced to flee, not for days but for hundreds of years. Well, perhaps the visionary dreamers were right. Perhaps the human race could die out. This morning the radio news announced that the city near the Chernobyl reactor had been evacuated. Fifty thousand people had had to leave their homes with no hope of ever coming back. The alarmists were right: nuclear power was a nightmare. Alexandre walked back to the farmhouse with his shovel on his shoulder, glancing at the sky. Country people had always lived in fear of the sky, and never more than now.

Their parents were already in front of the television, but they were unable to turn it on. Les Bertranges lay at the end of the power lines, and sometimes the current struggled to reach the house. A sign, no doubt, that in all the villages and farms round about, everyone had turned on their television. So their father asked Agathe to turn off her hi-fi, and all the lights. Every bulb was tracked down and extinguished, every pump and motor out as far as the barns, and the television came on. The evening news had just started. Alexandre almost wished it hadn't. Because this Wednesday night, on Antenne 2 and TF1 alike, the news was suddenly deadly serious, and frightening. Photographs taken by an American satellite showed that a second reactor had blown up in the USSR. From space, a second red spot was clearly visible. In reality, the Chernobyl reactor was still burning and there was no way to put it out. For days now, in the utmost secrecy, the Soviets had been bombarding the core with sandbags released from helicopters, to no effect whatsoever. The only solution was to send soldiers and firemen down into that hell, into the core, but with the burns and the radiation, men were dropping like flies. They collapsed after two minutes, and others had to be sent in their place, from towns further away, because if the uranium tanks and the graphite kept burning, they would produce clouds even more toxic than the first. Entire battalions of the Red Army were making the ultimate sacrifice, throwing themselves into the jaws of the eternal fire to smother the volcano of radioactive gas. It was unreal, insane. But there it was in front of them, on television.

Alexandre and his parents stood transfixed. The table still wasn't laid, though they needed to eat soon, and quickly, because tonight was the French cup final – Bordeaux against Marseille, a big match. But the knowledge that a second reactor at Chernobyl had exploded, with two others poised to do the same, made the football seem pathetically unimportant.

The absence of anchorman Claude Sérillon and his reassuring smile was an additional source of worry. His jovial, twinkly grin put everything in perspective, as a rule, but tonight's presenter wore an unshakeably dark expression, a sign that this catastrophe was indeed taking the world into the unknown. Would the earth recover? Would the fires continue to burn for weeks, would the radioactivity last for months, years, millennia? And that wandering cloud. Tomorrow, they said, it might float towards Monaco. Monaco, not France … How could a cloud the size of a country be so precise? How could it cast its shadow over the tiny principality, but not France? It was thanks to the anticyclone over the Azores, the one they'd been anticipating for weeks. Here it was, just in time to save the nation, but not Monaco. A Francophile cloud. Even their father was doubtful.

'He's lying!'

'Who?'

'Him, on the television, he's lying. You can tell.'

'But that's Bernard Rapp, Pa!'

The respected journalist co-hosted the eight o'clock news on Antenne 2 with Sérillon and Christine Ockrent. Lately, the trio had even lured viewers across from TF1 – an extraordinary feat.

'So?'

Report after report painted a grim picture. In the Nordic countries, people were being told not to go outside if it rained, nor to eat vegetables, while the Russian news said nothing at all about Pripyat, the evacuated city close to the reactor. Just then, the telephone rang. Caroline or Vanessa. At least they could reassure each other that everyone in the family was all right, in Toulouse and Paris alike, though Paris was so much further north … Before their parents or Alexandre had time to react, Agathe had shot out of her bedroom and picked up the receiver, thrilled to talk to one of her sisters. Bizarrely, half a minute later, she fell silent and stood motionless in the hallway, listening to someone, something. Finally, she came into the living room and addressed Alexandre solemnly, with an inscrutable expression:

'It's for you.'

The TV news had finished an hour ago. Agathe and their parents had eaten supper but Alexandre was still deep in conversation on the telephone. At first, he'd stood hunched over the hideous telephone table, with pins and needles in his arm as he rested it on the ghastly stand. Then he'd sat down on the floor. Now, he lay stretched out on the cold tiles. He felt uncomfortable, too, knowing the others would be listening, that they could hear everything he said. His mother had very soon realised it was the German girl calling, and whispered the news to his father, more perplexed than hopeful. Agathe, on the other hand, was full of excitement. For her brother to spend so long on the phone was an event in itself. At his end of the hall, Alexandre tried to think himself away from the family environment. He closed his eyes, immersed himself in Constanze's voice, pressing the handset to one ear, and the extra earpiece to the other so that all he could hear were her distinctive Germanic tones. He could almost smell her perfume, feel her warm mane of blonde curls. Her accent was more pronounced than five years ago, a sign of the distance between them. They were living worlds apart now.

She was in West Berlin. In West Germany, it seemed everyone was far more worried than in France, because in the GDR there were several reactors like the one at Chernobyl, and some even older – the first generation, built by the Soviets. Constanze felt trapped by the outdated, unregulated system all around her. A hundred kilometres west of Berlin, the East German authorities were about to open a new super-reactor, the biggest ever – four reactors of the same Soviet design as Chernobyl – and there was nothing they could do to stop it, no possibility of protest, in any form whatsoever. Her mind had been filled with apocalyptic visions over the past two days – cities emptied of their inhabitants, whole forests of desiccated trees, lifeless rivers, and that was why she'd needed to call. For her, Alexandre's world represented the exact opposite. It was a world of fields and hills and pure, clean air, and she could not stop thinking about it. The very first thing she had asked was whether the fields still smelled so wonderfully of fresh mint? Alexandre replied that it would be another two months before the mint was in flower, but yes, the grass was still rich and green with chlorophyll.

His father was watching the match now. In the living room, the crowd roared and the commentators' voices rose through the scale: 'Tigana, Giresse ... Di Meco coming on now ...' Alexandre took cover behind the wall of noise. Constanze told him what she had been doing. She had seen nothing of nature for five years, no wide-open spaces, just the city's parks. There had been no walks down sunken lanes lined with hedgerows, no chains of hills as far as the eye could see. Alexandre sensed that the spring of 1981, their escapade in the Renault 4L, three days out in the country air, had made their mark. Clearly, the memory had stayed with her. She told him outright: she still thought about the three days they had spent together, her first real contact with nature.

Alexandre was unsure how to interpret this distant show of loyalty. He even thought she might be calling solely for news of the landscape, the trees. Perhaps she wasn't interested in him at all? There wasn't much to tell, anyway. Nothing had changed. He felt ashamed of his solid, predictable existence, but it was precisely that which she had found so wonderful. Everything in

197

her world had been turned on its head: her father was working in the States now. She never saw him, but she saw her mother. Her grandfather was dead, and her grandmother was in hospital in the East. She refused to leave Leipzig, though she would have been allowed to. Apart from that, Constanze planned to make a career in humanitarian work, but it all came back to that blasted power plant. She wondered whether she should leave Berlin. She was mad with worry, convinced there would be more explosions. Her father had always told her that nuclear energy was safe, and she had always refused to believe it, though she trusted him deep down. But she knew he was wrong about this. She no longer knew who to believe or what to think. She felt lost.

At about ten o'clock, Alexandre's father stepped over him in the hall on his way to bed. Their eyes didn't meet. He'd lost interest in the match, probably dozed off in front of it, as usual. His mother changed channels, and the volume was lower now. Alexandre closed his eyes once more, sinking deep into the voice from Germany, the country beneath the great radioactive cloud. He wanted to feel her there beside him, to put his arms around her and hold her close, but she was hundreds of kilometres away, at the other end of the line. She said she'd never heard from Caroline, and that Anton and the other three had gone to prison. Thinking back, Alexandre felt a rush of anxiety. One thing was certain: none of them had ever said anything about the fertiliser. Constanze's voice brightened when she talked about Anton. Since his release, he'd joined a bunch of hippies who lived off the land, ex-militants from Larzac. They'd taken over a farm near Saint-Affrique, somewhere in Aveyron. Anton had gone there to lie low at first, but then he had embraced the way of life and decided to stay. Constanze sounded truly happy that this born-and-bred Berliner had decided to spend his life in the countryside, making cheeses and selling them at the market.

She felt quite envious, she told him. Alexandre was astonished. Listening to her, he realised that Crayssac, quite unintentionally, had been ahead of his time — an avant-garde figure, a role model for all these enlightened New Age types.

'Listen, could you come?'

'Where?'

'To see me.'

'No. You come here.'

'No, you come here.'

Alexandre's mother was stepping over him now, in her dressing gown, ready for bed. Half past ten. Late, for Les Bertranges. The music playing in Agathe's room was the only sign of life in the darkened farmhouse. Alexandre had no idea what to say. Travelling to Berlin would be quite a business, especially since he'd sworn never to take the plane. He'd be gone for a week, and he'd have to find someone to cover for him, or wait until the winter. Did he really want to find himself lost in a big city, utterly out of his depth? Even the thought of the impending journey would torment him, months ahead of time. In the silent hall, he heard his father knock three times on Agathe's bedroom wall. He lowered his own voice further still. If only this fucking spiral cord was ten metres longer he could have taken the call in the kitchen, or even outdoors. He detested feeling spied on from all sides.

'Or this summer. Perhaps I could come and see Anton this summer, and you could come and see us there. Is it far from you?'

'No, if he's near Saint-Affrique, it's not far at all.'

The clouds parted in Alexandre's mind. Naturally, they should meet in Aveyron. But he checked his excitement straight away. Would she really come in three months' time? And was it a good idea to see that crowd again — Anton, and the Basque, above all. Were they truly living a quieter life now? Perhaps they thought he owed them. Perhaps they'd ask for more favours. They'd done time in jail, thanks to him in part. Everything was complicated again.

Agathe must have put her headphones on, though her music could still be heard faintly. She must have turned the volume right up. The music she listened to was tense and angry. For the past two weeks, it had been U2 on a loop, those strained-sounding Irish guys, music by men from a country at war.

Alexandre waited for Constanze to have the last word before hanging up. He knew that as soon as he replaced the handset, it would all come flooding back: Chernobyl, the cold hallway, the farm under cover of darkness, the total silence that reigned outside. When he hung up, there would be not a trace of that voice left. They both hesitated for a long while, and then just as Constanze was about to go he suddenly, urgently, asked her for her number, the number he'd been searching for, without ever finding it, for months. And now he noted the precious combination of digits in the old notebook that always lay on the telephone stand. He found a pen that worked. Thank goodness his parents were organised at least.

Constanze ended the call at last. Alexandre replaced the handset. His ear was burning, his eardrum throbbing. The conversation had rekindled a thousand hopes, and a thousand fears. It was a miracle that she had called, and at the same time things would have been so much simpler if she never had.

Monday, 23 June 1986

'My brother's a true man of the woods! When we were kids, he was always hiding up a tree somewhere. He has a wild look about him, but he's a great guy, you'll see.'

Alexandre had never imagined one of his sisters could think so well of him. Vanessa had become remarkably self-assured since living in Paris, and more communicative than ever. No one even minded that she had moved so very far from the farm, in every sense.

She was visiting now with the photographer she'd been working for over the past year. He owned a big Paris agency, it seemed, and another one abroad. She'd started as an intern, but he'd taken her on, with a proper salary. The guy was about fifty, a leading light in the advertising world, so Vanessa said, and things were clearly going well, if only to judge by his car, an amazing vintage E-type Jaguar – an absolute gem, all shining chrome and glossy paintwork. An extraordinary sight out in the farmyard, parked opposite the barn. Most of all, it amused them to see that the old roadster had taken a battering along the sunken lane. The tyres had sprayed gravel all along the bottom of the coachwork, and the undercarriage must have scraped the ground. But from his considerable height, this didn't seem to bother Édouard one bit.

He was clearly one of the big names in his field – quite apart from his actual name, which was Édouard Revel de Montchamin. His shots featured in the ads you saw everywhere, in the newspapers, on billboards ... He worked with top models, all the big brands – DIM, Yoplait, Vittel and many more. But it was Vanessa who was in charge of preparing the equipment and finding the right location each time. As if she was the one who told him what to do, where to set up the spotlights, plug in the cables, position the reflectors, which lens to select from the big black case, and which camera to use.

To mark the occasion, their mother had roasted a chicken. A wry comment given that two days before, Montchamin had arranged the delivery of a huge coolbox filled with dozens of packets of ham – thin, uniform slices wrapped in clear plastic.

Their father could scarcely believe the guy was paying him for the right to take photographs of slices of ham in his fields.

'But of course we're paying you. Your farm is our set. A great location can name its price, believe me. When I hire a studio for a session, it's never less than two thousand francs a day, and double if you're shooting a film.'

Long and lean, Édouard devoured the beetroot and celeriac salad their mother had served as a starter. He explained that the executive who had scouted the site the week before was the agency's artistic director. When he'd approved the location, he had even told the production director that she shouldn't hesitate, whatever the fee. This was the place, and he wanted everything to go smoothly. Nothing was official yet, but Montchamin hinted that he planned to shoot the TV commercial right here, in the autumn – a full thirty-second spot.

'You'll get your money, have no fear. Money flows like water in this business, but wide-open spaces are gold dust!'

'Well, it's good to know business is booming. But it seems crazy to come all this way, to our farm in particular, to take photographs of ham.'

'How so?'

'For one thing, no one's ever reared pigs around here. You won't find a pig breeder within two hundred kilometres.'

'Is that because of the smell?'

'No – it's just that pig feed uses fishmeal and American soya. Obviously, the large-scale breeders are all near the sea.'

'Well, so much the better. When you're shooting an ad for ham, you'd better not catch sight of a pig or you'll frighten the consumer. You can't sell dreams by photographing reality; people get enough of the real world day in, day out. Unemployment, inflation, Chernobyl, AIDS, *Challenger* blown to smithereens while you watch ... that's reality.'

'So no cows in adverts for yoghurt?'

'Absolutely not! Cows won't sell yoghurts, but a buxom, rosy-cheeked milkmaid, fields full of flowers, a rippling stream, blue skies. Not an udder or a blade of straw anywhere. And no pigs, ever.'

Édouard knew what he was about. He had a grand manner, a fine way with words. But with his thick-soled Rangers boots and military-style clothes, dressed like a man who really did spend his working life out of doors, it seemed he was on their level, and affable with it. And he knew how to flatter his team – it was thanks to Vanessa's photographs, he was careful to point out, that he'd had the idea of coming here to Les Bertranges for the shoot. Since childhood, Vanessa had photographed her rural surroundings from every possible angle, filling whole albums with pictures of the river, the meadows, the huge trees, and the work in the fields. When he saw her pictures, he'd sworn he would work here himself one day.

'But don't worry, Monsieur Fabrier, nothing will identify the fields as yours.'

'Oh?'

'Well, of course – the product is the star. In the new pink-and-white packaging, with the new logo. The countryside, the fields, all that will be in the background.'

'Like Mitterrand's poster.'

Exactly! *La force tranquille!* Quiet strength! But we'll be focusing in on the packets more tightly than on Mitterrand, with a bit more light, more greenery. You don't sell a president like a packet of sliced ham, I'm sure you'll agree. And then we'll do another set down by the river, and another along one of your lanes, for the sales team, the B2B campaign, because this is truly a corner of paradise.'

'If you say so.'

Montchamin took a second helping of chicken. He had the equivalent of an entire sliced pig in his coolbox, but he preferred the chicken. He helped himself to more potatoes, too, soaked in the juices from the roast.

'With all this lovely sunshine, why don't you eat out of doors?

'Because of the wasps, and the flies, and the chickens wandering about, and the sparrows. Even the cows wouldn't eat out here …'

'Really?'

'We've never eaten outside here.'

Their mother was not giving Édouard the warmest of welcomes. Something about this long, tall man and his long, low-slung car bothered her. She suspected he was toying with Vanessa; perhaps they'd even started an affair, which was far from desirable given his age. Hence her next question:

'Where will you sleep tonight?'

'I'll be in my room,' said Vanessa, 'and Édouard can take Caroline's room.'

'Ah, no! No, I've booked a hotel, it's all arranged. I *love* staying in hotels, and I need a great big bathtub.'

'At Chateau de Mercuès?'

'That's the one!'

204

'But that's forty kilometres away,' Angèle objected. 'You should stay here.'

'Not at all, I won't hear of it.'

Strangely, their mother seemed to take umbrage at his categorical refusal. As if the farm wasn't good enough, as if he was too grand to sleep there. So much so that when she came to serve the apple tart, she told Montchamin that she would make up a room for him for that evening. He'd planned to spend three days at the farm, photographing his ham. He might as well sleep here, too.

'Apart from anything else, your car isn't made for our roads. It's too long to get around the tight bends, and the boar are everywhere at night. It'll be wrecked before you know it.'

Montchamin seemed to slump in his chair at her words, picturing the nightmare of a breakdown in this lonely stretch of country, with the nearest Jaguar garage an hour away by plane.

'No, thank you! But really,' he said, 'I'm a creature of habit! I get to bed very late, and I *love* reading in the bath …'

'There's a brand-new bath down at the grandparents' house. It's never been used.'

'Well, look, let's talk about that later. And now, to work!'

'You've got time for a brandy, Édouard?'

'Well, just a drop …'

Monday, 23 June 1986

After lunch, their mother went out in the Citroën. She loved to drive it, but never very far. She would take it to her mother's little apartment in Gourdon, or the hair salon in Souillac. This afternoon, she had an appointment at the bank in Cahors. At the wheel, she savoured a moment alone, in perfect peace, and most of all, a rare sit-down.

She'd had the same financial adviser for ten years. Once again, he told her that now was the time to borrow. Interest rates had dropped even further: 'Less than ten per cent, can you imagine?' Though that sounded huge to Angèle. Then, as he walked her to the door, he asked if they'd given any thought to dividing up the estate. What if the three sisters asked their brother to pay them their share?

'What do you mean?'

'They're entitled to their share one day, if they so desire.'

'My daughters would never ask for anything!'

'Provided everyone gets along, there's no problem, of course. But you never know with families. Children grow up, they may find themselves in debt. You need to be prepared for every eventuality.'

Angèle bid him a cold *au revoir*. She could never be sure whether his advice was self-interested, whether he was advising her as a fellow human, or a banker. All she knew was that there would never be any money trouble between Alexandre and his sisters. Never.

But she had reflected on the matter of the shared inheritance before now, and on the way home, she thought it through once again, turning it over and over in her mind. She decided to take the Cénevières road and stop in Le Paradou to take her mind off things. She made a point of visiting the café-cum-general-store so that the owner, Suzanne, would know Mammouth hadn't completely replaced the old ways. The same two customers were sitting at the bar, as always: Raymond and André. Sometimes, two or three others joined them there, but no one ever sat at the tables nowadays, and hardly anyone used the adjoining grocery store, which also sold bread. The familiar smell reached her as she entered, indefinable but fresh, an aroma of butter mixed with over-ripe bananas. The long row of sweet jars looked sorrier than ever: there were no children here now.

Angèle did her good deed, bought two packets of breakfast crispbreads and a box of Ricoré mix. Eighteen francs. She added a couple of tins of tuna and sardines, equally expensive. Then she went to the bar for coffee and a chat with Suzanne.

A third customer came in. Old Crayssac, heralded by the stuttering rasp of his moped. Angèle felt a kind of affection for the old goat breeder, though she knew he cursed them all. The Fabriers didn't farm, according to him – they ran a business off the land. She felt uncomfortable whenever he was around.

Crayssac seated himself at the bar and ordered a glass of white. Suzanne was slow on her feet. It took an eternity to attend to each client, marked out by the familiar sounds – the clink of one bottle knocking against another as she removed it from the fridge, the sharp rap of the coffee filter to dislodge the compressed grounds from the previous serving. Angèle seated herself at the far end of the bar near the cash register. She picked up the newspaper and began leafing through it to avoid joining in the conversation.

Their discussion resumed. The company bemoaned everything from the economic crisis to the weather, especially the inflation rate that was a constant worry, like high cholesterol. They were all in agreement on that at least – soon, money wouldn't be worth the paper it was printed on, like Germany in the 1920s, not to mention the price of petrol, which wasn't coming down. The OPEC countries wanted to bring the West to its knees. Besides, Europe was deciding everything now. Bad enough that the powers-that-be up in Paris had no understanding of rural life. But the suits in Brussels were even worse.

'No idea up there what it's like to have to take an hour's round trip on a moped to buy a loaf of bread.'

'True,' Crayssac agreed. 'And not a single communist in the government now. They couldn't care less about the rest of us.'

'Communists! Tomatoes, that's what we call them. Red on the outside, soft on the inside.'

'What do you know about tomatoes? Never grown one in your life!'

Angèle was happy to keep out of such talk. But she listened when they turned to discussing the motorway, a project that reared its head every twenty years, like the Loch Ness monster. But now, as prime minister, Chirac wanted to open up access to his rural and political heartland, Corrèze.

'Chirac's a blithering idiot. He'll resign after three months, like in 1976!'

'And good riddance,' said Crayssac, who suspected that Suzanne nurtured secret hopes the motorway would come through the neighbourhood someday soon, as if that would bring her blasted shop back to life.

There were plenty in the area who wanted the motorway to come. They could sell their land to the operating company at a very good price. The west side of the Massif Central still had no major trunk roads, and while the isolation was a blessing for some, others saw it as a curse.

Angèle looked at the three men, each with a cigarette dangling forgotten from his lip that curiously never came unstuck when they talked. She looked at the bar, the bottles of Côtes du Rhône, and the big, empty room. It would all go dark one day, like the train station opposite. The SNCF had closed the line, and now the tracks were overgrown with couch grass and brambles. The railway workers had given up treating it all with Roundup and nature was reclaiming the space, choking the rails and the red-brown rubble between them – the whole station soon enough. Theirs was a forgotten world. And if one day a motorway straddled the river, it would change nothing. Trucks would hurtle by on the viaduct at 130 kilometres an hour. Noise and pollution were all it would bring; the drivers would never stop. It would ruin the land. The final body blow that would kill the valley stone dead.

'We'll be like bloody Indians in the Wild West,' said Suzanne. 'If they bring their motorway through here, they'll wipe us off the map for good.'

Defeated by the fatalistic mood, Angèle got to her feet and produced two francs for her coffee. The coin clinked loudly in the heavy atmosphere, made denser still by the smoke from the filterless Gauloises. She prepared to leave, but Crayssac's voiced called her back. Crayssac, who hadn't spoken to her for more than twenty years.

'Don't you worry, Angèle. I have the ultimate weapon against their motorway, and I swear they'll never build it.'

His emphatic, determined air surprised them all for a second. But the counterattack was immediate – a hail of caustic retorts.

'A secret weapon? Ha! Got some big guns stashed away from Larzac, have you? Stole them from the 122nd Infantry Division?'

Crayssac ignored their taunts. He sat there coolly and calmly, fixing them with his stare and intoning solemnly: 'Better than that, believe me. Better than that.'

There was no towing hook on the Jaguar. When lunch was over, Alexandre loaded all the equipment into his tractor trailer. Besides the coolbox stuffed with ham, there were tripods of every sort, and lightboxes, and what looked like gigantic flashbulbs – all the gear the delivery driver had unloaded at the farm two days before, with a reminder of how much it was worth. Three huge logs would be used to display the sliced ham, plus two large stones for decoration. It was damned hard work. No wonder Montchamin dressed in combat fatigues. Alexandre didn't mind lending a hand. On the contrary, this nonsense was a welcome distraction. Climbing aboard the tractor, Édouard assured him he'd be paid as the 'assistant's assistant'. Five hundred francs in cash. A sizeable sum, but Alexandre told the photographer he was happy to volunteer. As Vanessa's brother, he felt it was the right thing to do, though she was glaring at him to take the money even as he spoke.

He started the tractor and they set off for the slopes above the Combe des Dames, driving into a west-facing field of tall grass. The light had changed and Montchamin declared it just perfect. There was the valley in the distance, the river lined with elms down at the bottom, a patch of sky. Everything was just as he'd anticipated. But when he'd picked out the spot that morning, there had been no sign of the enormous cow, an impressive beast that stood watching them now from the bottom of the field.

'What the hell's she doing there?'

'Who?'

'Your cow, down there ...'

'That's not a cow.'

'What is it, then?'

'A bull.'

'You've got a bull?'

Alexandre tried to explain: 'The old man isn't too keen on artificial insemination, all that business ... It's nature's way, Édouard!'

The photographer stared at the creature, plainly unconvinced by nature's way, in this regard at least.

'Perhaps. But we can't have any animals in the field.'

'Well, try telling him that!'

'In the field of vision, I mean.'

'Well, fine, we'll turn around and shoot the other way.'

Édouard's genial, commanding manner deserted him somewhat now. Alexandre and Vanessa began unloading the equipment, then Vanessa placed a packet of sliced ham on the logs while Édouard peered into his eyepiece to check the finished result. He was trying hard to concentrate, but he couldn't help glancing every thirty seconds or so to where Cosmos was standing down at the bottom of the field, near a clump of trees. Vanessa had set up a huge light source on a tripod. She alone kept her mind on the job, doing all she could to make sure everything ran smoothly. Reverently she lit the slices of vivid pink ham as if they were some sacred relic, then adjusted the reflector very slightly. The rays reached the retina of Cosmos's big, thickly lashed eye. He was staring fixedly at them now, fascinated by the big shiny umbrella.

'Couldn't you tie your bull up just for now, Alexandre?'

'Cosmos is the alpha male around here, he pays no attention to me at all.'

'Seriously?'

It was Vanessa who replied, calming Édouard's nerves with just a hint of superiority.

'Don't worry. He won't move.'

Alexandre added: 'If he *does* charge you, Édouard, the secret is to let him come and then at the very last minute, grab him by the ring through his nose. That stops them dead every time.'

The photographer straightened up and stared at Alexandre and Vanessa. They were a united front now. It was all right for them – they were country people in their element. The animals, the fields, these towering trees, this whole landscape was their natural environment.

He turned his back on the sliced ham, opened his arms wide and took a couple of deep breaths. Then suddenly he froze as if he had noticed something.

'Hear that?'

'No, what?'

'Nothing. That's it. Nothing. There's nothing to hear, no cars, no mopeds, no lawnmowers or heaven knows what ...'

'That's perfectly normal, Édouard. We're twenty kilometres from the nearest town. The valley road sees ten cars in a day, and half of those are driven by one of us.'

Again, Édouard filled his lungs with the fresh air and flung his arms wide.

'Dear God, I've never felt better. What a view! It would make a magnificent golf course, right here, a bit like Divonne-les-Bains, but without Mont Blanc in the background ...'

Alexandre stared at him in astonishment. This guy was overwhelmed, like Constanze, by the mere sight of their hills and valley. Montchamin gazed all around, as if discovering his ideal surroundings, though it was obvious he couldn't picture himself living here, not for one second.

'I was in New York when Chernobyl blew. When I saw the

pictures on TV, I was truly terrified that the radioactivity would frazzle the whole of Europe, that there'd be nothing left when I got back … Like a big explosion in a city, on TV. You think the whole place will go up with it. That's why it's so good to see this. If anywhere in this world can remain untouched, unchanged forever, it's here.'

They spent the afternoon photographing the sliced ham on the logs. Vanessa and Édouard handled the packets as if they were movie stars, lavishing them with care and attention. They turned on the huge lightboxes for each shot, though it was still broad daylight. Eventually the ham would sweat and steam up its plastic packaging, so they would take out a fresh packet and throw away the old one. Alexandre suggested they play some music – his tractor was fitted with speakers, but the battery was easily drained, so they left the engine running to keep it going. He put on his Supertramp tape, but Édouard rummaged through the assortment in the storage box beside the seat and pulled out a Pat Metheny. The racket reached the ears of Cosmos the bull. He was still glancing their way from time to time, but with the detached air of a breeding male who knows his work is done. A male no longer on the lookout for a rival.

At around six o'clock, they piled everything back into the trailer and drove down to the river to set up all over again. Now, the packets of ham were placed at the water's edge. Édouard sought to capture 'the simple things in life'. That was the ham's advertising slogan: THE SIMPLE THINGS … Which was just as well, because here at Les Bertranges, that was all there was. Past seven o'clock, the sky was still bright but the light was beginning to fade. There was nothing more they could do, even with all the flashbulbs. They took bottles of beer from the bottom of the coolbox, beneath the slices of movie-star ham, raised a toast and drank. Édouard was curious to know if Alexandre found it hard living here. His tone was very slightly condescending. What about going clubbing, or finding a girlfriend? With a rush of pride, Alexandre declared that he didn't need to *find* a girlfriend, there was already someone in his life, a German girl, a stunning blonde who lived in Berlin.

'Uh-huh. Can't be easy seeing each other though?'

Alexandre's pride was piqued. He assured Montchamin that it wasn't an issue, in fact he would be seeing her again very soon. Either he would go to Berlin this month, or she would come to France, somewhere not far away, in July. Not that complicated, really. Vanessa was suspicious of her brother's show of confidence, but she said nothing. She didn't know everything that was going on since she'd moved away. She had no idea whether the blonde bombshell from Berlin was really back on the scene or not. If she was, then Vanessa was happy for her brother, and relieved, more than anything, that he would take care of the farm. At least he had no qualms about carrying on, living off the land. Because if he gave up and left, or if anything happened to him, Vanessa couldn't see herself coming back here to help their parents. Nor Caroline. Certainly not. So they must pray that the beautiful German girl was back for real, and that she would want to live here one day ...

Monday, 23 June 1986

That evening, their mother felt obliged to serve another copious meal. She even piped *pommes dauphines* to accompany the rib of beef. Édouard watched the preparations. Ever the businessman, he pulled out his wallet and begged them to let him pay.

'Oh, but yes, this time I insist!'

'Absolutely not! You can lay the table if you like.'

Disarmed by their mother's rejoinder, Édouard towered over the table. Plainly, he had no idea where to start. Agathe was fascinated. She dreamed of working in fashion, and this photographer had come to them like a messiah – he'd worked in New York, he'd done photo shoots with famous models. Caroline of Monaco and Inès de la Fressange had posed for him! He was practically a god.

This summer, in anticipation of her future career as a designer of dresses that would appear in all the magazines, Agathe was going to spend two months working in a boutique in Rodez or Villeneuve, perhaps even the new Benetton store. Édouard told her he knew the family. He could get her a position in Paris, even New York or Tokyo. Though Villeneuve was great too, he added, seeing the look on Angèle's face.

After dinner, their father lit his Gitane at the table. Édouard ventured to take out a cigar, though he didn't dare light it. He didn't want to offend anyone, and preferred to smoke it outside.

'The very idea!'

For their father, a smoke at the table was the perfect end to a big blow-out meal. Still, he followed the photographer out into the yard.

Angèle returned to the kitchen and Vanessa sidled closer to Alexandre. Her curiosity was aroused.

'So apparently you're still seeing Constanze?'

'Yeah, of course. We're meeting up soon.'

'Really? Where?'

Alexandre did not want to lose face. He wished he could say 'Berlin', but if he announced that now in front of Vanessa and Agathe, he'd be forced to go there for real one day.

'She's coming to Aveyron this summer. I'm joining her there, with some friends. We'll spend a few days together.'

Vanessa stared hard at her brother. He didn't look like he was bluffing. And he was a terrible liar.


Jean and Édouard had seated themselves on the stone bench against the wall. They watched the sun dissolving slowly into orange, while an egg-yolk-yellow expanse filled the sky. To their right, the hills lay in shadow. The valley looked deeper now, and there was aura of peace all around.

'Impossible to do justice to all this in a photograph.'

'Oh really? Not even with one of your packets of ham in the foreground?'

'I sense a certain dislike of "my ham" …'

'I respect what you do, Édouard. Thanks to you, my daughter has a good job, she's learning a great deal, making a living. But all that plastic ham, it doesn't seem right to me.'

'Why not?'

'Well, for a start – it's pink. And *jambon blanc* isn't pink unless you feed your pigs on blackcurrants. As to keeping it for weeks in a plastic packet, well, it's bound to be pumped full of nitrates and colouring and flavours. "The simple things …" That ham's anything but simple, believe me.'

Alexandre's father knew only too well that when it came to rearing livestock, keeping things simple was increasingly complicated. The small independent butchers' shops were closing one after the other now that Mammouth and Euromarché were everywhere. The only thing people wanted to know about prepacked meat was the price; they never thought to ask where it had come from.

'I'll tell you this, Édouard, "simple things" are all very well, but nothing's simple now. No one knows where the animals are from. There are breeders in Nièvre who send their Charolais to North Africa for fattening, then re-import them. And the Brits fatten their cattle on soya and meal from South America. All those tonnes of frozen steak flying around the world. A cut of beef has done twenty thousand kilometres before it lands on your plate. This world is anything but simple.'

'But that's the course of history, Jean. You've got to expand your horizons. Look at your daughters: they're going out into the world to find work. And your son's staying here, but even he's got a German girlfriend! Globalisation will make the world a better place, it'll make us all better human beings. I'm sorry to have to say it, Jean, but we all need to keep moving in this life. Keep on moving forward … It's never a good idea to stagnate.'

'See my dog over there, the red one? He has an advantage over the other three.'

And what was that? Édouard wanted to know.

'He's deaf. He can't hear people talking nonsense! Get moving, keep moving … dear God, where's the sense in moving if everyone's doing it?'

'Travel broadens the mind.'

'Moving isn't what matters, it's being here, in one place.'

'Perhaps. There's room for both.'

'I know every last detail of the countryside around here, every nook and cranny. I've lived here always. Those trees over there, I know every one of them, only have to look at them to see which one is out of sorts, which one the ivy is choking, which one is thirsty, which one is pushing out the others. So if I was to get moving like all the rest, what would all the trees and livestock, the fields, the garden, those dogs, what would they all do without me, eh? What'd they do?'

'Jean, I only meant that ... Well, it's the way of history, the way of the world.'

'I'm the one who carries this world on my shoulders. It would never get along without me.'

'Sure. But that shouldn't stop others travelling if they want to.'

'Every bloody thing has to travel nowadays – cereal grains, cows, television sets, microwave ovens made in Hong Kong, Sony Walkmans made in Taiwan, and meanwhile we're selling our milk to the Chinese, and everything is crisscrossing this way and that in the sky, and out at sea. It's bloody nonsense ... You know what all this moving around is going to send this way, eh? Do you know what it's going to bring here, for me, my trees, my chickens, my dogs?'

'No, I don't.'

'A motorway.'

Édouard was confused.

'There. Right there, just across the valley. The scheme's all planned out. And they call it a motorway, but the "motors" aren't just cars. It's a truck route, is what it is. That's what they should be calling it. Ten thousand vehicles a day, and six thousand of those are bloody great trucks. That's why they're building it, that's where all this moving about gets us, that's what happen when no one can bloody sit still. It means trucks and planes all over the place.'

'But, Jean, surely no one's going to build a motorway here?'

218

'We're right in its path. A road bridge down there, to the left, across the Rauze valley, maybe even right here where we're sitting now.'

'I can't believe it.'

'Ever since Chirac was made prime minister. He dusted off the plans. As if there was suddenly an urgent need to link Corrèze with Spain one way and Germany the other. They want to turn France into a great tangle of roads, a gigantic roundabout between Britain, the Netherlands and Africa, with gigantic trucks full of plastic ham going round and round ...'

Édouard didn't know what to say. He gazed around at the landscape and the encroaching dark.

'Perhaps they will build a motorway, but not here ....'

'That's it. *Not here* ... that's what they all say. Not here. Like the Chernobyl cloud back in April. It's over there but it's *not here*.'

Édouard fell silent. He drove on motorways all the time, but he'd never given a thought to any of this. Never considered the thousands of small catastrophes it must have wrought, the thousand dramas that lay beneath every kilometre of concrete and tarmac, farms cut in two and farmers evicted, forests torn apart, homes sacrificed, lanes turned into dead ends and rivers diverted, the water table sucked dry ... Above all, he left unspoken the thought that had occurred to him all the way down here on the endless two-lane Nationale 20, and the country lanes he had taken after that, because it was a hell of a drive from Paris: a decent motorway wouldn't hurt, it would be good for the region. That was what he'd said to himself.

Saturday, 19 July 1986

Alexandre drove at a smooth, steady pace. He'd planned to reach Saint-Affrique around ten o'clock that morning, but now that he was in the area, he'd been going round in circles for an hour. Their place must be really remote. The farm didn't have a name and the hamlet they'd mentioned wasn't even on the map. There were no road signs, no houses either. He was relying on instinct, trying to locate the most likely spot for a sheep and goat farm. He turned south again. The landscape was less rocky now, and he saw a dirt track to the right that seemed to be in regular use. He turned off and followed it for about a kilometre. A group of buildings came into view, lower down. He felt sure this was the place he'd been looking for. This had to be the farm where the small group of friends were living, hidden from the rest of the world.

Everything pointed to this being the headquarters of their commune: there were ewes and goats in the fields all around, and a half-dozen battered old cars parked in the yard. But the most obvious sign of all was an array of colourful clothes hanging out to dry near the houses. The laundry had plainly been left overnight, and no true country person would ever do that. The buildings looked in good condition for a secret hideaway. Only one, over to the right, showed signs of work in progress. Alexandre shared his father's views on hippy, would-be farmers – you had to be born on the land to work the land. It was in your blood, in the same way as it was for a fishing community, or the Inuit out on the ice cap. That innate feel for your environment wasn't something you could work out for yourself, or learn.

It was past eleven o'clock. Alexandre cut the Renault's engine and sat looking down at the small knot of buildings, like a cowboy observing an Indian camp. Apart from the dogs lying stretched out in the yard, there was no sign of life. The most striking thing was the building to the right, its roof covered in plastic sheeting. The grand two-storey structure was clearly in a poor state of repair. It looked like an old priory, or perhaps the ruins of a Templars' commandery. The adjacent buildings included a longhouse and a series of smaller barns. He had pictured them all camped out in something far more rudimentary. Though Constanze had told him there were ten people living there altogether.

Alexandre was reluctant to drive down. He couldn't picture himself turning up and finding them all still crashed out. He was uncomfortable at the thought of meeting the group, and seeing some of them again. Not least Constanze. He didn't know whether they would hug and kiss, or just brush cheeks in the conventional way. Whether they were still lovers, or not. He was even afraid she might have come here with someone else. But he'd sensed from their telephone conversation that she wanted to see him. She was the one who had made the first move and contacted him. Still, he felt his usual wariness. He'd even wondered if this was a trap. Perhaps they wanted something from him again. The truth was, these guys had a hold over him: they could easily blackmail him, make demands in exchange for their silence. It was his fertiliser that had put them all in jail.

He was sure of it now. By coming out here to join the tribe he was walking into an ambush. But to get to Constanze, he had no choice. He must throw himself to these wolves. Like John Wayne hunting for Natalie Wood in *The Searchers*, he would face the Comanche. Except that these Comanche were a bunch of layabouts. They were still in bed at a quarter past noon.

Finally, Alexandre was the one to be taken by surprise. He had begun to nod off in the car when he heard the sound of a vehicle approaching from behind. There was a bend in the track, hidden by a clump of trees. He couldn't see what was coming around the corner towards him. He sat up straight, ready to get out of the car. The engine sounded like a van travelling at full speed, and straight away he thought of the local gendarmes. But the vehicle came into view, and he saw Indians at the wheel. An ancient Citroën Type H was headed straight for him at full tilt, despite the deeply rutted track. The bodywork was painted orange and green, and dirty, oily smoke belched from the exhaust. He didn't think he knew the driver, but despite the moustache, he recognised Anton in the passenger seat – that unmistakable steely gaze. And the other one, sitting in the middle. Xabi. The name came back to him when he saw the guy's face. The van was hurtling towards him, the driver clutching the wheel with an air of intense concentration. The Renault made the track even narrower, and Alexandre sprang out of the way just in time. Anton stuck his head out of the window as they passed.

'We can't stop or we'll stall! Follow us down!'

The van continued its descent, like a filthy, stuttering comet. Constanze wasn't with them. She was probably still asleep in one of the buildings down below.

## Saturday, 19 July 1986

They met in the yard. The guys were coming back from the market. They'd sold all of their cheeses. Two girls from the group, Kathleen and Lorraine, were still there on the vegetable stall. The others were indoors. They had got up later. Anton still had that crushing handshake, though he was more softly spoken, Alexandre thought, especially now that he spoke decent French. He couldn't believe the guy had spent two years in jail, and Xabi too, who greeted him coolly. At the sight of them both, he had no idea what to think – should he feel guilty? Perhaps they were grateful for the supplies he'd passed them five years back. The driver of the van was a nervous, highly strung type, busy unloading all their stuff, and making plenty of noise about it.

'That's Adrien. He'll say hello in his own time. Don't mind him, he's always on edge.'

'OK.'

'See where we're crashing now – not bad, eh?'

'Yeah, not bad at all … And Constanze?'

'What about Constanze?'

'Is she asleep?'

'No, she's arriving tomorrow.'

'Ah. She told me today.'

'Yeah, but her old man was in Toulouse for a couple of days, so she's seeing him, and some other people she knows down there.'

Alexandre followed them indoors, horribly disappointed. They entered a big room. Two guys and a girl were sitting around the table. Clearly, they were just waking up.

'Allow me to introduce Frédéric, Antoinette, and Thomas who's just joined us, since the spring,' said Anton.

Alexandre greeted them. He felt awkward, conscious of his rough-edged country manner, but hiding behind it, too. He sat down with the others while Xabi made coffee.

'See, Alexandre,' Anton continued, 'we're like you now, proper country folk.'

'I can see that.'

'It was you that got us into this, kind of; you were our role model!'

Alexandre knew Anton's ways – first the flattery, showering you with compliments, until, in the end, you could refuse him nothing.

Before fifteen minutes were up, Alexandre understood Anton's effortless control at the heart of the group. The others were easily led and saw him as a leader, some kind of guru. Xabi was more sullen than before. He said next to nothing now. Adrien, the guy driving the van, and his English girlfriend Kathleen were the group's pioneer couple. They'd been living on the farm for ten years. Frédéric and Antoinette, who looked after the sheep, had been the first to join them. The others had come later, and it seemed their line-up was constantly changing.

There was a lot to take on board, Alexandre thought, but when Adrien gathered that he, too, had a farm, he offered to show Alexandre around. They had no telephone or running water, but they did have electricity. The water came from three cisterns and a small spring just a short walk away. It seemed the goats provided about three hundred cheeses a month. They sold the ewe's milk to a cooperative for now, but soon they would be making their own *tomme*, and feta, and a kind of blue cheese like Roquefort but a hundred per cent natural, with no penicillium. They were thinking of calling it 'Roquedoux'. Alexandre nodded throughout. After that, Adrien showed him the kitchen garden. The ground was dry and stony, but Alexandre said nothing. The runner beans looked parched, and the leaves of the potato plants were overrun with Colorado beetle. The strawberries were eaten away. He'd never seen such a sickly-looking patch. The topsoil looked as if it had been brought up from a river valley somewhere – the farm stood on a chalk hillside. Adrien was visibly proud that they had got even this from such poor soil. There was enough to feed the group and sell the surplus at the markets every week.

'So, what do you reckon?'

'Not bad.'

'And all of it clean!'

'What do you mean, "clean"?'

'Clean – natural, no chemicals, nothing.'

'Well, now I see …'

'I don't know how you rear your livestock, Alexandre, but it all starts with respect for the soil. Look at the strawberries – I let the slugs do their thing. Normally, there aren't too many, but this year, with each new moon, there are loads. Too bad! Nature's in charge, so we'll eat fewer strawberries, but you won't catch me spraying them with copper sulphate or any of that filth … Hurt no living thing!'

The guy was dead set against pesticides and fertilisers, no point trying to argue, so Alexandre tried humour instead.

'Watering, that's your problem. Slugs love it.'

'Watering's the one thing I do!'

'Well, stop. Slugs love a drink.'

'Yes … But then there'd be no strawberries either.'

'Exactly. Like now.'

Adrien wore the closed expression of a man who knew he was being taken for a fool.

'Hey, only joking! But if you're going to grow strawberries and not get any to eat, you might as well not plant strawberries in the first place.'

'It's no laughing matter. You know they're running trials on genetically modified corn this year in Lot-et-Garonne? That's down your way, isn't it?'

'Not far.'

'Yeah, and you'll be using it soon enough.'

Adrien refused to lighten up. Now he was on to seeds – farmers had always done whatever they wanted with their own seeds, but now the Supreme Court in the United States had ruled that living organisms could be patented, and there'd been a clampdown on seeds.

'Can you believe it, no one's even allowed to re-sow their own seed after a harvest. The world's gone mad – you're turning a blind eye, but I can see what's happening right enough.'

Alexandre thought of Crayssac, who had no idea that a new generation was joining the fight. He needed to fit in with the group, anyhow. Best to keep a low profile, agree with them all about everything.

He went to give Anton a hand with a drystone wall he'd been trying and failing to rebuild for weeks. Then he helped bring the animals in for milking – just the goats, but it took forever. He was glad he'd never gone into dairy, because the fixed milking times would drive him insane. He had nothing in common with these communal farmers, but he saw a way to find his feet within the group. Most of all, he sensed a kind of respect towards him, as a true son of the soil.

It wasn't bedtime, but Antoinette and Kathleen asked him where he wanted to sleep that night – did he want to find a corner somewhere in the farmhouse? It would be quieter in the big building where the work was still going on. The ground floor was habitable, there was a decent mattress on the floor. And anyway, the nights were warm. Alexandre opted for the mattress in the big building. At least then he'd be out of everyone's way.

He quickly understood that everyone lent a hand getting dinner. So he rinsed three lettuces and shook them dry the old-fashioned way, in a wire basket, because plastic salad wringers were toxic. Then he began slicing a big joint of locally cured ham – thick, generous cuts, using a good, well-sharpened knife. But Antoinette and Frédéric stopped him right away and told him he had to cut thin – wafer-thin – slices, like roll-up papers. Which meant that with nine of them for supper, he'd need to cut thirty slices at least.

'No,' said Kathleen, 'the ham's not for nine. Frédéric, Antoinette and I don't eat meat. Nor does Lorraine.'

'So I'll cut enough for five.'

They ate at the big table, which had been moved outside. Alexandre felt he was in a different country: the high *causse* was dry as a bone, and the chalk and limestone radiated the day's heat. There was no drop in the temperature at night. He felt even more lost when some of the group began talking in English, and rolling joints he dared not refuse.

Adrien and Frédéric kept coming back to the subject of agriculture. Clearly, they were intrigued by Alexandre, with his hundred head of cattle in a valley that extended for fifty hectares or more. He was a real farmer, big time.

'Breeders today make a point of telling you their calves are reared on cow's milk, as if you could rear them on anything else …'

'Some of them mix it with eggs and sugar,' said Frédéric.

'And meat-based meal,' Adrien added.

'Yeah, some of them do that.'

Kathleen had been on her guard since the beginning of the

227

discussion, but she found it hard to see an ally in Alexandre. Now she cut the debate short, observing coldly: 'Two months ago, back at home, a cow went down with scrapie, the disease that usually affects sheep. That's what happens with your stupid, unnatural practices, you get cows with scrapie!'

'I don't know anything about what's going on in England,' said Alexandre. 'But scrapie isn't like the flu – they can't catch it – a cow can't get a sheep virus.'

'But they can.'

'How, by rubbing noses?'

'No, by eating sheep meal. They turn sheep carcasses into meal, and they feed it to calves.'

'In England, yes. Not in France.'

Anton brought the discussion to a close by asking Frédéric to play the guitar. Then they all decamped to the big oak tree under which they'd placed the remains of a couple of sofas. Kathleen and Antoinette lit candles that were dotted all around. In complete darkness, their effect was lovely. Alexandre smoked more than he ever did as a rule. Best just to switch off from it all, go with the flow, especially because they all looked severely stoned. The two girls had left a while ago, and he'd noticed their huge, dark, dilated pupils, probably because they'd been smoking hashish, or opium or something. He didn't want to know. Anton shot regular glances in his direction, making sure everything was all right. Even Xabi caught his eye and winked once or twice, the height of cordiality for him. Perhaps the two of them thought of him as an old comrade-in-arms. Alexandre hesitated to raise the subject. There'd been a new wave of attacks recently, at the Eiffel Tower, on the Champs-Élysées, and then aboard the TGV from Paris to Lyon, at top speed. Bombs were being set off all over France, even without them. Besides, he had no idea of the form with guys who had done time. Should he talk about it, ask them how it had been?

Anton was looking at him strangely – Alexandre could tell there was something he wanted to say, but he was just waiting for the right moment.

At about two o'clock in the morning, Kathleen and Antoinette walked him over to the building they called the 'chateau'. Inside the big building, the ground-floor rooms had no doors, and no ceiling in some cases. The girls gave him a lighter and a candle. He could wash at the standpipe out in the yard. Alexandre flopped onto the old mattress that lay on the floor. He'd smoked way too much of their resin, he knew that, some artisan-made shit that Antoinette had brought back from Himachal Pradesh. She said it was just like Aveyron, only in India. The farmers harvested stuff the old way there, mixing it with honeyed Camel tobacco. It had blown his head off and cut his legs from under him. Once he was lying down, he realised he couldn't get back up. He would stay where he was. He could feel their eyes on him, the newcomer, and most of all, the *modern* farmer. Or the *old-style* farmer, if you looked at it the other way round. Which was he? He no longer knew. But tomorrow Constanze would be there. Everything would be simpler. Or more complicated still.

Sunday, 20 July 1986

Alexandre looked twice at his watch. Yes, it was two o'clock in the afternoon, and he'd only just woken up. This had never happened to him before. He saw the dazzling sunlight outside, felt its heat, and knew he had fallen through a hole in space–time. He stood up and felt instantly dizzy. Blood pounded at his temples, and his throat was parched.

He emerged into the yard, not expecting to see anybody. To his surprise, he found everyone under the big tree. They'd moved the table to eat lunch in the shade. And there, in addition to the sunlight that hurt his eyes, and his discomfort at being caught red-handed after a long lie-in, he was transfixed by a bright blonde vision. Constanze was with them, sitting cross-legged on the bench. They all turned and signalled to him to join them, but Constanze was all Alexandre saw. He would have preferred a private reunion for sure, away from all these pairs of eyes, this sun, the cicadas and the dogs barking all around him …

Constanze got to her feet and walked towards him. She moved like some new vision, a creature of Himalayan myth, but she was real, this was her scent, and she took him in her arms and held him tighter and tighter, not kissing him. Then suddenly she released him and murmured something sweet in German, none of which Alexandre could understand. She switched to French: did he want some coffee? Or would he move straight on to the meal, the remains of which lay spread over the table? Cheeses, a slice of Swiss chard

230

and spinach pie. Still, he needed to wake up, so he made an effort to act naturally and asked her:

'When did you get here?'

'Yesterday. Yesterday lunchtime.'

'What?'

Everyone laughed out loud. Alexandre was perfectly prepared to believe he'd slept for forty-eight hours – four turns of the hands on the clock.

And with that, Constanze spoke with disconcerting affection in her voice.

'Have some coffee first.'

For the next three hours, Constanze felt obliged to stay with the group, talking to Anton and the rest. Only around five o'clock did she manage to break away. She and Alexandre set off on a long walk, and she immediately took his hand in hers. There was so much to say that for a moment they said nothing, unsure where to begin. He had so many questions about the five years that had passed, and about her plans for the future. She told him she should have been travelling in India last year, but when she found out about her grandmother's bizarre and disastrous medical treatments in the East, she had chosen to remain in Berlin to try to get to the bottom of things.

'Alexandre, can I tell you something I will only ever tell you and no one else?'

'Yes, of course.'

He did not show it, but he was overjoyed that she wanted to confide in him, whatever her secret was. It would connect them forever, like a pact, an intimate bond. They would be inseparable.

She hesitated, keeping him in suspense. And then: 'The truth is, I wanted my father to come and see me in Toulouse because he knows all the big pharmaceutical groups, like Bayer. But, well,

I didn't dare discuss it with him … Anyway, nothing's certain, nothing at all.'

Alexandre had no idea what she was talking about, so she explained. She believed Western pharmaceutical companies were conducting medical trials on patients in the East, her grandmother included.

'What would it change if you had proof?'

'But I do have proof! Sorry, I'm boring you …'

'Not at all, on the contrary.'

'No, we haven't seen each other for five years and here I am – I'm sorry, I'm being much too serious and heavy. Hold me.'

She fell into his arms, and nothing existed now but the two of them, and the landscape all around. They had walked a long way. Bells tinkled from time to time, in the distance – the group's flock of ewes. Alexandre and Constanze stood together in the most timeless setting imaginable and there was no date, no year, no century, nothing but the endless high pastureland and the far-off sheep, a scene like the cradle of humanity itself.

At dinner, Alexandre felt as if he was staying with a tribe that had retreated far from the world, to a secret hideaway from which they gazed in horror at modern society, something they all saw as oppressive, profit-driven and ready to explode. Listening to them talk, it seemed there was nothing but dreadful news in the world. Constanze expressed her critique in more concrete terms: she regretted the extraordinary run of victories scored by the West German football team in last month's World Cup because the West's supremacy pushed the GDR even further down into the doldrums. It was a humiliation for the East as a whole. And since Chernobyl, everyone knew that the Soviet bloc was not as powerful as all that, which made its humiliation all the more dangerous. Kathleen mentioned the thirty-five far-right deputies who had just been elected in France, plus the rising nationalist fervour in Yugoslavia. None of it augured well, and now Thatcher was on a high: she had survived an assassination attempt, while Mitterrand was mired in a hung parliament, a dinosaur trudging into history.

'Thing is,' said Kathleen, 'even to think that Mitterrand's on his way out and Thatcherism is the new ideology – just the knowledge that Tonton is finished, while that vile bitch might carry on for another twenty years, well, I could cheerfully murder someone ...'

'Hold on,' Frédéric retorted. 'Don't tell me you're a Mitterrand supporter now – you of all people, when he screwed us all over nuclear power!'

'Perhaps he did, but between him and the Iron Lady, I know whose head I'd blast off,' Xabi chipped in. 'It was a near miss, anyway. They almost got her.'

'Thatcherism will spread right across Europe, it's obvious, but is that any reason to blow up a hotel and kill five people. *Putain*, five people, that's vile ...'

Adrien voiced his thoughts without looking up at the group, but his tone was firm. He often sparred with Xabi, who was easily provoked.

Kathleen broke in, urgent and sincere: 'I'm British and I'm not fooled. What with the Irish in Vincennes, and the *Rainbow Warrior*, I should know – Mitterrand's no angel either.'

Her words brought Adrien to his feet, declaring drily: 'Don't forget that if it weren't for him, this would be a military camp, right here, and it wouldn't be the crickets you'd hear at night, but tanks firing rounds. Plus, it's you lot, all of you here, with your anti-nuclear nonsense back then, and your marches, your bombs; you're the ones who corrupted everyone's thinking, spread the fear, like Cousteau swearing blind that tonnes of plutonium had gone missing in Niger, enough to blow up a city the size of New York. You're the ones who frightened everybody stupid with all that shit.

It's never good to make people afraid ... End result, five years on and the Greens haven't got one single deputy, while the National Front have got thirty-five.'

'Ever heard of Chernobyl?'

'Fuck! I don't believe it, round we go again. You're missing the point. The problem with Chernobyl wasn't nuclear power, it was the Russians. Can't you see that with all your anti-nuclear crap, you're missing the real problem: acid rain, the ozone layer, greenhouse gases heating up the planet. Christ, we've known for a quarter of a fucking century that consumerism is the most significant threat to life on earth. Ever heard of the Club of Rome? A short memory is a dangerous thing, guys.'

Alexandre stared at Anton, surprised that he didn't say anything. He was probably keeping quiet on purpose, a thousand remarks jostling in his head, a thousand angry thoughts, a thousand regrets, but he stayed silent. Each time their eyes met, it seemed Anton was giving him a knowing stare, as if to say, 'Now that you're back, you owe me ...'

The conversation was stuck on politics. The one thing that united them all was the prospect of revolution. Alexandre said nothing throughout the meal. He and Constanze exchanged glances from time to time. They were in a different place, driven by other concerns entirely, anxious about the prospect of finding themselves alone later, in the same bed.

Again the group went to bed late, though at least two of them would have to set an alarm for milking at six the following morning. Constanze took Alexandre's hand and they headed for the chateau. Her bags had been taken into the farmhouse, but she wanted to sleep out there with him. It was the most natural thing in the world.

In the huge room, Alexandre did not light the candle. They were in total darkness, but he sensed that Constanze was undressing, that she had slipped between the sheets. He joined her and together they fell into the night, forgetting all sense of time and place, floating in the room with no door, spinning in an embrace that seemed unreal. Alexandre could scarcely believe it. For five years he'd thought of her, without the slightest hope, no illusion that they would ever see one another again, and now they were kissing. Constanze was there, he breathed the scent of her hair and felt her skin. But now, in total darkness, he could not see her, like during those five long years. The thought maddened him. But there was her scent, the golden sap of her fragrance, woody, warm and deep. He wanted to lose himself in it forever, for this moment to be the culmination of his existence, for nothing ever to come close to the desire that rose in them both, here and now. They rolled off the mattress as one, and embraced more passionately than ever, one body, one heat. Alexandre felt strong, and so hard, in her arms. Constanze was lost, undulating gently as if the whole room was water, then suddenly she sat up, gasped for air as if something terrible was about to occur, and froze. Alexandre could tell she was trying to see him, trying to look into his face.

'Alexandre, we can't.'

'What do you mean?'

'I'm sorry ... How can I say this? Have you got a condom?'

Monday, 21 July 1986

To wake up beside her in the morning light and watch her sleeping: he had dreamed this very scene a thousand times; but now that he was experiencing it for real he was full of regret. Perhaps Constanze had been right to stop things last night. For his part, condoms were not the first thing that sprang to mind when he thought about making love. Until now, he'd thought of AIDS as an urban disease, a disease of the big cities, certainly not the country. And although it was talked about on the news every day, although there were adverts for Durex on TV – that one with rabbits mating in their burrow – he had never thought the virus would affect him one day.

Ever since he'd known he would be seeing Constanze again, he hadn't given condoms a thought, not even for a minute, and even if he'd had the presence of mind to buy some he wouldn't have brought them along, for fear of jinxing their reunion. Also, he'd have to buy them in a pharmacy where no one knew him, where no one said 'hello' the minute he stepped through the door, where no one called him by his first name.

Besides loving a girl for five years without seeing her, besides the seismic shock of being reunited with her, he should have cast romanticism aside and thought about those ten grams of latex. The oversight had brought him cruelly back down to earth. Constanze's head was resting on his shoulder, and he dared not move, but lay pondering every possible way of getting hold of some. Constanze had told him he should ask someone in the group. She couldn't do that, she said, it would embarrass her. But Alexandre couldn't see himself asking Adrien, or Anton, still less Frédéric or the girls – it would presuppose a closeness they did not share. Worst of all, he would have looked like an idiot, incapable of forethought, and beholden to them as a result. If they'd given him a condom, it would have been thanks to them that he had been able to have sex with Constanze. And why just one? To ask for several, or two, or four, or five, would tell them much too much ... The joy of waking up beside her was turning into a nightmare, made worse still when he realised it was Monday. Here, even on an ordinary weekday, it was an hour's drive to the nearest pharmacy, but on a Monday even that was no use. On a Monday in the country, everything was closed. He would have to wait until tomorrow, even tomorrow evening, before they could make love, but tomorrow he must leave.

Alexandre knew already that the thought would prey on his mind all day. On rejoining the group, he knew it was too soon for him to ask such a thing. Scrounging condoms wasn't the sort of thing you did over breakfast. Worst of all, one after the other, they were all asking him if he needed anything: more coffee, the jam, more bread, or butter, or a joint ... Each time, he answered no, nothing at all. Constanze thought it was funny and stroked his head affectionately, but rather annoyingly all the same.

Over the course of the morning, he had several opportunities to take one or other of them aside and confess what he really needed. He began with Adrien, who was working in the vegetable patch. He had no idea how to broach the subject, especially when Adrien launched, as usual, into a virulent diatribe, this time against farmers who sprayed filth all over the place. Alexandre felt targeted and didn't dare mention condoms.

'The soil is hard here and even the weeds have trouble growing, but I see them down on the plain, they spread fertiliser before sowing, and after they've sown, there's so much fertiliser that the weeds shoot up before the seeds have even sprouted, so they spread weedkiller, and ten days later the greenfly attack the new shoots of their crop, obviously, because the weeds are all dead, and the greenfly have nowhere else to go, so they get out the pesticide, it just goes on and on ...'

Alexandre said nothing, but he had no desire to be indebted to this guy for his one opportunity to make love with Constanze. He went back to the house and found himself alone with Lorraine. He asked her casually if there was a pharmacy anywhere nearby, or if they knew any pharmacists.

'Are you in pain?'

'Sort of.'

'Go and see Kathleen, she can treat anything with her herbs and concoctions.'

He reckoned he'd have no better luck with Frédéric, and certainly not Xabi. And so, in despair, he went in search of Anton. Despite the heat, he was still fixing up his drystone wall.

'Anton, can I ask you something?'

'I knew you'd come and talk to me about it eventually.'

'About what?'

With that, Anton dropped the stone he was carrying, took a long drink of water, thought for a moment, then launched into a confession of sorts, about the explosives, the whole business. He said that Chernobyl had come five years too late. Five years earlier, the incident would have been a godsend for their struggle. The whole of France would have taken up the cause, but now it was too late; people had grown accustomed to nuclear power, to the idea that a reactor might blow its top. He regretted losing three years of his life and getting Alexandre mixed up in all that. He'd had time to mull everything over these past five years – in jail, obviously, but most of all here, in the peace and quiet, and the open air.

'Violence only accentuates fear, and when fear spreads, more people get worried, and the far right reels them in.'

His tone was solemn, and Alexandre felt awkward. Anton had confided something deeply personal, and he couldn't very well respond with a question about condoms. Anton carried on talking. Alexandre thought about tomorrow, when he would drive back home. He had seen Constanze. Three days together, but without making love. Unless they just went ahead tonight. He was prepared to do that. Or at least, he knew that in the heat of the moment it was a possibility that, this evening, that night, they would take one another passionately, with no thought for the virus, or death as the outcome of every embrace … Except that making love without a condom would ruin everything. But was it better to be in love with no sex, or to have sex and spoil it all? While Alexandre grappled with the vexed issue of sex, love, Durex and death, Anton was explaining that fighting against society meant defining your existence on society's terms, which meant you were subject to its rules, and society had won.

'I wanted to fight, but not to change the world. You need to fight, but not against a particular enemy. You can take action in your immediate surroundings, by restoring an old wall, for instance.'

Alexandre bent down to help him place the damned stone at last.

'You know what, Anton, you'd do better if you used a bit of cement, there's no law against it.'

But Anton wanted no cement. He wanted his wall pure and clean.

'Nature! See?'

'Whatever, Anton. Whatever.'

Anton was standing right in front of him now, staring him in the face.

'But I haven't forgotten, Alexandre. And you know that if ever you need my help one day, if ever you have a battle to fight, I'll be there.'

'What battle?'

'You never know, Alexandre. You're vulnerable, I can tell. In your work. You're vulnerable, exposed.'

Tuesday, 22 July 1986

Alexandre would set off tonight, as late as possible. If he drove through the night, he could spend a last afternoon with Constanze. He had been thinking about this girl for five years, and for the last two days he had refrained from asking her too many questions. Still, he longed to know how she felt about him. If they were some kind of couple. But to ask outright would make him look like a naïve kid. And he could see she had feelings for him anyway. She'd even told him how she thought about him often, and that she hadn't called because she didn't want to complicate things. It wasn't enough though, and Alexandre thought that before they parted, they should make plans to meet again, so as not to lose touch with one another.

They ate lunch all together around the big table. Adrien had roasted a leg of lamb. Kathleen and Lorraine didn't approve – even the smell made them feel sick. Alexandre felt suddenly grounded, far more so than these dreamers. He wondered, as he ate, what they would all be doing five years from now, or ten; who would still be here on this farm, and who would have left. He thought he knew already. Anton, for example, with his soft-soled leather shoes and polyester trousers, or Xabi with his black T-shirts in the hot sun; it was obvious the city was still part of them, and one day, sooner or later, it would catch up with them again. As for Constanze, her future was the easiest of all to read. The day after tomorrow she would board her plane back to Berlin. She talked of nothing but saving the world and coming to India's aid.

Constanze and Alexandre wanted to spend the rest of the afternoon alone, far from the group, and so they set out for the Trou aux Fées, a spring that they'd been told nestled amid tall grasses and shrubs. Alexandre was glad he'd brought the Renault – the haven of peace was some way off, and the track was narrow and badly rutted. It led to a deep-cut gorge with a stream at the bottom that supported an abundance of plants. There wasn't enough water to swim, hence there was no one else there. Holidaymakers preferred the riverbanks and lakesides. Small springs and streams like this one were like uninhabited planets, spared the presence of humankind.

They settled down. Alexandre was astonished at how spontaneously, how naturally Constanze got naked. She seemed to have taken all her clothes off in a single movement. He was obliged to do the same but found that he could not. For two nights they had shared the same bed, chaste but undressed, but to go naked now, in the bright open air, in front of her, seemed extravagant, unnecessary.

'You're so French!' she told him, before taking him by the hand and leading him to a broad, shallow pool, barely more than a puddle, where the water collected as it rose, before making its way leisurely down the slope.

Alexandre allowed himself to be led. He took off his jeans, his shoes and T-shirt, but not his boxers, then followed her into the water.

'Just think, this water is so pure, it's come from deep down inside the earth. It's unbelievable.'

Constanze marvelled at the spring like an oasis in the desert, prompting Alexandre to remark that perhaps she hadn't seen many natural springs before.

'I have! The Széchenyi Baths in Budapest. Baden-Baden. But they're not like this, in the heart of the countryside … *Komm, meine Liebe.*'

She thought they were all alone in the world. But Alexandre felt the presence of the bushes, the tall grasses, the birds and bugs all around them, the buzzard high above in the sky. He felt the gaze of the wild, and he found it impossibly hard to take off his boxers, just like when he played rugby. He'd never felt as comfortable as some of his teammates, who would strip off without a second thought. But at the sight of Constanze lying stretched out in the shallow pool, barely twenty centimetres deep, rolling in the water the way people do in the shallows at the edge of a beach, he felt a wild urge to join her. Her honey-coloured skin was even more dazzling when wet, tempting as gingerbread, and from that moment on his inhibitions vanished. There were no limits, no frontiers. Alexandre was overwhelmed by his own unthinking body, and he went to her in the tiny pond. The water was cold, but the sun burned hot. They put their arms around one another and sank immediately in a dizzying spiral, water mixing with each gulp of air, their hands endlessly searching. They touched, and spoke no more. Constanze laughed and threw herself into the game. Alexandre wasn't laughing; he was lost as they rolled over and over. Sometimes a rock hurt him, but the sun took the pain away, and the cold water was exhilarating. Nature conquered everything. Each time he tried to hold Constanze tight in his arms, she slipped away, fluid as a fish. Fleetingly, she offered him her mouth, he caught her breasts, her buttocks, but when he slipped his hand between her thighs, once again, she stopped him instantly, and pushed herself up, resting her upper body on her outstretched arms.

'I'm sorry, Alexandre, I can't.'

And then, to justify herself, she told him that she had had some flings over the past five years. Never a serious relationship, but some flings, and with hindsight, she was terrified at the thought. She was frightened of sex now. Frightened of love. It was as if the freedom to go to bed with someone just like that, for one night, had become a punishable crime. The world they had forgotten, just for a moment, intruded once more, and she told him stories her mother had told her, about the Western pharmaceutical companies that were testing new formulations on patients in the GDR, and the nurses' awkward silence. Since returning to the East from time to time, she had been gripped by fear. It was a kind of obsession, and now she dreaded everything – drugs, disease, medicine as a whole, and sex. And this world, where there was nothing left that she could trust.

We try to stand back from history, but it is always there, keeping us in its sights. The times you live in always catch up with you in the end. On their return to the communal farm, Alexandre found himself envying the rest of the group. They had chosen to drop out of history. They thought they had freed themselves from its grasp, from the world at large, living their happy, self-sufficient lives, with no hypermarkets, no rules and specifications, no controls, for the moment at least.

That evening, before he left, Constanze told him several times over that they would see one another again soon, that she would call him. She would call him all the time.

## Friday, 24 December 1999

For a week the radio had been talking about the oil slick caused by the *Erika* petrol tanker that had sunk off the coast of Brittany in the recent rough weather. This morning, they'd talked about more high winds on the way, perhaps even stronger than before. The forecast was clearer and more precise with each new weather bulletin: violent winds were very likely, of a strength seldom seen.

Since the total eclipse in August, nature had seemed more off balance than ever. Alexandre remembered how, five months ago, they had all come up to the farm to see the black sun. Everyone had gathered at Les Bertranges for the first time since their parents had moved down into the valley. Four generations all together. Because Lucienne had wanted to see it, too – the moon swallowing the sun, a once-in-a-lifetime spectacle. The children had run wild. Caroline and Vanessa feared one thing only, that their offspring would take off their infrared spectacles at the moment of the eclipse. But Angèle and Jean had been genuinely unnerved. The sun would disappear, if only for a few moments, and that was an ill omen, they said. They wouldn't go so far as to believe the nutcases who said this was the end of the world, the ones who predicted that the *Mir* space station would crash into Gers at that precise moment – and anyway, Gers was a hundred kilometres away – but still, no good would come of the eclipse, in their view. Their father said the valley was teeming with boar and deer that had come down from the high forest, as if the animals were fleeing the woods for fear the trees might fall on them. He'd never seen anything like it.

With the wind blowing from the north, as it was tonight, you could hear the work in progress. The site was hell itself. Thirteen million cubic metres of earth displaced, thousands of hectares of agricultural land devastated, hundreds of embankments, tunnels and bridges, not to mention the wild animals that the motorway would block when they emerged from the forest by night to roam the grasslands and find water. All so that Toulouse and Paris would have a direct route to Barcelona, The Hague and London. The cities dictated their own rules, and everyone else was forced to comply. They would sabotage the countryside to satisfy their thirst for unfettered trade, communications and transport, so that the inhabitants of one city could visit all the others. Their self-centredness was sickening.

Alexandre checked the M75 mortars. Before firing, they had to be half buried in the soil to keep them stable. Xabi had customised a rocket, tripling its explosive force. Alexandre would adhere scrupulously to his plan, to guaranteed effect. Old Crayssac had passed away, and Alexandre felt he had been walking in his footsteps ever since.

He took a shower before joining the family in the little house down below, though he had no desire to sit through the Christmas meal. Now, on France Info they were discussing the huge area of low pressure that was forming over the Atlantic, sending gusts of wind racing up the Breton coast. Storm-force winds from the south-west. That was bad luck. The response vessels would be unable to carry on pumping out the *Erika*'s tanks in six-metre waves. This whole century was going to end in disaster.

1991

## Monday, 4 March 1991

Now that he'd sold his goats, Crayssac no longer made a living from the land that had always sustained him. He'd been forced to give up the kitchen garden, and the cheese, because of his bad hip, and he obviously no longer went foraging or hunting. Nature, always such a bountiful source of food for him, now provided little more than mushrooms. For the rest, the grocery van sufficed. For as long as the small, ramshackle white van still made the detour and rattled up to his place, he would get all his food that way.

Since the Chernobyl cloud, everyone said mushrooms should be avoided. The ceps and girolles, and the ordinary field mushrooms, were contaminated with caesium-137. They would be inedible till the end of days. But that didn't stop Crayssac from collecting them. From long years of experience, he knew the best places and gathered them by the bagful. He was the only person in the district who still went out picking, and because nature moves in remarkable ways, it happened that mushrooms were lightweight, and he was still able to collect and bring back huge quantities of them.

'I couldn't care less about their caesium-137, or their 138 or their 139, at my age. You shouldn't believe all the blah, blah, blah you hear on the radio.'

There were times when Alexandre despaired of the crazy old man. He was the only one who went to see him in his cottage. Some said he was after Crayssac's land, and that was why he went on visiting the old-timer, but Alexandre wasn't the least bit interested in his stony fields. None of the Fabriers had ever coveted Crayssac's hectares. For him, the old man was the inspiration behind all the protestors and activists he had come to know, the anti-nuclear crowd and the anti-everything, all-purpose revolutionaries down in Toulouse, the hippy farmers up at Larzac, or Anton's gang, whom he had visited again that summer. Through Crayssac he had found a clan of sorts, a family of free spirits in which he liked to include Constanze, Anton and Adrien, even Kevin Costner in *Dances with Wolves*. Crayssac was, after all, the precursor of all the people who'd chosen to step aside and tread a different path; who removed themselves from the consumer society that was invariably presented as the only possible way forward. Now that the Berlin Wall had come down, ultra-liberalism and the free market was the only viable model, well organised and increasingly fast paced, the only form of civilisation that delivered the branches and outlets that were needed the whole world over, a world in which merchandise of every possible kind could be endlessly bought and sold.

The fall of the Wall had changed nothing in Alexandre's dealings with Constanze, however. At first, he'd thought things would be simpler. They would see one another more often. It would bring them closer together somehow. But it had been nothing like that. They kept to the old rites, a few days together each summer at Anton's place, a week when they would have trouble getting away from the others and ultimately promised one another very little. Alexandre had travelled to Berlin once for the Christmas holidays, a two-day train journey there, and another two days back. And from the six days he'd spent there, he took nothing but the realisation that the sun set at four o'clock in the afternoon, and two or three words of German that he could never pronounce correctly. Constanze had introduced him to crowds of friends, and while he should have taken that as a sign of her love, the language barrier made everything an ordeal. Only their nights were magical, in an old rococo hotel on the Kurfürstendamm, a bedroom with great red curtains that hung from the immensely high ceiling, with the contours of an entire world in their folds, a world for their eyes only …

'*Allô!* Anyone home?'

'Yes.'

'So tell me, why do you think the mushrooms get it all?'

'Get what?'

'The caesium-137!'

'I don't know.'

'Because mushrooms are nature's cleansers, they decontaminate the soil, they absorb whatever's bad for it, they suck it up and capture it in their flesh.'

'That's why you shouldn't eat them.'

'We all need our trace elements. Stop listening to nonsense on the television.'

Alexandre never checked out what the eccentric old man told him, but more than once events had proved him right. Like the telegraph poles treated with arsenic: twenty-five years had gone by, and none of them showed the slightest trace of rot, or woodworm. The trunks were clearly impervious to anything, steeped in a load of chemical crap that had definitely seeped into the soil by now. Crayssac was like some mad but clear-sighted old soothsayer, and that was why Alexandre had come to see him this morning. France Info had just announced the very first case of *vache folle*, in Brittany, and the entire herd had been slaughtered there and then to prevent the 'mad cow disease' from spreading. This was now the official advice. The outbreak must not become an epidemic.

'I told you no good would come of it when that cat died in England two years ago. You mark my words, one day the *vache folle* will pass to humans. We'll catch it like a cold, and there'll be panic in the streets.'

Crayssac was always critical of everything, forever declaring the world had gone mad, but it was getting harder and harder to prove him wrong.

'When that cat died, they banned meat and bone meal, and now they're finding sick animals that were born after the ban – Europe's been turning a blind eye. We let the English pass all their filth on to us so they'd join the Single Market, because without that they'd be off out and away. Bloody Brits. Believe me, the only thing the Brits know about cattle is that a cow's got four legs and is sold "by the pound". That's all. A pound's a pound to them, whether it's in weight or cash, it's all the same. No bloody wonder they're confused.'

Old-timers like Crayssac always prophesied the worst. It was a favourite strategy if you felt doomed in any way. If you predicted the end of the world, you had no regrets about leaving it. Alexandre glanced at his watch and leapt to his feet.

'Committee meeting, is it?'

'There's no fooling you ...'

Old Crayssac heaved himself up from his chair with difficulty. He crossed the room to the doorway, where Alexandre already stood poised to leave.

'I can reassure you about one thing at least, and I'll tell it to you because the others all take me for an old fool – they'll never bring that motorway through here, believe me. Even if the state mandates it, they won't be able to.'

'Why ever not?'

'Because of my treasure.'

When the old man began raving, Alexandre preferred to drop the subject, even sometimes pretending not to hear. He stepped outside, but Crayssac called him back, and his voice was unusually soft and kind. He turned back in surprise.

'You've got the treasure too, you know, at the bottom of your

252

field. You just don't know what it is yet, Alexandre. I'll tell you one day. Not now. I'll leave you to get on with your business for now. Your meetings and your blah, blah, blah.'

'What would you have me believe, Joseph?'

'Don't you worry, I'll tell you when the time is right.'

## Monday, 4 March 1991

Alexandre drove the Renault back down to Cénevières. The meeting would have started by now. Driving past Crayssac's now fallow fields, he wondered what ideas the goat breeder had got into his head. The old man often rambled but, as Alexandre knew, there was always something in the things he said. Always a grain of truth. Still, it was impossible to believe, even for a second, that this wilderness of brambles, juniper bushes and rampant weeds could conceal treasure of any sort, not even a water source, still less gold, or oil – it would have been discovered long ago.

Le Paradou no longer had its grocery store. Nor a bistro, really, in fact, just the bar. Old Suzanne stayed sitting in the empty dining area, seldom getting to her feet. Most of the time, her clientele served themselves. It helped if you knew how to use the old coffee machine: there was a knack to inserting and turning the holder for each fresh cup. But everyone knew how to flip the cap off a bottle or pour a measure of Ricard. Old Suzanne would get up to take the money, though. She trusted humanity as a rule, but she was the only one allowed to rummage in the till.

The Europe of the Twelve had ambitions to expand. France was destined to become the hub of a united continent, the beating heart of all Europe, especially because Britain would soon be connected by a tunnel, and tomorrow it would be quicker to get from London to Paris than from Rodez to Décazeville. Except for a hub connecting north and south, east and west, France lacked motorways. Which was why the project for the new A20 had been launched now in earnest.

Ever since the motorway had been announced as part of the master plan – since the state had taken the firm decision to build it – Le Paradou had become the headquarters for the committee meetings. The café had never been so full, a good fifty people at each gathering. The old bistro had been dying a long, slow death but now, ironically, it had become a vital asset for the wider area, far beyond the town and its rural surroundings.

The town halls of the other villages were too small and too scattered. Le Paradou became the venue for their public meetings, too – at least, for those of their populace who cared enough to try and stop their neighbourhood from disappearing beneath a vast strip of tarmac. Things had gathered pace since the beginning of the year. The project was still at the preliminary study phase, but already the motorway was on everyone's mind. The same people did most of the talking at the meetings, the ones who had a way with words, and knew how to hold the room: the local councillors. They would follow one after the other, illustrating their points with endless sketches and maps. A flip chart stood permanently at one end of the café now, adding a new top note all its own – the heady reek of marker pens – to the prevailing odour of stale alcohol.

'Oh, this could go on forever. For the moment they're studying several possible routes, alternative corridors through a broad, thirty-kilometre zone. The motorway could very well go east of here, towards Assier, or west, on the other side of Bouriane, but their preferred option is right here. A flyover above the valley.'

'When will we know?'

'They'll home in on the area at the end of the preliminary study phase. They'll identify a narrow zone one kilometre wide, and three hundred metres beyond that, and then it gets serious.'

'What do you mean, it gets serious? The work begins?'

'Yes. Once the three-hundred-metre strip is identified, nothing can stop them.'

'Who's "them"?'

'The state!'

Tonight, the local deputy had shown up in person to explain the situation in greater detail. Le grand Bernard, trusted by everyone because he spoke with their local accent, and because he sold agricultural equipment. He knew the land all around, he was born there, and yet he wasn't opposed to the motorway scheme. Far from it.

'The thing you need to get clear in your minds is that this motorway is in the public interest, in everyone's interest, and to that extent it takes precedence over our own, personal interest – do you understand? Well, yes, that's democracy, because if there's one thing you need to keep in mind, it's that none of us is alone on this earth.'

'We're all alone, here.'

'Well, you're not as alone and cut off as you might think.'

That was enough for the mayor of Cénevières. This was more than he could take. This area, these villages, the tiny country roads, had been neglected for years. The train stations were closing one after another, and now the bistros too. All your damned public interest brought here was closures – the post office, the grocery store, and soon enough this bistro, too. They had suffered from spending cuts in the public interest, and the cuts had left people more and more isolated, further and further from everything, and now all of a sudden, they would be forced to accept a motorway, disfiguring their valley, in the self-same public interest ... Well, no. He wouldn't stand for it.

Whistles and boos rang out around the room, but their deputy reminded them that it was as much his job to represent the interests of local people to the state as it was to represent the interests of the state to everyone here.

'So let's be clear: blocking a new motorway scheme is the same as blocking the traffic once it's built. Do you see?'

'No.'

'I mean that stopping a motorway from being built is the same as blocking one that already exists. It's a criminal act. Crim-in-al.'

'But we don't want to block the motorway, we just want it to take a different route. To the east, over the *causse*. There's nothing there but wild juniper – no one minds about that. But here in the valley there's good land. That's easy enough to comprehend.'

'If everyone was like you, there would have been no railways in the nineteenth century – imagine that. It was far worse back then: tens of thousands of kilometres of railways were built, the same ones you regret being shut now, though not one of you ever takes the train.'

'Of course no one ever takes the train: have you seen what's left of your precious railways?'

'Whatever. But no one has the right to stand in the way of the public interest – and if you do, that's pure selfishness.'

Alexandre looked at his father. The Fabrier men stood and listened but said nothing because, inside, their stomachs were knotted. No one cared about them, or old Crayssac. No one cared what they thought. Only one person said it out loud but they all thought it: the easiest thing was to run the motorway overhead, up there, across the Fabriers' land. The solution suited the landowners along the axis of the route, on the north and south sides alike. They were all waiting for precisely that – for the motorway company to buy their land, because they'd never sell it any other way. Around here, permission would never be granted to build on it otherwise, and everyone knew there were no farmers to carry on in future. They'd be saddled with useless land forever. Old Taillade was even prepared to sell ten hectares to the Autoroutes du Sud de la France or ASF for a quarry, because they'd need stone to build the motorway, and that way they'd have all the rocks they could want right there: local scree for their embankments. They could even build a cement works. Win–win, and everyone would cash in.

'I'll be frank,' Taillade Senior intervened. 'We all know there'll be half as many farms around here in the year 2000 as there are now. Here, it'll just be wasteland and wild trees, so instead of freezing worthless land, I'll tell you right now, I'd rather sell at a good price for the motorway and be done with it ...'

Alexandre and his father found themselves out on a limb. Around them, most were prepared to sell. They would keep their cool until they were certain, but it would be a catastrophe if the motorway passed over the valley. Apart from cutting their land in half, and the hellish din, it would mean a road bridge eighty metres high, straddling the Rauze. Years of earthworks and construction sites, not to mention the endless nuisance. And so Alexandre's father was determined to speak up, because the deputy was there. Crossing the valley made no sense, he said. The simplest thing would be to build the motorway on the flat land to the east.

'No. That's where you're wrong. Taking it out and around to the east adds kilometres to the project. The simplest thing for them is to straddle the valley, right along the Brive–Cahors axis, in a straight line.'

'But a viaduct will cost a fortune!'

'Not a problem for the motorway company. On the contrary, the costlier the project, the more it generates in tolls and subsidies.'

His father was speechless. Alexandre said nothing but he swore to himself that a motorway viaduct would never come near Les Bertranges. Never would he allow that landscape to become disfigured. If it came to that, he would ask Anton, Xabi and the rest of them for help, even Crayssac and all the old guard. They would form a resistance. He had no idea how he would set about it just yet, but bulldozers would never tear into his fields of wild mint, never disfigure the scenery Constanze loved so much.

Seated in the middle of the room, old Suzanne followed the debate, but didn't take part. She was just happy to see her café full of people. Apart from that, as far as she could tell, the difference between cars and trains was that trains used to bring people here, while cars allowed them to get away. And when the meeting was over, the thirty or so cars parked outside the bistro all drove off, disappearing into thin air virtually all at once. Only the three regulars remained, leaning on the bar. Not setting the world to rights for once, but the motorway. The ticking clock could be heard again, filling the room as it always did, and the boiler's muffled roar, punctuating the tedium.

Vanessa had brought an AT&T phone back with her from the States – a white cordless phone with a long, telescopic aerial like the one on the car. At last, thanks to his sister, Alexandre could hold long conversations without having to stand in the hallway. By pulling out the aerial, he could even take the phone out of doors.

He and Constanze spoke at least once a fortnight. Typically, she would call from work. Alexandre could contact her when he wanted to, provided it was during office hours and he reversed the charges. He found it humiliating to go via the operator and wait for Constanze to accept the call, or not, but he went ahead all the same, especially because often they would talk for long periods of time, and it would have cost him a fortune if he'd had to pay.

Their long-distance relationship gave Alexandre the unexpected feeling of being in another place. Through Constanze, he experienced cities, lives, worlds he would otherwise never know. And he'd been to Berlin – an amazing, long journey that he wanted to repeat sooner or later, but to see Constanze, not the city. He'd be more confident next time. For her part, Constanze found in Alexandre a refreshingly straightforward character, a man who lived free because he lived in the heart of the countryside. He was dependable, her one fixed point, especially since the death of her grandmother. The fall of the Wall had not been enough to save her, and with all the upheavals that had ensued, her mother was quite losing her mind. Her familiar frame of reference had vanished, things were in a constant state of flux, while Constanze's father flitted all over the world for Airbus. Her country was reunified but still in two halves. Constanze herself was working for an NGO now, a job for which she would be travelling more and more.

Alexandre was immune to the wanderlust that seized them all – his sisters and Constanze alike. Countries were opening up to one another; the world seemed at peace; the superpowers were talking about disarmament now, and in this calm, prosperous bubble people and goods knew no frontiers. Globalisation was a happy phenomenon that saw millions of people piling onto planes. He saw more and more of them each night, up in the sky, and the thought sickened him. The whole planet was accessible to everyone, even to him, with his white telephone and its extended aerial. Each time Constanze called he was transported to Berlin. It felt a little as if he were there for real. The ritual was set in stone: on two Fridays a month, she would stay late at work and call the farm. Curled up in his room, Alexandre could hear his parents calling him to come and eat or it would get cold. They couldn't help it. He was almost thirty now, but still they spoke to him as if he was a kid.


When Alexandre came down to eat that evening, it was past nine o'clock. The TV had been turned off – a sign that no one was in the mood for entertainment. His mother fetched a cold steak from the kitchen, with a resigned air. There was salad, too. And fried potatoes, also cold.

'Don't bother, Ma. I can eat in the kitchen.'

'Sit down.'

Alexandre saw straight away that his parents wanted to talk. The price of beef was down again. His parents delivered the information in a tone that seemed to hold him partly responsible – it was since the fall of the Berlin Wall, anyway, that the scheme to import meat from the East had given everyone a serious fright. As if Alexandre was behind the former Communist bloc's conversion to a market economy, as if being in love with a German girl made him somehow complicit in the changes that were afoot. As always, he replied that the solution was to plant even more corn, so that they could be sure of increased revenues, but for that they'd need to buy a new tractor. Massey had just brought out a 170-horsepower model: it would cost them about ten thousand francs a year, but they could manage that … There was worse news this evening, though. His father was worried. The new director at the hypermarket had produced a report, a document full of charts and photographs that showed how the meat from cattle reared outside was a duller red than the meat obtained from cattle that were kept inside. The lighting in the huge stores was specially adjusted, but even so, good meat with a high pH had less sheen to it than a flaccid cut from an animal that could barely move around. So beasts like theirs, beasts reared in vast meadows, in the open air, beasts with fine, herb-flavoured muscle, produced meat that looked dark and unappetising when it was sealed under plastic. It was one hundred per cent better beef, but in a polystyrene tray under the neon lights, it wasn't selling. And the thought of that drove his father crazy.

## Sunday, 14 July 1991

Seeing them all out in the yard, Angèle thought again of the intuition she'd had once, long ago: the dread that one day her family would end up like all the rest, scattered to the four corners of France or the world, only ever coming together for big occasions – New Year, holidays, weddings, funerals. It made her sadder still to think that they weren't all here now, for Bastille Day. Agathe had not come. She should have been there, but she had taken it into her head to open a franchise boutique in Rodez, and now none of them quite understood what she was doing with her life, only that she had gone into partnership for the money, and that she was too young to be saddling herself with so much debt.

Saddest of all for their mother was to see how detached her daughters had become from the farm. Nothing about them suggested that they had lived within these walls until they were old enough to leave home. When they visited, they never even went out to see the fields or the cattle, they never set out along the footpaths to breathe the air of their childhood. They barely stroked the dogs, and with no real show of affection. They seemed not to remember that the animals were born of the same landscape, the same air, as them.

Now that Caroline was a mother herself, her behaviour was more and more that of the oldest sister. And now that she was teaching *collège* pupils, aged eleven to fifteen, she had assumed an even greater air of authority. She had tried to take control at lunchtime: it had been so hot these last few days that she wanted to make the most of the fine weather and move the table outside. But her parents stood their ground, especially because Lucienne and Louis were coming, and they couldn't subject them to the ordeal of eating outdoors, with wasps buzzing around.

'Little Chloë, she's the image of her grandmother.'

'No, her great-grandma, look, she has the same hazel eyes.'

'Really? Did you have curly hair when you were a baby?'

'What do you reckon, Alexandre?'

Alexandre had not taken to his tiny new niece. Since her arrival, all they ever talked about was her face, her hair, her teeth, her little dress or her new dolly. No one at Les Bertranges had ever been so besotted with children before; no one had ever doted on one of them that way. Anyone would think the newborn baby was some kind of miracle, when all around them the farm pulsed with life. Things were born all the time, thirty or more calves each year, not to mention great armfuls of kittens and chicks, litters of puppies, a whole multitude of animals around the farmhouse, plus the pheasants that nested in the hedges, the boar and roe deer that lived hereabouts, and the pairs of doves in the great walnut trees opposite. Things were born everywhere on the farm, all the time, bursting out all over. The place was a factory of new lives, plus all the vegetables and crops sprouting over hectares of land, and yet the coming of this tiny girl into the world seemed a thousand times more extraordinary to them than all that … The tableful of people cooing over baby Chloë was really getting on Alexandre's nerves.

Fortunately, there was Vanessa. A certified Parisienne, she approached her role as auntie with measured enthusiasm. Sometimes, Alexandre tried to steer the conversation back to the farm, the motorway that was becoming more and more of a reality, but his anxieties barely elicited a response. Caroline was unbothered, asking in a matter-of-fact way about compensation if they were forced to sell. How much was the motorway company offering per hectare for the land it needed? Vanessa saw the motorway in a positive light, too. She was convinced it would bring new business and boost the regional economy. Alexandre saw no one he could turn to. Jean and Angèle were resigned and fatalistic, far too law-abiding to stand in the way of a project of national importance. His parents and grandparents alike were docile, public-spirited citizens, determined their whole lives long not to make trouble.

When the meal was over, their parents relented and took their chairs out of doors for coffee. Alexandre seized his chance to bring up the subject of the motorway, but again their father and mother refused to take the bait, and Caroline cut him short, crossly. There were other, far more disturbing things to worry about – in Europe, where hostilities had broken out in Yugoslavia, and in the wider world, where George Bush and Saddam Hussein risked sending the Middle East up in smoke. A motorway was the last thing anyone was going to worry about.

'It won't come right through the house, anyway!'

'How do you know?'

Caroline made no attempt to show sympathy, all she wanted was for Alexandre not to spoil their Bastille Day lunch with this business about the motorway, as he had done last Christmas.

The only person who seemed genuinely concerned and ready to listen was Philippe. As Caroline's husband, he was careful not to contradict her, but still, as a history teacher, he could see the bigger picture, and he at least understood that a four-lane highway would be a catastrophe for the valley. He wanted to know more.

'What's the worst-case scenario? Would it pass a hundred metres from here, two hundred metres? What can you hear from a motorway two hundred metres away?'

'We'd lose between five and ten hectares of land, but worst of all is the viaduct. It would take years to build, and the noise would be hellish; even if it's half a kilometre from the farm we'd still hear it. Living right next to that is unthinkable.'

Alexandre had raised the subject of the motorway once again for another reason, too. This was his way of gauging where his sisters stood in relation to the farm. One evening, Agathe had called their parents and asked outright for an advance on her share, to help with the racket she was getting into with that man of hers. Since that blow, Alexandre had feared they would all do the same. They had all walked out, but they were still entitled to know if he had signed a contract as his parents' tenant farmer, or whether he owned the property already, though instinctively he felt it was none of their business. The question would come up one day: what right did Alexandre have to be the sole heir to the family farm? It already provided him with a roof over his head and a salary. Sometimes, he even felt guilty, though he never delved into their personal affairs. He would never dare ask Caroline or Philippe what they earned as teachers in the state system, or how much they still owed on their mortgage.

It was hot, but rather than lounge in the shade, Alexandre wanted to go and check if the cattle had enough water. Philippe said he would come along. After a wet, cool spring, the sun had shone in cloudless skies for the past three weeks. The grass in the fields was tall and abundant, the green more reminiscent of Normandy than the south-west. A rare sight in mid-July. Philippe sat awkwardly on the tractor. He was getting shaken about but clung on, and Alexandre sensed his brother-in-law was enjoying the ride. He had a countryman's soul, deep down, though he had never had much contact with nature, still less with life on a farm. Now, he was savouring the new experience with relish.

To take water to the cattle, they first had to fill the mobile tank at the spring, but the flow was inadequate. Alexandre decided to pump the river. Philippe held tight, on the tractor's footplate. He felt like a character in a western, riding a steam engine.

'You're a cowboy at heart,' he said.

'You reckon?'

'Absolutely! Your life is cattle, and the great outdoors, the river … There are even Indians lying in wait!'

Alexandre thought Philippe was referring to his sisters as some sort of enemy, but his brother-in-law was thinking about the motorway company. To get a better idea of what might be involved, he asked Alexandre to point out the site of the viaduct, should it ever come to pass.

'The most logical thing for them would be to take it straight across. Straddle the valley right overhead, north–south.'

Alexandre connected the pipe to the tank and activated the pump. Philippe admired the scene all around. Looking up, he tried to picture a viaduct, eighty metres high.

'You could organise a defence committee, take action, everyone should get involved.'

'Who's "everyone"?'

'Well, everyone affected.'

Alexandre explained the situation. The high ground was of no interest to anybody any more. Most of the farms had ceased operating, one after another. Apart from Les Bertranges, none of the farmers did anything with their land now, and most of them were waiting for a chance to sell it to the motorway company.

The pump stalled. Philippe stood by while Alexandre fired up the engine again. He walked a little way along the river. Surely the scheme was crazy – a road bridge carrying an endless stream of cars and trucks seemed extraordinary amid all this natural beauty, a pointless waste of money. He couldn't understand why Caroline was not more shocked. He turned and saw Alexandre struggling to restart the pump. His brother-in-law looked strong and tough, but he was a fragile soul, so much more fragile than he seemed, and entirely alone. He had no weight, no clout, in the face of hundreds of tonnes of concrete and tarmac. And he was powerless against the state. An impervious, pitiless state that decided where it would put its highways and expropriated people's land without a second thought. A thousand such dramas preceded the building of every motorway. Endless regrets and evictions like this. This cowboy was only a wisp of straw in the face of a concerted ambush from the motorway company, the state's road transport plan, and the civil engineers. Philippe swore he would look into the matter. He wouldn't say anything to the others. But already he feared there was nothing anyone could do to halt the inevitable process that led, one day, to a decision by the state to run a motorway across your land, right in front of your house.

He walked back to where Alexandre was standing, and together they drove back up the track to the high meadow. The tank was full and heavy. They had more than enough water to fill the three troughs.

'Goodness, how they drink!'

'When the sun's beating down, you need to watch out. A cow can drink a hundred litres or more, especially mine. They have a salty diet!'

Philippe was discovering the realities of life on the farm. They were of no consequence to him, but he showed the same open-minded curiosity that had led him to long years of study, deciphering the world through books rather than out in the field. He enjoyed experiences like this. Where he saw only a field of grass, Alexandre was talking about ryegrass, and fescue, and clover.

'Have you ever produced milk?'

'Milk? Are you kidding? I'd never go into dairy.'

'Oh. But surely a cow is a cow?'

'Dairy cows have to be pumped morning and night; there's always someone harassing them, whereas these are free — as you can see. They go where they please, no one bothers them.'

They drove into another field and Alexandre lined the tractor up beside a drinking trough. He filled it up. From the far end of the field, the cows began to amble over.

'You know, Alexandre, history is like nature. The point is not to try and understand everything, but to know how to learn the right lessons. The thing I've learned from the history of protest is that people need to organise.'

'What's that got to do with me?'

'The motorway. Seems to me you're on your own, especially since your parents don't seem to want to put up a fight.'

Philippe gazed around at the scenery, where there was not another soul to be seen. Then he drew closer to Alexandre and lowered his voice.

'You know, your sister told me once, vaguely, about what you got up to a long time ago. If I understood right, you were something of an activist?'

Alexandre's heart thumped hard and fast. He was profoundly shocked by his brother-in-law's remark, but he was determined to let nothing show. How could his sister think that of him? That he'd been far more deeply involved, one of the extremists, even planting bombs ... He said nothing, gave no reaction.

'So?'

'So nothing. I'm not a rebel at heart.'

'Too bad.'

Alexandre shut off the water. Almost before Philippe had time to climb onto the tractor, he had pulled himself back into the driver's seat and set off into the next field. A thousand thoughts ran through his mind. He was jealous of the three of them, finally — of Caroline, Philippe and their baby girl. He would have done anything, given up this life, to be where they were right now, with Constanze. Small pleasures, simple joys on public holidays. To be part of a family you had made for yourself.

For now, all he knew was that he'd be seeing her again in August. But this time, she'd be at Anton's for just two days. She had to travel to Greece after that, and then to India again. She was a free spirit, but he knew that one day she would want to settle down and live a quieter life. She told him once that family life represented everything she was running away from, that she could never understand the need for routine, and self-imposed limits. But she didn't like the communal life at Anton's farm either. She said that was worse – a commune was a kind of outsized, totally invasive family. Freedom was all that mattered to her. One day, when they were walking on the Larzac plateau, she had confided that she thought being a couple was the height of conformity. Alexandre had nodded in agreement, wanting to make the right impression and, above all, not reveal his true feelings.

Philippe had no inkling of the doubts and questions his remarks had stirred in his brother-in-law's mind. He carried on talking, standing proud on the footplate while the tractor barrelled along at thirty kilometres an hour.

'You know what Uncle Ho used to say when he was lost in the forests of North Tonkin?'

'Uncle who?'

'Ho Chi Minh!'

'No idea.'

'"Let he who has a gun use his gun, and he who has a knife use his knife." Well, I'd add "let he who has a tractor use his tractor!"'

Alexandre shot his brother-in-law a perplexed glance. Philippe seemed to see himself as some kind of sage, a figurehead of revolt, clinging on to the footplate as the tractor plummeted down the hill.

'You know what, I envy you a little.'

'Oh really? Why's that?'

'At least you know which battle you need to pick.'

Alexandre slowed the tractor and his brother-in-law stepped back down to earth. He asked him if he was taking the piss, just a little.

'Not at all, I promise. I envy you ... Your sister and I met when we were Student Union activists. We wanted to turn society on its head, have the world at our feet.'

'And?'

'And the opposite happened. Nowadays, it's not that I've lost the will to fight. I just don't know who or what – even the socialists are on the right now. But at least you know your enemy. You don't know how lucky you are, believe me. You should remobilise, like the old times, back when you were helping them plant their bombs ...'

Saturday, 3 August 1991

On meeting Constanze at the station in Albi, Alexandre felt something had changed, if only in the rather awkward way they embraced one another. For once, they were reuniting under the gaze of strangers, the summer holidaymakers who thronged the station. This was not like before. They stood for a moment holding one another close, saying nothing, not even looking at each other. Alexandre felt Constanze's arms tight around his body, clasping him without a word, as she might a person she was trying to console.

It had been near-impossible to agree on a place to meet. They'd spent two weeks studying every possible alternative. Constanze had to visit Paris first, but getting from the capital to Anton's farm was not as simple now as it had once been. There were fewer trains and Rodez, the nearest station, was a long way from Les Bertranges. Hardly anything stopped at Millau anymore either, and even then, the connection meant a two-and-a-half-hour wait, making it an eleven-hour journey overall. Finally, Constanze had taken an early flight from Orly to Toulouse, and then the train from Toulouse to Albi, where she arrived at noon. The world was opening up, but the foothills of the Massif Central were more and more difficult to reach. Rail services were dwindling, stations were closing, as if everything was conspiring to make it more and more difficult for Constanze to come and see him.

Rather than go straight to Saint-Affrique to join their little group, Constanze wanted to take a detour to Rougier de Camarès. She was determined to see the vivid landscape of red rock set amid green hills. People had told her it was a corner of France that looked more like Africa or India. Most of all, it was a pretext to talk to Alexandre alone. She was in no hurry to see Anton, Xabi, Adrien and all the others right away. Over the years, she had become gradually more detached from the group.

Alexandre was suspicious of her sudden need to be alone with him. He feared she had something to tell him. Perhaps she wanted to discuss their too-long-distance relationship. Perhaps she wanted it to end.

They set out along narrow country roads bathed in light. Rows of plane trees stretched their branches towards the sun, their shadows moving over the trunks. The Renault's windows were wound right down, and it was hard to hear one another speak as they bowled along. Constanze pressed EJECT on the cassette Alexandre had already put in the deck. *Cowboys and Angels* popped out. Alexandre was embarrassed to be caught listening to George Michael. He hadn't expected she would take it out. Had he known, he would have chosen Bowie or Nirvana. Constanze rested her hand on his knee and gave him a look that seemed to say everything was all right.

The famous expanse of blood-red rock was fifty kilometres to the north. They passed through a small village where Constanze spotted a restaurant in the square. She liked the name: Hôtel des Voyageurs. A slate board on the terrace announced ICI MENU VRP.

'What does "*menu VRP*" mean?'

'It means they do a special menu for *voyageurs représentants*, travelling sales representatives.'

'And the P?'

'I don't know, Constanze.'

'Don't you want to stop here? I'm hungry, aren't you?'

Each time she came back to these remote corners of the French countryside, Constanze was overwhelmed by how time seemed to stand still – the feeling was both alien and restful. On entering the auberge's dining room she looked around – as if in a museum – at the formica-topped tables, the faded tiles, the endlessly repeated wallpaper motif (a farm in a picturesque scrap of landscape, colourful against a white background). She ran her hand over the huge, white-painted, cast-iron radiator, and its cold mass felt good. The old-fashioned ambience soothed her. Immediately, she felt at home. Finally, they took a table out on the terrace, despite the heat. Without a second thought, they ordered the *menu du jour. Entrée, plat, dessert.*

Constanze marvelled at everything: the little square that lay before them; the old bridge over a river they could not see but which ran deep in the gorge below, so it seemed; the warm-coloured buildings with their stone roof tiles that merged with the surrounding hills. Alexandre had no desire to curb her enthusiasm, but he pictured the village in three months' time, with the terrace closed for the winter, and the swollen river raging around the piers of the bridge, and the fog rolling in on the back of the icy damp that turned the stone walls of the houses black. She asked him for news of the farm. He told her about the motorway they wanted to build over the valley, and how property values would plummet. He didn't want to darken the day, but it was the truth. To make up for it, he told her that this year the fragrance of the wild mint was lovelier than ever, there were flowers by the thousand. Walking in the big field on the hillside opposite the farm was like diving into a sea of fresh mint.

The waitress brought frogs' legs on a stainless-steel dish. She was a good-looking woman in her fifties, dressed in a navy skirt and a small white apron, like a professional serving in a big restaurant full of diners. Constanze asked her what VRP meant. The woman confided instead that there were fewer and fewer VRPs these days.

No one had time to stop here now. Or they travelled by plane.

'Same for the holidaymakers. People want to go further afield now, and I don't blame them. Club Med makes them feel like millionaires, everything laid on – the all-you-can-eat buffet, free water-skiing – while the *camping* at Camarès has two showers for the whole site.'

Constanze still had no idea what the P stood for. She watched as Alexandre filled their glasses, pouring the wine and the pitcher of cool water. She noticed once again how he sat straight in his chair, squaring himself up to his plate, resting his big frame on his left elbow. She felt a sudden need to say something she had never told him before, to look back at the moment they first met, the way people do when they revisit a life-changing event years later.

'You know, when we first met, I was going out with Anton.'

'Oh, really?'

Alexandre couldn't believe what he had just heard. He hadn't noticed anything at the time, though it was something he'd feared later, because Anton radiated charisma. He was the sort of guy people always listened to. A strong personality, a leader.

'Well, you know what, the funniest thing is, he was the one who told me about you. Just after you met in the kitchen. He said: "I've just met a really good guy, straightforward, clear." I remember those were his words, "straightforward, clear …", *ein klarer Kerl*. I was intrigued. And it was partly thanks to Anton that we were paired off to deliver the letters.'

Alexandre was convinced she had something to tell him now. This meeting was quite different from the others, that perfect, timeless bubble that had cocooned them for the past ten years. Here and now, everything seemed firmly anchored in the real world. Perhaps it was their age. They had both just turned thirty. And yet, for his part, he would have been happy to carry on just as they were, seeing one another very little, loving one another very much, and talking over the phone the rest of the time. But her tone was grave now. Listening to her, he acknowledged her bravery at least, her determination to clarify things, whereas he wanted nothing to disrupt their finely balanced relationship. The situation suited him just fine; he could carry on like this for another ten years.

'Alexandre, in eight years' time it'll be the year 2000. Have you thought about that?'

'What about it?'

'Well, time goes by so fast. I can't ask you to wait for me any longer. I don't want to hold you back. We're thirty now, do you understand? At thirty, most people have laid the foundations of their lives. It's the age when couples settle down, but look at us, we're still living like a pair of teenagers who get together once a year for their summer holiday then say goodbye and "see you next year" when August comes around. Doesn't that bother you?'

Alexandre could neither nod stupidly in agreement, nor deny her words. Perhaps she was right. She was holding him back in a way, but his life was on hold anyway. Being a farmer meant being confined to a single place, far from everything. But that didn't bother him one bit.

'Constanze, you're the one who told me once that the idea of living with someone terrified you. You said the very idea of life as a couple was depressing – true or false?'

'True. And I still think that now.'

'Well, then there's nothing to stop us carrying on exactly the way we are. We're anything but a couple, you and me, we don't live together. You should be happy with that!'

Constanze fell silent. She seemed uneasy, burdened with something. The waitress brought their grilled lamb steaks with runner beans and tomatoes. The air felt hotter still, even here on the terrace, in the shade.

'What if we just stay here, Alexandre?'

'Where?'

'Here. I don't want to see the others, not right now, not tonight. I want to spend the night here, get a room and sleep here tonight.'

'Like a couple of VRPs?'

'No. Like a couple.'

That morning, their father noticed one of the cows was lame. He knew the source of the problem, and it wasn't some ancient curse emanating from the stone slab buried deep in the earth beneath his field. Incensed, he fetched the tractor and, with Alexandre not there to tell him otherwise, he hitched up the rotary mower. He was determined now to mow the hectares of pasture that Crayssac had left to grow wild since getting rid of his goats. To Jean, the sea of tall grass and weeds was a badge of shame, a jungle teeming with creatures, not least vipers and foxes, almost certainly badgers, too, and entire generations of boar. A hellish bestiary of creatures issued constantly from out of the overgrown scrub. Over the past three years, he had asked Alexandre a hundred times to cut it back, but out of respect for Crayssac, Alexandre had left it untouched. He would suggest it in vague terms to the old Red when he went up to call on him, but Crayssac insisted everything should stay as it was. It was his right, after all, to let his land get overgrown, to leave his woodlands untended. And he had a lot of land, a whole expanse of high pasture from here to the cliffs above Cénevières. But today, Jean had found a beast with a bruised foot, and though it was said a viper could never kill a cow, he remembered a heifer that had been bitten on the lip when he was a boy. Louis hadn't sent for the vet that day – it would have taken hours for him to reach the farm – and the poor creature had died in agony. The image had stayed with Jean since childhood, like a guilty secret. It had been a terrible thing to see, the huge Limousin cow with her fine, red hide, unable to draw breath. Louis had shown him the marks left by the viper's fangs. That snake had killed a cow, for sure.

Jean rode fast over the fields, swearing that old Crayssac's land would harbour snakes and lizards no longer, not to mention the wasps' nests that multiplied there unchecked.

Sitting beside his radio set, the old countryman saw the big tractor down below, driving full tilt into his field. His first thought was that he should clean the glass: it was hard to see through the window that he kept shut against the hot air outside. But when he saw the machine moving back and forth across his field, and the huge mower cutting the undergrowth, he got up from his chair as quickly as he was able and prepared to go out, despite the hip that would no longer bear his weight. Opening his door, he was overwhelmed by the heat, then turned towards the chest underneath which he hid his gun. He weighed the decision in his mind – whether to take it and chase the old fool away – but then he thought of the gendarmes, and all the old trouble, and decided to leave it where it was. Angry and flustered, he dropped his stick, and incapable as he was of bending to pick it up, he kept on just like that, without his stick or his gun, marching out empty-handed to meet the tractor.

Jean saw the old hermit emerge from his shack and shuffle towards him. He felt a pang of pity. He hadn't realised old Crayssac had such difficulty walking, especially here in the overgrown field. The poor old fellow was the image of the eternal peasant, of people who lived off their land with no thought of anything beyond supplying their own needs. But he'd had enough of this blasted mess. He pressed down on the accelerator, fired up the Massey's full seventy horsepower and plunged into the heart of the scrub that tore and splintered on contact with the mower's blades. Turning at the far end of the field, he spotted the old man a couple of hundred metres to his left. He was hobbling more and more now, struggling with difficulty through the tall grass and brambles, but still headed straight for the tractor. Jean averted his gaze. He preferred not to talk or argue with him, nor to try and scare him away. Best just to finish cutting the field and be done with it. He glanced to his left one more time. But now Crayssac was nowhere to be seen. The old man must have stumbled in the *maquis*, trapped in a wilderness of his own making. Jean slowed down, softening the din of the engine. He felt slightly guilty now, and stared all around, watching for Crayssac to reappear. He stopped the tractor, disengaging the power take-off, but he must have driven the mower a bit too hard – the pedal stayed down, and the blades were still turning, like the engine. The whole damned thing kept on running. Jean stood up at the wheel to get a better view, and hollered at the top of his voice:

'Joseph! Hey! Joseph!'

The mower was making such a racket that Jean could not tell if the old man had answered or not. Rather than try to disengage the power take-off one more time, he cut the ignition. After the noise, the silence seemed even more profound to him than it actually was.

'Hey! Joseph …'

Jean got no answer. He began to walk through the wasp-infested undergrowth. The brambles caught at his legs. In this heat, he had dressed in shorts, and the thorns snagged his calves. Struggling through the tangled scrub hurt like hell. The old man must have collapsed somewhere in the thick of it, perhaps on contact with his tractor. The thought made Jean retch. Perhaps he'd killed Crayssac. He cursed his own hot temper. Dear God, it never did any good to get angry. Now he was the one who dreaded getting bitten by a snake, or a tick. With each new step, he had no idea what lay underfoot. This was hell indeed.

He found the old man sprawled in the grass behind a juniper

bush, his foot caught in a hole. He was lying on his back, inert, as if turned to stone, eyes wide open to the sky.

'Christ! You might have answered me!'

Jean's fear was so great that it turned again to anger. Old Crayssac was unable to move. It seemed his hip had given out for good.

'You've bust my leg, Fabrier!'

'Never! I never touched you!'

Jean bent down to try and help him up, but the old man was in tremendous pain, and a great dead weight to boot. Cautiously, gentle as a nurse, Jean placed a hand under his back. With the other, he caught hold of Crayssac's belt, then heaved him up like a dead bullock. At last, the old man struggled to his feet, and for Jean it was as if the whole of nature, the cicadas, the birds, the buzzard circling high overhead, all of it had sprung back to life. He could hear it all now, as if time had stood still for the past two minutes, and everything was starting over.

'You've bust my leg.'

Jean gave no reply. He wasn't a doctor. His sole aim right now was to get Crayssac indoors out of the sun, to place him back in his shack, like a figure in a rustic Nativity crib. Just that, no explanation. An end to it.

They made their way back slowly, without a word. Crayssac's face twisted in agony, but at length he began to speak in vehement tones despite his pain.

'Ah! You love parading about on that tractor, think you're the biggest and strongest, but when it comes to opening your mouth in the meetings, you take a back seat then, all right.'

'What on earth do you mean?'

Crayssac's arm was thrown around his saviour's neck. With a huge effort, he pressed his hand to Jean's cheek and forced his neighbour to look him in the eye.

'The motorway. You're scared to death about it, aren't you? But when it comes to standing up for yourself in front of the committee, it seems you've got nothing to say. You're like your father, and your grandfather before him, always looking out for yourselves and no one else. Looking out for your own is all very well, but when you're in trouble you're not up to the fight, and there's no one you can count on. Isn't that right?'

Jean stared at him, taken aback. He was pouring with sweat, horrified to see the old man so weak and infirm, to feel his weight. He had never so much as touched him before. They reached the house, but Crayssac was incapable of taking another step. Jean sat him down on the bench beside the door, in the shade. Stricken with anxiety, he went inside to fetch a glass of water.

'You've given me nothing but trouble, ever, with your blasted tractors, your poisoned poles, your aerials, your cars, and now you come over here trying to mow my wild pasture! What's the matter with you, are you bloody mad?'

Jean held out the glass.

'Water? Is that some fucking joke?'

'Joseph, you can't neglect your land like this, it's not right.'

'Let nature take its course.'

Jean inspected the old man's ankle. It had swollen to twice its usual size. The skin was taut, with a blueish tinge, marbled with streaks of grey. There was on old wound there, too. Some kind of ulcer, and pus.

'We need to get you to a doctor.'

'Never!'

'Joseph, you must.'

'You bastard! You want to put me in hospital – I see your plan – then you want them to stick me in the old people's home at Saint-Sauveur. That's it, you want me out of here.'

'But you can't stay here with your leg like that. It looks gangrenous – that's not just from today.'

Jean examined the leg in horror. It reminded him of the cow's shank after the snake bite; it had turned blue just like that.

'And so, what if I peg out right here? Don't tell me that would bother you in any way at all, you haven't spoken to me in forty fucking years.'

'I'm going to fetch the car.'

Joseph clutched Jean by the wrist. His grip was astonishingly tight, and painful.

'Now get this: there is no way on earth I'm leaving here in that car of yours, do you hear me? Not in anyone's car; no one will take me away from here, not even the doc or the ambulancemen.'

Jean said nothing.

'If I die, I die right here. Not in some home, can you understand that at least?'

The old man released his wrist. Jean stood for a moment in silence, then turned on his heel and set off again for the field, bare-legged through the brambles. Joseph watched as he walked away, certain he had taught the other man a lesson. Perhaps he'd leave now, just like that, turn around and take his tractor away, leave the mowing unfinished. He chuckled to see Jean suffer as he made his way through the undergrowth. Then he saw him down at the bottom of the field, rummaging about in the tractor, but not firing up the engine. And now he was coming back through the brambles, legs bleeding, holding a small white case.

'Know about first aid, do you, Fabrier?'

'I've treated more cows than you've milked goats.'

For once, Joseph said nothing in reply. Jean poured pure spirit onto a fat wad of cotton wool and rubbed it over the purple, scratched ankle. Joseph felt nothing, it seemed. He was silent now.

He let Jean go about his work, like any wounded deer, any damaged creature that relents and puts itself in the hands of its healer, without resentment, no longer even trying to flee. Jean pressed the wound gently and a dubious-looking liquid oozed out, too yellow for pus. He handled the ankle carefully, attentively, making sure to do the right thing, but anxious above all to identify the cause of the trouble. At the very least, he needed to know if the old man was running a fever. Already, he was figuring out a strategy to get him some antibiotics, but for that he'd have to go to the pharmacy in Villefranche or ask the vet what he thought when he came to check on the herd that Thursday. Yes, he would wait for the vet.

'I saw you that time, when you took the digger out. Did you know that, Fabrier?'

Jean wasn't listening. He was transfixed by the stench emanating from the leg, and the skin that came away in shreds each time he lifted the wad of cotton wool.

'Don't you remember? That old digger of yours.'

Something stirred in Jean's memory at these words. His old digger ... He hadn't touched it for years.

'Oh? When was that?'

'When you dug that trench? Ten years ago. Ten years exactly.'

At this, Jean stopped what he was doing, surprised to learn that the old man had seen him that day. That he'd been watching from some hiding place or other.

'Yes. And so?'

'And so you should have kept on digging, you'd have come right up to my place, my field, and if you'd kept on further still you'd have come out at the other end on the right, in the Vielmanay wood. My overgrown jungle, as your lot call it.'

Jean stared at Joseph. He couldn't believe what he was hearing. Joseph was talking about the sandstone slab he'd found two metres

284

underground, the conduit sealed with mortar, the vestiges he'd taken for some ancient tomb, or a dried-up spring.

'I never said anything to your boy because he was just a kid and couldn't be trusted. But I'm sure you won't say anything, you never say anything to anybody. I know you'll keep quiet about it.'

'About what?'

'See your machine down there?'

'The mower?'

'Well, the day something happens to me, you take that machine down to the bottom of the Vielmanay wood, and you go and dig out the undergrowth there, the acacias and brambles, and you'll see what I mean.'

'But what *do* you mean?'

'And you'll go and tell the mayor, and the mayor will tell the prefect.'

'Fine. But what?'

'Tell them why they'll never put a motorway through here.'

## Sunday, 4 August 1991

It was their first real breakfast alone together, sitting at a table after a real night in a real bedroom, on their own, as a couple. Almost without knowing, they were sampling what life together might be like. Except that this slice of everyday existence, the ordinary life that people live day after day, was for them something extraordinary. Spontaneously, they had both chosen to take breakfast downstairs rather than in their room. Instinctively, they agreed about everything. For Constanze, that mattered. There were no other guests in the dining room, or else they had all got up and left earlier.

'What kind of life do your dream about, Alexandre?'

'What do you mean?'

'All around me, I see more and more people who've stopped dreaming. The craziness of the seventies has all gone. We've gone from Pink Floyd to Enigma, Roxy Music to Nirvana ... All anyone dreams about today is a life just like everyone else's.'

'Well, not me. I couldn't live a life like everyone else – no way. That's not for me.'

'Because of the farm?'

'Yes. And because that's not what I want.'

'Do you really mean that?'

'Yes.'

There and then, Alexandre decided to speak the truth, not what

Constanze wanted to hear. He told her plainly that his only concern was the health of his livestock, and his parents, and his land. The things that preoccupied him and took up his time were the calculations for his compensatory allowances, and form-filling, and compliance with the ever-changing standards, not to mention the motorway that threatened to plough straight through the middle of his fields. The constant battle to protect his corner of paradise. He was permanently anxious, as if he was responsible for the entire world, not merely his own small patch.

'Taking care of dozens of hectares of hillside, fields and riverbanks is like taking care of your own private world.'

Constanze said nothing. She held her glass of freshly squeezed orange juice in both hands and sipped it like some precious nectar. She wanted to save the world, and he wanted to save his. Alexandre caught her staring at him over the rim of her glass, as if she was trying to read his thoughts. If she asked him what he was thinking, he had an answer ready: 'Nothing.'

He had only ever experienced this sort of interlude with Constanze. When he'd gone out with Aline, the girl from the insurance office, two years earlier, he'd never felt anything like this – for one thing, Aline never said much, and dreamed even less, not even of going out for a meal, just watching television night after night. Véronique, whom he had been seeing more or less since the winter, was the exact opposite. Véronique was talkative, open. She went out to the Metropolis or the Sherlock three times a week, chatted constantly to her girlfriends and colleagues, but always about stock turnover in the preserves section, or biscuits, and market share. At twenty-nine, she was a section head at Carrefour. She dreamed of self-building a detached house – her parents would give her the plot of land. Véronique was sexy, she could have any man she liked, and she planned to have a baby as soon as she turned thirty. All her girlfriends thought that was perfectly normal. The others, the ones who dropped out of their bowling nights one by one, were all at home looking after their newborn babies.

'What are you thinking about?'

'Us,' he lied.

They went back up to their room to collect Constanze's things and threw themselves onto the still-unmade bed. They could take their time, they had nothing planned for the rest of the day. The window was open, and the room was bathed in sunlight. The air was warm, and they wrapped their arms tightly around one another and rolled over, first onto his back, then hers. Constanze saw the box of condoms on the bedside table. It was unsightly, intrusive, though making love one more time would be one way to forestall the moment when she would say what she had to say, when she would tell this boy that she liked him more than anyone else, but that to carry on seeing one another like this and phoning each other was pointless. Or else they should do things differently and just call each other as friends, for news. Yes, as friends. But that was impossible. He would never understand, he would always delude himself that there was more. And this was all her fault. Last night, she had told herself they would not make love, not ever again, that she would talk to him, but in the end she had let herself be carried away on a tidal wave of the senses, by the summer, the warm night, the plain, simple bedroom in a hotel in the middle of nowhere, a space out of time.

'Alexandre, I think it's best if we don't see one another any more.'

'What?'

'I want – I need to travel for work, for a charity in India, and now that we've got the project up and running, I have to go out there, and live there for several years.'

'Well, there are planes, airports, I don't know ...'

'Didn't you tell me you were afraid of flying?'

'No. I just don't want to fly, ever.'

They lay on their backs, staring at the ceiling. Soothing small-town sounds floated through the open window, scraps of conversation on the café terrace, the hum of passing cars, the river running over the rocks in the gorge below, and above it all, the cries of swallows and starlings. Constanze spoke softly, Alexandre listened, and what she told him sounded just a little crazy. She talked about the downside of the green revolution, the evils inflicted by the Western world on developing countries under the guise of helping them to feed themselves. Now, the soil was saline and full of pesticides and fertilisers. We had taken those countries out of famine to save them from communism and now communism was finished, and we were doing nothing to help bring their soil back to life. Perhaps she thought she would rally Alexandre to her cause when she told him that eighty per cent of the population of sub-Saharan Africa lived in rural environments, as did almost three-quarters of the population in India. Her concerns were his, in a way. She wanted a return to the soil, too, but another soil, far away. She turned to look at him, pressed her face close to his.

'I want us to be absolutely honest now, you and me, because I haven't always told you the truth. There were times in Berlin when I desperately wanted to come and live with you. Each time we called I felt as if I'd had a moment away in the country, I felt soothed, and calm, as if I was living with you surrounded by nature. I really did dream about that.'

'So you see, you've given up dreaming too!'

'But no, I haven't. I want to be useful. I want my life to serve a purpose. I was never able to fight communism, and now I can't fight liberalism, the free market either. But I want to help the countries that are paying the price of our greed.'

Alexandre felt no urge to dissuade her, to try and make her stay with him instead of going off to save the world. It was impossible. He felt bypassed, left behind, but above all he knew that if he tried to make her stay, to hold her back one way or another, she would resist, and so he didn't dare. And in his eyes, she had always been far beyond his reach – too intelligent, too beautiful … He would never get the chance to meet another girl like her, to spend time with someone like her, be their friend, become their lover. He felt he was being sent back to where he'd come from, forever. He was returning to his natural state – a country bumpkin. He was losing her, and with her, his passport to a world quite different from his own. His mind reeled at the thought, but he wouldn't let it show. Perhaps you should never step outside your world after all. Perhaps it was best not to try. There was a whole tier of society to which he had no access whatsoever, and here, right in front of him, was the living proof.

'Shall we go, then?' he asked.

'Go where?'

'To Anton's of course. You're not planning to walk there, are you?'

'There must be a bus … or I'll hitch. Don't worry.'

Alexandre got to his feet, brisk and soldierly. He gathered up his wallet and watch, his small handful of things.

'I need to see Anton and Xabi, Constanze.'

'Oh really? Why?'

'I've got battles of my own to fight, you know. And I need some advice.'

'Alexandre, watch out for them, will you? I didn't like the way they used you, ten years ago. Things could have turned out very badly for you – don't forget it.'

Alexandre took her words as an affront, as if he'd been a mere puppet, as if he'd been duped and manipulated over the affair with the fertiliser. But what she said was true, and that made it hurt all the more.

'That's just it. Now I'm going to use them. They owe me that much.'

'For that business with the motorway? You're not going to ask them to show you how to use the fertiliser?'

'Why not? I've got a world to save too. My world.'

1996

Tuesday, 18 June 1996

Since his parents had moved to the small house down in the valley, Alexandre had the farm all to himself. In the morning, he didn't hesitate to turn the radio up as loud as he pleased, switching stations whenever an advert came on, or a topic he found boring. Voices. He needed voices; he switched smoothly from RTL to France Inter, and from Europe 1 to France Info. Every morning, the same line-up of familiar voices accompanied him from the bedroom to the bathroom, after which he would grasp the big Telefunken radio by the handle and take it downstairs to the kitchen, where he made his coffee. France Info suited him because they gave constant time checks. The jingles helped him wake up, then punctuated the bulletins of increasingly outlandish news.

This morning, it seemed India had declared itself ready to accept the cattle that Britain was preparing to slaughter by the million. The proof that mad cow disease could kill humans, too, had provoked widespread panic. Nothing frightened people more than a further reminder of their own mortality – and over 2 million beasts would now have to be slaughtered across the Channel. People in India saw the epidemic as a sign the gods were angry. They said they would take in the condemned cattle: at least they could live out their lives and die naturally, provided Britain paid for their transport, which required the chartering of hundreds of cargo vessels. Cambodia had offered to take in the accursed cows, too, and put them peacefully out to pasture. The cattle would not be eaten but allowed to roam free in as yet unstipulated parts of the country, as a way to trigger the landmines that still mutilated hundreds of farmers each year. Alexandre drank his bowl of scalding coffee and stared out of the window. Nothing astonished him in this world any more. He knew already that the madness would spread, that his entire herd would suffer, and that even though his cows ate nothing but grass, he would pay for the misdeeds of others.

Inevitably, the talk of India led his thoughts to Constanze. She'd called him a month ago, from Bengal. She had called him regularly over the five past years. But as a friend. On that point, too, she had won. Sometimes she wrote him a letter, with photographs of the fields managed by the NGO she worked for. In one of them, she stood in a white sari, beautiful and radiant. The picture of her had left him stricken. When she called, it was usually to ask his opinion – a farmer's opinion, though he knew nothing about land affected by salinity, any more than he knew how to cultivate rice or cassava. The telephone meant she was reachable, but unforgettable too, omnipresent yet utterly absent. Often, he thought of the things old Crayssac had said, as he lay dying: 'Nowadays, we open our doors to the world, so as not to know what's happening in our own homes.' He had been unable to move, due to his hip, and had refused surgery. One evening, when Alexandre had gone to see him and take him his food, he'd been astonished to hear Crayssac say he wanted to buy a television. Two days later, the old revolutionary had blown himself into the hereafter with his shotgun.

Now that the hedges were cut low, you could see from the yard Crayssac's land off in the distance. Alexandre noticed a small van parked in front of the old farm cottage. The goat breeder's tiny house was used as storage for the excavation work now. An important project, so it seemed, though there were seldom more than two people working on it, and no one at all most of the time.

Alexandre took the Renault and drove across to see them, turning right and taking the long way around by the lanes. The Vielmanay wood had been cleared of undergrowth now, the trees felled, and their roots dug out over an area covering almost two hectares. The space had been opened up so that the two archaeologists could get to work. Alexandre enjoyed watching them – the tall, gangly man and the girl in her army fatigues, both of them constantly on all fours. From a distance they looked like a couple of kids busily piecing together a giant jigsaw puzzle. They had been searching the soil for months, not with a mechanical digger but with trowels, paintbrushes, brooms, sometimes even a scalpel. Millimetre by millimetre, they had revealed the foundations and floors of structures that had stood there in some far-distant time. The whole thing seemed crazy to Alexandre, crazier and more outlandish even than India. The thought that right here, exactly two thousand years ago, there had been a vast villa with other buildings and houses all around, and farm buildings, and thermal springs, and water tanks fed by two aqueducts. It was quite mad.

'Still worried about your field?'

'No, no. Just came over to say hello.'

The girl and the man stood up to greet him.

'Guess what: we've found pips.'

'Pips from what?'

'Grapes!'

'Ah. And so?'

'And so? It means they were making wine here. There were vineyards all around. We wondered about it but now we've got proof ... There was probably even a cellar down there. It's an astonishing find.'

Alexandre was both curious and suspicious about their explanations. These two were telling him about a world more distant still than India, or Cambodia, or Africa, a lost world two thousand years from here, that was still revealing itself, right before his eyes, under his feet. His great worry was that they would start digging in his own fields, to uncover the buried aqueduct along its full length, in which case they would ruin all his crops. Fortunately, they already had too much to do over here. The project would take at least another two years. Alexandre followed them as they guided him around their squared-off zone, treading carefully as if on some priceless tapestry, proudly pointing out the remains of a water tank here, a bathing pool there, a bakery (he would never have thought people made bread two thousand years ago). And laid out all around the area under excavation, an infinite quantity of fragments – jugs, pitchers, amphorae dug up even from the deepest levels they had uncovered. The deeper they went, the more they found.

'But when you've dug everything up, who will it belong to?'

'The state!'

Alexandre left them to it and drove off in the Renault. Passing the abandoned farm cottage he thought of the old Red rebel. Even in death, Crayssac had taught him a valuable lesson. It was thanks to his wood that the motorway had been rerouted. When the old goat breeder died in the spring of 1992, Jean had kept his promise and set about clearing the impenetrable tangle of brambles, blowndown trees and creeper, a veritable jungle, untouched by human hand, and there they had found the strange ruins and stonework, hidden amid the greenery. The mayor had been alerted, and taken the information straight to the prefect. Any thought of planning permission was stopped dead in its tracks: even if the company charged with building the motorway had acquired the land, they would be responsible for the dig, and would have to pay the archaeologists. Worst of all, the excavations would halt the earthworks for the motorway for two years at least. And so the 'three-hundred-metre zone' had been pushed west, towards Cénevières, and though it was said the motorway would still go straight over the Rauze valley, it would pass at least two kilometres from Les Bertranges.

What Alexandre didn't know was how much noise a motorway two kilometres from his home would make. He had no way of telling whether the endless stream of cars and trucks crossing the viaduct would produce a hellish racket or a gentle background hum. The mayor had joked: 'You'll have your own weather forecasting system – in the evening, with a west wind, you'll hear the motorway, and with an east wind, you won't hear anything at all, so you'll know the weather's set fine.'

One thing was certain, at any rate: the old goat breeder with his wood and his two-thousand-year-old basement had managed to get the viaduct located further away, just as he had helped save the Larzac plateau fifteen years before. He had lived on the margins of the modern world, but with the power to change its course nonetheless.

Tuesday, 18 June 1996

For a while now, each time Alexandre went over to Véronique's place, he had felt overcome with tiredness. Since the scandal of mad cow disease, he had hardly slept. Almost the minute he arrived at her house, he would sink into an exhausted stupor on the huge white sofa, something he had never done before, and certainly not up at the farm. Perhaps because there was no sofa there.

Véronique kept the television on all the time. She would put it on as soon as she got in from work. She said it was to keep her little girl occupied, though the kid showed barely any interest in the screen, despite the endless succession of brightly coloured, frenetic cartoons – a blue octopus, yellow turtles, the BaBaLoos (a bizarre gang of nocturnal household items), or Goscinny's series about Iznogoud, the wily Grand Vizier of Baghdad. A constant racket of voices underscored by jumpy, enervating music, none of which distracted the child from her games on the rug, seemingly indifferent to it all. She played endlessly with the Hungry Hippos, a horrible, moulded plastic game that made a horrible noise.

Alexandre would have preferred Véronique and the little girl to come and live at the farm, but Véronique loved her detached house and garden on a new development in a fake village six kilometres from Cahors. She had risen through the ranks at Carrefour, and never finished before seven o'clock in the evening now. Alexandre could see that, for her, it would be a long drive up to Les Bertranges after work, and there was the little girl to collect, too, from her childminder or her father's place. Life was complicated enough.

They had followed the same unchanging routine since getting back together. Alexandre would sleep at hers twice a week and every other weekend. Often, Véronique needed help with something that had stopped working, and Alexandre would tell her he'd see to it the next time, before getting up from the sofa five minutes later to see if he could discover what was the matter. Véronique's garden was not large, but it was fitted with all manner of equipment that constantly needed fixing – the automatic watering system, the lighting around the lawn or the automatic electric shutters, not to mention the grass itself, the hedges and the flowers that had stopped growing. And to cap it all, the small swimming pool, with some critter forever drowned or drowning in the filter. Véronique's eight hundred square metres generated almost as much work as the farm.

Once the little girl was in bed, Véronique and Alexandre would sit at the table like a proper couple, but with the television turned down. The microwaved ready meals saved a huge amount of time. They were not madly in love, but they had found one another again in spite of everything. Véronique's partner had walked out three months after their baby daughter was born. Alexandre heard stories just like this all the time, the guy who leaves as soon as the kid is born. Whereas he had come back, though not to step into the father's shoes.

Véronique was full of energy, which suited Alexandre perfectly, especially as she was the only girlfriend who'd taken an interest in the farm, in his work. Often, she would ask him to tell her about it. But she had very fixed ideas. Since becoming a section head she had developed a confident businesswoman's manner and she liked nothing better than to tell Alexandre what he should do, as if her professional success made her some sort of expert in everything.

One thing was certain: her job gave her real expertise in buying, selling and negotiating. Less so, on the subject of cattle. But

301

according to her, a livestock farm should be run like a store, so that when Alexandre despaired over the crisis of mad cow disease, which had sent prices plummeting and destroyed consumer confidence, she saw it as an opportunity to bounce back. She even told Alexandre it was a blessing in disguise— at least now people would pay more attention to what they were buying, because they had learned the difference between cattle reared for beef, and dairy cows.

'Believe me, people really have realised that dairy cows slaughtered for meat were the problem, not cows kept for milking. When the market revives, you'll need to adapt, build up the herd, that's obvious. You're in a far better position when you can offer a hundred head of cattle instead of just one.'

As head of fresh produce at Carrefour, she had insider information about the future centralised purchasing system. It would be huge. She even told him a large group was planning to take over the abattoir in Murat and that the meat would be processed at the same plant. Sodavia and Codéviandes were merging to form a huge group that would cover the whole of France, under the name Coopavia.

'This is a boon for you, Alexandre. In five years' time you'll be just off the motorway, you'll have no trouble securing a bank loan, and if you go up to two hundred head of cattle, you'll be the king of the hill, believe me!'

Alexandre listened. He was sure she was right, but he was reluctant to launch into something so big, to conform to that other world. Still, he knew he would have to, sooner or later. Transport was the key to the market nowadays: roads, ports, airports, the whole world was one big network.

In bed, Alexandre would lie awake, his mind buzzing with all the changes he would have to take on board. They made love only at the weekend, and even then only when the little girl was away.

Véronique said her presence in the next room bothered her. Each time Alexandre moved closer, to put his arms around her under the sheets, careful not to make any noise, the kid would wake up and start crying. Véronique felt she was the one at fault.

Unable to sleep, Alexandre thought back over everything they had said that evening. Perhaps she was right after all. His sisters all said the same, too: expand the herd and feed them on soya meal, as well as grass. There was plenty of room for two hundred cows up at the farm, provided they built modern, well-ventilated sheds. Two buildings, each eighty metres long, and another for forty incoming store cattle. He saw his sisters only rarely, but he knew what they were thinking – they never stopped telling their parents that they should make use of the motorway that would soon be coming their way, and the closer the better in truth. It was an opportunity he should seize. It would make trading and deliveries so much easier … Alexandre suspected his sisters were pushing him to invest because they knew that under the arrangements of their parents' living will, they would be compensated once the work was finished. And all three of them needed the money.

His sisters always got their way. Even over Constanze, in the end. Caroline and Agathe had opened his eyes: he had been blind to carry on waiting, hoping for anything at all from his long-distance German girlfriend. She had been stringing him along all the time, or she would never have gone to live on the other side of the world. He saw that now, thanks to them. Often in life, the things that you refuse to see are the most glaringly obvious.

As if to honour the memory of old Crayssac, and his Uncle Pierrot, Alexandre had put goldfish back in the water troughs – the old ones down on the lower ground, and the tanks up on the hillside. The fish ensured that they were kept free of algae and mosquito larvae, but you had to keep an eye on the water, to make sure it was clean, and the levels were maintained, so that the cows didn't swallow the fish. Sometimes, Alexandre watched his animals as they drank. They weren't bothered by the goldfish wriggling about down there, though the fish always seemed agitated when the cows were drinking.

On the days when his sisters came, like this Bastille Day, Alexandre would clean the bottom of all the tanks and troughs. He took his time over it, as a way to spend as little time as possible up at the farmhouse with the three of them.

It was unusual for them all to be at Les Bertranges together. The last time the siblings had gathered at their childhood home was when Louis had died three years earlier. Now that their parents were living in the little house down in the valley, the farm was Alexandre's private world. The buildings and equipment had never been new, but now they looked worn out and old fashioned. When their parents moved out, it was as if the house had suddenly aged. The aniseed-green tiles in the bathroom looked sicklier than ever, and the yellow light bulbs and undusted lampshades certainly didn't help. The kitchen was no longer in use, and it showed. The gas cooker sputtered and gasped, and the cupboard doors were ill-fitting or askew.

Alexandre went up to the farmhouse towards seven o'clock in the evening. The three sisters had brought out the kitchen table and chairs, behaving as if they still owned the place. But Alexandre said nothing. He hated to spoil things, and really didn't care if the furniture was taken out of doors. All that really mattered to him was the Telefunken, which they had taken outside too, letting the children play with it unchecked. Worse still, the three kids kept putting on that blasted 'Macarena' and doing the dance. This had to be the hundredth time in the last two days that they had wound the cassette back and played it again. They listened to nothing else. The sound of the song, each time he came home, was torture to Alexandre's ears. It was as if the three kids had seized power. Hearing the grim, mechanical rumba pounding out through the speakers of his old friend, the radio-cassette player, made it somehow even worse.

Rather than scold the children, Alexandre suggested he fetch their parents and grandmother from the little house down below. Caroline had insisted on preparing a big farmhouse dinner so that everyone could get together at Les Bertranges, like the old days. She and Vanessa had been baking pies all afternoon – potato pie, cheese pie, courgette pie, all manner of peculiar things that smelled better, according to them, than a leg of lamb roasting in the oven. Alexandre told his parents about the meal when he arrived at the house.

'What are they making, did you say?'

'Five pies!'

'But we can't just eat desserts.'

'No, Mamie, I told you, courgette pies …'

'Courgettes for dessert? Really, there's something wrong with those girls.'

Lucienne was becoming confused and forgetful. Since the death of her husband, Angèle and Jean had become the fixed points of her world, guiding her from the moment she woke to the moment she went to bed. While he waited for them to get ready, Alexandre went outside to take a look at the vegetables. His parents could still cope with the kitchen garden, but at the turn of the millennium, they would both be seventy, and he felt sure they would be calling on him to help them soon enough after that. Or perhaps they would need to hire someone. The problem with producing crops was bending down to tend them, which got harder and harder with age. The beans and salad leaves, the onions and strawberries, the parsley – all that produce, sold by the gram, took its toll on the body. Discreetly, he kept an eye on his parents, watching how they sat down or got to their feet, looking for signs of lower back pain, the pain he himself felt more and more often, especially in winter. He felt guilty, to think that already, at thirty-five, he suffered from aches and pains occasionally. He stared at the strawberries, and again he remembered the vision of Adrien and Anton's plot. At least here there were no slugs, and the leaves were still whole.

'Shall we go?'

He turned and saw the three of them standing in front of their small detached house, so square and neat. It was odd, but each time his parents dressed up, it made them look suddenly much older. His father in a suit jacket, his mother in a blouse and necklace; they looked more like grandparents than parents. Which is what they were.

Sunday, 14 July 1996

That evening, Alexandre was even more of a spectator at the family dinner table than usual. Back when they were kids, he would watch the nightly show put on by his three sisters, but now the cast extended to Caroline's two girls and Vanessa's boy. There was so much noise they hadn't even bothered to turn on the TV. The Bastille Day dinner was like Christmas all over again. Agathe arrived late, as always, and speedily updated everyone on Greg, her associate, who had been disqualified as a director and wanted her to take over their business, which meant she would be in the firing line if any new difficulties arose. Meanwhile, they had been forced to sell their first boutique, and things were no better with the second one: Benetton wanted to cancel their franchise. Agathe was at pains to make it clear that none of this was her fault – the Italian giant was moving out of fashion and investing in motorway companies, toll bridges and airports. As further justification for their setbacks, she added that the fashion sector was suffering the fallout from the latest marketing fad – 'fast fashion'. People nowadays wanted to buy lots of clothes, very cheaply, so that their wardrobes were constantly changing. This trend had left her on the starting blocks, too. First Zara, then Naf, Kookaï and all the rest: the big labels were outsourcing their manufacturing; soon everything would be made in Asia. So that now, in Rodez and Villefranche alike, she felt like a lost soul in the centre of town, crowded out by fake 'luxury' boutiques with their clever merchandising and fancy cardboard bags, while on the outskirts La Halle aux Vêtements and all the hypermarkets sold denim dresses for under twenty francs. She was under attack from both sides. Vanessa took up the refrain. Things were no better for her: the money had run out in advertising. Contracts were melting away, no one would hire an art photographer to take pack shots of sliced ham now, advertisers weren't doing costly campaigns like the old days, and, looking ahead, digital technology would make things harder still. Anyone would be able to create an authentic farmhouse backdrop on their computer for next to nothing …

Alexandre sat and listened. His family was like a world unto itself, he thought. Still, the bad news fuelled their conversations, which were livelier than ever. They actually seemed to relish all the trouble and conflict. In the midst of it all, he watched his nephew Victor, small and silent – the boy Vanessa had had with an ad executive, 'one of the suits', as she put it, as if the child was fatherless, not even born of man, but of a suit. Vanessa had never lived with the guy and had refused so much as a centime of his money, of course, though she had none of her own, and if business didn't pick up soon, she would be forced to sell her studio, the tool of her trade, the way she made her living. And in Paris, the cost of living was exorbitant.

Now that they saw one another just twice a year, the three sisters had a huge amount to tell. Alexandre listened to everything they said. His sisters were unafraid to share even the most personal details, as if their bank statements or blood test results lay spread out over the table. Caroline and her husband Philippe offered some reassurance to their parents at least. The other two girls had ignored common sense and messed up their lives. Angèle and their father were horrified by what they heard. Privately they told themselves that everything would have been so much simpler if they had stayed out here rather than rushing off to the city.

The meal of quiches, pies and salad was at an end, and just like last year, the kids were complaining that there were no fireworks. Again, just like last year, Alexandre took it on the chin while his sisters piled on the guilt.

'Absolutely. Tonton Alex could have bought some rockets ...'

'*Oui!* Tonton! Rockets! Rockets!'

'Your Tonton's no fun at all, is he?'

Alexandre bit his tongue, though he'd had enough of his sisters' jibes, the implied criticism that he never paid enough attention to his nephew and nieces, never made enough of an effort when they were around.

'*Allez, Tonton!* A firework display! Fireworks!'

Alexandre silenced them by rising from the table and addressing them all in his severest tones: 'No! Never play with fireworks. Fireworks aren't toys, they're explosives, and they're dangerous.'

He felt his three sisters' eyes on him as they turned to stare. *Explosives*. He was the one who had spoken the word, the absolute taboo that only the four of them understood. For now, at least.

Finally, they all went down to Cénevières in four cars, for the torchlit procession. Le Paradou had closed two years before, and only a handful of people still lived in the village. The torchlit procession was a sorry sight compared to what it had once been, twenty years ago. Back then, there had been fifty children or more. It had been fun, really, to see all the little flaming torches winding through the village at sunset. There was a purpose to these things when a lot of people were involved. But now, there were just eight in the whole procession, and they didn't seem to be enjoying themselves much at all.

## Monday, 15 July 1996

Next morning, the jibes were sharper still. The sisters laid into Alexandre at breakfast, telling him he might have made an effort. If cash was the issue, they would advance him the money next time, but he really might have thought to buy a dozen rockets, even some flares, silver comets, golden rain, one of those fountains that crackles, with blue, white and red sparks. Some fun for the children. Because they always used to have fireworks for the *fête nationale*. Alexandre put up with their comments, saying nothing. His sisters felt distant, somehow disembodied, and listening to them he thought of how the purple tinge came from saltpetre. Potassium nitrate produced violet-coloured sparks when it exploded, whereas the blue came from copper sulphate, which was a powerful pesticide, too. Barium chloride gave those beautiful green comet tails, and the yellow came from sodium nitrate, the stuff they put in pork and ham to give it that fresh, pink colour.

One good thing – this year Bastille Day fell on a Sunday. There was no public holiday midweek, no 'bridge' to or from the weekend, when people sneaked the days off in between. His sisters wouldn't stay around for long, and his parents had managed to get an appointment with the solicitor for today, July the fifteenth, to read through the proposition they had been finalising for months. Caroline and Vanessa had been manoeuvring behind the scenes, by telephone, and Agathe had come up several times from Rodez, officially unbeknownst to Alexandre, though he saw everything

310

from his vantage point up at the farm. Agathe had been visiting their parents regularly for the past two years. Even without spying, his sister's red Austin Mini was easily spotted when she parked in front of the little house down below. He knew she was paving the way.

The solicitor sat alone in the middle of one side of the big meeting-room table, with a huge quantity of paperwork spread out all around him. The Fabriers, all six of them, sat facing him on the other side. Alexandre observed the small man sitting bolt upright, so straight and tall in his chair that he looked bigger once he had sat down. His prestige was enhanced by their parents, who addressed him constantly as *maître*. Caroline and Agathe called him Monsieur Loupiac, but their parents used his official title at every possible opportunity. Philippe had stayed up at the farm, keeping an eye on their grandmother and the children.

Maître Loupiac acted in an exemplary fashion. He spoke clearly, with the air of a doctor, or a curate – a doctor examining them all, or a curate attentive to their needs and sensitivities, the way men of the Church can be when planning a family funeral. The meeting had that ceremonial feel to it, though it was unclear exactly who was burying whom, or what. The farm, their parents, or Alexandre? Or his sisters? The whole procedure was their doing, at any rate. They were the ones who had wanted to set everything in order while their parents were still alive. And the family had opted for a *donation-partage*: their parents would sell the farm to Alexandre and use the money to pay the three girls their share straight away. Provided Alexandre saddled himself with a sizeable debt.

Until now, the farm had remained the property of his parents. They had rented the business to their son. As their tenant farmer, he had paid them a sum of money each month. Clear and simple. But his parents were getting older, and after much scheming and discussion on his sisters' part, they were convinced that they should plan ahead, that everything should be in order before the turn of the millennium. Above all, Agathe and Vanessa would no longer have to wait for their money.

'Permit me to tell you something in confidence …'

'Of course, *maître*!'

'Well then, let me tell you this one thing, and believe me, it's not something I say often: that farm of yours is magnificent, really, a superb property, with good soil, and all of a piece, with a splendid view, sizeable buildings, though they need to be brought up to the current specifications – you know that as well as I – and there's no getting away from the fact that at your age, the banks will be reluctant to lend. Whereas for your son, it'll be an entirely different matter, in fact quite the contrary, they will welcome him with open arms … With him as the owner, well, it's very much for the best.'

'Absolutely.'

Maître Loupiac always took the sisters' line. Anyone would think he was acting for them alone. Every five minutes, he was careful to point out that their decision made perfect sense for the future, in the name of progress. Once Alexandre had secured his loan, he would pay each of his sisters their share – almost a hundred thousand francs apiece. But to get to that stage, to obtain the loan, he would have to secure approval for his plans. He would need to make a really good, solid case, and that would take time.

Alexandre went along with everything. He had no choice in the matter. The barns were leaking, the fences were collapsing and the cowsheds no longer met the current regulations. Listening to them all trot out the same comments over and over brought him out in a cold sweat. He would never show his doubts, frankly how scared he felt at the idea of committing himself to investment on such a huge scale. If he did, they would all decide he wasn't up to the task, that he lacked the strength to shoulder such a burden. And there was someone else pushing him constantly, too, besides all of them: Véronique. She had a perfect grasp of emerging markets, knew all the supply chains, and the grants he could access under the CAP. She knew that with a bigger herd he could unlock much bigger subsidies and grants. The more animals he kept, the more cash he would get.

'Yes indeed, Monsieur Fabrier ... Monsieur Fabrier *fils*. What do you say to that?'

'I'm sorry ... To what?'

'To extending your tenancy until the end of 1999 – why not set 1 January 2000 as our target date for the handover. A powerful symbol, don't you agree?'

'Yes, very good, *maître*, let's do that.'

'There's absolutely no need to hurry. You'll need a thoroughly prepared business plan. But that motorway is heaven-sent – you'll have no difficulty attracting a large retail partner; they'll sign you up with their eyes closed.'

'But the motorway won't be ready for another five years.'

'Exactly. The year 2000, as I said! Mark my words, the new millennium will change everything. I can't predict what will happen in the wider world, but I can tell you this: the year 2000 will see the winds of change blowing through Les Bertranges!'

## Wednesday, 6 November 1996

That morning, France Info announced that Bill Clinton had been re-elected president of the United States, and that he would be going out for his morning jog as usual. At the same moment, Boris Yeltsin was back in hospital for a five-way heart bypass. Alexandre was late, but he took the time to make himself a proper coffee. The main thing he registered from the newsflash was that Bill Clinton had just turned fifty, and Boris Yeltsin was sixty-five. The details had struck him. The questionnaires the bank had asked him to complete recently had left him preoccupied with the question of age, unsure whether thirty-five was still young or not. Perhaps he was in between. By launching into a plan he was to pay for over the next fifteen years, he was tying himself down, hands and feet, until he turned fifty. Not merely attached to the land that lay all around him, but literally bound to it, body and soul.

Véronique had said she would be at the farm by eighty thirty in the morning, with the guy from Coopavia. Alexandre had been unable to change the date of the meeting; he would have to march them briskly around the property. Véronique would take it badly, no doubt. She'd think it strange that he was rushing them through the visit, but he had no choice. If he was to get to the airport by half past eleven, he would have to leave here by ten at the latest. Constanze had told him only yesterday that she would be in Toulouse today. It had all been decided in a panic. She had booked the first available flight, unsure what exactly had happened to her father. Yesterday, when he heard the news, Alexandre hadn't dared postpone this morning's meeting. Véronique had gone to so much trouble, fitting it into her schedule so that the chairman of Coopavia could make it in person. And to be here by eight thirty, she would have skipped breakfast, not to mention the long drive and arriving late for all her morning meetings at Carrefour.

At eight thirty-five, Alexandre saw her little red Clio at the top of the lane, followed by a big BMW 4×4. A rich man's car. The Coopavia guy was eager to flaunt his money. Alexandre walked out to meet them and open Véronique's door for her. He was surprised when she kissed him full on the mouth in front of the other guy. He didn't need to know they were going out.

Alexandre offered them both coffee, which they drank quickly in the dining room, before a tour of the buildings. He saw no point in viewing the fields, but the Coopavia guy wanted to see the meadows along the hillside, top and bottom. They all climbed into the big 4×4. The interior was spotless, and the guy had no walking boots. He gasped at the extent of the property – the fields were vast and well laid out, sheltered by mature hedges, but above all, the pasture was astonishingly rich for November. The grass was still tall in places. Several times, Véronique asked Alexandre if everything was all right. Yes, he told her, though all he wanted to do was race off to Toulouse. But he had to continue the tour.

When the guy had seen enough, he suggested they go back to the farmhouse so that he could show them his plans. He'd brought plans for the buildings, the feed-distribution system, the straw bedding, the different stabling models, the quarantine sheds – with individually isolated stalls, but wide, which was important – all conforming to the very latest industry standards. There was no way Alexandre could refuse, and so they went back to the farm, where the guy produced fat rolls of paper from a briefcase, spreading them out over the dining-room table. Alexandre felt

315

obliged to make them some more coffee. The guy recommended two new buildings, one eighty metres long, for the weanling calves, and another for the cull cows and milkers – why not? Anything was possible. According to him, they had the wherewithal to create a superb fattening site at Les Bertranges.

'A fattening site?'

'Yes, that's it. With the space you've got here, not to mention the motorway, you're looking at two hundred head of cattle, easily, perhaps even three hundred, no problem. You need to think big …'

Véronique agreed with the head of Coopavia on every point, nodding enthusiastically. The guy was accustomed to working with hypermarkets, and in any case she worked with him already. Alexandre listened to the two of them producing figures that made his head spin. He began taking notes, so as not to miss anything. For a start, if he signed with Coopavia, they would commit to take seventy-five per cent of his production, with a guaranteed minimum price, plus all the grants for fattening the young beef cattle, and since every cloud has a silver lining (as they say), mad cow disease meant there would soon be a *label rouge* certificate for the traceability of premium-quality beef. As for the bull calves, Coopavia would take care of them too. The French ate cow meat as a rule, but Coopavia would pay a good price to transport the bullocks to Italy. The motorway would cut hours off the journey, so the animals would arrive in far better condition, and lose less weight on the road.

Alexandre's attention was focused on one thing only – the time. The issues they were discussing were crucial, huge; they would govern life at the farm for the next thirty years, but it was already ten past ten and there was no way he could tell Véronique that he had to rush off to Toulouse to meet an ex at the airport. He was incapable of lying to her anyway. He was a terrible liar: he always got muddled and gave himself away. He let nothing show, but he found this whole business profoundly depressing. The big shot with his plans for buildings as tall as an aircraft hangar, his colourful brochures showing animals parked like rows of cars, fine-looking bullocks, superb Charolais with labels punched into their ears but no names. That was the worst of it – rearing the animals over such a short space of time, three or nine months, fattening up the store cattle, with no time even to choose a name for them. No more Caramels, or Blondies, or Trompettes, or Venuses ... The thought appalled him, but he had no choice, and he would get used to it. He said yes to everything and hoped to get the meeting over with fast. The guy hadn't drawn up a draft contract yet, or he would have signed it there and then, so that everything was settled and he could get away to Toulouse.

Finally, it was Véronique who said she would have to go, there was a meeting of the section heads scheduled for ten thirty and she was late. Alexandre breathed a sigh of relief. Everything speeded up after that. They left their coffee unfinished, and the guy forgot his plans and his brochure on the dining-room table – or else he left them there on purpose. Alexandre snatched the keys to the Citroën CX. He had thought he would take the Renault 4L at first, for old times' sake, for the pleasure of sitting in it again with Constanze, stirring up old memories, old feelings. But the Citroën was faster and he was in a hurry.

The guy said he would call next week – they had plenty of time, the motorway wasn't finished yet, and the Coopavia plant would be ready in 1999. Ideally, everything would be up and running for the year 2000, with a brand-new operation.

'Sound good?'

'Sounds good.'

Wednesday, 6 November 1996

Past Caussade, the traffic on the N20 was heavy, with roadworks every ten kilometres. Alexandre had never really noticed all the building going on around Caussade, and then Montauban, all these out-of-town business zones with their endless succession of hypermarkets, sports stores, DIY and garden centres, and vast furniture showrooms, and every five hundred metres they put in a roundabout to channel the traffic generated by all these car parks and new roads. The urban environment was becoming unrecognisable. Craziest of all, the land they were paving over, the land on the outskirts of the towns and cities, was the best land there is – flood plains, valley bottoms. They were pouring concrete onto prime agricultural land to sprout more hypermarkets.

It was twenty-one minutes past eleven when Alexandre reached Blagnac Airport. Wasting no time, he parked in a reserved space then raced into the terminal and stared at the arrivals board. Naïvely, he had assumed the flight was direct from Delhi, when obviously Constanze had changed planes in Paris, Brussels or Munich, though he had no idea which. He felt lost amid all these flights *en provenance de*, but above all he had no way of contacting her, and it was by sheer chance that he saw her from behind, right at the far end of the terminal, talking into a telephone in the row of cubicles, with a small suitcase at her feet. She hung up just as he reached her. Turning, she saw him, heaved a huge sigh of relief, and wrapped her arms tightly around him.

They had seated themselves at a brasserie table on Place du Capitole. Constanze wanted to sit down to eat a piece of meat and above all some chips. She would not be allowed to see her father until tomorrow, when he would be out of intensive care, but she was relieved that he was in a French hospital. To Alexandre, she seemed utterly at a loss – the only cash she had was rupees and a few dollars, not having had time to stop at the bureau de change, and she couldn't find her old French bank card. Besides which, she had no keys to the small apartment her father kept in town, and no way of getting hold of any. She would sleep at a hotel tonight because she had no desire to try contacting old acquaintances, to have to explain to them why she was here; she just wanted to see her father, reassure herself that he was all right, and get back to Delhi, where she had abandoned the rest of the team at work. She felt bad – she had barely called her father in two years, or her mother. Bad, and guilty.

'But what did he have done anyway?'

'A five-way heart bypass. His secretary called me.'

Alexandre thought of the newsflash on France Info that morning, the re-elected jogger, and Yeltsin undergoing surgery. Constanze said it was a stroke of luck that it had happened during a trip to France. This was the best country in the world for healthcare, she reckoned. Alexandre had never seen her eat with such an appetite: she devoured her plate of chips, savouring each one as if it was a rare delicacy, then called the waiter over to order some more. After hours aboard the plane, and the anxiety of her father's emergency operation, she was becoming her old self little by little. Alexandre couldn't take his eyes off her. Something about her had changed. She would probably think exactly the same thing, looking at him, except that she wasn't looking at him; she avoided his gaze constantly, as if she dreaded giving him ideas, in case he started believing in them again.

'Thank you, anyway. Thank you for coming to get me, for taking care of me ... Feeding me.'

'The least I can do.'

She was strong, he could see that. She had jumped on a plane, knowing her father's life hung in the balance, and flown halfway around the world to be at his bedside, with no money on her, and no idea where she was going to sleep, and in spite of all this, she sat straight up in front of him, relatively unperturbed, when anyone else would have slumped in defeat, exhausted, jet-lagged and probably irritable and snappy too.

'Alexandre, this really isn't the best time to tell you but ... Well, I wasn't sure at first, and then I didn't dare tell you – that's why I haven't called since the summer – but I've known for certain for a month now ...'

'Oh really? What?'

'I'm pregnant.'

She spoke the words joylessly, her expression dull, as if apologising for the fact. Alexandre was astounded. Quite simply, it had never occurred to him that she might fall pregnant. In a vague, unformed way, he had always secretly believed that Constanze would come back to Toulouse one day, perhaps even to Les Bertranges. He had nurtured the illusion, though it was impossible in reality. At least now everything was clear. Especially when she began to tell him a little about the father, a German guy she worked with at the charity. She had met him out there, in Delhi. He was five years older than her. And then a second blow struck Alexandre right in the gut, even harder than the first.

'He's an engineer,' she said innocently. 'An agronomist.'

Alexandre felt more keenly than ever that he was a mere farmer. He bore no comparison to a guy like that.

Constanze lightened the atmosphere, changed the subject. She told him about her work, her charity's mission to 'help countries in the developing world'. Alexandre let nothing show, but his world was collapsing around him. The brasserie, the Capitole, the whole of Toulouse had been flattened by a great, silent tremor. He stared out of the windows, at the women walking past on the huge square. There were always plenty of women in Toulouse, but he saw only her ... How had he managed to persuade himself over the past fifteen years that they were made for each other? He had never felt so intimate with anyone else, so close. He had never loved anyone else. No other relationship had felt so complete, so symbiotic, as with the girl sitting there in front of him. Constanze eclipsed all the others, cast them all into the shade. And here she was, doing just that, with her back to the window, filling his field of vision.

'I'm sorry, but I have to ask – do you think you'll make your life out there?'

'I don't know, Alexandre. As a German citizen, it's like I owe them a debt. I feel like I went out there to right all the wrongs done to them by Hoechst and the other big chemical groups. They've been poisoning everyone in India with endosulfan for twenty years, drowning them in pesticide ... Three-quarters of the population are rural farmers, but pesticides have destroyed the soil, and the government says nothing. Quite the opposite, they push small-time farmers to use more and more chemicals – it's never-ending. At first I thought I'd be righting the wrongs of the green revolution, all that supposedly generous help we gave them for years, but there's no way out of it in reality ...'

It wounded Alexandre to the core to see her there, devoting herself to another person, another place, to the farmland of India, a country so far distant it seemed almost unreal. He felt a sudden horrible stab of jealousy. And so, dreading she might say something, anything, about her German boyfriend, he kept her talking about Indian agriculture, what they sowed, and what grew there. From now on, she would be nothing more than a distant colleague, a grower like him, but of a rather different kind. She said people in India were vegetarian because they were poor, but very soon, around 2020, two-thirds of the planet's middle classes would be in India or Asia, and when that day came, they would move away from a diet of cereals, to one based on sugar, oil and animal protein.

'It's completely crazy, believe me. The planet is doomed. Everywhere will be poisoned with organochlorides. That's why it does me good to call you now and then – you don't realise it, but you're living in a kind of Eden up there, your own paradise on earth.'

Alexandre thought of that morning's meeting, of Véronique in her heels and two-piece suit, and the big shot with no walking boots, both of them hardly daring to step out of the BMW and walk in the high pastures. He thought of the plans for the vast new buildings, the brochure, and the motorway that would be up and running in five years' time. His corner of nature.

'Does the wild mint still flower?'

'Yes. Well, not now, in November, but in the summer it does. There are even more flowers, if anything.'

'You should get into old varieties, you know?'

'Old what?'

'You told me you harvested saffron before, and sage, and that you had lots of wild berries and red fruit. Well, all those medicinal, aromatic plants are coming back into fashion; people are turning back to those old varieties, all the berries you showed me, and the lime blossom, the walnuts. That's the way you should go – the past is the future.'

And there and then, Alexandre had to tell her – about his sisters, how he must pay them their share, and the two huge sheds he would have to build, the unnaturally large herd, all the investment that would be needed for the future so they could start afresh in the year 2000, make a clean break from the old world, walk in the path of progress. Constanze said nothing.

They emerged from the brasserie, uncertain where to go. Alexandre took a couple of hundred-franc notes from a cash machine. Anxious to take her somewhere safe, he suggested they go to the hotel across the street. He would see her into the foyer, no further, and pay for her room. Constanze said that was a good idea, she would nap for an hour or two, just to come back down to earth and recover, and tonight she would go to bed early, skip supper, so that she was on top form tomorrow. Alexandre had to get back up to the farm anyhow, to bring the cows in. There were two Salers ready to calve. They were a breed that could manage perfectly well on their own, but with all the rain they'd had lately, it would be just his luck for them to drop straight into a puddle. Sometimes nature has a way of ruining everything all by herself.

Constanze had a return ticket for the day after tomorrow. She told Alexandre she would call him, not this evening but tomorrow. It would depend on how her father seemed. Already, he knew she would not.

Friday, 24 December 1999

'They'll get a show for their money ...'

Nervously, Alexandre repeated the phrase irritably to himself as he checked the cases of mortars. For years his sisters and their kids had been pestering him for a firework display. Well, now he'd give them one, the best show ever, with a hundred and twenty 75mm mortars, blowing everything sky-high with them. One hell of a firework display.

Alexandre stowed everything away in the barn. He locked the door and added a padlock, too, then went indoors to change before going down to his parents' house, though he had no desire to sit through the usual Christmas Eve dinner, surrounded by all the family. Making the so-called festivities last till midnight would be torture. Family meals were rare now, and they always took place at the little house in the valley, with his sisters and their four children. They would be the centre of attention as usual; the whole family revolved around them. Tonight, Alexandre had forewarned them, he wouldn't be putting any presents under the tree, but he had promised a fantastic firework display to see in the year 2000. An amazing pyrotechnical extravaganza that would start on the stroke of midnight, New Year's Day, marking their entry into the new millennium.

The farmhouse was in a mess. Caroline and her family were sleeping down at their parents', but Vanessa, Agathe and their kids were up here. There was no heating, because of all the building work, and so they only came back up to sleep. Even their parents never came up to Les Bertranges now. They hated the two huge buildings that had only just gone up, and the stabling that was almost finished and stood like two vast aircraft hangars, two cathedrals without walls. Jean and Angèle could see them when they looked up from their little house, and though the roof structures were solid wood, with laminated wood panels, the new arrivals filled them with horror. Yet it was they who had forced Alexandre to buy the farm, they who had wanted everything settled while they were still alive, they who had wanted to share it all out with an immediate cash payment from Alexandre to his sisters, so it was their fault that the new buildings had sprung up, the stabling for the cull cows and the weanlings, six metres from the floor to the apex of the roof, with a state-of-the-art quarantine shed for the incoming cattle and two equipment stores – five new buildings that had ruined the view and disfigured Les Bertranges forever. Now it really did look like a 'fattening site', a farming 'operation' – not really a farm any more.

Alexandre had agreed to everything. For a year, he had put up with all the work, on top of which, this summer, the earthworks had begun for the new motorway two kilometres away. Day in, day out, he heard the muffled roar of dozens of bulldozers and mechanical diggers, the daily blasts that shattered the bedrock, and the ear-splitting whine of the trenchers, fitted with blades three metres in diameter. In six months, construction would begin on the viaduct: two more years of this hellish racket. He had gone along with it all, felt the anger mounting inside him over the past twelve months, an anger that grew and grew. A rage that had increased tenfold this autumn, when he had sold the herd, making a clean sweep so that the work could be completed.

The trouble was, this life – the one waiting for him – was a life he did not want. And so he had sworn he would blast everything sky-high and cash in on the insurance. They'd get their money, everyone would have their share and that way they'd leave him in peace. Never in this life would he raise two hundred head of cattle, standing motionless in a shed from dawn to dusk. The specifications in the contract were crystal clear: the animals were never to be put out to pasture, their feed must be controlled, quarantine must be strictly observed. They were never to be allowed out in case they damaged their feet, or got fluke, or some other disease. They had to remain in the sheds, fed on hay from overhead feeders, and their feed had to be measured down to the last gram, using a mechanical feed distributor – factory farming for him and the animals alike. And so rather than live that reality, he would prefer nothing was left of Les Bertranges. He would bring it all down. Never would he fatten up two hundred cows like cars on a production line.

The plan was to recover just enough cash to buy the small estate next door back from the state – Crayssac's fields and woodland – and then to do nothing but live quietly in the old cottage, especially now the archaeologists had fixed it up a little before they left.

To ensure everything would blow up exactly as planned, at midnight on 1 January of the year 2000, Anton and Xabi had proved invaluable. They owed him that much. They hadn't batted an eyelid when he explained his plan and asked for their help. They insisted on one thing only from the outset: they would never set foot at Les Bertranges. They couldn't risk being spotted and identified by the gendarmes, or anyone else. Alexandre visited them three times. Three return trips to Saint-Affrique. But Xabi had come over last Tuesday, nonetheless, just to be sure everything was in place, to check the precise location of the explosive device, so that the insurance would suspect nothing. The trickiest point, he reckoned, was the positioning of the detonator. The detonator that Alexandre had stolen one night from the motorway site. For the rest, Anton's instructions were to break the roof tiles on the old barn, then stow everything away, well under cover in the new equipment store. Keep all the products together in the same place, then dampen the fertiliser so that it swelled up, and position the diesel tank and pesticides as close together as possible. Line up the cocktail of ingredients. Xabi had planned everything down to the last detail. He had even set the angle at which the mortars would fire the rockets when Alexandre set them off at midnight. Most important of all, he had calculated the precise angle of the rocket that would fire at eight minutes past midnight, not straight up into the stars like the others, but out sideways, for a direct hit on the equipment store.

Down below, they would all be standing outside the little house to watch the display – proper fireworks at last, fast and furious. There'd be no complaints, no disappointment now. Especially because, according to Anton, that amount of ammonium nitrate would produce a huge fireball, and everything within a two-hundred-metre radius would be blasted to smithereens. It would all come crashing down, the new buildings and the old. Even the farmhouse would be unlikely to withstand the shock; with that amount of ammonium nitrate the old stone-built house and its stone-tiled roof would be reduced to a heap of rubble.

Alexandre wanted to look smart before he went down to share the Christmas capon. He took the big battery-powered Telefunken into the bathroom, shaved and took a shower, though there was no hot water. Tonight, he would put on a proper pair of Terylene trousers, and a nice white shirt, just to shut the three of them up. For a week now, the radio news had talked of nothing but the *Erika* – the vast oil slick that had blighted the coast of Brittany, but now panic was rising over the Millennium Bug. An expert said that the turn of the year 2000 might prove catastrophic, almost apocalyptic! Alexandre grinned. He'd heard talk of the year 2000 since he was a kid. The year

2000 was a kind of glorious horizon, rich with a thousand promises, but the closer it got, the more frightened everyone became. France had even invested 120 billion francs to protect against the computer bug that would send everything haywire on the stroke of midnight. Machines would stop working – microwave ovens, trains, planes, nuclear power plants – and the whole planet would grind to a halt. But Alexandre was smiling because one thing at least was clear, the Bertranges Bug would be huge. Their precious cash would blow sky-high while they watched, then come floating down to earth in a thousand incandescent fragments. A cold shower was not the best thing in winter. He rubbed himself vigorously with the towel to warm up, listening out as he always did for the weather report, right after the jingle for farmhouse guinea fowl from Gers. The weatherman Joël Collado announced gale-force winds, gusts of over a hundred kilometres an hour north of the Loire, with worse to come – hurricane-force winds in two days' time. Perhaps he was joking – a Christmas prank. But there was something different this evening in Joël Collado's voice, the voice that meant the most to him out of all the familiar radio voices that filled the farmhouse, because he listened to it religiously, every day. It sounded deeper than usual tonight, and strange, almost choked.

## Monday, 27 December 1999

To switch on the TV and see Paris turned upside down, to see the capital brought to its knees, trees tossed across its streets, cars crushed and rooftops blown away, to see parts of the Bois de Boulogne and the Bois de Vincennes devastated, was a truly unimaginable spectacle. Eighty per cent of the electricity substations around Paris were out of service – no electricity up there in the Île-de-France, that most favoured of regions, though the studios at TF1 and France 2 seemed to be up and running. For Vanessa, down in the valley, the sight was more horrifying still. She even panicked about whether the top-floor apartment she rented in Montmartre was still standing. She began making calls that no one picked up, neither her neighbours in the building, nor her friends round about. Each time, the call went straight to their voicemail. Alexandre tried to ease the tension. If one day Paris really were cut off from the rest of the world, how would anyone know, because every radio and TV station in France was up there, in Paris!

Their parents loathed Paris, but this was no laughing matter – just imagine, a storm of that intensity, gusts of two hundred kilometres an hour, and a blackout three days away from the year 2000. It was a bad sign. A bad omen for the new century that was just around the corner.

They had all gathered around the television, from the start of the eight o'clock news – even the children. Each new report showed unbelievable scenes, such as the park at Versailles flattened, hectares of centuries-old oak trees uprooted, and rare specimen trees too, like the tulipwoods planted by Marie-Antoinette, and Napoleon's pines – proof that there had never been a storm of this power until now. This was a first. Never in France had there been such a furious onslaught from the elements. An expert from Météo France said the phenomenon was not merely exceptional but 'almost impossible'. And clearly, it had taken a heavy toll: dozens of people had been killed, thousands injured. Motorists had been killed by falling trees, others had perished under collapsed walls, or been crushed by falling chimneys, even whole houses. But the death toll might have been far higher, in the hundreds, if the storm had not struck at night on Christmas Eve, but during the week in the rush hour. Some parts of the country still could not be reached.

Alexandre was not smiling now. For once, his feelings were attuned to the rest of the family. They sat together, petrified, staring at the television, the panorama of chaos. If the west wind had blown that strongly the day after the Chernobyl disaster, he thought, the radioactive cloud really would have been pushed back from the French border, at two hundred kilometres an hour … Straight away, he thought of Constanze. She had called him once in three years, to announce the birth of her daughter. She said she was afraid to raise the child out there in India, because of the air pollution; that she missed France, especially the countryside. But he had heard nothing since. Yesterday, his heart had stopped when Caroline asked if he'd heard any news of her. Just like that, out of the blue, almost kindly. Alexandre told his sister that Constanze had been living in India for the past eight years, that he hadn't heard anything for three years, that she had stopped calling. It was then that Caroline had surprised him most of all. What she said was a kind of revelation, a shaft of light, an intuitive suggestion that had never occurred to him: perhaps Constanze had stopped calling because she was unhappy, and she didn't want him to know. Alexandre had stared at his sister, unable to conceal the profound gratitude he so suddenly felt. He had never thought of it like that.

They drank their soup, though it had cooled now, but they all put down their spoons when Claude Sérillon appeared at the end of the TV news with the same grim expression he had worn on the night of the Chernobyl disaster, the same wan voice. He announced that another storm was heading towards France. He sounded almost as if he could not believe his own words. Another cyclone was on its way, at least as strong as the previous one, but further south this time. It sounded like a joke, because the unthinkable could not happen twice in a row; exceptional events did not repeat themselves just a few hours apart. But on a live link to La Rochelle, the local prefect informed the nation that already the wind was blowing hard, and there was no electricity, that nobody should go outside, that the station building had been blown away, and the Maritime Museum too, and reports were coming in of numerous fatalities. He begged anyone with a mobile phone not to use it, so as to keep the airwaves clear for the emergency services.

A new Atlantic depression was clearly visible on the weather map. It would sweep in rapidly during the night, moving east and gathering strength, up to storm force around midnight, with gusts of over 150 kilometres an hour in places, not on the coast but inland. Right there, where they sat. There was no time tonight for Sérillon to talk about the other great ecological disaster of the moment, the *Erika*. Over the closing headlines, images of rescuers collecting petrol on beaches were intercut with scenes of armoured police vans pushing back trees that lay strewn across the motorway. Even the television set was showing signs of fatigue. The picture blinked and broke up; the aerial up on the roof must be getting blown about because now there was nothing but a screen of dancing white dots.

And so the Fabriers battened down the hatches, locked all the doors and shutters tight, snuggled down indoors, made some more coffee just in case.

At ten o'clock sharp, the wind began to howl wildly. Their father and Alexandre went outside, nonetheless, to the top of the steps. They could see nothing from down there in the valley, but they heard trees thrashing in the wind, though they didn't have any leaves. But still their branches were flailing, some had already broken off, and others were giving way. It was extremely unusual to see trees blown about to that extent by a gust of wind when they were not in leaf. Alexandre stepped a little further out into the open. Horizontal rain stung his face and arms. Bits of twig, even small branches shot by like a hail of arrows. Shocked at the fury descending on them from the sky, he decided to go straight up to the farm. There was not a moment to lose. His parents and sisters tried to dissuade him. He pulled on his waterproof jacket and hood, and made ready to leave, but his nephews and nieces burst out crying. The noise from outside was terrifying now: gusts that howled like sound effects in a film, and made the little house shake as if it had been struck. All around them, trees were bent almost horizontal. But he absolutely must get up the hill. The rain-soaked wind must be prevented, at any cost, from penetrating the equipment store, tearing off the door, or the roof, and messing up the complex chemistry he had prepared inside, ruining all his plans. Besides which, he had had no idea whether the new buildings would hold out in the storm, even whether they were still standing now.

'There's nothing you can do. Why on earth try to get up there? There are no cattle there now, nothing to worry about ...'

'I need to make sure everything's all right, Ma. I didn't even close the shutters on the house.'

Suddenly, the lights in the small house dimmed, then the electricity cut out altogether. They were plunged into total darkness. No television, no light in any of the rooms. The house felt like a frail shack shuddering in the storm, caught in the great blast of air that was being sucked down into the valley. With no electricity, nothing was working now – the boiler had stopped, soon the radiators would be cold, everything was black, and to make matters worse the four children had spurred one another into a frenzy, crying and screaming in unison. Alexandre decided to calm things down. He closed the door and took off his boots and his waterproof. At the sight of him hanging up his things, at least, the children stopped crying. Their mother fetched candles and the old hurricane lamp. There wasn't even a battery-powered radio in the little house for them to find out what was happening in the outside world. And so the whole family huddled together, listening to the increasingly violent din outside by the light of candles. Like the old days.

When he woke next morning and opened the shutter, Alexandre understood the scale of the disaster. Plainly, the new buildings had not held, certainly not the biggest one, though from down here he couldn't see the others. Without stopping even for a coffee, he took the Renault and drove up towards the farm. The road was blocked by several fallen trees, so he turned off across the fields. Halfway up the hill, he saw that sections of the Noailles wood had been flattened entirely. The road along the bottom of the valley must be closed as well. Clearly, no cars were getting through.

At the farm, the two newly constructed sheds had been destroyed. Further along, the old barn roof had partly blown away. The equipment store had been decapitated and everything inside was soaked. Ruined. Only the old farmhouse stood intact. The door had blown open, but the shutters had been slammed shut by the wind, as if the storm had taken care to protect the place and close them tight. There was no electricity up here, either. Alexandre made for the bathroom and turned on the big battery-powered Telefunken radio. The only thing that still worked, as if nothing had happened.

From the radio he learned that last night's storm had been far worse than the first, the day before. Across the country, hundreds of pylons and wires had been blown down or severed, as if tens of thousands of small bomb attacks had taken place all at once. Millions of people in France would be without electricity for days, even weeks. Which meant that Les Bertranges would be last on the list to get its current restored. Alexandre pictured the scene: his parents, sisters, nephews and nieces would all come here to the farmhouse. They would take refuge in the old homestead, because here at least there were working fireplaces, candles and firewood. The whole family would spend New Year just like in the olden days, warming themselves around a log fire, by the light of the oil lamp. There was nothing else for it – he knew perfectly well that EDF would concentrate on Paris and the other big cities first, then the outlying residential districts. Houses all on their own, deep in the countryside, would be the last to be repaired.

His mind was racing. But he was certain of one thing. Constanze would try to call. She would call just as she had the day after Chernobyl. She would call to find out if everything was all right, if the farm was still standing, and if the wild mint still flowered in the field. Perhaps she had done the same as Véronique. Perhaps she had already split with the father of her child. No doubt about it – the exact same scenario, and so this time he would tell her straight, he would ask her to stop charging all over the world, and come and settle here. This time he would tell her outright: stop running away and settle down. Perhaps it would take her by surprise, perhaps she would think twice. He'd tell her he was ready to grow nothing but fragrant mint, and lemon balm, and hawthorn. Nothing but walnuts, and hazelnuts, and root vegetables, and saffron. They'd do whatever she wanted with the land, make few demands of it, and cultivate it naturally. The purest, cleanest land in the world.

He checked the telephone, lifted the handset and listened for a dialling tone, but it was just as he had feared – nothing, no sound at all, not a peep. He ran into the barn and fetched his toolbox. He would never touch a fallen power line, but he knew how to lift a severed telephone cable, strip it back and reconnect the wires; he could use the pack of Scotchlok connectors that Xabi had used for the electric detonator. He'd left a whole bunch behind, said he never travelled with stuff like that in the car. With his past, you could never be sure.

Alexandre found the telephone cable lying on the ground at the end of the track, beside old Crayssac's fields. The poles had all blown down, too, and the cable was cut in one place. Alexandre bent to pick it up, like a poor wounded animal begging to be restored to life, a cable that he knew, in just a few hours' time, would open the world to him like a final inrush of air. Constanze would call, and Crayssac could never be thanked enough for not having fired on the gendarmes, for having finally agreed, one day, and for all time, to allow the rubber cables to festoon the edges of his fields. She will call, and he will – he must – tell her that theirs is a story that can never fade. That even when she is far away, when she gives not the slightest sign of life, the air at Les Bertranges is sweet with nothing but the scent of patchouli.